Body Not Recovered

Other Books by Alan Spector

(aaspector.com)

Baseball: Never Too Old to Play "The" Game

Hail Hail to U City High

Your Retirement Quest (with coauthor Keith Lawrence)

University City Schools: Our First 100 Years

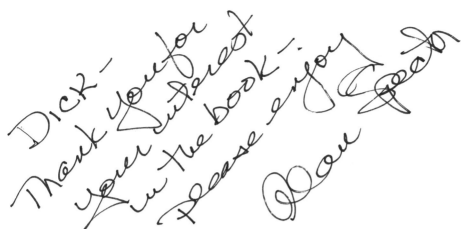

Body Not Recovered

A Vietnam War/Protest Movement Novel

Alan Spector

Body Not Recovered
A Vietnam War/Protest Movement Novel

Copyright ©2015 by Alan Spector

ISBN: 978-1-63110-169-4   paperback
ISBN: 978-1-63110-170-0   epub
ISBN: 978-1-63110-171-7   mobi

All rights reserved. No part of this book may be reproduced or transmitted in any form or by any means, electronic or mechanical, including photocopying, recording, or by any information storage or retrieval system, without permission from the author, except for the inclusion of brief quotations in a review.

Photo Credits: Keith Tarrier and Leena Krohn
Cover Design: Kyle Sandy

Printed in the United States of America by
Mira Digital Publishing
Chesterfield, Missouri 63005

DEDICATION

This book is dedicated to high school classmate, M. J. Savoy, who was killed in a plane crash into the South China Sea off the coast of Vietnam on June 17, 1966. He is listed as "Killed in Action/*Body Not Recovered.*"

This is also dedicated to my University City (Missouri) High School Class of 1964 and all of the classes from all of the high schools during the Vietnam War era— some of us fought; some of us dodged; some of us protested; some of us died; all of us were affected.

ACKNOWLEDGMENTS

Thank you to all of those who gave me your time, energy, and insights as I navigated the development of *Body Not Recovered*.

- Vietnam veterans Marc Tenzer, Mark Tucker, Ord Elliott, and Jack Zerr— for sharing your experiences and for providing your constructive critique
- Beta readers Jill Chapin (Maggie thanks you also), Joanna Baymiller, Laurie Friedman, Keith Lawrence, and Dana DeBlasi—for not allowing me to get complacent
- Research supporters Dr. Alan Halpern, Carol Strelic, Ed Friedman, and Grant Phillips—for filling in the gaps
- Cover concept reviewers Elaine Unell, CarolAnn Cole, Jill Chapin, Joanna Baymiller, and Laurie Friedman—for your artistic eye

A special thank you to my wife, Ann, for urging me to take on the intimidating task of writing a novel and for being beta reader, cover reviewer, moral supporter, and forever partner.

CHAPTER 1

DISTANT, SAD, AND LOST

June 3, 1964
University City, Missouri

JR Spears hesitated outside the double doorway longer than usual. After watching exuberant schoolmates rush headlong into the heart of the midday chaos that was the University City High School cafeteria, he reluctantly entered and sidled along the periphery of the large room, until he settled into his usual chair at his usual table in the farthest corner.

"Where's your lunch," asked Mouse.

"Don't feel like eating," JR mumbled.

"You need to put some meat on those bones," Mouse said, mockingly waving his finger and sporting a phony scowl.

JR smiled, but it faded quickly, "That's what my mom used to say."

Although never comfortable where throngs of students congregated in the school, JR felt even more claustrophobic in the oppressive humidity and lack of air movement in the lunchroom that was located in the basement of the neoclassical three-story brick building that had opened in 1930.

The lunchroom clamor had been growing for weeks. Not only were students, especially seniors, excitedly anticipating the end of the school year, but heated discussions about America's growing military involvement in Vietnam were becoming the norm. Many a conversation began, "Did you see Walter Cronkite last night?"

There were regular nightly news reports of U.S. combat casualties. Two American carriers had been positioned off the coast to provide air support to South Vietnamese ground forces. And the words "Agent Orange," "napalm," and "escalation" were being used more frequently.

For senior boys, the prospect of going to Vietnam loomed in their future. JR and many others had already registered for the military draft as required by law when they turned 18.

On this day, talk of Vietnam played a smaller role in the incessant din. Seniors had become increasingly animated about their impending graduation only seven days away. Most had shut down business as usual—grades had been well established, many teachers had given the seniors a reprieve by cancelling final exams, college choices had been made, and summer jobs had been secured. But the greatest reason for the racket was the distribution of high school yearbooks.

Students darted from table to table amidst the aroma of hamburgers and tater tots to ask classmates to write something profound in their books. Occasionally, a student or two or three would take the time to exit the single door behind JR's table to catch a smoke in the blacktopped courtyard that was tightly bounded by three stories of brick building before returning to the fray.

No one knew most of the 600 with whom they would graduate, and few had more than a handful of close friends whose words of wisdom they really cared about. Yet the annual and frenetic ritual of getting as many signatures as possible was underway.

With head down, eyes closed, elbows on the table, and hands covering his ears, JR tried desperately but unsuccessfully to ignore it all. "This is bullshit. I could care less about this yearbook, this class, or this graduation," he blurted out.

"Come on, JR," implored Mouse. Larry Hegel was JR's best friend. His protruding ears and weak jaw had earned him the nickname that would probably stick with him for eternity. "You never thought you'd get this far. That should count for something."

"Yeah, you're right. I'm surprised I'm still in school. Since my folks' car wreck, school and life have been really screwed up. In fact, things weren't so hot even before the accident."

Early in his sophomore year, JR was out late on a Friday night. Despite trying to be as rebellious as any teenager, he had always made the effort either to be home on time or to let his parents know where he would be. That night, he lost track of time.

As they frequently did, JR and his friends had stopped at Hamburger Heaven to get a late-night burger and fries with tangy "H Sauce." After devouring their food while standing outside the hut-like takeout joint and avoiding being hit by cars in the cramped parking lot, they walked across the street to the large city park, where they started a game of two-on-two touch football on the lighted and abandoned tennis courts. The cool fall air and the freedom they felt on the illuminated oasis in the otherwise dark and silent park kept the game going.

When it was well past his time to be home and they had not heard from him and being less angry than concerned, JR's parents walked to the turquoise 1957 Nash Rambler station wagon in their driveway. Knowing where he normally hung out and with whom, they headed toward Hamburger Heaven.

The Spears drove steadily down Olive Boulevard, which was wide open in the late-night lack of traffic. They cruised through the green light at the Hanley Road intersection as they had done a thousand times before and never saw the car that ran the red light and drove their Rambler into the stone and black wrought-iron fence that surrounded the cemetery on the southwest corner of Olive and Hanley. Neither the Spears nor high school senior, Jules Cooper, who had run the light, survived.

The sound of the crash and the emergency vehicles traveled through the otherwise quiet section of the city. JR had heard the screeching metal-on-metal noise but would not know until later what had happened. Although he could only speculate, he would never know for sure why his parents were out that night.

An only child, JR moved in with his aunt Jane, his mom's single sister, with whom he had not been close. She made arrangements for JR to live with her in her small two-bedroom bungalow and set aside the small amount in his parents' estate for him. Although he knew she was being kind, the relationship was and always would be remote. Even though he continued at the high school and had his few friends, JR felt alone.

"JR, would you sign my yearbook?"

"Are you sure you want me to, Barb," JR asked, as he was overcome by her Shalimar perfume.

"You bet. We had World History together. That makes us lifelong buds," Barb twittered as she hovered over JR, shoved the book in front of him, and held out her pen.

JR opened the black matte-finished faux-leather bound book with the gold-colored silhouette of the head of the school's mascot, the Indian, embossed on the front cover. Having leafed through the pages to find his senior photo, JR accepted the pen from the perky brunette varsity cheerleader. As he bent over the book to write something, he paused and studied the surrounding photos of his classmates, who smiled broadly in stark contrast to his distant, sad, and lost expression.

Others had long lists of school activities to accompany their photos; Junior Varsity Water Polo, School Newspaper Editor, Intramural Sports, Senior Cabinet Social Chairman, Pep Club Board Member, National Merit Finalist, Fencing Club, Student Government, Future Teachers of America, Varsity Football, and on and on.

Each senior photo was accompanied by a personalized quotation called a "quip" that had been chosen to reflect an admirable trait. JR had no activities listed, and his quip that someone had decided suited him read, "There is no man but may make his own paradise."

"What the hell does that mean?" JR thought.

After staring at the empty space that would have held his list of high school activities and recognizing that Barb was getting anxious to move on, JR wrote the most profound thing he could think of, "Barb, great year in World History—good luck. JR"

Barb gave him a superficial hug, pushed the book in front of Mouse and then Lenny, and was off into the frenzy.

"OK, we've been friends forever, we're about to graduate high school, and you've been holding out all of these years. It's time you told us what JR stands for." It was Lenny, who was the only one of the group of friends who was in any way connected to the broader high school experience, because he was six-two, had a sweet jump shot, and was second-team all-conference.

"I've been telling you for years, that's my name. The other day, my aunt showed me a box of pictures and papers. There were photos of my folks from when they were growing up and when they were married. There were even a few of me with them."

It took a few moments for JR to continue, as his face maintained its faraway stare, "There was also a copy of my birth certificate. My name is JR. That's all it says. It doesn't stand for anything. It's just JR. I asked my aunt about it, and she didn't know why my parents chose it."

"OK, just JR," Lenny said with an exaggerated grimace of unresolved disbelief, "we'll take your word for it."

After another round of classmates pestered them for signatures and left, Mouse said, "So, JR, are you still considering enlisting? I can't believe you've even been thinking about it. Who wants to go half way around the world to get shot?"

"Great question," JR responded. "Sometimes that's exactly how I feel and sometimes I think the army would be the best thing for me. Anyway, I might work for awhile before going in—if I don't get drafted first, that is. I'm really not sure. The more I hear about Vietnam, the more it all seems wrong to me. And besides, I've never been in a fight of any kind in my life."

"Remember, the offer is always open. My dad's a United Steelworkers labor organizer. He says he's pretty sure he can get you into the union and find you a job right away."

"Yeah, Mouse, that might be the plan. Tell your dad thanks."

Lenny chimed in, "My brother is thinking about enlisting. He says we need to win this war or the next thing we know, we'll all be Communists and speaking Russian."

"That's bullshit, and you know it," Mouse said.

JR opened his own yearbook, stared again at his picture, feeling as blank inside as his face showed outside, and said, "You know, I'm not sure it matters whether the war is right or wrong. I'm not sure it matters whether I enlist, get drafted, go, don't go, work, whatever. I just don't know and I'm not sure I really care."

Before anyone could respond, a tall classmate with a flattop came over to the table with yearbook in hand. John Muccelli, paying absolutely no attention to anyone but Lenny, put his yearbook in front of his varsity basketball teammate. "Lenny, sign this."

JR looked up from his yearbook at the figure looming over their table and felt the hair stand up on the back of his neck.

"Sure, Mooch, be glad to. Sign mine too," Lenny responded.

When signatures had been swapped and Muccelli had left, Lenny said, "He's the only one I know who's already dead certain what he's going to do with his life. Look," shoving his book in front of JR and Mouse, "he signed my book, 'FBI Agent John 'Mooch' Muccelli.'"

CHAPTER 2

THE SHED

July 17, 1964
St. Louis, Missouri

"Yeah, Mouse, your dad was great," JR said, speaking into the telephone in the living room of his newly-rented apartment. "It feels great being in my own place, and I'm sure my aunt was happy when I moved out. It's not much, but you'll need to come by to see it. By then I'll have a fan—it's hotter than hell in here. And wait till you're riding in my '55 two-tone Chevy Bel Air."

Mouse's dad had delivered on his promise. The day after high school graduation, Bob Hegel began pulling strings to expedite JR's union membership and even got him on the most prestigious job in town, the construction of the St. Louis Gateway Arch. Although he was just a base laborer doing the most menial tasks, he was employed and making reasonable money.

"That's great, but slow down," Mouse chuckled, "You've only been on the job for a week."

"I just needed to make it as much a life of my own as I could."

"Hey, man, I'm excited for you. How's the job going?"

Before he could answer, JR heard a click, some deep breaths, and another click.

"Sorry, that was someone on my party line. Job's good, but I'm only a rookie trying to find my way. No surprise—I think everyone else has been working there since excavation began in early '61, and they're longtime union brothers. Nobody pays much attention to me, unless they need me to do something, but that's fine with me. I need some time to get used to all of this anyway."

"Keep me posted, JR, and I'll definitely come by to see your place."

Uncertain how things worked, on his first work day, JR had wandered around a bit before finding an isolated area not far from the carpenters' tool shed to eat lunch. From his solitary lunchtime perch on a concrete retaining wall, JR would soon learn that he was not the only outsider working on the site.

Each day, three Negro workmen walked by JR on their way to a wooden, flat-roofed shed, laid a piece of plywood across two sawhorses, and used crates as chairs to eat on the shady, downwind side. Combined with the wind-blown dust of the construction site, the heat and humidity of the St. Louis summer made shade and shelter a valuable commodity. The trio and JR were in sight of each other, but although he could hear the rumbles of their constant conversation, JR could not make out what they were saying.

On JR's second Friday, an early-morning rain teased the construction workers with a brief respite, but when it passed, the sun and humidity combined to make it as though a hot wet blanket covered the worksite. At lunchtime, JR settled gingerly on the hot concrete of the retaining wall and laid a wet cold washrag around his neck, having learned to wrap the rag around ice cubes in his insulated lunchbox.

When the three Negroes walked past him on their way to the shed, JR heard reference to Reverend King, Freedom Riders, and Goodman, Schwerner, and Chaney. He knew these names and their implications, because he had begun paying attention to the nightly news, something he had not done much of since his parents died. Most evenings, he watched his 13-inch black-and-white Zenith television as he ate dinner on a TV tray placed in front of his threadbare couch and relished the breeze from his Emerson Electric rotating fan; the TV, couch, set of TV trays, and fan having been garnered from Goodwill. He found himself increasingly interested in the war in Vietnam and the civil rights movement, both issues brought to life by CBS news anchors Walter Cronkite nationally and Max Roby locally.

Being curious, but not wanting to be obvious, JR only occasionally looked up from his lunch to follow the three as they sauntered toward him. When they were several steps past, he kept his eyes on

THE SHED

them the rest of the way. It was then he noticed one of the Negroes, despite having his hands full carrying his lunchbox, tool belt, and a bottle of Coke, had managed to reach into his back pocket, pull out and open his wallet, and unfold a newspaper clipping. As the man tried to maneuver the wallet back into his work overalls while showing the clipping to his friends, he missed his pocket. The wallet fell to the ground, as the men walked on.

JR waited to see if the man would notice and return. He did not. He and his workmates continued to their usual spot behind the shed. Leaving his lunchbox on the wall, JR left his perch, retrieved the wallet, and followed the normally dusty path that had been dampened by the morning rain. As the three men saw JR approach, their high-energy conversation came to an abrupt halt.

"Excuse me. You dropped this."

"Thank you, sir."

"No problem."

As JR relinquished the wallet and turned to get back to his lunch, he heard, "Hey, my name is Walter. Walter Rawlings. Would you like to join us?"

Walter's companions gave him a look that was somewhere between, "What do you think you're doing?" and "Have you lost your mind?"

Turning back to face the men, he hesitantly said, "I'm JR. JR Spears. Are you sure?"

Walter looked at each of his friends, then back to JR. "Sure, grab your lunch. We've got room for an extra crate."

Returning with his lunch, JR found a crate in the shed and sat at the open side of the makeshift plywood table.

"This is Oliver Davis or 'OD,' and this is Mitch Wise—we call him 'Not So,'" Walter declared with a broad smile on his face.

Mitch glared at Walter, nodded a short-of-polite greeting to JR, and settled into a stretch of not-quite-comfortable silence, which Walter finally broke, "What's JR stand for? Junior?"

"No, it's just JR. That's what my birth certificate says."

Hoping to get a clue about what to say or at least to get his bearings, JR looked from face to face. He had never been this close to Negroes where he was expected to know what to say or how to act. All three men were much older than he. Each had gray hair sprinkled throughout their moderately-cropped afros, with Walter's gray clearly on its way to winning a 50-50 battle. The men were clean-shaven, bright-eyed, and seemingly as curious about him as he was about them.

Again Walter broke the silence, "You just started here, didn't you?"

"Yeah, I graduated high school just a few weeks ago and got the job."

"Must have pulled some strings. There's a waiting list at the union hall to get on this job. And they stopped hiring our boys again after we got on," Mitch griped, taking advantage of the opportunity to make a fervent point as was his habit.

"Young man, did you know that Negroes have only been accepted into the local unions since '58 as part of an out-of-court settlement of a discrimination lawsuit?"

"No sir, I didn't know that," JR said, avoiding any comments that might get Mr. Hegel into trouble.

"One of these days," Oliver said, "we'll have a better chance of getting good jobs. If Martin had his way, we'd all live the dream. But it's going to take some head knocking."

"OD, we've got to keep it peaceful like Martin says, or we'll lose what support we do have," Walter said with conviction.

"Oh, I know the party line, but that didn't stop the KKK from killing Goodman, Schwerner, and Chaney."

Mitch jumped in, "Killing those young men, especially with two of them being white, was a big mistake. They'll be martyrs."

"Not So, you see if the guys around here give a shit about those killings. I doubt it. They'd as soon it been us that got lynched," Oliver said, sitting up straight and glaring at Mitch to emphasize his point.

It was clear to JR that his presence had not prevented the three from settling into the heated topic of conversation that he assumed they had every day. Every so often, JR noticed Walter staring at him and a couple of times detected the beginning of a smile on Walter's lips.

Mitch checked his watch. "Time to get back on the job, or they'll have our black asses. Only thing that keeps things on an even keel is that we're good at what we do. Damn, we spent a lot of time doing our work before the unions were forced to let us in, and now they found ways to limit how many of us they hire."

They packed up their lunch waste, returned the plywood, sawhorses, and crates to the shed, and began to walk back toward the arch. "Join us for lunch Monday, JR?"

"I don't know, Walter. It's not that I don't want to, but do you think it's OK?"

"JR, the only thing that's right is what you have in your heart to do."

This would not be the last nugget of insight that Walter would impart to JR over the next 15 months, nor would it be the last time he shared this particular bit of wisdom.

"Then I'll see you on Monday. Thanks."

CHAPTER 3

THAT'S HOW I SEE IT

July 24, 1964
St. Louis, Missouri

Over the weekend, JR relentlessly pored over the *St. Louis Post-Dispatch* and the *Globe-Democrat* and even got his hands on the *St. Louis American*, the Negro community newspaper. Focusing on everything he could find about the civil rights movement, he supplemented his reading with the most recent issues of *TIME* and *Newsweek*. Wanting to intelligently participate in his inaugural discussion, he also watched and listened to every newscast he could on TV and radio.

When lunchtime came on Monday, JR was prepared to join the civil rights discussion but got surprised. The topic was the St. Louis Cardinals, who, despite having four all-stars, were only a disappointing three games over .500. Tuesday's conversation was about where to find the best fried chicken in the city. Wednesday—how was the Negro community going to make any headway if the schools weren't educating their children?

JR found himself beginning to get in a word or two, "Kenny Boyer's my favorite Cardinal." "None crispier or juicier than Golden Fried Chicken."

On Thursday, JR would be late to lunch. On his way to the shed, he saw a worker that he recognized but did not know coming his way. Expecting to simply pass the man, JR was taken by surprise when the man stopped just short of him and violently grabbed his upper arm. "Having lunch with the niggers again today?"

"Let go! It's none of your business!" JR tried to free himself, but he man was too strong.

"You're making a big mistake, kid." The big man held on, tightened his grip, and leaned in close enough that JR could smell his fetid breath and sweat-soaked clothes. "The niggers don't belong here."

JR finally wrenched himself free and surprised himself with a sharp, confident response, "If they don't belong here, neither do I!"

"That's the point, kid. Watch your step."

Again, sounding much more in control than he actually was, JR said the only thing that came to his mind, "Fuck off."

"Like I said," the man growled, pointing his finger within an inch of JR's face, "just watch your step."

JR's adrenaline had taken over, and he slapped the hand away from his face. Realizing what he had done, JR took two steps back and was ready to run, when the man turned and walked away.

As JR stood in place, it took him a few minutes to steady his wobbly legs and thought, "Should I heed the warning or head for the shed?"

"Hey, JR, thought you were going to skip out on us," Walter said as JR approached.

"Uh, sorry, I had to talk to somebody about something," JR replied, trying to sound as casual as possible.

"You OK? You seem edgy," Walter persisted.

JR's head was down. He couldn't look Walter in the eye. Should he tell them? If he did, what would they do? Seemed like that would mean more trouble. He decided to keep the incident to himself and looked up to meet Walter's stare, "No, I'm OK."

"JR, what do you think about the Vietnam War?"

"Oh, Walter, I don't know," JR began, glad to be talking instead of thinking about what just happened, "When we were talking about it at school, I thought I didn't care. I thought about enlisting right after graduation, just for something to do and probably would have if I didn't get this job. I'm still thinking about it, mostly because I guess I need to decide what to do with my life."

"Our black boys are over there getting killed for no reason," Mitch asserted. "We're trying to free the Vietnamese, and we're not even free here."

"That's not how I see it," Walter said, with a fierceness in his eyes that JR had not seen in their brief relationship. "People who are being oppressed anywhere have to be helped. We can't allow it. You know, a Jewish guy came to speak at church a few months ago. He was a Holocaust survivor. He said that we all have to fight against oppression. Said our struggle was his struggle. If people would have spoken up and fought the oppression of Jews in Europe, maybe the Holocaust would have never happened.

"That made sense to me. So, if the Vietnamese are being oppressed, even if we're struggling here, we need to help them out. That's how I see it."

This was the first time JR had heard a rationale for the war that made sense to him on a gut level, and he felt good jumping into this discussion, "My high school had a lot of Jews in it. We even had two who were children of Holocaust survivors. And we had a classmate, a Jewish guy, who was trying to get a local skating rink lined up for a senior class party. This guy met with the owners to make arrangements but found out they didn't allow Negroes in. We didn't have any Negroes in our school, but this guy comes back from the rink and says, 'No way. We can't have a party at a place like that.' The party was moved.

"Everybody seemed to feel good about that. So, I guess you're right, Walter. And that's how I see it," JR said, feeling a deepening bond forming between the two.

When the work day had ended, JR ran into Walter as they were both heading toward their cars in a far corner of the parking lot. "You're a good kid, JR," Walter said as he put his hand on JR's shoulder.

"Get your goddamned hand off him, nigger!"

It was the big guy who had grabbed JR earlier, and he had a couple of others with him, both with powerful arms crossed over their barrel chests and both glaring at Walter and JR.

"Not meaning any harm," Walter said, slumping his shoulders in deference and averting his eyes.

"He's not bothering me," JR said softly, trying to ease the situation.

"Well, the nigger is bothering us."

"I'll just be on my way," Walter mumbled.

"The hell you will."

The punch was quick and unexpected. Walter doubled over gasping for breath and holding his gut.

"Hey, stop..."

JR's voice trailed away as he was hit from behind. He didn't remember hitting the ground, but when he looked up, he saw the boot and felt the successive blows to his stomach.

"OK, let's go. I think both niggers have learned their lesson," JR heard from behind him.

JR had lost track of Walter, but when he rolled over to confirm the attackers were gone, he saw Walter bleeding from the mouth, writhing on the ground, and having trouble breathing.

JR crawled over and was barely able to get the words out, "Are you OK?"

It took Walter a few seconds to respond, "I've had worse. I don't think anything's broken. How 'bout you?"

"I feel like I have to throw up."

And he did. Several times.

"Let's go tell someone, a foreman, the police, someone," JR implored, wiping vomit residue from his lips. "That guy can't get away with..."

"No, son, let's not," Walter said quietly, but firmly, as he struggled to raise his head to look JR in the eye. "Nobody'll do nothing anyway."

"But what if those guys do this again?"

"We're OK for awhile," Walter said as he struggled to get up. "Every so often, they need to show who's superior. You and me being together was just an excuse. We'll go about our business and they'll go about theirs. For now, we're OK. I need to get home. Can you make it?"

"It hurts, but yeah, I can make it."

"JR, even if it hurts like hell tomorrow morning, come to work. And at lunch, you make sure you join us. You can never show weakness to bullies—they breed on it. Let's get out of here."

JR and Walter helped each other up and slowly and silently made their way to their respective cars. Although it was clearly not the case for Walter, this was the first beating JR had experienced. He was aching all over, but the thing he remembered most and understood least about the incident was the hatred these men had shown and the fury they unleashed.

CHAPTER 4

THE UNTOUCHABLES

September 26, 1964
Palo Alto, California

Having arrived at Stanford University a week early to get acclimated, John "Mooch" Muccelli also used the week to schedule time with Dr. Gabriel Almond, the Chair of the Political Science Department. Mooch dressed well for the appointment, made sure he was on time, showed respect to the secretary who greeted him, and was ushered into a classically unkempt academic office. After introducing himself and thanking the chair for seeing him, Mooch politely asked, "Dr. Almond, what do I have to do to get my degree in three years?"

A week before he was to leave for Stanford, Mooch lay in his tiny bedroom that barely held a mismatched dresser, desk, and bed. As he listened to the sportscaster on KMOX recap that afternoon's Cardinals 5-to-1 loss to the Phillies, a book about the history of the FBI rested on his chest. He had spent the summer reading everything he could about the FBI, studying the bureau's job qualification requirements, working in a local warehouse as a replacement for vacationing employees, and preparing for his trip west.

After turning off his Zenith clock radio and just before he dozed off, Mooch grinned at a new insight and declared out loud, "Not only am I going to be an FBI agent, but I'm going to do it in record time."

Not realizing that his pronouncement was as loud as it was, he could only smile when he heard his dad call from his parents' bedroom across the hall, "Sounds like a good idea to me, Mooch. Good night."

John Muccelli's dad, Mike, began calling him Mooch right after he was born, and the nickname stuck. Mike had been an officer in the St. Louis City Police Department, where his promotions through the ranks were well earned. With growing resume and reputation, Mike applied for the open position of Chief of the nearby suburb's University City Police Department, and he was appointed to the job during the summer before Mooch's eighth-grade year.

When Mike became Chief, the Muccelli family stretched their finances and moved into a three-bedroom brick home in University City within walking distance of City Hall and Police Department Headquarters. Mooch attended Hanley Junior High School and joined his University City High School Class of 1964.

When they moved into their new home, the basement was unfinished, and Mooch helped his father convert it into a rec room with wood paneled walls, linoleum tile floor, and recessed lighting in an acoustical tile ceiling. The room was perfect for continuing a tradition Mike had begun when he worked in the city of St. Louis, hosting frequent gatherings of his police friends. Mooch grew up surrounded by the language, loyalty, and lore of the police brotherhood.

On nights when Mooch's favorite crime-fighting shows were scheduled, he would get his homework done early and head down to the basement, where the family's combination TV and stereo hi-fi RCA console was located. Tuning in the right channel and constantly adjusting the sensitive vertical hold, Mooch would escape into the world created by *Dragnet, Naked City,* or his absolute favorite, *The Untouchables.*

Mooch's academic work ethic and his athletic ability were a perfect match for the high standards of his new schools. He loved his classes and could not understand why classmates complained about homework. He became a Merit Finalist, was ranked number one in his class, and was selected valedictorian.

Mooch played varsity basketball, but his real love was baseball, where he played left field and batted fifth on the team that won the Missouri state high school championship when he was a junior. He was also involved in student government, in choir, and with Kay Jenkins. When Mooch applied to Stanford with a nearly perfect grade point, high SAT scores, and his breadth of activities, he was accepted by the prestigious school and received sufficient scholarship funds to ensure he could attend.

Not knowing this young man and hesitant to make any commitments, Dr. Almond was not initially encouraging about an accelerated degree, but Mooch was politely persistent. The tone of the conversation changed when Mooch shared why he was interested in cutting a year off of his degree path.

After several consultations over two weeks, Dr. Almond endorsed a plan Mooch could live with. Combined with having placed out of 15 hours of required freshman courses, Mooch would take an extra course or two every semester and maximize his summer course load. Barring unforeseen circumstances, he was on his way to a three-year undergraduate degree, a key step toward an earlier FBI career.

During his first month of freshman classes, Mooch developed two important connections outside of his schoolwork, one that he initiated and one with help from his father. When he felt he had his college routine reasonably well established, Mooch visited the Stanford campus police department and said to the officer at the front desk, "I'd like to speak with someone about a part-time job."

"I don't think we have part-time jobs, but the chief is in."

The desk officer led Mooch to the office of Chief Gordon "Gordie" Davis and said, "Chief, this guy's looking for part-time work."

Davis looked up from his paperwork and scowled at the officer, who quietly retreated to his desk. Davis glared at Mooch and growled, "Haven't ever had a student ask for a job before."

"Chief Davis," Mooch jumped in sensing that he needed to begin to explain before being summarily dismissed, "My name is John Muccelli. I want to learn as much as I can about law enforcement. My dad is a police chief back home in Missouri, and it's my goal to be an FBI agent. I thought working here could get me some experience, and to be honest, it probably wouldn't hurt my resume for the FBI."

Mooch stood quietly at near-attention for what seemed like a few minutes as he watched the chief stare back and mull over the possibilities; the scowl slowly receding from his face.

Because he had been dealing with an ever-increasing level of student unrest and disdain for authority, Davis found himself intuitively liking this kid, impressed by his honesty and show of respect. Here was a forthright young man who, at least on the surface, appeared to respect what Davis stood for. And his dad was a cop, part of the brotherhood.

"Mr. Muccelli, I need to think about this and do some checking. No promises, but maybe we can work something out. If you don't mind going through some on-the-job training without pay first, then we might find some work for you on the weekends. I've been using overtime to manage the weekends anyway; so you'd cost me less than I'm already paying, and the officers would rather have as much weekend time off as possible. So, like I said, no promises, but I'll get back to you in the next couple of days."

"Thank you, sir. I'm also planning on being here over the summers, so if you need me then, that would be great," Mooch responded almost before Chief Davis had finished.

"One step at a time. I'll let you know what our plans are for your training if we proceed. And again, no promises. Let the officer at the desk know how to contact you. Thanks for coming in, Mr. Muccelli."

"Thank you, Chief Davis," Mooch said as he smiled, shook the Chief's hand, turned to leave, but stopped short of the door.

"By the way Chief, call me Mooch."

That conversation led to three years of Mooch's first job in law enforcement, albeit as a part-time dispatcher for a campus police force. But that was fine with him; it was a start.

Mooch called his mom and dad at least weekly and after getting the dispatcher job, he was proud to report, "Dad, guess what I'm doing. I'm working part-time for the campus police."

"I'm proud of you, Mooch, but I have to tell you that I already knew. Chief Davis called me. I had to think about it for awhile, but," his dad couldn't help from laughing, "I decided to give you a strong recommendation."

"Thanks, Dad."

"Now that you're officially in the law enforcement business, I've got another option for you. I don't know if you would remember this, but back when I was a lieutenant in St. Louis, we conducted a joint investigation with the FBI. The lead agent on the case was Special Agent Paul Marcus. Straight shooter, a standup guy. Came over to the house a few times, but you were pretty young, so you may not remember him."

"I remember you talking about the FBI case. But, no, I don't remember him."

"Well, Paul and I kept in touch even after the case was over. He put in a good word for me when the University City job came up. About two years ago, Paul was transferred from St. Louis to the San Francisco office. We talk every two to three months now. Last week, I was telling him about you being at Stanford and about your interest in the FBI. Paul said that if there was anything he could do to help, we should let him know. He's only about an hour from you. Would you like to connect with him? I can give you his number to get in touch?"

"That would be great, Dad!" Mooch screamed into the phone, unable to contain his excitement.

CHAPTER 5

THE DOORBELL RANG

April 22, 1965
Tunkannock, Pennsylvania

The Blessings homestead was nestled amongst the trees on a hilltop in Pennsylvania's Endless Mountains, foothills to the Poconos, overlooking the Susquehanna River. Their dinner table rested in front of a bay window providing panoramic views of their small pond, the rolling hills, and the river in the distance. The sweet scent of early spring coming through the open screened windows added to the idyllic setting to which Maggie and her parents sat down to dinner. Yet the serenity of the evening and their lives would soon be shaken to the core.

Margaret "Maggie" Blessings was an active and attractive Tunkhannock High School senior. Long, untamed red hair framed a delicate heart-shaped face and bright green eyes. Her energy, engaging smile, good looks, and sleek frame drew a large circle of friends.

Maggie's high grade point average, presidency of the student government as a junior, and involvement in every aspect of school life bode well for her future. Throughout the year, she had spent hours sorting through the stacks of mailings from colleges across the country that were urging her to consider them for the following year. She arranged and rearranged piles into what she called "preferred," "possible," and "no-way" schools. The preferred pile sat neatly on the front right corner of the old study desk in her room—the other piles were less tidy and filled shelves on the tall worn wooden bookcase next to the desk. Materials from her final choice, Penn State, lay atop the preferred pile

Her brother, Matt, had led the way through the local school system a year ahead of her. He did well in academics and was recruited heavily by colleges interested in the football, basketball, and baseball all-star. But from the time he was a small boy, Matt knew he wanted to be a soldier like his dad and grandfather before him. He considered the military academies, having been recruited by each of them to play football, but he opted to volunteer for military service with the intent of choosing later whether to apply for Officer Candidate School.

The day after he graduated from high school, Matt Blessings enlisted. After basic and advanced infantry training, he was deployed to Germany and settled into the routine of his new life. He and his barracks mates talked often about the expanding war in Vietnam and the likelihood that they would be sent into the fray. Matt made his point of view clear, "This is what I signed up for. If we're needed in Vietnam, that's where they'll send us. In fact, that's where the real soldiering is happening."

Being among the first of those deployed to Southeast Asia early in the 1965 U.S. troop buildup, Matt and his new unit immediately found themselves supporting South Vietnamese troops and entangled in jungle warfare.

The Blessings were proud of Matt and his service to their country and supported the war; at least, Maggie's father did. Maggie's mom talked little of the war itself. When the topic came up at the dinner table or on the news, she would typically assume a faraway stare and heave a great sigh, "Matt, Matt, Matt."

Only caring about Matt and hoping he was safe, Maggie did not think much about the war itself; that is until Matt's letters began to change in frequency and content. Previously, he had been writing routine everything's-fine letters to the whole family a couple of times each week. Then Maggie began receiving almost daily letters from her brother, who knew it was her chore to pick up the mail from the box at the foot of their driveway where she was dropped off by the school bus. Each envelope contained a single letter to her or two letters, one clearly marked for her and one marked for their parents.

Matt's first letter written specifically to Maggie read in part, "Mags, Mom and Dad would never understand what I'm dealing with. And I don't want them to be afraid for me. I'm plenty afraid for myself. Never show them the letters I'm sending just to you.

I'll write separate ones for them. I just need to tell someone what's going on over here."

Maggie's previously stable existence was shaken, as she spent more time locked away in her room reading, rereading, and trying to make sense of Matt's letters. Having had a life in which everything had gone so well, she struggled to deal with the adversity. Her zest for school, her interaction with her mom and dad, and even her appetite waned, as she carried the burden of knowing Matt's feelings but being unable to share them with their parents. She even bore occasional twinges of resentment for Matt putting her in this position, but those passed quickly when she reminded herself that his burden was much greater than her own.

While she continued to love and admire him, Maggie no longer thought of her brother as the invincible pillar of strength. Although each letter was different in its detail, there were two common themes. Matt found everything about the war to be abhorrent, and he was dead-cold terrified.

Just that morning, Matt's letter to Maggie read, "Yesterday we were on patrol with a South Vietnamese unit looking for Viet Cong—the guys call them "gooks"—that had been firing into our base camp every night. We came across a village. I can't imagine what we looked like to the villagers as we approached—armed to the teeth. We saw only women, children, and old men. Our lieutenant decided that meant the young men were Viet Cong and hiding in the jungle poised to attack. With nothing but a quick look around, he hollered, 'Burn it down.' A couple of our guys carried flamethrowers, and the thatched roof huts went up in flames in seconds. They didn't even check to see who was inside. I couldn't do it, Mags. I just couldn't. I hate this place—I hate this war."

Matt followed, "We'll never be sure if we were at risk from those people. What we are sure of is that we killed 17 of them. We counted. And later, the lieutenant reported the 17 as enemy body count. What he didn't report is that all 17 were women and children—just folks—like us."

He finished, "Mags, I was scared all the way out on patrol, in the village, and all the way back. I'm scared even when we're at our base and I'm sitting here writing you. We're surrounded by jungle and who knows what or who else. I hate this place—I hate this war. I can't wait to get out of the army and come home. Take care of Mom and Dad, Mags. I love you."

Maggie reread the letter several times and realized she was shivering from both anger and fear. She was angry with the situation, getting ever angrier at the war, and in fear for her brother. The one redeeming constant was Matt's use of the pet name only he used for her, "Mags." It reminded her that he would always be there for her, no matter what.

Her self-reflection was interrupted when her mom called from the kitchen, "Margaret, it's time for dinner. Set the table and get your father. He's out back doing something in the yard. And turn on Walter Cronkite."

Maggie took a moment to hide the letters and stop shaking, found her father, and settled in at the dinner table. She felt her spirits bolstered somewhat by the wonderfully mixed aromas of dinner, the cool breeze coming through the screens, and the comfortable presence of her parents. Harold Blessings led the family in prayer, thanking God for his wife and daughter, for their meal, and for his son who was proudly serving his country. Amen.

"Jenny, did you read Matt's letter today?"

Maggie's mother, who had been in town most of the day, quietly said, "No dear, what did it say?"

"It's on my desk, but in a nutshell, it said how proud he was to be serving. He misses us and would rather be home, but he understands he and his buddies have a job to do. He's proud to be a soldier and following in Pop's and my footsteps. He sounded great in the letter."

"We are blessed," said Jenny, assuming her distant stare, heaving her sigh, and concluding, "Matt, Matt, Matt, I miss him."

"We all do, Mom," Maggie forced herself to say and fought the urge to recoil at the vast gulf between the reality of Matt's situation and what he was telling their parents.

They were quiet for awhile, each alternating bites of meat loaf, mashed potatoes, green beans, and homemade bread while watching and listening to Cronkite whenever he spoke of the war. It appeared things were going well for the Americans, who were winning battles and amassing enemy body count daily. When the news was not about the war, the Blessings enjoyed the peacefulness of their pond and rolling hills outside the window.

Maggie also found herself paying attention to a report of an antiwar rally. Although she could tell her dad was listening and not happy with the information, her parents pretended to ignore that segment. Earlier in the year, Maggie had heard about the protests but did not pay much attention. She recalled something about a group called the SDS and their antiwar rally at the University of Michigan that had spread to other campuses. She knew about a larger protest in Washington, D. C. and draft-card burnings at Berkeley. At the time, the incidents did not seem real or relevant. Now they took on a new meaning, and news about protests began to feel more personal.

Matt's letters had raised her awareness about both the protests and the occasional report of an American atrocity in Vietnam. Walter Cronkite was saying, "CBS News has learned that President Johnson has labeled CBS reporter Morley Safer a Communist and ordered him investigated because of Safer's report of American troops' destruction of the Vietnam village complex called Cam Ne. Safer, who was with the troops on what their Captain referred to as a 'search and destroy' mission, reported that the Americans entered the villages and, without warning, began torching the houses using everything from Zippo lighters to flamethrowers. Nothing was spared as could be readily seen in the film footage that Safer sent."

Cronkite concluded the piece, "After a thorough security check, President Johnson was informed that Safer wasn't a Communist, just a Canadian. Johnson's response was, 'Well, I knew he wasn't an American.'"

Maggie, who immediately connected the CBS story to what she had been reading from Matt, was looking at her father for a reaction when the doorbell rang.

"I wonder who that can be. I'll get it," Jenny said.

A moment later, Maggie and her father heard her mother wail, "Harold!"

When Harold and Maggie ran to the front door, they saw a uniformed soldier on either side of Jenny, holding her up. They rushed to her side, keeping one eye on Jenny and the other on the soldiers, who had backed away once Jenny had family support.

"Mr. and Mrs. Blessings, I'm Chaplain Ralph Summers. This is Staff Sergeant William Atkins. May we come in?"

Silently, the Blessings, still huddled together, moved from the door to the living room with the chaplain and staff sergeant close behind. The Blessings made no pretense of bravery as they collectively sank into the sofa. The soldiers remained standing, erect while not at attention.

"We are sorry to have to inform you that your brave son, Specialist Matthew Blessings, was killed in action in Vietnam yesterday afternoon."

Jenny was already in tears. When she had opened the door, she knew immediately but did not want to believe what was happening. Harold held her tightly and sat seemingly emotionless, unable to speak, react, or even breathe.

Maggie exploded from her seat at the chaplain, who was closest to her; fists pounding on his chest, screaming, "No, you're wrong, it's not Matt! It's a mistake!"

The chaplain gently held Maggie to him. Her rage was replaced with uncontrollable sorrow. Screams became wails and tears. She pushed away and returned to the hugs of her parents.

"How did this happen?" Harold was barely able to get it out.

Sergeant Atkins explained, but the Blessings were too numb to hear, and subconsciously each of them decided that, at least for now, it did not really matter. Events over which they had no control thousands of miles from home had dramatically and forever changed the course of their lives.

CHAPTER 6

GHOST-WALKING

May 20, 1965
Tunkannock, Pennsylvania

When they settled in for dinner, Harold Blessings led the family in prayer, "Thank God for my wife and daughter, for this meal, and for my son, who proudly and honorably served his country in an honorable war. Amen."

Only four weeks earlier, the Blessings had learned of Matt's combat death. During that time, with appreciated help from the Army and the local VFW Post, Maggie and her parents had arranged for Matt's funeral. Although they had been offered a military burial at Indiantown Gap National Cemetery about a two-hour drive south of Tunkhannock, they had opted to bury Matt locally at the Dixon Cemetery in Factoryville, only a few miles from the house.

Maggie had returned to school but was ghost-walking through each day. Her previously comfortable status quo had been disrupted when she began to get Matt's letters. Since his death, the friends that used to energize her were like shadows. The classes and hallways she once relished were like empty rooms with but muted sounds. The activities in which she used to take pleasure were now a burden.

Coming home to her family should have provided some relief, but it did not. The place that should have been a haven was far from it. In the short time that seemed like an eternity, her mother had not stopped crying and had aged before Maggie's eyes. Her father spoke of nothing except how his son had died a hero, serving his county with honor and commitment. Only Maggie knew that Matt wanted nothing more than to come home from the war he hated, but she could not talk about it with her parents. Having no outlet for her sorrow, Maggie grew more despondent and isolated, turning down dates, invitations to parties, and requests to get involved in school projects.

Normal conversation at the Blessings home had ceased; a deathly quiet permeated the home that had once been filled with love, laughter, and banter. They still sought to maintain the routines, trying to return to some semblance of normalcy, but it was a ruse. When they sat at the dinner table, the view of their once-beloved pond and hills was now shrouded by closed curtains. The once-idyllic homestead would never be the same.

The only thing that had seemed to maintain some semblance of normalcy was the evening news with Walter Cronkite. Reports of progress on the war continued, but there was increasing attention to protests and the growing antiwar movement.

On this evening, there would be neither Walter Cronkite nor dinner. Following her father's prayer, for the first time in her life, Maggie, without saying a word, left the table and ran out of the room. She went to her bedroom, slammed and locked the door, collapsed onto her bed, and sobbed.

Every other evening after dinner, she had been going to her room. Instead of attending to homework, which no longer had meaning, she spent her time reading and rereading Matt's letters, trying to make sense of what had happened to him and of what had happened to her life.

As her weeping subsided, a sense of clarity began to surface. But Maggie's innermost thoughts were interrupted by a banging on her door and a jiggling of the locked doorknob, "Unlock this door, young lady!"

"Not now, Daddy."

"Yes, now!"

The unusually sharp tone from her father prompted Maggie to rise slowly and reluctantly open the door.

"Why did you leave the dinner table?"

"It's not an honorable war! Matt hated the war! I hate the war! You should too!" Maggie screamed at her father through the remnants of her sobs.

"Matt died a hero in a just cause!" He screamed back.

"Maybe a hero, Dad, but not a just cause," Maggie squeaked out, no longer having the emotional energy to scream and unsuccessfully trying to stave off the shivers.

Her father had lost none of his steam and bellowed, "We'll not have that talk in my house!"

That statement refocused her thinking, and Maggie was about to lash out at her father when her mother came into view and stopped just outside the bedroom door, tears streaming down her cheeks. Maggie could not continue in the face of her mother's tears, so she returned to her bed and rolled over away from her parents. She heard and felt the door slam.

After waiting to ensure they would not return, Maggie rose, walked resolutely to the full-length mirror, stood erect, and stared into her own green eyes. A steady, purposeful young woman stared back. The clarity that had been building inside her had rushed to the surface when the door slammed.

Maggie found herself able to draw on her reserves, muster her intellect and logic, and develop her options. Perhaps without really knowing it, she had been near a decision before dinner and now knew with certainty what she needed to do. Her school was no longer hers. Her family was no longer hers. Her life was no longer hers. She needed to leave. More than that, she needed to do something for Matt. She needed to do everything within her power to help stop the war.

CHAPTER 7

BEAUTY AND ENERGY

July 26, 1965
St. Louis, Missouri

Walter had been right. Despite soreness, anger, and embarrassment, JR had come to work the day after Walter and he had been attacked a year earlier. Everyone on the job site, including the rogues who had done the beating, acted as though nothing had happened. And, as Walter had predicted, there were no repercussions for their attackers. JR's soreness and embarrassment faded, but his anger would not.

JR had also joined his lunch mates again that following Monday—and he continued to do so every day. That meant a lot to Oliver and Mitch, who had fully accepted JR despite their initial wariness.

Unlike any other time in his life, JR sensed what it was to be intellectually stimulated, as he became deeply involved in the daily conversations. Topics wandered from civil rights to the war, from the St. Louis Hawks to barbeque, from construction techniques to politics, and everything in between. One day when the group was discussing cars and bemoaning the poor quality of St. Louis drivers, JR felt comfortable telling them about how he lost his parents.

Then, as Walter, OD, and Not So were stunned and saddened to silence, JR added with both melancholy and appreciation, "With my parents gone and only seeing a couple of high school friends when they're home from college, if it wasn't for the three of you, I'd be pretty much alone."

JR joined the silence.

As was the norm, Walter seemed to know what to say, "Bunch of ways to get over the loneliness. You can find yourself a lady friend or two or more; never a bad idea. You can get in good with the union brotherhood; always a bad idea. You could spend the rest of your life with us; doubt if you want to do that. Or you could join the Army."

Glad to be on a different subject, JR said, "There's that Army thing again, but I just don't know if it's right for me."

Before they could get deeply into the topic of JR and the Army, it was time to get back to work. With plywood, horses, and crates put away, they trudged up the dusty path toward the Arch. JR and Walter were side-by-side, and Walter had slowed the pace, causing them to fall behind OD and Not So. Feeling Walter's hand on his shoulder, JR turned his head toward his friend and was caught off guard when Walter asked, "Would you like to come over for dinner one night? I've been telling my wife about you, and it would be great if you could join us."

JR realized that until this invitation, he had not thought much about Walter having a family. For some reason, except for him telling his story about his parents' crash, family had not been a topic of discussion at the lunch table, and he certainly had no interest in dredging up his memories any further.

"That would be great, if you're sure."

"Not only am I sure, but I think Mary would kill me if you didn't say yes."

"Well, we can't have that happen—need you to stick around for awhile. Sure. Thanks. When would you like me to come by?"

A week later, JR drove along Page Avenue on his way to Walter Rawlings's home on Ella Avenue, a quiet street of small well-kept brick homes in the predominately black community of Wellston. As he approached, JR noticed that many of the Rawlings's neighbors were outside visiting with each other, and that they warily had their eyes riveted on him as he parked and got out of the Bel Air.

JR had recalled that every time he visited another family with his parents, his mom would bring flowers. He carried his bouquet from the car to the house, but did not have to knock. Walter came out to meet him on the front porch, waved to his neighbors, and welcomed JR into his home, where an appetizing aroma wafted through the small, neat, and brightly lit space. A single window air conditioning unit groaned as it labored to keep the heat and humidity of the St. Louis summer at bay.

"I'll bet those are for Mary. Right? Very thoughtful of you. Let's head for the kitchen, and you can make the presentation yourself."

"Uh, Walter?"

"Yes?"

"Thank you for asking me over."

"You're in for a treat. Mary's a great cook. And Karen will be home any minute."

"Karen?"

"Yep, my daughter. She's been out with friends today, like most days. But she'll be home shortly."

"Mary," Walter called out, "special delivery."

As they entered the kitchen, Mary Rawlings was busily moving from bowl to pot to platter. She turned her head, and JR noticed that the slim, graceful woman was doing about as well as Walter in her battle with gray hair.

"Welcome, JR. Walter's told me so much about you. Give me a moment, and we'll get a chance to visit. Oh my, are those for me? You're a real charmer, JR. Thank you."

JR handed her the bouquet, "It's nice to meet you."

Mary left her bowls, pots, and platters to adeptly snip the stems, find a suitable receptacle for the flowers, add water, sniff the bouquet, and place it in the middle of the table that occupied one end of the small space that served as living and dining room.

Then she bustled back to the kitchen saying, "You two visit, and we'll eat as soon as Karen gets home."

When Walter and JR had settled into the sofa, Walter offered, "I'm not a big beer drinker, but I always have some around the house for neighbors. Want one?"

Never being a drinker himself, but not wanting to offend Walter, "Sure, thanks."

"Walter, while I have a moment with just you, do you mind if I ask why, with all of the lunchtime discussions we've had, no one has ever mentioned their families before? I hope you don't mind me asking."

"It's a taboo subject for the three, now four, of us. Let me tell you a story. There's always been racial tension in this city, and much of it has had to do with white folks fearing us black folks would be taking their jobs.

"Not So has been a rabble rouser since day one, and about ten years ago, he had become a real thorn in the side of the unions—being very vocal about why we weren't being let in. When they had the chance, the union guys hollered back. It was all verbal until one night, when Mitch went to a meeting trying to get others to step up and step out. While he was gone, a mob of white folks went to his home and just set it on fire with no warning.

"Mitch comes home to fire trucks and police cars, the charred remains of his house, and..."

Walter searched for words as tears filled his eyes. JR didn't know what to say, so he simply added to the silence.

"...and Dionne," Walter finally able to force out a gravelly whisper, "his pregnant wife, who had been trapped inside the house and died."

JR, who did not like to talk about or even think about his parents' accident, immediately understood why Mitch, Walter, and Oliver avoided discussions about family. He sat quietly with Walter in mutual grief.

"Hi, Dad."

The mood changed immediately as JR was transfixed by the beauty and energy that had exploded into the room. Karen, dressed smartly in a plaid skirt, knee socks, and a white blouse that emphasized her dark, smooth skin, was as tall as JR and had the body and grace of an athlete. Her afro created a four-inch halo around her classic face and engaging smile. JR involuntarily rose and leaned forward as if drawn into Karen's personal space.

"Hi, princess. This is..."

"Hi, JR, glad to finally meet you." JR did not quite know what to do with himself when Karen bear-hugged him.

"I'll be right back," Karen called back to them as she whisked through the room and headed for the kitchen. "Need any help, Mom?"

"Well," Walter said with a grin and obvious pride, "she sure does make an entrance."

Still off balance, JR could only nod.

"Mom says dinner's ready. I guess I was too late to help. Come on, JR, sit next to me."

"You can bring your beer if you'd like, JR," Mary said as she approached the dinner table with the first of the serving platters. "I hope you like pork chops, baked potatoes, and green beans."

"Yes, ma'am, thank you."

"It's Mary to you, young man. Not ma'am," Mary chided and smiled.

As the four settled in, Mary and Walter joined hands on the table as they sat next to each other, and Mary extended her hand to JR, making it obvious what he should do. Walter did the same to Karen, who firmly grabbed both her father's and JR's hands. The Rawlings bowed their heads, so JR followed suit.

"Dear God, bless this meal we are about to receive. Bless our friend, JR, and help him to do what is right in his heart."

JR snuck a quick peek. Walter, eyes closed, was smiling as though he knew JR was watching.

"Bless this family and the love we have for one another. Dear God, keep us safe, especially Walter, Jr. as he fights for his country in the jungles of Vietnam."

JR snuck another peek. Walter's face had turned solemn.

"Amen."

As Walter raised his head and noticed JR staring at him, he explained, "Karen's brother was thinking about college, but thought and prayed long and hard about it. He decided that it was right to enlist in the Army. He decided that being a soldier and fighting for his country was in his heart to do. We're proud of him."

Karen changed the focus of the subject from her brother to JR, "Dad tells me that you're thinking about enlisting."

"Well, I kinda go back and forth on it."

Finding himself feeling perfectly at ease in the midst of the Rawlings family, JR continued, "I'm not sure how I feel about the war. The more I learn about it, the more I'm confused. It seems we can really help those people, but it seems like a long way away to be fighting to help ourselves. I'm also trying to figure out what's right for me. I'm starting to think that being in the Army could help me find my place. I really don't know."

"The only thing I know about the war," Karen responded, "is that I want Walter Jr. home from it. I'm scared for him."

"We all are," Mary added, "but we also know that he is doing what he chose to do, and we respect that and are proud of him."

While listening to Mary, JR noticed out of the corner of his eye that Walter was staring at him. He turned his head, and his eyes met Walter's. JR began to feel what was in his heart to do. Walter smiled knowingly.

CHAPTER 8

A GOOD NIGHT'S SLEEP

August 7, 1965
Tunkhannock, Pennsylvania

Since the confrontation with her father and her realization that perhaps the best thing for her to do was leave home, Maggie struggled with that prospect, knowing instinctively not to act on impulse. She found it heart-wrenching to turn away from her roots and decided the best thing to do was to stay at least through graduation, hoping time and the significance of the event might change things.

During the weeks leading up to graduation, she dutifully went to school and did everything she could to give her parents a chance to reengage with her, with reality, and with life.

Every evening, Maggie would attempt to prompt a conversation at the dinner table, but to no avail. She also tried to engage with each of her parents separately; seeking out her father when he was absentmindedly piddling in his garden; finding her mother sorting through laundry that she had already sorted several times. Not knowing whether it was their fault or hers, Maggie was unsuccessful at making any meaningful connection.

Dejected, she would retire to the solitude of her room, reread Matt's letters, and look within herself to search for a reason not to leave. But each time she played her options out in her head and her heart, she found the reasons to stay, her family, her friends, her future, to be less compelling than the choice to leave.

On graduation morning, Maggie dragged herself through the motions of getting ready, sat silently in the back seat of the family car on the way to the high school, left her parents to find her appointed place, dolefully marched with her classmates, and settled into the first of the many rows of white folding chairs that had been arrayed on the football field.

Less than two months earlier, she was looking forward to this day with great anticipation, but now she could only sit in her cap and gown with shoulders slumped and think how meaningless it all seemed. What is a high school graduation compared to losing Matt? What is it compared to becoming estranged from her family?

Impervious to the beauty of the cloudless comfortable day and with the ceremony droning on in her background, she considered the prospect of going to Penn State, having gone through the motions to prepare to do so. But that too seemed inconsequential. The only thought that continued to come to the fore was that she owed it to Matt and herself to do something to end the war that had consumed them both.

She looked up and spotted her parents sitting alone in a far corner of the bleachers and knew their hearts were not in what should have been a joyous lifecycle event. Maggie did not join her classmates when they threw their mortarboards into the air but quietly waited to join the march out of the stadium. She walked straight to the car to meet her parents for a ride home that was without conversation or radio—the whirr of the tires on the rural roads the only sound.

Not knowing exactly when and how to leave, Maggie started her summer as she had for the past three years, working at Reese Florist in downtown Tunkhannock. Despite offers from friends, she chose not to go out in the evenings while continuing to find no solace at home.

One Friday night, Maggie looked herself in the eyes in the bathroom mirror and knew it was time. "I just can't do this anymore," she said quietly but resolutely. She left her room, looked for her mom, found her sitting alone in the living room, and asked if she could borrow the family car Saturday morning to meet some friends for breakfast at the Shadowbrook Golf Course restaurant, at one time not an uncommon occurrence. Before going to bed that night, Maggie located her large duffle bag, chose the clothes and incidentals she would take with her, packed the bag, and put it in her closet.

Fearing that she would not be able to sleep, she was surprised when she awoke Saturday morning, having had her best night since she began getting Matt's Vietnam letters. Surmising that the good night's sleep was a reflection of her being at peace with her decision to leave home, Maggie loaded the bag in the trunk of the car.

She loved her mother and father and was distraught about leaving without telling them she was going or where or why. She knew she was piling on additional pain, but she also knew there was no way to have the conversation. Maggie had considered that when she pulled away from the house, she might never be back, never see her parents again, and possibly never even talk with them. It hurt, but she was convinced staying would hurt more and, she rationalized, staying would not relieve her parents' deep suffering. Once again, she concluded that she was at peace with her decision.

Maggie hugged her mom, tighter than she had planned, kissed her quickly before her mother noticed the tears welling in Maggie's eyes, and went looking for her father. She found him where he spent much of his time, in his armchair stoically staring at Matt's photos on the mantel—Matt in graduation cap and gown; Matt in his football uniform; Matt waving from the backyard pond; Matt in full and formal military uniform.

"I'm going, Daddy."

"Huh? OK, g'bye."

"I love you, Daddy."

"Uh-huh."

Maggie bent over and hugged her father, who pressed his head only slightly into hers but did not hug her back. She knew he would not notice her tears.

"Bye, Daddy."

No answer.

Maggie took a deep breath and headed out the door to the car. She had not figured out a way to let her mom and dad know how to get the car back or even where it was, but she would deal with that later. She started the lime gold Ford Fairlane 500, took another deep breath, and headed down the long driveway on her way to the Scranton bus station, about 45 minutes and a lifetime away.

Despite her uncertainty, Maggie felt energized by her new sense of purpose and freedom. The tears faded, and she sat erect behind the steering wheel as she turned toward town.

Maggie had two stops to make before she went to the bus station. From her years of work at Reese Florist and occasional babysitting, Maggie had accumulated nearly $2700 for her college fund. Knowing the bank was open on Saturday mornings, she stopped to withdrew her money, hid most of it deep within her duffle bag next to Matt's letters, and headed east on Route 92.

Her next stop was the one she dreaded most. It was time to say goodbye to Matt. As she had hoped, the cemetery was deserted, and she was able to visit with her brother alone. Although anxious as she got out of the car, Maggie was calmed by the silence, serenity, and scent of freshly mowed lawn.

She approached and stared at the gravestone that rested in the shadow of an ancient oak tree, visualizing Matt from the last time she saw him—broad smile, broad shoulders, knowing eyes. "Matt, I've made a decision that I know is going to hurt Mom and Dad. But, it is the only thing I can do to make things right for me. If I don't try to do something to make sense of what's happened, I'll go crazy or worse.

"You made a difference in my life before you left. Then you trusted me with your letters. Then you were gone, and that made a difference in my life again. The war took you from me and destroyed our family. Now, just like you, I hate this war. My only choice is to help stop it. It's what I need to do. For you. For me."

Maggie knelt and laid her hand gently on the gravestone, "I love you, Matt."

The cooling shade and the mild breeze added to the tranquility, giving her time to think about what she had decided to do. Now that she had declared her intentions to Matt, there was no doubt. She rose, walked steadfastly to the car, and began the journey into the rest of her life.

Maggie found a spot in the free parking lot near the bus station. As she walked toward the building's entrance, she noticed a post office across the street. With a twinge of regret and responsibility, she bought a postcard and stamp and wrote simply, "Your car is in the parking lot of the Scranton bus station. I love you. Maggie"

She was afraid to write more, not wanting to give any clue to where she was going, which was easy because she really did not know herself. She also did not want to get into an explanation or write anything that would give her pause. Wanting delivery of the postcard to be delayed, Maggie purposely used the wrong address so the card would be delivered to the Swansons down the road, knowing they would get the card to her parents. Opening the heavy metal mailbox door, she held onto the postcard for a few seconds, dropped it in, let the door slam shut, and crossed the street.

Maggie had no particular plan when she entered the chaotic bus station, but she knew she wanted to get involved with the antiwar movement and a bus could get her closer to the action. All she knew about the protest movement was from television and newspaper reports and, at the time, she was thinking East Coast, for no other reason than it was reasonably close.

When she was 14, her family traveled to Washington, D. C., the only vacation they had taken outside of Pennsylvania. When Maggie looked at the bus schedule in the Scranton station and saw there was a Greyhound to Washington, she rationalized that maybe the city would feel familiar. She also recalled reports of large protest marches in Washington. Two hours later, she was in the back of the bus heading south on I-81 passing through Wilkes-Barre.

The good news was that she was now free to travel where and when she wanted, she was looking forward to expanding her horizons, and she was on her way. The bad news was that she was neither travel-wise nor streetwise, and she could not fully shake the effects of having left home.

CHAPTER 9

THIS IS MAGGIE; SHE'S WITH ME

August 7, 1965
Washington, D. C.

As Maggie had considered leaving home, she knew she would begin without a place to stay and without knowing anyone. At the time, she surprised herself to discover that the uncertainty did not seem all that intimidating. But as her bus approached Washington D. C., Maggie felt more than just a pang of anxiety, and her senses were on full alert. Fighting for control, she whispered to herself, "It's OK, Mags, you can do this and you have to do this."

She smiled at her use of the name "Mags" and knew Matt was with her on the bus and would be with her wherever she went.

With duffle bag in tow and Matt in her heart, Maggie stepped into the D. C. bus station, which was far more unsettling than even what she had experienced in Scranton. The size was disorienting. The echoes of unintelligible announcements being made, of piped-in music, and of vendors hawking their wares were jarring. The smells of too-old frying oil and grease from the food court were overwhelming. The bustling of passengers to and from buses and streets was chaotic.

After a number of deep breaths, Maggie forced a confident bearing and headed for the middle of the station to figure out her next move.

As she was about to find an exit to get oriented on the D. C. streets, Maggie noticed a striking young woman with wild curly long black hair, dressed in jeans, a black sleeveless tank top, and sandals, and very clearly not wearing a bra. Behind the woman was a chair acting as an impromptu easel supporting a poster that read,

THIS IS MAGGIE; SHE'S WITH ME

"Bring the war home." She was handing out leaflets to anyone who would stop. Few did.

Maggie was drawn to the young woman, who remained persistent despite the lack of interest in her flyers. As Maggie got closer, she heard the woman shout to a passerby, "The war is unjust! The war is an atrocity! Bring the war home!"

Maggie reached for and scanned a mimeographed leaflet. There were photos of whom she assumed were Vietnamese standing in front of burning huts. Matt's stories exploded in her mind's eye. Maggie looked up to realize the woman was staring at her. "Hi, I'm Bernie. Are you against the fucking war?"

"Why, uh, yes. In fact..."

"Well what the hell are you doing about it?" Bernie interrupted.

"I...I don't...I'm not really...doing anything...yet."

"Well..."

It was Maggie's turn to interrupt, and she spoke in rapid fire, "I want to do something. I really do. It's just that I don't know what to do. But I'm ready to help. I want to. I have to. I'm Maggie. I just got off the bus from Scranton. I want to help."

"OK, OK, Maggie, I get it. I'm about out of leaflets, tired of being on my fucking feet, and need some coffee. Wanna get some?"

Not waiting for an answer, Bernie left the remaining pile of leaflets on the chair, put the poster under her arm, threw her large green canvas bag over her shoulder, and started out at a brisk pace. Bernie was her first link to her future, and Maggie was not about to lose her in the crowds of the bus station or the streets.

But even before leaving the station, Maggie bumped into bustling travelers, each time putting her farther behind. Determined to stay close, Maggie leaned forward, concentrated on maneuvering her duffle through the crowds, and ran to catch up. She knew she had done so when she stepped on the heel of Bernie's sandal, nearly causing them both to fall.

Once on the streets, Bernie walked and talked nonstop about the absurdity of the war and the U. S. government's role in the oppression of the Vietnamese people. Then without warning, she turned into a nondescript doorway about six blocks from the station. It took awhile for Maggie's eyes to adjust to the candlelit room. It was small, smoky, and smelled of coffee, human sweat, and some odors she could not identify.

"This is Maggie; she's with me," Bernie said to no one in particular and everyone at the same time.

About 15 people were scattered among small tables that were barely big enough to hold a few cups and glasses.

"A few more people stopped to talk and take a flyer," someone said from the darkness. "How did you do, Bern?"

"Likewise, but there are still too many assholes who just don't get it," Bernie sighed.

Maggie had heard what she thought was her fair share of cursing among her friends at school. But looking back, all that had seemed forced compared to how Bernie's language flowed so naturally.

"Can I get you something, Bernie?" The voice seemed to emanate from behind a small counter in the back.

"Yeah, a cup of that fucking mud you call coffee, Mort. And one for my new best friend, Maggie."

"Thanks," Maggie was barely able to get the word out. She had never been in a place like this or met anyone like Bernie before. She wanted to dive right into her new experience, but would clearly need some time to adjust.

"Maggie, how do you want your coffee?" Mort hollered as if he had said it several times and had not been heard.

That was a tough question. She had never had coffee before. "Just regular," she said sheepishly, vaguely remembering her dad saying that and hoping it would answer the question.

"Where are you staying, Maggie?" Bernie jumped back in.

"I haven't figured that out yet."

"Mort, Maggie's crashing with us tonight. OK? Of course, it's OK."

"Sure, Bernie, the more the merrier. As long as she doesn't mind sleeping on the floor," Mort declared with a semblance of authority.

THIS IS MAGGIE; SHE'S WITH ME

"Bullshit, Mort. You sleep on the floor. Maggie's going to sleep in the bed with me. We're not having my new best friend sleep on the fucking floor."

Bernie led Maggie to a table near the counter. Because sound was unmuffled in the compact coffeehouse, it was easy to hear every conversation taking place, and almost every statement was about the war, racial inequality, and what to do about each. Maggie could do little but listen with mouth agape as she had two overwhelming reactions. It seemed that she had stumbled into protest-movement-central, and she was surprised that this collection of whites seemed to care as much about racial issues as they did about the war. Where she came from, race was only a topic of discussion on the TV news and in an occasional current events class.

After Mort brought the coffee, Maggie ventured a first sip. Noticing the pained expression on Maggie's face, Bernie said, "I told you it was fucking mud. It's an acquired taste; kinda like Mort himself."

"I have to admit—I've never had coffee before. In fact, I've never been in a place like this before or met anyone like you."

"I can't wait to hear your story. Let's get out of here. It's late anyway."

In the excitement of her day, Maggie had lost track of time. It was late and she had not eaten except for the few snacks she had packed for the bus ride. "Where can I get something to eat first?"

"We'll find something upstairs."

"Upstairs?"

"Yeah, that's where Mort and I crash. He's never told me how or why, but he owns this building. I pay him some rent and keep him warm at night. C'mon, let's go."

Bernie said good-bye to no one in particular and everyone at the same time and led Maggie out of the coffeehouse, down a dark, narrow walkway between it and the adjacent building, to a creaky wooden stairway. Compared to the rundown, dimly-lit, cramped, smoky, smelly coffeehouse, the two room apartment, while clearly old, was comfortable, neat, and inviting.

"Dump your bag in the bedroom—you're sleeping with me. You can catch a shower if you'd like. I'll find us something to eat."

A shower and something to eat sounded great. Maggie took her bag to the bedroom, put it on the floor in the corner as far out of the way as possible, pulled out a Tunkhannock High School tee-shirt and a pair of sweat pants that would serve as pajamas, and headed for the shower.

As the hot water enveloped her body and steam rose to surround her, she allowed herself to escape from the emotions of the day—from hugging and leaving her parents to saying goodbye to Matt, from the anxious moments of the bus ride to the uncertainty of the bus stations, from meeting Bernie to the new world of the coffeehouse.

Maggie's moment of meditation came to an abrupt end when the water went from hot to cold in an instant, and she realized she had been in the shower a long time. Turning off the water, she dried off, put on her makeshift PJ's, and refolded her clothes in her bag.

The cathartic effect of the shower lingered, helping Maggie to think about what was next instead of what had been, and the order of business was something to eat. One step at a time seemed to be working out. She came out of the bedroom to a sight she had not expected. There was Bernie, placing plates with sandwiches and glasses of wine on the small table in the corner of the room that served as kitchen, living room, dining room, guest room, and whatever else was needed. And except for her panties, Bernie was stark naked.

Maggie stared, trying to gain her composure before Bernie looked up. She had seen other girls naked before at slumber parties and in the showers after gym class, but she had never seen a body like Bernie's—breasts large but firm, stomach flat, hips perfect, legs long and shapely. And she had never seen anyone so comfortable with her body as to just be casually naked. Pretending all of this did not affect her, Maggie tried to appear nonchalant as she said, "The shower was perfect."

"Great. Hope you like turkey and cheese, because that's what we have. And I hope you like this wine, because that's what we have."

Struggling to keep from staring at Bernie's breasts, Maggie said, "Turkey and cheese is great. But another confession—I'm not a big wine drinker. In fact, I've not had much more wine in my life than coffee. But I'll try it."

"I don't know your story, Maggie, but I'll bet there are a lot of things you'll be trying for the first time very soon."

"OK, confession time again. I've never eaten with a naked woman sitting across the table from me either."

"Just naked men," Bernie smirked.

"No, no, no—no one naked. Bernie, you're beautiful."

"Thanks, Mags."

Maggie was shocked. "Mags" sounded as natural coming out of Bernie as it had from Matt.

"At one time, I wasn't comfortable with this either. But we're part of a fucking revolution. You'll get used to it."

"I'm not so sure," Maggie confessed while lowering her eyes.

They ate in silence for awhile. Maggie finally tried the wine and liked it. It gave the warmth from the shower a booster shot, and she asked for more. As she poured another glass for each of them, Bernie cautioned Maggie to be careful not to overdo it too soon.

"You know, Mags, I've been on my fucking feet all day and I'm beat. Mort's working late tonight. Why don't we hit the hay and let him fend for himself when he comes up?"

While Bernie was in the bathroom, Maggie sat on the side of the bed not knowing what to do. When Bernie entered the bedroom, she did so having also removed her panties and got into bed. Maggie left her PJ's on and stiffly lay down on the other side.

"Mags, I know I can be a little overwhelming at times, especially to someone who meets me for the first time. I know absolutely nothing about you except that from the moment you came up to me in the bus station today, I knew I liked you. Sleep well and we'll talk in the morning."

Maggie had never shared a bed with anyone, let alone a beautiful, naked woman she had only met a few hours before. She was more than a little intimidated, but Bernie had made her feel comfortable, and Maggie sensed she knew she could not have asked for a better start to her new life. She was starting to nod off when Bernie leaned over and kissed her on the cheek and hugged her. It was intimate, but not offensive. Maggie found herself returning the hug and said, "Good night, Bernie."

Bernie fell asleep immediately. As she lay on her back, eyes wide open and listening to Bernie's light rhythmic snoring, Maggie thought about her day's journey. She had awakened in her own bed and was now going to sleep in a stranger's bed. She had left her family and friends behind, but to her great surprise could begin to envision a new future. Maggie could also not help but wonder whether she had made and was making the right choices. Was it really OK to have left her parents, especially without telling them anything? Was it OK to be in Bernie's bed? Was it OK to be living moment to moment? Or just in general, was she OK? Before she could answer herself, Margaret Blessings fell asleep.

CHAPTER 10

WE'RE GOING TO BERKELEY

August 8, 1965
Washington, D. C.

When Maggie awoke, Bernie was not in bed. After stretching, wiping sleepers from her eyes, and hearing talking in the other room, Maggie went to join Bernie and Mort and gasped.

They were only inches apart and facing each other on the sleeping bag Mort had used, each fully naked. Interrupted by the gasp, they merely looked up and said "Good morning" before returning to their conversation.

"We need to talk, but I've got to go open the coffeehouse," Mort said, pulling Bernie to him and kissing her.

Bernie broke the kiss and said, "I'm really serious about doing this. I'd dig it if you would come with me, but if not, I'll just go by my own fuckin' self. I need to get more deeply involved and I feel locked in here—not by you, but by the lack of action. We need to be doing more."

"I'll see you later today, and we'll figure it out," Mort responded as he stood, helped Bernie to her feet, and hugged her.

Their bodies fit together so well. Although she really wanted to look, Maggie turned away and asked over her shoulder, "Do you want me to leave?"

"No, Mags, don't be silly. Mort has to go anyway, so there'll be no nookie for him this morning."

Maggie did not know what that word meant but could make a pretty good guess. Mort picked up his clothes from the day before and stumbled while trying to get into his pants. Bernie reached to support him and chuckled while hugging Mort once more after he finally got dressed. "We'll talk later," she said as he walked out the door.

When Mort had left, Bernie walked over to Maggie, gave her a big hug and a kiss on the cheek. "Let's make some toast and coffee. We've got stories to tell. Do you want to tell them with clothes on or naked?"

When Bernie was dressed, they sat at the table, worked on breakfast, and talked. Maggie went first and was surprised how easy it was and how relieved she felt to tell Bernie everything; that is, everything except that until now, Matt was the only one to call her "Mags."

Bernice Williams grew up in Brick, New Jersey, aced high school without having to study much, spent a lot of time in the back seat of guy's cars, and decided to go as far away for college as she could. She had a cousin who lived in Sacramento and who went to college at the University of California, Berkeley. That sounded far enough, so she told her parents, who could afford any college she chose and just wanted what was "best for their baby." She enrolled at Berkeley for the fall 1964 semester.

"When I first got there, it was easy to get into the sex scene. What was new for me was the drugs. Sure, some of my high school buddies were druggies, but it never appealed to me. That changed at Berkeley. It was everywhere, and I guess I was ready to experiment. Oh, don't get me wrong—I was going to classes. But in between, I was smokin' pot and fuckin'."

Bernie hesitated, "Mags, I'm sorry. Does that bother you? I mean, really."

Maggie's faced reddened, "My only...um, experience in high school was with a boy I dated for a few months. One night on the way home from a movie, he stopped the car, leaned over and kissed me. Oh, we had kissed before, but this time it was different. I was kissing him back when he put his hand on my breast over my blouse and just held it there. I've never told anyone else this before.

"I guess it was OK, but when he tried to unbutton my blouse, I told him to stop and he did. I think he was more relieved than I was that we stopped. Until this morning, the only time I've ever seen a boy naked was when I accidently walked into the bathroom one time when Matt had just gotten out of the shower. I ran out, and we never talked about it."

"So, does it bother you? I mean the way I talk and the way I act."

"It doesn't really bother me, but I'm not used to it."

"Anyway, Berkeley started off being classes, sex, and pot. But that didn't last long. I guess I never thought about it before I went there, but I didn't really have any direction in my life. Maybe no one in high school does—I don't know. So, whether I knew it or not, I was looking for some sense of direction, and boy did I ever fucking find it at Berkeley.

"Berkeley was protest central. Everyone had a cause or two or more. At first, I went along with the throngs just to be there, but soon I was paying attention to what students and faculty were saying, and it started making sense. I was hooked.

"When I got there, people were still talking about the protest at the Sheraton Palace—4000 people, mostly students, rallying against the assholes with racially biased hiring practices. That must have gotten it started. During my first semester, a CORE leader..."

Maggie interrupted, "What's CORE?"

"Congress of Racial Equality," Bernie said, and assuming that would suffice, continued.

"The leader was arrested for violating the university's new rules against student activism. Thousands of us surrounded the police car, and some took turns making speeches from the top of the car. And you know what? The next day, the fucking administration signed a pact with leaders of the student groups. We won. The whole experience was energizing and fun. But I still didn't have a clue what it was really all about.

"I started spending more time with people who were deeply involved in the protests. It was listening to them that got me to understand what was really happening in this country—the racial shit, the fucking war, and the assholes who were running the country and lying to us. The protests took on a new meaning for me. I found my life direction. I needed to make a difference."

Bernie had gotten more and more agitated as she went on, realized it, took a deep breath, smiled at Maggie, and said, "You may be able to tell that I really care about what I'm doing."

"I did get that idea," Maggie said as she smiled back. "So, why aren't you still in Berkeley?"

Bernie wiped some jam off of her lips. "I get home when the year is over. I'm feeling like I own the world and can make a difference in it. I can't wait to lay this all on my friends and even my parents. I had seen them over Christmas and semester break when I didn't really have my shit together. But by June, I was more than just along for the joy ride. I was serious. I had become a leader. I was speaking out on my own. I was committed. Then the shit hit the fan."

Maggie had not taken a bite and was leaning into Bernie's story.

"A few days after I get home, my parents sit me down for a talk, asking me what happened to my grades. They were used to all A's and I was getting B's and C's—oh, and a D. I proceeded to tell them that grades weren't as important as other things and let the whole thing out. I told them about the protests, how I had gotten involved, how I was now an active leader. Then I told them about the arrest."

"You were arrested?"

"We were at a draft board sit-in and were ordered to leave. A bunch stood up to go, and I started shouting to them to sit their asses down. The cops figured I was the leader, which I sorta was. When many of us wouldn't move, the pigs picked me up first and carried me to the wagon they had outside. About ten of us were taken in, lectured to, and released with a warning. So, I wasn't really charged, but I was hauled in. Anyway, I told this all to my folks, who just sat there with their mouths wide open. They couldn't say anything, so I walked out of the room.

"When I got back in from a late night with my high school friends, my parents were waiting up for me. They never did that, but there they were. They proceeded to tell me that I wasn't going back to Berkeley. They gave me shit about my grades, about the arrest, and about just generally being involved with all of those hippie protestors. They said I could either go to school closer to home or get a job until I figured out what I really wanted to do with my life.

"I told them I already knew what I wanted to do with my life and it sure as shit wasn't doing nothing about what was going on in this country like they were. We yelled at each other for awhile—I can't remember what we said, but I was pissed and, for what I think was the first times in their lives, so were they. They'd always given me what I wanted, let me do what I wanted to do. But they were so fucking establishment, they couldn't accept what I was into.

"I screamed that they couldn't stop me from being who I was, and I would leave. My dad said that maybe it would be best if I did. My mom broke down and cried, which caused us all to take a deep breath. 'Look,' I said, 'I need to be myself and do what I think is right. If I can't do that here, I need to leave. I'll let you know where I am, but tomorrow morning, I'm gone.'"

Bernie shrugged as if to indicate she did not really care that she made the choice, but her sheepish smile gave away her deeper feelings.

"What did they say?"

"Nothing. Dad focused on getting Mom to stop crying. I turned around and went to pack. Since then, I've kept my promise and let them know where I am. Mom sends me money every month; I guess hoping that will make me want to come home. She just doesn't fucking get it.

"So here I am."

"And, so here I am."

Bernie reached across the table, took Maggie by the hand, looked her in the eye and said, "Are you up for an adventure?"

Maggie met Bernie's stare, "I left home knowing that's what my life would become, an adventure. And I know every step will take me farther away from home, and that's not the most comfortable thing yet. But, sure, I'm up for it."

"OK, then, we're going to Berkeley."

CHAPTER 11

LOSE THE PJ'S

August 9, 1965
Washington, D. C.

When Mort returned later in the day, Bernie told him about their decision to head west, fully expecting him to be tied to his coffeehouse and to Washington, D. C. "Bernie, I don't want you to go, but if you have to, I wish you well. You can crash here as long as you'd like. Maggie too."

That night, Maggie slept on the floor in the other room but barely got any sleep with all of the noise from the bedroom. It was not the noise itself that kept her awake; it was the stirring she felt deep inside her—did she want to be in the bedroom too?

In the morning, Mort ambled toward Maggie in only his tee-shirt looking for his pants and absentmindedly playing with himself. He yawned. "Hey, Maggie. Sleep well?"

"Not exactly. I was a little distracted," she said, finding herself staring at Mort's penis.

Mort noticed her attention, "Oh, well next time, if you feel like it, just come on in."

He paused, took on a more serious look, and removed his hand from his crotch, "Actually, there won't be many next times. Will there?"

Mort found his pants, put them on, picked up his shoes and socks, and without looking back to say goodbye to either Maggie or Bernie, walked out of the apartment.

Maggie got up from the sleeping bag on the floor and went into the bedroom to check if Bernie wanted any coffee. She found Bernie under the covers, lying on her back and staring at the ceiling with a hint of a tear in her eye. While she had only known Bernie for less than 48 hours, Maggie could not imagine her ever being vulnerable. "Are you OK?"

Bernie did not immediately answer but slowly brought her gaze into focus and looked at Maggie. "Mort's a good soul, and I'll miss him."

Bernie's face changed to a devilish grin, "Oh, and he's a great fuck too. Mags, I didn't get much sleep last night, so I'm going to settle in for awhile."

"I didn't sleep much either. Like I told Mort, I was a little distracted."

"Well, why don't you bring that red hair, those green eyes, and that great body to bed? I'll sleep better with you here. When we get up later, we can figure out how we want to head west. Oh, and Mags, lose the PJ's."

Maggie recoiled, took two steps away from the bed, and thought to herself, "Coffee for the first time—no problem. Wine for the first time—no problem. Seeing Bernie casually naked—I can handle that. Seeing Mort naked from the waist down—surprisingly, a little exciting. But..."

"Bernie, I don't think I'm ready to do that. I hope you don't mind."

"Your call, Mags," Bernie said casually, yawned, and stretched, "but we both need some sleep."

Maggie, PJ's still on, crawled into bed. Bernie smiled, kissed Maggie on the cheek, and as she rolled over, whispered, "Sleep well, Mags," and dozed off.

Once again, Maggie had time to think after Bernie fell asleep. Although she was becoming more comfortable with Bernie, Mort, and a level of intimacy she had never experienced, she was not ready for so much so quickly. But as she watched Bernie sleep, Maggie considered her new friend and smiled at how comfortable, safe, and relaxed she was beginning to feel. She leaned over and returned Bernie's kiss on the cheek, closed her eyes, and fell asleep.

When Maggie awoke, Bernie was not in bed. Maggie stretched, pulled off the covers, and found Bernie, dressed in cut-off shorts and a tee-shirt that read, "Make love, not war" across her ample chest.

"I thought I'd get dressed for you, Mags."

"Bernie, I hope you didn't mind that..."

"Mags, no worries. Maybe some other time; maybe not. Like I said, 'Your call.'"

"Thank you," Maggie said and initiated their hug.

"We've got some planning to do. It's time to get serious."

Over a sandwich, they made several decisions. Their goal was to get to the Bay Area, but they would not hurry themselves. They would stick around Washington until they were fully ready to leave and then choose interim destinations that would be both meaningful and fun. They thought they'd have enough money, but agreed that if they needed to stop someplace and work for awhile, that was alright too.

CHAPTER 12

SOUNDS LIKE A PLAN

October 31, 1965
San Francisco, California

On the Sunday following the call to his dad, Mooch was on a mid-morning bus to San Francisco to meet FBI Special Agent Paul Marcus for lunch. He had called the agent immediately after hanging up with his father, and the two agreed to get together.

As promised, Marcus met the bus. They had described themselves on the phone and had no problem finding each other. What Marcus had not mentioned was the scar that curved from his left cheekbone, around the corner of his mouth, to the center of his chin. Mooch worked hard not to stare.

With greetings out of the way, the pair made their way to a small well-worn diner across the street, settled into a small booth whose faded red vinyl seats were split exposing their foam padding, ordered from the limited menu, and began a conversation and relationship that would continue over the years.

After a few moments of compulsory small talk to get to know each other, Marcus honed in on the reason that brought them together, "So, Mooch, your dad tells me that you're beyond interested in joining the FBI. In fact, he used the word 'committed.'"

"He's right, Agent Marcus."

"I told you over the phone and in the station and I mean it—call me Paul; at least when we're on our own. If you ever come by the office, we'll get more formal."

"OK, Paul," Mooch said, still uncomfortable using the first name of someone his parents' age, "Thanks. Anyway, I've been interested in law enforcement ever since I can remember. I'm sure it's all because of my dad and his friends. I really don't know where the specific interest in the FBI came from, but I also can't remember when I wasn't...what was Dad's word...committed."

"I can relate. That's how I felt. Not as early as you, but I really wanted the bureau, and I'm glad I chose it and they chose me. I get it that you're committed, but the key question is why. It's not important because I'm curious—although I am. It's important for you to know."

"I guess I like the way cops act when they're together. The work seems challenging and exciting. I think I'd be good at it. And, if you promise not to tell Dad..."

Mooch hesitated, waiting for a sign that Paul was willing to hold a confidence from his old friend. Paul responded with a nod and a smile as if he knew what was coming.

Mooch sat up a little straighter and finished his thought, "I want Dad to be proud of me, and I know he'd bust his buttons if I were an FBI agent."

"No doubt. You know he's already proud of you, right?"

"Yeah," said Mooch, reddening a little.

Paul leaned into the conversation, focused his eyes on Mooch's. "All of that's well and good, but I gotta tell you—you sound like a three year old who just saw a shiny red fire engine go by with lights and sirens. When it passes, the mom asks the kid, 'What do you want to be when you grow up?' 'A fireman, Mommy!'"

Mooch held the eye contact, but was taken aback. He thought to himself that Dad said Paul was a straight shooter, but...wow.

Mooch was glad when Paul continued so he would not have to respond, "Look, Mooch, I don't doubt that you really want to be an agent, and it's likely that you'll be one someday. But, you're old enough to be thinking more deeply before you make a lifelong commitment to something. Why do you think your dad is a cop?"

Lunch was delivered, giving Mooch some extra time to think about an answer. But before he could respond, Paul answered the question himself, "Your dad does it because he is dedicated to making a difference in people's lives and in the community. Simple as that. Makes him feel good. Guess what. Even though I started out because of the excitement, challenge, and even the ego of it all,

I'm coming out where your dad is. I make a difference and that feels good."

Mooch took a bite of his cheeseburger, wiped the grease and pickle juice from his mouth with a napkin, and thought about what Paul said. Paul also ate quietly, giving Mooch time to process this seemingly new thought.

Apparently, Paul was ready to leave Mooch with the unstated expectation that he would think more about why he wanted the FBI, because he changed the subject, "So, Mister Committed, how are you going to get from this hole-in-the-wall restaurant today to the FBI out there in your future?"

"Well, I'll graduate in three years instead of four, go to law school, get as much practical experience as I can along the way, and apply for the bureau."

"Sounds like a plan. Listen, Mooch, I'm not sure what I can do to help, but I'll be glad to do anything I can. I'll check around to see if there's any way to grease the skids. No promises."

"Wow, that would be great!" Mooch could not contain his excitement. "Sorry," he said, trying to calm himself. "That would really be great. And I understand; no promises."

For the next hour, Mooch told Paul about his campus police job, but mostly, he picked Paul's brain about the FBI, and Paul was able to talk about some of his cases and about how he did his work.

During a lull in the conversation as they were finishing their lunches, Paul looked up and caught Mooch glancing at the scar. Paul explained, "About eight months ago, I got a message that there was a protest planned at Berkeley. We expected a lot of students to be sitting in at a local hotel to demonstrate against racially discriminating hiring practices. The bureau had some information that the protest was being incited by a group from the Midwest, and we wanted to identify the instigators. So, several of us dressed casually and went over to Berkeley.

"The local Berkeley police intercepted the 200 or so that were walking to the hotel and chanting slogans. When the protestors found themselves surrounded, they got frustrated and belligerent and started picking up anything on the street within reach and throwing it at the locals. I was behind a police line, but something hit me in the side of the face and tore it open. Next thing I know, I'm in the hospital getting stitched up."

"I'm sorry it happened, Paul," Mooch said.

"I'm sorry too. It took awhile for it to stop hurting like hell, and I had headaches off and on for a few months. But, it's part of the job. It's not like I'm in a potentially violent situation on a daily basis, but it's to be expected."

Paul paid for lunch.

"Thank you, Paul."

"I owe your dad a lot, Mooch. The least I could do is buy you lunch."

"No, that's not what I meant—but, yes, thanks for lunch too. I meant about spending this time with me and..."

"I know what you meant. My pleasure. Anytime."

On his bus ride home, Mooch revisited every word of his meeting with Paul, especially the discussion about why he wanted to be in the FBI. It was more than his dad being a cop; more than being around cops his whole life; more than loving *The Untouchables*. Although he could not yet articulate his reasons, he felt good about taking on the challenge of being able to do so.

CHAPTER 13

THE HUG

November 1, 1965
St. Louis, Missouri

Early in the week, unusually warm fall temperatures had caused the open ends of the two base legs of the St. Louis Gateway Arch to expand beyond tolerance. On Thursday, after a night during which JR and others hosed water on and in the giant curved legs to cool them down, the keystone, the topmost and center section, was installed to complete the majestic landmark.

Despite the installation of the final segment of the monument, work at the construction site continued. The Museum of Western Expansion located underground beneath the Arch was being completed, and there was the inevitable post-construction cleanup and landscaping to be done. Like the other workers on the site, JR had begun to think about where he would be working next. He could not have imagined the devastating circumstances in which that answer would come to him.

Before JR had left the Rawlings's home the last time he visited, Mary had invited him to join them again on Monday. Karen and he had also planned to meet at Steak 'n Shake for lunch on Saturday, neither admitting to themselves it would be considered a date. Were it not for the overt stares and a few just-loud-enough-to-be-heard comments from staff and other patrons, they would have thoroughly enjoyed their time together. St. Louis was not ready to see a white boy and a black girl together.

JR spent Sunday with the flu, throwing up, fighting diarrhea, or both at the same time. Barely able to stand, he opted out of both work and the dinner invitation the next day.

By Monday evening, he was getting some strength back and was no longer tethered to the bathroom. As he was about to doze off, his telephone rang, "JR, come down to Barnes Hospital now. Dad's been hurt. He's in the emergency room. He asked for you. He needs you here. I need you here. JR…"

"Karen, what happened? Never mind, not now. I'm on my way."

It was only the adrenaline that broke through his weakness and got him to the car. Barely remembering the drive, JR arrived at the hospital, parked, and ran to the emergency waiting room, where he saw Mary, Karen, Oliver, and Mitch huddled together in a far corner.

"It's not good." OD said just above a whisper as he stepped out to intercept JR before he got to the Rawlings.

"What happened?"

"Remember that guy who beat on you and Walter that day? Well, we were heading for our cars after work today, and he and his goons stop us, and he says something like, 'I understand your nigger daughter is screwing your white friend.' Then he asks where you are."

"You mean this is all my fault?"

"Whoa, man. No. Fault's only in one place—that guy. Walter says, 'You can say what you want about me, but leave my daughter out of this.' Next thing we know, Walter gets a crack on the side of the head with a sawed-off two-by-four. He goes down and is bleeding. The guy stands over Walter and shouts, 'You just keep that nigger daughter of yours locked up if you know what's good for you and her.'

"Mitch and me, we start to move toward Walter, but the two other guys bear hug us and throw us to the ground. The guy comes over to us with board in hand and hits us both across our backs. I could barely breathe, let alone get up. Off they go toward their cars."

"Are you OK now?"

"Yeah, Mitch and I are sore, but Walter's in a bad way."

JR and Karen made eye contact, which drew them together into a long voiceless hug they knew meant, "I'm here for you and I'm sorry for what has happened and whatever happens next, I'll still be here for you."

When Mary wrapped her arms around the two of them, JR realized that for the first time since he lost his parents, he was fully part of a family. And one family member was fighting for his life.

"They moved him into ICU, and we can only go in to see him for five minutes every hour. Only one of us can go at a time. Karen and I had our turn, and Walter specifically asked for you—you're next," Mary said in a gentle but firm way that made it clear it was not just a kind gesture, but a command.

"When?"

"In about 15 minutes."

"How is he really?"

OD, who had assumed the role of medical liaison for the family, stepped back into the conversation, "Walter's skull is cracked, and he has what they're calling an epidural hematoma. They're deciding whether to operate to relieve the pressure. But there's a risk to the surgery, because it may cause blood clots, and that means other problems. He's been in and out of consciousness since the attack, and even when he's lucid, he's disoriented."

"When do the doctors say he'll be OK?"

"Well, they haven't been real optimistic. Most of it has been, 'we'll have to wait and see.' I don't like what I hear or feel." OD's shoulders, normally square and tall, were slumped.

"What do I say to him, OD?"

"Just say what's in your heart."

JR spent the next ten minutes holding hands, wiping away tears, both his and others, and trying to figure out what to say to Walter. OD's advice about saying what was in his heart did not seem to be all that helpful.

A volunteer from behind the emergency room waiting area desk respectfully called out, "Would someone from the Rawlings family like to visit in ICU?"

Barely supported by weak knees, JR rose and walked toward the desk. Mary joined him and gently answered the unasked question on the face of the volunteer, "He's family."

Through the double doors, he encountered the bustle of nurses, doctors, and aides as they darted in and out of closed-curtained treatment areas that surrounded a central work station. JR felt a chill but could not tell if it came from the room's temperature, his bout with the flu, or from his emotions. The volunteer turned him over to a nurse, who caringly held JR's elbow and guided him to Walter, asked JR to wait outside the curtain, and disappeared inside. Just a moment later, "You can come in. Remember, only five minutes and call me if you have any problems."

"Thank you," said JR as he entered through the curtain the nurse held aside for him.

Walter's head was bandaged and his eyes were closed. He was surrounded by tubes, machines, and a faded scent of disinfectant. The sight of Walter laying there was almost too much to bear, but JR inched forward, leaned down, and whispered into the ear uncovered by bandages, "Walter."

No response. Closer and a little louder, "Walter."

Eyes opened slightly. "Hi, JR."

"I don't know what to say," was all that JR could think to say.

Silence.

"Walter," JR hesitated and surprised himself, "I love you."

OD was right—it had come from his heart.

"You have become my family. I want you to know that. You are a big part of my life, and I am indebted to you. I want you to get better for both your sake and mine. I need you, Walter. I love you."

Walter strained to speak. "JR, you don't need me. You'll always do what's right. You'll be just fine."

Walter's eyes opened wider and there was a faint and fleeting smile on his face. Then his eyes closed as if exhausted by the brief conversation.

JR bent over, kissed Walter's cheek, and said, "Good-bye, Walter, I love you."

The nurse escorted JR back toward the waiting room.

"Was he awake?" Karen had rushed to JR's side.

THE HUG

"Yes, and he was giving me advice, just like he always does," JR said while attempting a brave smile.

"Thank you for being here," Karen whispered in his ear as she held him close.

"I belong here...with all of you. I belong here."

After joining the others in their corner of the waiting room, JR and Karen sat silently, holding hands and just waiting. JR broke the silence, "OD, how about joining me to get drinks for everyone from the cafeteria?"

"Good idea. We'll be right back."

"OD," JR said, when they were out of earshot of the others, "what's happening to the guy who did this? He can't get away with it."

"Mitch stayed with Walter, and I called the cops after I called the ambulance. We told them what happened and who did it. But here's my guess. They'll pull the guy in and ask him about it. He'll likely say that we attacked him and that he responded in self-defense. He'll say that his goon buddies can vouch for him—and they will. Maybe he gets a slap on the wrist; maybe none at all."

"You've got to be kidding. That's not fair."

"You're right, but for now, that's the way it is."

"Well, I'll tell you this, OD. Until that guy gets more than a slap on the wrist, it won't be over for me. And that's the way it is," JR said with all the anger he could muster through his concern for Walter and the residual weakness from the flu.

OD put his hand on JR's shoulder, stopped in the hallway, and said with determination, "Look, JR, for now, let's focus on Walter. But I can assure you, Not So and I will not let this go. I'm not sure what we'll do, but that guy will not get away with this."

They continued their walk in silence, bought the drinks, and turned to go back upstairs. "OD, can you handle the drinks? I'd like to just sit here for awhile. I'll be back up shortly."

"Sure. Take your time."

JR found a table in the back corner of the cafeteria, pulled back the heavy metal chair that screeched along the linoleum, and slumped into it. He placed his Coca-Cola on the table, absentmindedly unwrapped the straw, and inserted it into the drink. He then tried to clear his head.

Do what's in my heart to do. Oppression anywhere needs to be confronted. Walter, Jr. committed to Vietnam. Do what's in my heart to do. I'm not really permanently tied to anything. The Rawlings will need help no matter how Walter does, but OD and Not So and their neighbors will be there for them. Do what's in my heart to do. Oppression anywhere needs to be confronted. The Army would provide me with direction. It's time to make a decision. Do what's in my heart to do.

With another screech from the chair, JR rose from the table and walked back to the waiting room. He had made his decision and wanted to tell Karen, Mary, OD, and Not So. But most of all, he wanted to tell Walter.

He entered the waiting room. They were no longer silently holding hands in the corner but were wrapped around each other and collectively crying. JR knew immediately what had happened. He would never get to tell Walter about his choice. He joined the hug without a word—none was necessary.

CHAPTER 14

BY GOD, IT'S NOT POSSIBLE

November 3, 1965
Washington, D. C.

Although they had made a firm decision to head west, Maggie and Bernie were still in Washington, D. C. three months later. Bernie wanted to spend more time with Mort; there was more planning to do; and two events occurred that almost kept them in the area indefinitely.

Maggie and Bernie heard about the first incident in Mort's coffeehouse, where a guy whose face Maggie could barely make out, was struggling to read the newspaper by candlelight. Reporting to no one in particular and everyone at the same time, the guy said, "You won't believe this. The headline in the paper is 'Man Burns Self to Death at Pentagon, Baby in His Arms Saved from Fire before Hundreds.'"

"Let me see that," Bernie commanded, as she strode into the dark corner and snatched the paper.

She held up a candle and continued the oral reading, *"Yesterday morning, Norman Morrison, a devout Quaker and father of three, immolated himself outside Secretary of Defense McNamara's office at the Pentagon. Morrison had driven from Baltimore and brought his infant daughter, Emily, who had to be rescued from Morrison's arms."*

The story went on to reveal more details. A close friend of Morrison's said that the Quaker had been struggling with the war for months and suspected that Morrison was moved to action after reading an article in *I.F. Stone's Weekly*, a popular antiwar paper. The *Weekly* article reported on an accidental bombing of a South Vietnamese church by an American aircraft. A priest, who was wounded in the church bombing, had said, *"I have seen my faithful burned up in napalm. I have seen the bodies of women and children blown to bits. I have seen my village razed. By God, it's not possible."*

Morrison had included the *Weekly* article in a note he had written to his wife before leaving the house that morning; a letter in which he included that he "must act for the children in the priest's village."

The incident at the Pentagon reinforced Bernie's and Maggie's view of the horror of war, and it reminded them that the seat of decision making about the war was in Washington. Should they stay?

The coffeehouse was also abuzz with anticipation of the planned March on Washington for Peace to take place later that month. Prominent speakers and sponsors were stepping up. Dr. Benjamin Spock, chairman for The National Committee for a Sane Nuclear Policy, and Carl Oglesby, president of Students for a Democratic Society, were both going to speak, as were celebrated authors, artists, and actors. Reverend Martin Luther King was going to be there. Upwards of 25,000 people were expected to march on the White House.

During the past few months, Maggie, Bernie, and Mort had settled into a comfortable routine. In deference to her, Bernie and Mort found time to be together when Maggie was out of the apartment, which she was more frequently. Maggie had gotten to know the coffeehouse denizens and began joining them as they went out to spread their antiwar message.

Morrison's death and the upcoming march as well as their shared lifestyle prompted Maggie to ask Bernie, "Should we stay?"

Bernie hesitated, something she was not accustomed to doing, "Maggie, I've been thinking about that too, but I'm convinced the real action is in the Bay Area. I can't believe that guy set himself on fire. And the march is going to be great. And being here with Mort has been working. But the heart of this movement is in Berkeley—I can feel it. I'm ready to go."

"I'm with you."

CHAPTER 15

DO SOLEMNLY SWEAR

January 3, 1966
St. Louis, Missouri

JR Spears entered the offices of St. Louis County Draft Board 101, walked up to the first occupied desk he came to, and said, "Where do I enlist?"

"Sorry, son, you've got it all wrong. We administer the draft—enlistments happen at recruiting stations. Here's a map to the closest one. It's about 15 minutes from here. Good luck, son."

The last thing JR needed was a complication that gave him time to think. On the drive to the recruiting station, he revisited his decision, as he had been doing continuously since making it, but he stayed the course, parked, and entered. The cramped office was filled with posters, pamphlets, and an imposing, uniformed recruiter, who stood, walked from behind the small gray-metal desk, and extended his hand, which enveloped JR's.

"Is this where I enlist?"

"Yes, thank you for coming in and thank you for choosing to serve your country in the United States Army. What questions can I answer for you before we have you sign some papers?"

"Just tell me what I need to do. I'm ready to go now."

"Great. If you'd like, I'll get you in the group going through MEPS as early as Wednesday morning."

"What's that?"

"The Military Entrance Processing Station. It's downtown. They'll give you an aptitude test and a physical, and they'll interview you. I'm sure you'll do just fine, but we need to make sure you're mentally and physically able to be a soldier. If all goes well on

Wednesday, you're on your way. Assume you'll leave for basic training from MEPS that day."

"Let's schedule it," JR declared.

The recruiter collected some preliminary medical information, had JR fill out the paperwork, gave him a scheduling card for Wednesday, and sent him on his way with, "Thank you and good luck."

JR walked out of the recruiting office with a military bearing and more than a hint of pride.

As he headed home to begin making final arrangements, he realized that except for Mouse, there were not any friends he really needed to tell.

JR had already told Mary, Karen, Not So, and OD about his decision, and he felt fortunate to have met and told Walter, Jr., who had returned home on bereavement leave. After the funeral and after streams of family, friends, church congregants, and neighbors paid their respects, JR was sitting in his usual place at the Rawlings's dining room table. Walter's absence loomed as large as had his presence.

Walter, Jr. sat erect in Walter's chair in an attempt to bravely convey that he had accepted the responsibility of having been thrust into the role as the male head of the family. But the look on his face revealed the pain of his loss and the uncertainty of a future without his father, mentor, and friend.

"I'm enlisting in the Army," JR quietly declared after OD had finished saying grace.

"I know," said Mary.

Karen, who had not let go of JR's hand after grace, squeezed it.

Not So and OD simply nodded as if there was no more to say.

Mary broke the silence, "Now I'll have two sons in Vietnam. I'm proud of both of you."

Although they had only met that morning, JR and Walter, Jr. looked at each other and knew that Walter's death had brought them together and that he would have wanted them to treat each other as brothers. Two nearly imperceptible nods crossed the table.

After dinner, JR found Walter, Jr. bundled against the stiff cold breeze in one of his father's coats and smoking a cigarette in the chain-link fenced backyard. "I grew to love your father. It was an honor to know him."

"He wrote to me about you. Told me that when he first met you, you seemed a little lost, without much direction, but you were finding yourself. I certainly know that Dad could have that effect on folks. He did on me. Dad taught me to figure out what I believed in and then act on it. That's why I'm wearing this uniform."

"And that's why I'm going to be wearing it. What's it like in Vietnam?"

"Hard as hell. Sometimes you live on pure adrenaline for days when you're on patrol; then seems like you might die of boredom in between. Getting shot at; seeing guys get killed or injured; resisting getting into the drug thing. Hot and rainy or hot and dry. Long list of shit, including the extra crap I take for being black. But I know what I'm there for and get satisfaction from that. Although I'll be glad when it's over, I'm OK with doing what I'm doing. I'm convinced it's in my heart to do."

"That last part sounds vaguely familiar," JR said with a knowing smile.

"You got that right."

As JR's thoughts returned to the present, he continued his drive home from the recruiting office and thought about the arrangements he needed to make. What would be the problem if he just walked away from his apartment, car, and job? He thought of his parents and felt good that a deeply-rooted sense of responsibility would not allow him to simply leave. He called Mr. Hegel, thanked him for all of his help, let him know about joining the Army, and asked him what he needed to close out his association with the union. He called Mitch Wise and made arrangements to give Not So his car. He stopped by to see his landlord to break his lease.

Barney Passman would have been six-foot-three had he been able to stand erect, but he was no taller than JR. His military haircut, clean-shaven appearance, and bright eyes counterbalanced his broken body.

"Hey, I was in the Army in the second World War," the landlord said, putting his arm around JR's shoulder in a fatherly way.

"That's why this bad back and limp. Almost made it through D-Day unscathed. But you'll be fine," he continued, reacting to the look of concern on JR's face. "Anyway, no problem on the lease."

"I've got to figure out what to do with my furniture. Do you want it?"

"Just leave it in the apartment, and the next tenant can use it if he wants. Do you want it when you get back?"

"I have no idea how long I'll be in or what I'll do or where I'll go when I get out. So consider everything yours. And thanks."

As they shook hands, Passman gripped firmly, placed his left hand just as firmly over JR's right, and said, "Good luck, son."

JR got around to calling Mouse, finding the conversation awkward. Despite Mouse being his best friend, they had not been in contact lately.

"Stay in touch, and you be careful," Mouse said after the brief discussion.

"Will do," JR responded, although he intuitively felt that might not be the case.

Would he see Mouse or the Rawlings family or Not So or OD or anyone he knew from St. Louis again? He hoped that he would, especially when he thought of Karen, although he could not quite sort out why that was.

Early Wednesday morning, JR packed a few odds and ends in a small duffle bag, picked Not So up at his home, drove to the military processing station, gave his friend a sincere hug as they silently remembered Walter, and turned over the keys. A couple of hours later, after taking a written aptitude test, having what seemed to be a cursory physical examination, tolerating a brief interview, and signing some more papers, JR joined the hundred or so others who went through the morning routine with him to take his oath.

The windowless gray walls of the Ceremony Room were bare except for a photo of President Johnson. An American flag lay limp on a wooden floor pole at the front of the room.

"We will administer your Oath of Enlistment and get you on your way to Fort Leonard Wood. Please raise your right hand and repeat after me."

JR proudly declared, "I, JR Spears, do solemnly swear that I will support and defend the Constitution of the United States against all enemies, foreign and domestic; that I will bear true faith and allegiance to the same; and that I will obey the orders of the President of the United States and the orders of the officers appointed over me, according to regulations and the Uniform Code of Military Justice. So help me God."

CHAPTER 16

THANK YOU

January 15, 1966
San Francisco, California

The damp morning chill tried to penetrate, but it was no match for the warmth Maggie and Bernie shared inside their wraparound blanket. Having attended a free open-air evening performance of the racially-charged *Civil Rights in a Cracker Barrel* by the San Francisco Mime Troupe, they had spent the night in the middle of the Panhandle of Golden Gate Park with about 20 others in tents, sleeping bags, and makeshift bedding.

Maggie had both hands wrapped around a cup of hot coffee; the aroma reminding her more of home than of Mort's coffeehouse and triggering a short-lived twinge of regret. She had come a long way, in large part thanks to Bernie, both over miles and as a person. She smiled at her good fortune to have met Bernie so early in her new life, turned her head, and replaced her smile with pursed lips. She kissed Bernie gently, hugged her friend, and cooed, "Thank you."

They had only been in the Bay Area for a week, having zigzagged their way across the country after having left Mort's apartment a couple of months earlier. While still in D. C., Bernie had contacted a former Berkeley student friend, who made living arrangements, such as they were, for Maggie and her when they arrived.

They had planned their cross-country itinerary to meet who Bernie had identified as protest action-leaders. Their first stop was New York City, where they sought out David Miller, who in late 1965 had been the first to burn a draft card. Having been arrested several days later, Miller was out on bail and able to meet them near his apartment just east of Columbia University.

In Ann Arbor, Bernie used connections to meet with Robert Alan Haber, the first President of the Students for a Democratic Society, whose inaugural organizing meeting had taken place at the University of Michigan. The SDS was at the core of the antiwar movement, and along with U of M faculty, had also organized the first-ever teach-in on the Vietnam War. The teach-in model spread to other campuses, including Berkeley, where the largest of its kind took place only two months after the Michigan event.

Meeting Miller and Haber affected Bernie and Maggie in different ways, but with the same result, an increased dedication to the cause. Bernie, who was used to talking with experienced and articulate antiwar leaders, came away having further validated her point of view, "See, Mags, that's what I mean. These guys are making a difference and we can too."

Maggie, whose exposure to the antiwar movement had been limited to reports from Walter Cronkite and a still-brief relationship with Bernie and her coffeehouse friends, left the New York and Ann Arbor visits in awe, "Bernie, these guys are doing more than talking about it—they're taking action. That's what I want to be part of."

Maggie and Bernie made their way to Madison to meet the organizers of the University of Wisconsin teach-in, but instead ended up in a loud confrontation with several ROTC cadets they ran into in a smoky local bar frequented by Badgers. The straight-laced cadets were far from pleased to hear Bernie's blatant belligerence about the war. It was the first time in their relationship that Maggie took charge, as she ushered Bernie out of the bar before the confrontation went beyond verbal.

"We've got to stand up to those militaristic assholes who think the way to help people is to decimate their country," Bernie screamed, hoping the cadets would hear her, as she wrested her arm from Maggie's tight grip.

"Standing up is one thing—taking on four guys in a bar is another."

"Mags, I'm just not sure that peaceful protests and teach-ins are going to do the trick. At some point, we need to shake people up to make them realize how fucked up this war is."

There was a fierceness in Bernie's eyes and a strain in her voice that was beyond even her normal aggressiveness. But she must have seen the concern in Maggie's reaction, because Bernie quickly calmed down, hugged her friend, and said, "OK, I'm not going to run back in there and take on the infantry. But somehow we need to find a way to do more."

For the remainder of the trip, the two women were less focused on the war as they made their way west. They had learned a lot along the way and built new relationships among and respect for the protest community, but they took joy in dedicating the final three weeks to solidifying their own relationship.

On their travels from Washington to Madison, they had spent virtually all of their time on a bus or in the presence of others. Now, despite the wintery conditions across the plains, they were taking breaks from the drone of the bus ride and spending time together by stopping to see the sights or just relax.

Although they knew nothing about the town, both Maggie and Bernie had grown up watching TV westerns, and Cheyenne, Wyoming sparked their interest when they realized it was an upcoming bus stop. They decided to spend a few days there.

Their choice of where to stay was easy. The downtown station was just two blocks down Central Avenue from the Plains Hotel. A short walk later, they were in their room with two twin beds. It did not take long for the two women to realize that while they were expecting the wild-west Cheyenne of the TV westerns, what they got was a downtown business area not far from a railroad yard. Although the location and the winter weather made for an experience less than they would have liked, they had a cozy room, the hotel's Wigwam Lounge, and each other.

After dinner in the small café across the street, they leaned into the frigid temperature and gusting wind to return to the hotel. Since that first glass of wine in Mort's apartment, Maggie had learned to enjoy an occasional drink or two. She had also become increasingly appreciative of Bernie and their growing friendship. As they entered the hotel lobby, Maggie looked at the entrance to the Wigwam Lounge then at Bernie and made a choice she had been considering for several days.

"I'm beat, Bernie, let's head upstairs."

When they got to the room, Bernie looked at Maggie and said, "What's that silly grin for?"

THANK YOU

"Bernie," Maggie said as she pulled her sweater over her head, "I'm going to bed and you're going to join me. And, my friend, lose the PJs!"

Most of their remaining time in Cheyenne was spent in bed, at the lounge, and in the Cattlemen's Café; in that order. Although they were enjoying their private wild west, Maggie and Bernie were also anxious to get to the Bay Area. The remaining bus ride took them through rolling cattle country, past the Great Salt Lake, through high plains, over and around mountains, and finally to the West Coast.

With help from Bernie's friend, they had no problem establishing themselves in the Bay Area. For Maggie, despite living as a transient, she quickly felt at home.

CHAPTER 17

HULK

February 11, 1966
Fort Leonard Wood, Missouri

JR's sense of purpose continued to grow as his newly-developing life took him from recruiting office to processing station and to and through his first few weeks of basic training.

Although it was only 140 miles down Route 66 southwest of what had been his home, Fort Leonard Wood might as well have been on the other side of the world. On the bus trip that brought him to basic training, it came to him that one of the reasons he may have been initially hesitant about enlisting was a subconscious concern about being away from familiar turf.

JR had been outside of his hometown only a couple of times in his life, not counting occasional Friday night rides with Mouse, Lenny, and sometimes others across the Mississippi River into East St. Louis to listen to jazz at the Blue Note and have dinner at Stoplight, the all-you-can-eat fried chicken place. Sixth-grade sleep-away camp took him 50 miles from home. And the summer before his parents' accident, the family, who could not afford extended trips, took a long-weekend vacation to Chicago. All he remembered from that trip was the coal mine at the Museum of Science and Industry and the fear of driving on the highway for the first time. Although he was not yet old enough for his driver's license, to his great surprise, his dad had asked him if he wanted to drive part of the way home.

In but a short time after getting off the bus at Fort Leonard Wood, JR was yelled at, lined up, issued uniforms, and yelled at some more. He had his head shaved, marched to his first Army meal, was assigned a bunk and issued a foot locker, and was yelled at some more. Despite the whirlwind introduction to boot camp and the beginning of the verbal abuse and physical challenge that would last for eight weeks, JR did not mind it at all. Maybe army life was for him; maybe he had made the right decision.

His barracks mates spent most of their infrequent free time complaining about Drill Sergeant Harding, who they referred to as Hardass when he was not around, the strenuous and constant physical demands, and the food. But JR felt good—his mind and body were developing to a place they had never been.

As he was growing up and through his high school years, he aimlessly drifted from one day to the next. His parents had been his only source of grounding—then came the accident. Although he felt a sense of responsibility to his job at the Arch, it never seemed to him to be what he wanted to do with the rest of his life.

Through the early weeks of basic training, JR found satisfaction in his commitment to a cause, approached every physical activity eagerly despite the degree of difficulty, and felt good about his growing strength, endurance, and especially his newly-discovered marksmanship ability.

Yet despite his personal progress and growing self-confidence, JR still felt like an outsider. He was surrounded by guys who seemed to have instantly bonded; sharing everything from back-slapping, grab-assing good times to long philosophical talks about the war, to stories of sexual conquests back home.

JR watched all this going on, occasionally and unsuccessfully tried to participate, felt badly about it, tried to decide if he cared or not, and watched some more. He could not seem to break into the camaraderie.

On a Friday afternoon, having just finished an 11-mile full-pack and weapon hike through the remnants of the snow that had fallen a couple of days before, JR was in his bunk with his eyes closed, trying to take full advantage of the unusual 30-minute break they were given before mess. Sensing a presence, he opened his eyes and was looking up at the biggest man in his training company and for that matter, the biggest man he had ever seen up close.

"Hey, Hulk, what are you doing hanging over me like that?"

Virtually every trainee had acquired a nickname that would stick with him at least through his time in the service. For most, the nicknames fit pretty well—Hulk's certainly did, as his biceps always seemed to be fighting to break out of his uniform. JR had some previous experience with nicknames, but nothing like this. There was "Mouse" with his ears. Lenny was "Swish," the sound the net made when he took that sweet jump shot. And there was that guy in his elementary school class whose nickname was "Monkey," because he went through a phase of eating a whole banana for lunch each day, peel and all.

"Waitin' for you to wake up."

"I'm awake; just resting my eyes."

"Do you know what tonight is, Speargun?"

JR and his nickname came together on the first day of weapons training, when he demonstrated an uncanny ability to hit anything he aimed at, despite never before having had a gun in his hands.

"It's the only night in the first four weeks of this circle-jerk that we have off and a later lights out. I'm goin' to go drink a beer at the EM Club, and you're comin'," Hulk declared.

Hulk was Bill Carlson, who JR guessed to be at least 6'4" and 250 pounds. His square jaw and blond hair framed blue eyes and a quick and frequent grin. Other than he came from somewhere in South Dakota, JR knew little about Carlson's personal story.

JR had done little drinking in high school and had that one beer during his first visit with the Rawlings. After his third beer at the Enlisted Men's Club, he was feeling somewhere between good and disoriented.

Calling the building a club was a bit of a stretch. It was a converted corrugated sheet-metal walled barracks that looked like it had been there since Fort Leonard Wood was established in 1940 and not been maintained since. The cigarettes and beer were cheap, one of the reasons for the dense smoke and odor. There were few tables and chairs, but plenty of standing room. The only element of class in the place was a band playing in one corner—the Lyndells were a garage band from the nearby college town of Rolla. They could barely be heard above the noise, as basic training and experienced soldiers mingled, told stories, drank, smoked, laughed, bragged, hollered, lied, and drank some more.

Hulk, who had been downing beers like they were water, had gathered their training squad in a far corner opposite the band. For the first time in four weeks, JR felt like he belonged. Whether it was the beer or Hulk's having drawn him in, he did not care.

"Hey Speargun, you must've been shooting all of your life."

"No, Pucker, never did. Just luck I guess."

Pucker was Eddie Planck, a short wiry guy from West Virginia whose lips seemed to always be pursed for a kiss.

"Bullshit! I've been huntin' all my life, and I can't get your scores."

"I'm telling you, Kit, it's the truth. No guns, no shooting, no shit."

His last name and his endless stories of tracking and hunting in his native Upstate New York had earned Wesley Carson his nickname. When he realized he had the floor, Kit, as he was wont to do, began to settle into a story, "So it's the first day of deer season and my factory is officially shut down like it's a holiday, which it is, and because none of us would have showed up anyway. My buddies come over to my house at oh-dark-thirty, and my mom fixes us a hunter's breakfast you wouldn't believe. We get in my truck and head for..."

"After we burned the village, we grabbed the fucking gooks and fucked 'em up real good until they talked." The declaration from the nearby group of regular soldiers was loud and offensive enough to even stop Kit Carson from continuing his story.

JR, Hulk, and the others were silent and stunned but could not help but listen.

"Our interpreter was sketchy at best. He kept telling us that the gooks were saying they weren't soldiers. Bullshit. It didn't fucking matter. We'd been getting reports for weeks of VC being in and out of that fucking place. Our patrols were getting ambushed. It was time to torch the whole village. No doubt—every one of those women and old men were aiding and abetting."

Everyone else was now silent, as the soldier got louder and wild-eyed, seemingly reliving his experience. The Lyndells stopped playing, instruments in hand but inert, leaving the only sounds in the room to be the drunk and the background whirr of the beer cooler.

"Only two days before, my buddy had been killed within four klicks of that fucking hellhole. We burned it to the ground. Huts went up in flame and were gone in minutes. Gook women cryin'. Old men screaming at us. Had to beat on them to shut them the fuck up. Don't know where the kids went. Never learned a fucking thing about the VC. All we got out of it was some body count."

His buddies were trying to get the guy to finish his beer and hustle him out of the place.

"Just fucking glad my tour's over. No more jungle rot; no more gooks; no more fucking helicopter rides in the fog. Time to turn it all over to these new boys."

The drunken loudmouth was finally ushered out of the EM Club. Conversations slowly restarted but were much more subdued. The Lyndells chose a set of slow, quiet numbers.

"That is exactly why my dad and I tried like the dickens to keep me from getting drafted, but it just didn't work. I'm not sure what we're getting into, but I don't like it," Hulk said quietly but firmly; his smile long gone.

"What we're getting into, Hulk, is keeping the communists over there so they don't come over here."

"How the hell did you get into this man's army, Peepers? You can barely see, even when you've got those Coke bottles on your nose. You certainly can't see reality staring you in the face. Burning villages and beating old men is not about communism. Treating people like animals is not about communism. Being the oppressor instead of defending them from oppression is not about communism." Hulk was getting more intense as he responded to Dan Prince, whose thick glasses were his most distinguishing feature.

"You gotta do what you gotta do, and by the way, I can see just fine. Or at least good enough for the doc at my induction physical," Peepers said and shifted his focus to his beer.

JR was not quite ready to jump into a war versus antiwar discussion, especially because it did not feel right that his fellow soldiers were even having the conversation. Weren't they there to be trained to fight a war? Hadn't he enlisted for that reason? Wasn't he energized by finally doing something with his life that really seemed to matter?

He was trying to sort this all out through the haze brought on by what was now five beers, as he struggled with a new thought. Although he had been aware that many if not most of the basic trainees had been drafted versus having enlisted, Hulk's comment brought the fact to the front of JR's mind for the first time—a lot of these guys really wanted no part of being in the Army or going to Vietnam.

CHAPTER 18

WE WON'T GO

April 9, 1966
Palo Alto, California

Mooch sat in the tiny room that housed the switchboard in the back corner of the campus police station. His headset covered his ears and his communications microphone rested in front of him along with his open but unread political science text book. It was not uncommon for Mooch's weekend shifts to be uneventful, and this Saturday was particularly slow—the switchboard lights were dark and had been for some time. With eyes closed and a contemplative expression, Mooch had taken a break from his studies to reflect on his time at Stanford.

He thought about his plan to finish in three years, knowing that the accelerated degree carried consequences. Unlike his high school career in which he was involved in almost everything and with almost everybody, his sphere of activity and his circle of acquaintances at college were limited, spending virtually all of his time in his dorm room, at the library, in class, and at the campus police station.

He would have liked to have gotten involved in intramural sports but could not find the time. When dorm mates gathered to release some energy at a local bar, he would have liked to join them, but Mooch forced himself to hit the books.

Confined to the cramped dispatcher room, once again he struggled with whether his restricted campus life bothered him or not. But every time he considered the alternatives, Mooch concluded that his focus on doing everything he could to accelerate his path to the FBI was right for him. He was at peace with his choices, and his expression of contemplation was replaced by a knowing and self-confident smile.

There were only two diversions that broke into his college routine. Mooch continued his periodic bus trips to see Special Agent Paul Marcus and was thrilled that Paul had begun to invite him to visit the San Francisco bureau offices.

Mooch's other avocation was far different from the time he spent with Paul. Civil rights and antiwar activism had been something to read about, hear about on the TV, and discuss at the Muccelli family dinner table. But at their first meeting, when Paul related the story of the student protest that resulted in his facial scar, Mooch's curiosity was piqued.

Mooch began seeking out campus activists. There was no shortage of those willing to talk to him. Each wanted to spread his or her particular agenda, whether it was defense research, ROTC activities, Selective Service policies, racial injustice, or free speech issues.

Mooch learned that in the early 1960s, Stanford had been a hotbed of civil rights demonstrations. During the "Freedom Summer" of 1964, his university had the largest contingent of the thousands of college students from around the country that converged on Mississippi to help register Negroes to vote. The antiwar protest movement on campus had grown out of this civil rights activism.

Mooch found much of the civil rights discussion making sense. Although he had grown up in a home that fostered respect for the nation's institutions, his mom and dad followed the news closely, and dinner table conversations were frequently about how courageous the Negroes were who were standing up to discrimination. His family had instilled in him the value of law and order combined with intolerance for injustice.

Mooch learned a lot from his conversations about the antiwar political philosophy and about plans for upcoming meetings and protests. It did not dampen protest leader's enthusiasm when they found out Mooch was working part-time for the campus police but merely encouraged them to try harder to convert him.

Although he was moved by the passion with which the students and faculty expressed their opposition to the war, Mooch was initially unsympathetic. But as he learned more, his personal philosophy about the war paralleled that of his civil rights position—

maintain law and order but be sensitive to injustice, regardless of the perpetrator.

The phone rang and a switchboard light illuminated, tearing Mooch from his moment of reflection. Flipping a switch, pulling the microphone closer, and assuming his professional voice, Mooch answered the call, "Stanford University Campus Police Department, John Muccelli speaking, how may I help you?"

The caller was jittery and speaking almost too quickly to be understood, "This is Jim Berkman. I manage the campus bookstore. A mob of about, oh, I don't know, maybe two to three hundred students is assembled across the street. They're overflowing toward the store, carrying signs, and hollering. It doesn't look good."

"Thank you Mr. Berkman. Does it look like they are staying there?"

"No, they're leaving now, heading up Lasuen Mall toward..."

Berkman hesitated and then continued in an even more agitated state, "They just knocked down two coeds who were leaving the store!"

"We'll get someone there quickly, Mr. Berkman. Thank you for the call," Mooch said, as he tried but failed to recall if he had heard about plans for this demonstration in any of his recent conversations.

"Chief Davis, I'm calling about a student protest," Mooch said, following the new protocol to inform the chief first whenever the issue was an incident of campus unrest. Mooch relayed the information from Jim Berkman.

"Mooch, call everyone in and get the guys on duty ahead of this thing. Tell them to take no action unless provoked. I'm calling the Palo Alto police and the FBI."

The call to the Palo Alto police had become routine for such an incident. The FBI call was a more recent policy, requested by memo from Director J. Edgar Hoover to all college campus presidents and police chiefs. Hoover wanted his people involved to help them identify who the instigators were. Stanford President Sterling, who was glad for any help he could get, directed Chief Davis to agree to the request, which had been worded more like an order.

"Yes, sir, Chief. I'll make my calls," Mooch said, but the chief had already hung up.

The entire switchboard was now lit up. He struggled to call all of the officers, both on and off duty, to pass on the chief's directions while also answering a flood of calls from students, faculty, and a dean or two. Fortunately, the officer who was to replace Mooch at the end of his shift came in early, figured out Mooch needed immediate help, got a 30-second update, and squeezed in beside Mooch at the switchboard.

The two answered the phones, tracked the movement of the student protestors, answered an occasional call from the chief's car, and generally tried to remain calm. An hour later, the full campus force was in place, the chief seemed reasonably satisfied, the frequency of phone calls lessened, and Mooch finally had time to breathe.

"Go ahead, Mooch, I'll take it from here. Great job."

"You sure?"

"Yep."

Mooch smiled at the officer, informally saluted, grabbed his book bag, and headed for the door. He had planned to go back to his dorm after his shift to study for his LSAT, which he would be taking in June. A solid LSAT score to complement his close-to-4.0 grade point average would position to get into an elite law school.

But there would be no studying that night. Mooch's curiosity impelled him toward The Oval Park, where he had learned the demonstration had settled. As he did, he found himself in the midst of hundreds of other students headed that way, mostly because they shared his curiosity.

"What's going on," Mooch asked a coed who was scurrying beside him.

"Don't know, but I don't have anything else to do tonight." She surprised Mooch by taking his hand and picking up the pace. "Come on. Don't want to miss anything."

By the time Mooch and his new friend reached the site, they came upon a frenzied scene. It had grown dark, making it easy to see the fires that had been started in 55-gallon drums amidst the gathering of shouting, sign-carrying protestors. Some signs read simply, "Freedom" or "Resistance." Others more specifically described the reason for the rally, "Burn Draft Cards not Children,"

"Draft Card Burning Here and Now," "The War is Obscene," "Bring the War Home," and "Fuck the Draft."

Mooch estimated the demonstration to be much larger than Berkman's original estimate, but it was difficult to tell how many were really demonstrating and how many were there just to watch, like his coed friend, who had released his hand and melted into the crowd.

The local and campus police had deployed along the perimeter of the park. The media had begun to arrive. For now, everything was peaceful, but tense.

Mooch then heard a girl shouting through a bullhorn. The sound traveled well, especially when everyone assembled grew quiet. Mooch could barely see the speaker, although she was somehow elevated above the crowd, perhaps on someone's shoulders.

"We are gathered here to declare that the war in Vietnam is obscene. We are killing innocent men, women, and children in the name of protecting them. We are burning them and their homes. Fuck the war."

The protestors waved their placards and responded, "Fuck the war."

The police lines noticeably tensed. News reporters forced their way toward the voice. The crowd quieted again as the speaker raised her hand.

"My name is Bernie, and I hate our government for sending our young men off to die for a lie. It's an atrocity. The liars have to be stopped. We are fighting back. Bring the war home."

"Bring the war home," the crowd response having gotten even louder.

The police line instinctively inched forward. Mooch worked his way around the crowd and police line to flank the protestors, craning his neck to see what was going on. He was slowly closing in on the center of the protest and better able to see the woman calling herself Bernie, who was illuminated by the glow of a nearby fire.

"Last week, four comrades in Boston burned their draft cards to protest the war, its atrocities, and its illegality. They refused to fight in an unjust war. The pigs arrested them. Tonight, we will honor their courage and declare that their arrests were unjust. The Boston burners are merely young men who know the war is illegal."

The word "pigs" prompted every officer to take two more steps forward—the distance between the protest leaders and the police was decreasing.

"Tonight, your brave comrades will burn their draft cards as well. Join them. Fuck the war."

Bernie had brought the crowd to a peak of excitement and kept them there. And her commanding presence brought them to silence every time she raised her hand to continue. This time Bernie raised her hand, but instead of speaking, gave the bullhorn to a young man who had been quietly and patiently waiting next to her. Bernie got down from the stepladder, making room for the young man.

He spoke quietly, but firmly. The crowd strained to hear. "I just returned from a tour of duty in Vietnam. We are killing and being killed needlessly. I've seen us burn whole villages to the ground, killing women and children. I've seen my buddies killed. I've seen what no one should ever see. If I knew then what I know now, I would have burned my draft card. This has got to stop."

The protestors cheered as the young man descended the ladder. Another young man took his place. "I am a student here at Stanford University. I intend to burn my draft card tonight, because I abhor the war. Here is my message to LBJ. Hell no, we won't go!"

The chant began as a low hum, gained strength, and continued for several minutes, until Bernie ascended the ladder again and raised her hand. Silence.

"If you have a draft card and are ready to tell the government that we won't go, join us. We're going to burn the cards over there," Bernie said, pointing to one of the drums from which flames were leaping.

The next 30 minutes were a blur. As young men from throughout the demonstration made their way toward the fire, police repositioned themselves. Mooch moved closer. His more rational self wanted to observe the police tactics as they dealt with this certain confrontation. At the same time, his more prurient self was drawn to the raw excitement of the scene.

As the first young men touched their draft cards to the flames and held them high for everyone to see them burning, the police moved in. With directions from Chief Davis and the Palo Alto Police Chief, their intent was noble, to arrest the first few card burners as a way of preventing too many young people from getting into trouble. In 1965, Congress had amended the Selective Service Act to prohibit destruction of draft cards. With cards on fire, the protestors had crossed the legal line.

As the police targeted the first card burners, the crowd pushed toward the center of the protest. More young men wanted to burn their cards. Others in the crowd wanted to stop the arrests. Despite being ordered to minimize violence, the police, sensing a loss of control, responded with force. Initially targeting only the card burners and those who seemed to be a physical risk to the police, officers wielded their batons.

Mooch found himself trapped inside the police perimeter. Although he tried, his attempts to get out of the action were hampered by the size and convergence of the mob. His heartbeat raced as he realized he looked no different to the police than other students in the area. Trying to stave off panic, Mooch frantically searched for and finally saw an opening in the perimeter, but just before he could take a step toward it, he felt a sharp pain in his left shoulder. Down he went.

As he struggled to get up, he felt a hand grab his left arm, magnifying the pain. As he tried to free himself from the grasp, he heard, "Officer, I'm Special Agent Paul Marcus, FBI," and after showing his credentials, declared, "I've got this one."

When they had cleared the mob, Paul shook Mooch just enough to ensure he had his attention, "What the hell do you think you're doing?"

"Paul, I was only here to see what was going on. I heard about the protest at the dispatcher's desk, and..."

"OK, think about this conversation. 'Yes, Mr. Hoover, I was arrested at an antiwar rally, but I really want to be in the FBI.' How do you think that would go down?"

"I'm sorry, I just wanted to..."

"Sorry is after the fact. You need to be buttoned up in every respect. Never, I repeat, never get yourself into a situation where you need to say you're sorry."

"You're right, and thank you," Mooch said.

"Now get the hell back to your dorm, and I'll get in touch when this calms down. Can you do that with your shoulder?" Paul's tone softened.

Trembling, Mooch responded, "Yes sir, Agent Marcus. I can. Thank you."

Mooch turned toward the dorms, took a number of steps, looked back to confirm that he was escaping the action, and ran headlong into a beautiful redhead, knocking her flat. "Oh, I'm sorry. Are you OK?"

Maggie Blessings reached up to grab Mooch's offered hand, pulled herself up, and said, "Yeah, I'm OK, thanks."

Mooch, whose main interest was getting back to his dorm room, was surprised when the redhead continued to hold his hand, smiled, and said, "This is the third time I've been knocked down, but only the first apology and help up. Thanks again. Have you burned your draft card yet?"

"Er...uh...no, not yet," Mooch said as he broke hand contact, turned, and ran toward the dorms.

Hours later, when Paul and Mooch were settled into a booth and had ordered sodas, Mooch began, "First of all, thanks again. I get what you're saying, and I'll never let anything like this happen again. But, I've got to tell you, even though I know that those guys were breaking the law and I don't agree with how they are trying to make a statement, I don't totally disagree with what they are trying to say. Is that a problem?"

"Mooch, there's a distinction between how an FBI agent feels about things and his dedication to upholding the law. I don't have this conversation at the office, but there are things about the war that I don't like. Because my job is to enforce the law, I need to be able to compartmentalize the two. That's what makes me a good agent. I'm sure your dad has sympathy for some of the folks he has to arrest, but when they break the law, it's his job."

BODY NOT RECOVERED

"I got it, Paul. I remember dad saying many times that he had to arrest someone he felt sorry for. By the way, I knew that Chief Davis would be calling your office, but why?"

"The FBI wants to know who is inciting the unrest to make sure they're not violating any laws. For example, that girl who was apparently the leader—her name is Bernice Williams. She's not a student, but she helps organize protests here and elsewhere in the Bay Area. We want to keep an eye on her and others like her to make sure this whole thing doesn't get out of control. We've offered to help local officials, like your Chief Davis. Director Hoover has made this a priority. You know, it's more than a little difficult, because we look like FBI agents, not like students. We need to find a way to get more intelligence about what's going on much earlier and easier than we do."

CHAPTER 19

JUST DOESN'T FEEL RIGHT

April 10, 1966
Berkeley, California

"Mags, are you OK," Bernie asked with a wrinkled brow.

"I'm just not comfortable with this. It's getting out of hand," Maggie responded, forcing her words through quivering lips.

"Let's start with the physical part. Are you OK?"

They were sharing a sleeping bag and some blankets in the corner of the living room at a friend's apartment near the UC-Berkeley campus. The previous May, the friend had been involved in organizing the two-day, 35,000-person antiwar protest at Berkeley, at which the Vietnam Day Committee was formed. Since then, Jill Golding had been an active VDC member and was glad to have Bernie and Maggie involved.

After they had arrived in the Bay Area, Maggie had been introduced to the broad network of friends Bernie had developed when she was active on campus two years earlier, most who were still deeply involved in the movement in one way or another. Some were active with the Free Speech Movement; others with the VDC; many were associated with the SDS; and some were profoundly antiwar but not part of a given organization.

As they had expected and hoped, Maggie and Bernie found the movement to be alive throughout the entire area, from Berkeley to Oakland, from Stanford to San Francisco and Marin County. And they had no problem finding places to crash. Jill's apartment was unusual, however, in that they were the only guests. In most places they stayed, there were any number of people coming and going from day to day and night to night.

"Well, last night at Stanford, I got knocked down three times and barely avoided getting clubbed and arrested. I can count the bruises. Then this morning, we were this close," Maggie held her right thumb and forefinger two inches apart, "to getting blown up at the VDC office."

Bernie leaned over and kissed Maggie's thumb and forefinger.

Maggie hesitated, shivered, and then said, "If we'd been five minutes earlier, we would have been in the office. Thankfully, no one was seriously injured, but Jill's still in her room sleeping off the effects of the bomb concussion.

"Then when you and others began marching down Telegraph Avenue to protest the bombing, I felt like I had to join in. But everyone was so angry that I knew it wouldn't end well. When the police showed up and weighed in, down I went again. That's the one that really hurt," Maggie said as she pointed to her right butt cheek, which Bernie also kissed.

"So, yes, I'm all in one piece, but I'm sore, and to be quite honest with you, Bernie, I'm scared."

"Mags, I'm sorry that you're hurt, and I understand that you're scared. But think about what we accomplished in the last 24 hours. We helped those guys burn their draft cards in front of the TV cameras, and the bombing shows that the pro-war assholes are scared shitless about us getting the message out. We're making a difference.

"I'm becoming more and more convinced that we need to be getting even more aggressive to continue to make our point. I don't want anybody to get hurt, especially you. But it seems that the more violence there is, the more attention we get. And attention is exactly what we want.

"Right now, the horrifying violence is in Vietnam—that's what we want to stop. If people here can't relate, they'll never get it. We've been saying 'Bring the war home'—violence here might just be the way to do that. Show people what it's like to be at risk, just like the Vietnamese villagers, and maybe they'll start giving a shit."

Maggie looked into her friend's eyes, "Sorry Bernie, but when you talk like that, it scares the hell out of me. It just doesn't feel right. Do violence to stop violence? I don't know."

"Well, Mags, we don't need to sort this out right now."

Bernie slowly found and kissed each of Maggie's bruises, put her arm around her friend, closed her eyes, and was quickly asleep. Maggie was comfortable in the embrace, but as often happened when she had a quiet moment to think, she felt a twinge of homesickness.

An hour later, Bernie rolled over to find the sound of Maggie's sobs, "What's wrong, Mags?"

"I can't fix it."

"Fix what?"

"I didn't tell you, but before we left D. C., I wrote my folks. I knew that when we decided to go to California, I'd likely never see them again. I just needed to tell them I was sorry but knew I couldn't do it by phone. One of the reasons I left was that I couldn't even talk with them when we were face-to-face. What could I possibly say over the phone?

"I told them I was OK and sorry for what I did to them. I didn't try to explain why I left—no way they'd understand. But I knew I piled more hurt on them after Matt died. Then I told them that I couldn't say where I was going but that I might keep in touch. I think that was a stupid thing to do, because I'm not sure I ever will. It hurts, Bernie.

"Maybe I should write. Maybe I should call. I just don't know."

"Do you think you should go home to see them?"

"No. I'm convinced of that. None of the reasons I left are likely to have changed. So, why add even more hurt by going home and then leaving again? I feel I'm in the right place right now—thanks to you. Like I said, I can't fix it, but I'd like to."

"I wish I could help, Mags."

"Just being here helps a lot."

Bernie and Maggie embraced—an embrace of deep friendship and more. With a hand resting gently on Maggie's bare hip, Bernie closed her eyes and was back to sleep.

Maggie had stopped crying, feeling better for having shared her feelings. But, as she looked at Bernie and was reminded of her increasing references to becoming more aggressive, her thoughts went from her parents to her friend. Although she could not fully articulate her concerns, Maggie felt that something was wrong and about to get more wrong.

CHAPTER 20

ENGAGE AND DESTROY

May 20, 1966
Fort Polk, Louisiana

When JR graduated from basic training in March 1966, he did so with a hard body and a focused mind. He was confident in his abilities, connected to his comrades, and feeling more certain of his place in the world. On the day of his graduation, JR crowded around the free-standing bulletin board outside the mess hall and found his name on two separate announcements. He had earned his accelerated advancement to the rank of Private E2, and his orders were to report to Advanced Infantry Training in Fort Polk, Louisiana.

"Why the hell are we going to Fort Polk, Hulk?"

"I hear there's a section filled with jungle, a simulated Viet Cong village, and it's as close as they can get us to a Vietnam-like climate here in the states. They call it Tigerland. Someone told me that the army considers it the second worse place on earth. Guess what the first is. Anyway, Speargun, as uninviting as it sounds, that's going to be home for a couple of months."

Over the final four weeks of basic training, JR had grown close to Hulk and had opened up to him as he had never done with anyone before, except perhaps Walter. He felt comfortable sharing his history, including losing his parents, his initial ambivalence about soldiering, his relationship with the Rawlings family, and how Walter's guidance and death had helped him make the enlistment decision. He even shared that he had lingering feelings for Karen Rawlings and that he looked forward to her letters.

JR also learned a lot more about Hulk, who had not always lived in South Dakota and had not always carried the moniker. Bill

Carlson was born in Seattle, where his father founded and owned an import business that was so successful he was able to fulfill a lifelong dream of owning a ranch. When Bill was 13, the Carlsons bought and moved to an 8,000-acre working cattle ranch about 15 miles northwest of Mitchell, South Dakota. Bill spent his youth working on the ranch, attending festivals at the Corn Palace in Mitchell, playing high school football, and growing strong. When Marvel Comics introduced *The Incredible Hulk* during Bill's sophomore year, a football teammate made the connection and gave Bill the nickname—it stuck.

Unlike JR, Hulk had traveled extensively. Although his father had reduced his level of involvement in his import business, he made occasional trips to visit suppliers across Asia. He took his wife and their two boys, Hulk and his older brother James, on a couple of those adventures, one to Japan and South Korea and the other to the Philippines and Thailand. Hulk had fond memories of those trips and especially liked Bangkok, where they stayed with the Jattawan family, who were not only a supplier, but friends.

Annan Jattawan was about Hulk's age and spoke English well. The boys hit it off, and they were allowed, with some limitations, to go around Bangkok by themselves for a couple of days. Although his tall, broad, blond presence caused him to stand out in the crowd, Hulk was very comfortable in Asia in general and in Bangkok with Annan specifically.

"You know, Speargun," Hulk said at mess one evening at Fort Leonard Wood, "I wouldn't mind getting back to Bangkok some day."

"Well, it's likely that we're going to be just around the corner in Vietnam. Maybe we can drop in when we're in the neighborhood," JR said with a smirk.

"Oh yeah, fat fucking chance."

When Hulk graduated from high school, his father, who hated what the United States was doing and about to do in Vietnam, unsuccessfully tried to use his wealth and influence to keep his son from being drafted. He had rubbed some local ranchers and politicians the wrong way when he had first stormed into the area as a brash outsider, and those wounds had never healed. Wanting to work on his father's ranch after high school, Hulk instead found himself drafted and on his way to Fort Leonard Wood.

From that first evening they spent at the EM Club in Fort Leonard Wood, the two had been inseparable, and now Hulk and Speargun were heading to Fort Polk together. They had both been assigned to Alpha Company, 4th Battalion, 5th Training Brigade, along with Peepers, Kit, Pucker, and others from their Fort Leonard Wood Company.

Most of those on the plane and bus ride to Tigerland slept all the way.

"I wish I could just fall asleep like that. I understand once we get to Vietnam, sleep will be hard to come by," JR whispered to Kit, who was in the next seat on the plane, as though he were afraid of waking someone; highly unlikely given the others were already sleeping through the stuffy, bumpy, and noisy ride.

"I gotta tell you, JR, I'm not looking forward to the next couple of months or to being deployed. I know there's not much I can do about it, but I wish there was some way I could just go home. I know you enlisted, but not me," Kit said with a mixture of anger and sorrow in his voice.

JR tried to help, "Think about it as hunting season, just like back home."

"Yeah. The problem is that this prey will be shooting back. Speaking of shooting, maybe when we get to Nam, I'll just shoot myself in the foot. That should get me home."

JR was about to smile at his comrade, until he realized from the look on Kit's face that he was dead serious. They continued the plane ride in silence, and JR could still not fall asleep.

As the bus from the airfield approached Fort Polk, it became even clearer what their upcoming training was all about.

"Check that out," Hulk elbowed JR, who had not fallen asleep but had at least been able to keep his eyes closed for awhile.

JR looked up to see the rough-hewn sign at the entrance to Fort Polk. Across the top was painted, "TIGER LAND." Down the left side was "FIGHT" and "WIN." Down the right side was "ENGAGE & DESTROY." In the center of the sign was:

BIRTHPLACE
OF
COMBAT INFANTRY
FOR VIET NAM

"This looks familiar," JR said to no one in particular, as he picked a bunk and began to stow his gear.

The barracks at Tigerland mirrored those at Fort Leonard Wood, devoid of color, smelling of disinfectant, everything in its place. The long rectangular room had bunk beds protruding from each of the long walls at a precise distance from each other; the distance being prescribed by the width of the lockers wedged between. The 40 men who slept in each room alternated head to foot in adjoining beds to minimize the temptation to talk versus sleep during lights out.

Boots were to be lined up on the floor at the foot of each bed and helmets positioned atop lockers. Fluorescent light fixtures formed the border between the two sides. Windows positioned high along the walls provided the daytime lighting, although that did not matter much, because they would seldom be in the barracks during the training day.

The next eight weeks drove JR, Hulk, and the other trainees at Fort Polk relentlessly closer to Vietnam. Although they continued to refine skills learned in basic training, they were also exposed to hand grenade instruction, the operation of high-powered weapons, advanced hand-to-hand combat, map reading, survival skills, live-fire exercises, advanced first aid, and the Geneva Convention.

Each day began at 0430, when they were awakened by drill sergeants yelling and cursing while beating metal trash cans with sticks, and the day was long and intense. Regardless of the activity, it commanded their full attention, because what they were learning could help save their lives and those of their comrades.

Toward the end of AIT, although it was only May, temperatures were reaching 90 degrees, and the humidity kept them in a constant state of dampness. "Get used to it, men," their instructors preached during and after each march or other high-exertion session. "This is nothing like what you'll feel in Nam."

Despite the intensity, heat, and humidity, JR continued to hone himself physically and psychologically. Being well aware of the dangers ahead of him, he was also aware of his growing sense of purpose, self-esteem, and belonging. He knew where his life was going and why, and his decision to enlist was shaping up to be the best one he had ever made.

This Friday marked two milestones for JR, his 20th birthday and his graduation from AIT. There was little doubt in his mind that deployment to Vietnam was imminent.

CHAPTER 21

MAKE US PROUD

May 26, 1966
Fort Polk, Louisiana

"Alpha Company, it has been an honor to train such a fine group of young patriots. Congratulations on your graduation from Advanced Infantry Training."

The company had been mustered on the sparsely-grassed parade grounds just after noon mess. Both the temperature and humidity were 90-plus under what baseball players refer to as a high sky. The trainees had anticipated this day as a company and as individuals with mixed emotions—a level of pride and excitement coupled with more than a healthy dose of anxiety. Each of them knew that President Johnson had ordered another major troop buildup in Vietnam, and their completion of AIT made them prime candidates to go.

"You'll be loading onto World Airways 707 contract planes at 0600 on Monday; refueling at Moffett Naval Air Station and in Okinawa before landing in Cam Ranh Bay, Vietnam. Know that your mission will be to help establish a safe perimeter around Cam Ranh Bay's port and airbase to ensure they continue to operate smoothly. You'll also be securing supply routes both north and south on highway 1A."

Their training had included enough about the geography and terrain of Vietnam that to a man, they could envision the map. Cam Ranh Bay, with its port and its airfield in the southeast of the country along the South China Sea, was vital to the resupply of troops and materiel. Highway 1A ran the length of Vietnam and was the essential ground supply link.

Captain Jenkins scanned his assembled company and gave them time to absorb what he had said. "The safety of Saigon to the south, materiel movement to the north, and the operations at Cam Ranh Bay will be in your capable hands. You were chosen because you're the best damned training unit in this man's army.

"That being said, we will no longer operate as a company. When you arrive at Cam Ranh Bay, each of you will get your specific orders to join units throughout the area. I wish you the best. Make us proud."

CHAPTER 22

WELCOME TO VIETNAM

June 1, 1966
Cam Ranh Bay, Vietnam

JR joined his comrades, each carrying their 50 pounds of gear and their emotions onto the cramped 707. During the long, bumpy flight, excitement and anxiety gave way to boredom and nausea. The refueling stops at Moffett Air Station at the southern end of San Francisco Bay and in Okinawa, just south of Japan, did little to help JR regain his bearings. Upon deplaning at the Cam Ranh Bay airfield, fatigue and disorientation were joined by a full frontal assault of heat and humidity.

Having grown up in St. Louis, JR thought that he would have been accustomed to the feeling of relentless dampness. His boyhood summers included streaks of days over 100 degrees and over 80 percent humidity. Then his time at Fort Polk should have steeled him to the conditions in and around Cam Ranh Bay. But neither St. Louis nor Fort Polk prepared him for what it felt like when his boots hit the platform ladder just outside the airplane doorway. The air even smelled oppressive.

As the troops carried their packs to an appointed assembly area, JR saw air conditioning units protruding from the Quonset huts to his right. But the brief promise of relief was just that, brief and a promise.

"Listen up. At ease and drop your packs. In the next 15 minutes, check the bulletin board. It will confirm your unit and your assembly area. Welcome to Vietnam."

In the time he had, JR checked the board and had a few moments to look around. He noticed that the Quonset huts and other structures were surrounded by waist-high walls of piled sandbags.

WELCOME TO VIETNAM

He noticed craters in the earth and repaired cracks on runways. He noticed the lush green hillsides surrounding the airbase and port. Although he had only just landed, his training enabled JR to put these observations together--Cam Ranh Bay airfield was a sniper and mortar target.

While still at Fort Polk, JR was pleased to have learned that Hulk, Peepers, Kit, and Pucker had been assigned to the same area, and the bulletin board reported that all of them would be in his platoon and Hulk would be in his squad. Their packs were once again on their backs, and they were heading toward the assembly area from which they could hear the rumble and smell the fumes of idling jeeps and deuce-and-a-half troop carriers that were waiting to transport them to their new units.

JR was less than 30 meters from the assembly area when he simultaneously heard a whistling sound and multiple shouts, "Incoming!"

As they had been trained, the newbies first looked for a protective area and finding none nearby, hit the ground to minimize their profile as targets. Incoming mortar rounds exploded within 80 meters of their location, and sand, rocks, and smoke flew up from the impact area.

Cam Ranh Bay personnel quickly located the source of the attacks, and a full-fledged counterattack was underway from base artillery batteries and attack helicopters. What seemed like hours was more like ten minutes before the firing stopped on both sides. Everyone got to their feet except Kit. A pool of blood had formed under him. "Medic!"

This was the first of innumerable times, JR would hear that shout. And as he would become accustomed, the medical personnel arrived quickly. Two men, each with red crosses on their helmets and medical insignias on their sleeves, had been waiting in a jeep in the assembly area, saw the shelling, and with seeming disregard for their own safety, drove their jeep to Kit's side and began working on him.

"Back off, soldier," JR heard one of the men yell at him, and he realized he had run toward Kit and was hovering over him, making it difficult for the medics to maneuver.

JR moved back but only just enough to get out of the way. Kit was alive and conscious, but a gnarled metal fragment had penetrated the front of his right shoulder.

"In country for less than an hour and hit already. Great start. Yeah, welcome to Vietnam," Hulk, who had come to JR's side, said with both anger and fear in his voice, yet barely loud enough to be heard over Kit's moaning.

"It looks like Kit found his way home," JR replied, recalling the conversation he had with Kit on the plane to Fort Polk.

Two experienced soldiers had been playing horseshoes nearby and had been the source of the "Incoming" shouts. They too had hit the ground. But unlike JR and his newly-arrived comrades, they seemed to take it all in stride; returning to their horseshoes as if nothing had happened.

JR eyed the two as they threw ringer after ringer and whispered to Hulk, "This must happen all the time."

"I think when we walked out of that airplane door, we left civilization behind."

Within moments, 19-year-old Wesley "Kit" Carson was stabilized and taken on the medics' jeep to the base medical facilities. JR and the others would learn later that although Kit survived, he would lose partial use of his right arm. Kit had been evacuated to Clark Air Force Base in the Philippines on his way to the US Army Hospital in the Ryukyu Islands off the eastern coast of Okinawa and then home. They would never see him again.

CHAPTER 23

M. J. SAVOY

July 6, 1966
Cam Ranh Bay Perimeter, Vietnam

JR had received fewer than ten letters since leaving St. Louis and none in the last few weeks. All but two of his letters had been from Karen with one each from Mary and Mouse. His platoon mates seemed to be getting mail almost daily when the company was not on patrol in the bush or nestled into a bunker on some defoliated hilltop waiting to be blown to bits by a mortar round.

"Mail call," Corporal Baker shouted as he unsealed the thick plastic mail bag that was designed to keep out the humidity, rain, mud, blood, and any other detritus.

"Peters, Wallace, Planck, Small, Spears...Spears..."

Having numbed himself to the staccato calling of names of those who had received mail, JR was not prepared to hear his. "Spears."

The return address simply read, "Mouse"

Although he had convinced himself that he did not care whether he received mail, he had to admit it felt good. He opened the envelope with anticipation, only to be jolted back to reality. "JR, YOU be careful," Mouse began. "We want you back in one piece. You probably haven't heard, but we just found out that M. J. Savoy was killed in Vietnam."

M. J. had been what JR thought of only as a high school acquaintance, but they had shared some common bonds. They had kidded each other about neither having a real first name. Each of them had been outside the arena of high school activities. And before JR's parents were killed, they and M. J.'s parents were part of a larger group that got together from time to time to go ballroom

BODY NOT RECOVERED

dancing on the Admiral, the excursion riverboat docked on the St. Louis riverfront.

Mouse's letter continued, "M. J.'s name is all over the local news and every classmate I run into or hear from is talking about him. It's awful, JR----YOU be careful. I enclosed the clipping from the newspaper. He only spent one day, actually part of a day, in Vietnam. I can't believe it."

JR carefully unfolded the article and saw the headline, "*Local Navy Boy Killed—Lost at Sea.*"

"*Recent University City High School graduate M. J. Savoy was killed in a plane crash on June 17, when the C-130 Hercules he was riding in crashed at sea just after taking off from Cam Ranh Bay Air Station. Witnesses aboard the USS Fortify, a Navy gunboat, said they saw an explosion about 1000 feet over the water and another when the plane impacted the water. The C-130 had been in the air less than 20 minutes.*

"*The Fortify was on the scene in minutes and launched a search mission. Four days later, on June 21, the deep-water search was terminated. The remains of only two of the 14 on board, eight crew plus six passengers, had been recovered. The remaining 12 men are listed as Killed in Action/Body not Recovered.*

"*Savoy, a Navy airman, and his crewmates had flown a supply mission that had begun at Moffett Naval Air Station, California and proceeded to Kadena Airbase, Okinawa, Japan, then to Cam Ranh Bay Air Station, South Vietnam.*"

The article went on to report on arrangements for M. J.'s memorial service and for a plaque to be placed in the library of University City High School, the later having been organized by his classmate Eddie Friedman. By the time JR finished the article, he felt empty. M. J. dead. Plane crash. Lost at sea. Body not recovered.

JR looked around at the expressions of others reading their letters and concluded they bore good news. He felt like he wanted to tell someone what happened, but it just did not feel appropriate to do so.

He recalled Walter's words, "Bunch of ways to get over the loneliness...you could join the Army."

Well, he was in the Army, but despite his relationship with Hulk and his increased sense of belonging, at this moment, he was surrounded by platoon mates but very much alone.

Mouse's letter ended, "YOU be careful. And get in touch when you get back. Mouse."

"Hey, Speargun, you finally get a letter and you look like it gave you the shits. What's up?"

"Well, Hulk, aside from the fact that I can't get rid of this jungle rot, I haven't slept more than two hours at a time for a month, I can't remember what a shower feels like, and R&R is a lifetime away, I'm doing just great."

He seemed to have deflected any discussion of M. J.

"Yeah, I'm not sure whether it's better to be on patrol and scared of being the next one to die or back here being bored to death."

As he met Hulk's stare and settled into a moment of silence, JR realized he was being given the space to let it out, which he did, "A high school classmate was killed in a plane crash near here. They didn't find his body. Apparently, he was on the ground in this hellhole for only a few hours, then bam—his plane exploded over the water."

"Oh man, I'm sorry to hear about your friend."

"Well, he wasn't really a friend," JR said, unsuccessfully trying to distance himself from his memories, "but we talked at school, and our folks knew each other."

Hulk instinctively knew to let JR live with his thoughts for awhile and then said, "Hey, I'm going to find a couple of beers before I try to get some sleep. I hear we're heading out into the jungle tomorrow at o-dark-thirty."

"Thanks, but I..."

"Look Speargun, the only thing we've got out here that makes any sense is each other. Get your ass in gear and follow me."

JR gave Hulk an over-ceremoniously correct salute, smiled, and said, "Well, if you put it that way—OK, Hulk, I'll have that beer. And we're drinking to M. J. Savoy."

CHAPTER 24

FIND EM! KILL 'EM! COUNT 'EM!

July 10, 1966
Am Dat, Vietnam

Early in the morning after learning of M. J. Savoy's death, JR and Hulk assembled with the rest of Bravo Company at the landing zone near the command post for the First Battalion. The post was located in the highlands, four kilometers west of Cam Ranh Bay and of the memories of the Quonset hut air conditioner units.

In the six weeks they had been in-country, JR and the other newbies had become accustomed to the routine of assemble, fly out, trek, fly back, and wait for the next set of orders. Although they had seen some light combat to date, their patrols had seemed more like search-and-avoid than search-and-destroy. All they had encountered were heat, humidity, jungle rot, mosquitoes the size and ferocity of Huey gunships, skin lesions from elephant grass, leeches on all kinds of unpleasant body parts, plenty of fear, and waves of boredom.

This morning, they were to be flown 30 kilometers south near the village of Am Dat, where convoys were being attacked by sniper and mortar fire from high ground along a five-kilometer stretch of Highway One. Casualties of both men and vehicles and the disruption of supply lines to the troops protecting Saigon were to be stopped.

The UH-1 Huey troop transport helicopters were warmed up and ready to go. The signature WHOP, WHOP, WHOP of the helo's blades was a sound they would come to recognize from miles away, as did the enemy, who would lie in wait to fire at machines and men they knew were approaching. Staff Sergeant Elton Trainer led his eight-man squad, Bravo One Three, onboard for the 20-minute flight. They would be among the first wave to land and had the responsibility to secure the landing zone.

Although it was still two months from the start of the monsoon season, heavy rains had again begun to fall. "Are we really gonna fly in this? I can barely see my hand in front of my face."

Trainer was quick to pounce, "Hey pansy ass, these pilots can and will fly in anything. They're the best, and it doesn't hurt that they're all a little crazy. Wait until you see them tackle the monsoon rains and the fog. Can't see a fucking thing, but they get it done. Yep—they're good—good and crazy."

Train's maniacal laugh was the only sound breaking through the steady rain. The squad leader had earned his nickname less for it being a play on his name than for how he relentlessly ran over guys. And Train could be as loud as his namesake. He was on his second tour in Vietnam, having returned to what he did best, as he put it, "Find 'em! Kill 'em! Count 'em!"

The target of Train's current rant was Billy Davis, a short wiry black from Albany, Georgia—his high-pitched voice having earned him his nickname, Cricket.

After a terrifying flight in the torrential downpour, they landed, secured the LZ, awaited the full complement of the company to arrive, and headed toward the nearby hills, the reported source of the sniper and mortar fire.

Over the next few days, the rain was intermittently heavy, leaving a blanket of humidity behind when it stopped. JR felt as though he were in a trance; hour after hour, tediously hacking through dense jungle growth, maneuvering over and around hilly terrain, and going through the motions of establishing secure base camps each night. He tried to keep alert, knowing that any moment he could be someone's target, but he also began to believe this would be just another mission with no encounter with the enemy.

"We've been out here for four days and still haven't had an eyeball on a single gook," griped Train. "Maybe the little fuckers are holed up somewhere dry, although I never seen rain stop 'em before."

"Well, the good news is that they haven't eyeballed us either," Hulk countered.

Train was in Hulk's face in no time, "That's pretty surprising given the noise you and the rest this damn squad makes. Probably the only thing that's kept us invisible has been the rain."

It was easy for Train to be eye-to-eye with Hulk—they were the same height, although the staff sergeant did not carry the same bulk. Train was long and lanky, but intimidating nevertheless. Among his squad-leading counterparts, he seemed to be first among equals. And Lieutenant Grand, who led Bravo Company's first platoon, appeared to be incapable of taking a step without making sure Train was in agreement.

Bravo One Three had secured a perimeter as the platoon took a break while awaiting orders. Train was on the radio, "Roger, LT, we can take the hill."

"OK, listen up. The lieutenant has orders to secure a better vantage point. Hill 254 is about three klicks east." Train pointed. "Bravo One One and One Two will flank it on either side, while we go right up the belly of the beast. We'll all come together at the top. Intel isn't sure whether there's gooks on the hill, so we'll just have to improvise. We're up and at it in five."

JR had just enough time to apply salve to the peeling skin on his feet and to change into his other pair of socks, which were damp but not as sodden as those he had on. He was amazed how quickly the constant heat, humidity, and trekking through the oozing sludge created by the rains had degraded his body. His skin was peeling off from the jungle rot that found its way into the ever-present cuts and scrapes from the elephant grass. Leeches sucked his blood, transmitting God knows what disease. He could barely keep enough fluids in his body with the persistent state of having the runs, occasional bouts with vomiting, and frequent delays of water resupply. And that said nothing of the welts resulting from the swarms of aggressive mosquitoes. He was sure he had taken on the smell of the jungle, if not worse. But what bothered him most was that he seemed to be getting used to it all.

"Move out."

The going was slow, but it always was in the combination of dense vegetation and soggy jungle floor. Five hours later, they were at the base of the hill. "Well, they either didn't see us through the rain, or there's nobody home. Should be a cakewalk," Train said as he signaled the squad to keep moving.

Just as Train dropped his arm, all hell broke loose. The whistling sound JR had heard on the first day in Cam Ranh Bay was repeated as was the shout, "Incoming!"

Men and their 50-pound packs hit the ground. All but Train, "We're going up, not down, you pussies. Let's go, hump it."

JR and Hulk made eye contact, sharing the unspoken fear of imminent demise. Soaked to the bone, they rose, assumed their positions with the squad, and followed Train up the hill. JR strained to see where the firing was coming from, thought he saw something in the thicket up the hill and to his right, and fired into it. The firing stopped from that position, but not from others. Before he was able to take his next step, JR heard a scream to his left, looked over, and saw Cricket on the ground not more than ten meters away, blood spurting from his neck. "Medic!" JR shouted as he ran to Cricket and crouched at his side.

Doc joined JR within a minute, urgently pulled dressings from his bag, and leaned over Cricket to stop the bleeding. But the medic hesitated, reached down to check for a pulse, and finding none, respectfully closed Cricket's eyes and put the unused dressings back into his bag.

JR had frozen to watch the scene play out. For those brief moments, the sound of the firefight, the wetness of the hillside, and the smell of gunpowder were gone. His world was moving in slow motion as he saw Doc turn toward him and shake his head as if to say, "I'm sorry, there was nothing I could do."

JR returned a nod that said, "It's not your fault, Doc."

It was then that JR shuddered at the thought that despite being in potential combat situations for six weeks, Cricket was the first death he had witnessed. He also recoiled at the realization that there was likely another death on that hill; one that he had caused. Was there a young man in the thicket up the hill; a young man who was likely lying dead by JR's hand? Intellectually, he knew that this was what he had been trained to do—this was why he was here. Yet, despite the "Kill! Kill! Kill!" training of boot camp and AIT, he felt emotionally drained.

For a moment, JR was unable to move, but that changed with the adrenaline rush caused by a mortar shell landing close enough to deposit bits of the jungle floor on both Doc and him. The sounds, sights, and smells of the hillside returned with an even-greater intensity.

"Halt, hold your ground, find cover," Train yelled to the squad as he grabbed the radio.

"Big Batt," Train shouted, referring to Battalion headquarters, "this is Bravo One Three, pinned down on Hill 254. Requesting air support—target hilltop."

Staff Sergeant Elton Trainer had no qualms about bypassing the chain of command when he knew what their eventual decision would be. He had checked with neither the platoon leader nor the company commander.

Apparently, battalion headquarters also had no qualms about responding to Train, because within minutes, the platoon heard the WHOP, WHOP, WHOP of three Huey gunships that strafed the top of the hill with machine gun and rocket fire. The hilltop was stripped bare, and when the gunships stopped firing, JR knew, or at least hoped, he would no longer be at risk.

"Why the hell didn't we just start with air support? It seemed like our job was to be the bait, to draw fire, so we knew where to call in the strike," JR said to Doc after looking around to make sure Train was not within earshot.

"I don't know. Seems like we sacrificed Cricket to control the hill and take the pressure off of the supply routes. Does that make it worth it," Doc asked.

"What do you think Cricket would say? This whole thing stinks," JR said quietly but with emphasis.

When the hill was secured, there was still plenty to do. First Platoon, Bravo Company, took advantage of VC bunkers and rocket craters to make their digging easier. Lieutenant Grand called in medevac for Cricket and two others from other squads who had been seriously wounded. They turned to the task of counting enemy bodies.

A churning in his stomach told him not to do so, but JR headed down the hill toward the thicket into which he had fired during the assault. Had he actually killed a man? If he had, how would he feel? Was it justified because the guy was trying to kill him? Was it justified because this was war and that is exactly what is supposed to happen? JR reluctantly but methodically searched for the thicket.

The rain had stopped, allowing JR to hear the man before he saw him. Weapon poised, JR inched toward the moaning. What he saw took his breath away.

Lying on his back in the mud, blood seeping from a wound in his neck similar to Cricket's, eyes open but barely, was not a man, but a boy who looked to be no older than 13 or 14. The boy stared into JR's eyes—a stare filled with fear; a stare asking for help. In the next 30 seconds, which seemed never-ending, JR watched the youngster's eyes slowly, ever so slowly, become a blank stare as his life drained away.

JR knew in his heart that he had killed him. No longer able to control the churning in his stomach, he vomited, feeling as he did when Walter and he were beat up. This time it was not a physical kick in the stomach, but an emotional kick to his psyche.

JR collected the boy's weapons and ammunition and in doing so, came across a photograph in a small bag. It was of the boy and apparently his mother, father, and two sisters. All were smiling. A family—already torn apart by war; now torn apart by death. Would they ever smile again? Were the others even still alive? An enemy combatant? Yes. An enemy? No.

JR slogged back up the hill to report the kill and turn in the weapons and ammo. The photo of the boy's family was in his pocket and in his mind's eye.

That night, while others guarded the perimeter, Hulk and JR settled into a bunker next to Arnold "Doc" Timlin to get a breather, debrief the day, and open rations.

"How long have you been here, Doc?"

"My whole life, which is about eight months."

"How the hell do you do it? I could barely keep from upchucking when I saw Cricket go down."

"First one, Hulk?"

"Yeah."

"Won't be your last."

"So, how do you do it?"

"Well, I worked for an ambulance service in New York City right after high school. When I got drafted, it seemed to both me and the Army that I should be a medic, so after basic training at Fort Knox, I had ten weeks of combat medic training at Fort Sam Houston. Despite all that, nothing prepared me for what I've seen here. I know what I'm doing is saving lives," Doc hesitated with his head down, "sometimes. But even so, what has become the toughest part is that I no longer believe that all of this has any purpose. I'm not sure I ever believed it."

"I'm with you, Doc," Hulk said.

"If there was something, anything, I could do to stop this war, I'd do it," said Doc, as he stood. "Hey, I gotta get some sleep."

"I just can't get Cricket out of my head," JR said.

For now, that was as far as he could go. He was not yet prepared to share his experience with the Vietnamese boy, not even with Hulk.

Doc looked down at JR, "I have this album in my head of every guy I treated over the eight months, and I just keep going through the pictures. And you know something? It doesn't matter a bit whether the guy I've tried to help is white or black or even Vietnamese—they're all the same. This has just got to stop."

JR gently put his hand over the pocket that held the Vietnamese family photo and thought to himself, "Have I begun my own album?"

The following morning, just as the platoon had settled in to their newly-gained hilltop, they were given orders to return to base. Apparently, the hill was no longer of strategic importance.

CHAPTER 25

GOD BLESS THEM

August 12, 1966
Cam Ranh Bay Perimeter, Vietnam

Sleep was hard to come by, even between patrols when the troops were relatively safe at base camp. Except for the few fortunate ones who could doze off even when standing against a tree in the jungle, sleep was nearly impossible. Deprivation resulted in a constant state of fatigue that put everyone on edge, affected morale, and made everything much more difficult to get done.

"This is depressing. Did you know the really heavy rains haven't even started yet? I'm tired; I'm wet; I'm sick; I'm caught somewhere in between being dehydrated and having the shits; and I'm pissed off."

"Well, Pucker, other than that, what's your issue?"

"Laugh if you want, Speargun, but you're in no great shakes either. You can barely walk on those fucked up feet of yours. When do you think they'll be dry enough to heal? Just when our bodies get a little relief, it's time to head back out in the slop again. If we live through this hellhole, we'll still be falling apart when we get home.

"And to top it all off, I'm having a tough time even breathing since that asshole pilot dropped napalm in our back pockets last week," Peepers coughed.

"Peepers, you're lucky you can see at all. How can you know what got dropped where," Hulk asked, always ready to jab Peepers about his eyesight.

"I could feel it, smell it, hear it, and even taste it. I didn't need to see it," Peepers roared back.

"If it really got that close, you're probably feeling the effects of the carbon monoxide that the fires let off and of the smoke being in your lungs. Much closer and you'd be in deeper shit, especially if it got on you. Burns in an instant and hurts like hell. Nothing and no one is left in an area we hit with that stuff. That's why we use it," JR added while shaking his head in disgust.

"Yeah, that's all well and good as long as what we hit ain't our guys," Peepers scowled.

That previous Friday, Bravo Company was on a search-and-destroy mission that had been going on for ten days. Supplies were short, as were nerves. It was not just a walk through the jungle. Around every hill and in every clearing was a new battle. Casualties throughout the company were heavy, mostly men who were wounded, some seriously. Two were dead.

The operation had been coordinated with air support to help the ground troops find and kill the enemy, to medevac the American dead and wounded, and to drop napalm where and when called to do so by ground commanders.

Bravo Company finally got orders to hike its way back to base camp, where Alpha Company would give them a breather. The last medevac flights of the mission would be flown that afternoon. A landing zone needed to be cleared of both jungle growth and enemy threat.

Bravo One Two, the squad that both Pucker and Peepers were in, was on point to secure the LZ once the area was cleared by the napalm drop. The men were on a small hill within two klicks of the targeted area, close and high enough to see it over the jungle growth.

The squad heard the A-1 Skyraiders first and then caught sight of the three single-propeller aircraft, whose wing positions were loaded with ordnance. Unaffected by light enemy fire, the three planes flew relentlessly toward the would-be landing zone and began dropping napalm and firing rockets with deadly accuracy.

It was then that Pucker pointed and shouted, "There's one more!"

From the horizon came a fourth plane, similarly loaded, but its bearing was different from that of the first three. In fact, Pucker's next shout was, "That son-of-a-bitch is heading our way!"

The next few minutes got increasingly dangerous as the last plane began releasing napalm far from the target area and within a couple of hundred meters of Bravo One Two. While the squad did not take a direct hit, they felt the debris from the nearby strikes, the heat of the incendiary devices exploding on impact, and the smoke from the flames entering their lungs.

Although a full disaster had been narrowly averted, it took all the grit and composure the squad could muster to reorganize themselves to secure the LZ. Peepers was closest to the blasts and still felt the effects a week later.

"OK, Peepers, I get it. You nearly got burned to death, and you're having trouble breathing. But I'm thinking about it another way. Every time we drop some of that shit, we burn away age-old jungle, destroy a village, ruin farm land, or kill a bunch of folks— some of them, maybe most of them, who are just like us; trying to make it through this fucking war alive. We're supposed to be saving this country, but we're burning it up. Does that make sense to you?"

"Hulk, you're on your soapbox again. But you do have a point. These people didn't ask us to come over here. Even the guys who we're fighting against are guys just like us—called up to lay it on the line for some noble cause that isn't very noble," Peepers coughed a response.

"How long do you think this war would last or if it would have even been started if the politicians had to fight it or send their kids here," Hulk asked the rhetorical question.

"You know, Peepers, the story doesn't stop there," Doc jumped in after having listened quietly to the napalm story. "You guys get the LZ set to go. Then WHOP, WHOP, WHOP—in come the medevac copters. It's raining like a motherfucker, but what's new? If these guys were back in the states and in that weather, they'd be somewhere sitting back and drinking coffee.

"But no. Those two pilots are hell-bent on evacuating our guys and God bless them for that. I gave a report to the crew chiefs on each guy, and both birds took off to head for the evac hospital and about ten minutes later, as I hear it, the rain that couldn't be any heavier got heavier. One of the choppers clips the side of a hillside. The pilot goes into a controlled crash, if there's such a thing. To

BODY NOT RECOVERED

his credit, everyone who wasn't already dead in that thing survived the crash.

"The other pilot sees it all happen, completes his flight, drops off his wounded guys, and heads back out. Lands his bird in an impossible place, transfers the bodies to his chopper, and brings them back.

"These guys are fantastic. The good news is that he saw the crash and knew the coordinates to find them again. Can you imagine looking for a crash site in the fucking jungle or if a copter crashed into the sea? It would be next to impossible to find."

JR recoiled as he remembered M. J.—crash at sea; body not recovered.

"Yeah," Hulk added, "and I remember Train saying that flying in the rain is nothing like flying in the fog, which I guess we'll have to do at some point."

JR, Hulk, Pucker, Peepers, and Doc huddled in silence under ponchos that served to keep at least some of the rain at bay, each contemplating the many ways their time in Vietnam could end, most of them bad.

CHAPTER 26

VUNG DONG

September 3, 1966
Hill 356, Cam Ranh Bay Perimeter, Vietnam

"Where did you get this, Salt?"

Bravo One had quickly taken hill 356, ordered to do so to commandeer the highest ground in the area, enabling Bravo Company to set up a looking post among the highlands northwest of Cam Ranh Bay. Enemy resistance had been light and aside from some minor scrapes and bruises, the platoon was unscathed. Once the hill was secure and the platoon was dug in, those not on perimeter guard duty had some time to relax.

As was becoming the norm when they had the chance, JR, Hulk, Pucker, Peepers, and Doc gathered to share stories, rations, and camaraderie. On this day, Salt had joined them.

Pucker opened a can, and despite peaches being his favorite, performed his ritual of offering some to the others, who knew better than to accept the offer—also part of the ritual. Peepers lit Sterno to make coffee. Doc burned a leech off of Hulk's right butt cheek and suggested he could put a tattoo back there while he was at it. All lit cigarettes except JR, who methodically applied salve to his rotting feet.

Business as usual—except when Salt handed Hulk the newspaper. The first thing Hulk saw was the newspaper's name—*FTA*.

Jack Morton's last name, which appeared on the blue canister with the girl and umbrella in virtually every household in America, earned him the nickname. He was a couple of years older and more educated than most soldiers in the company. After high school, he had entered and spent five semesters at the University of Michigan.

"Well, Hulk, before I tell you that, let me give you all some background. During my sophomore year, I was taking a sociology course at U of M with a Professor William Gamson. Great guy—I really loved his class. Anyway, in early '65, he led an antiwar effort among the university's professors, who had generally supported Johnson's election campaign.

"The faculty felt they backed the right guy, because Goldwater wanted to bomb everything in sight. But Johnson reneged and started bombing the hell out of North Vietnam with Rolling Thunder. Gamson and other faculty members got together and decided to take action.

"They declared a one-day moratorium from teaching their regular classes. Instead, they spent that day teaching interested students about U. S. involvement in Vietnam. It was the first teach-in in the country, and the idea spread to other campuses.

"So, I go to the teach-in with about 600 others, and I'm blown away by what I learned. I was hooked and focused my full attention on antiwar activism. I got so involved that I rarely attended class, and my grades went down the toilet. My junior year starts, and I drop a couple of classes—they just weren't as important as everything else.

"Big mistake. I lost full-time student status; my draft board rescinded my student deferment; and I was drafted. I went from Jack Morton, University of Michigan student, to Salt, Vietnam Hill 356 soldier in less than six months.

"Now that I'm here, I hate this war even more than when I was at Michigan. And I'm going to do everything I can to bring it to an end. I just need to do it in a different way and need to be careful. I don't want to be prosecuted for subversion.

"Anyway, about a week ago, I overheard a conversation between Hulk and Peepers that led me to believe that you guys might be open to doing something about this war. Since I see all of you together a lot, I decided to take the risk and raise the subject."

After Salt had shared his Michigan to Vietnam story, Hulk held up the newspaper again and asked "OK, Salt, where'd you get this, and while you're at it, what does FTA stand for?"

Salt grinned broadly, "Don't you know the army recruiting slogan? FTA—fun, travel, and adventure."

Hulk shared the grin, "Yeah, but somehow, I don't think this is army-sanctioned."

"Not exactly."

Salt's grin turned into a hearty laugh, but then he got serious, he riveted his eyes on Hulk's and took the risk of opening the subject, "There's a growing antiwar movement within the military, and its spreading rapidly. These underground newspapers are cropping up on bases everywhere. Some guy in Fort Ord thought *FTA* would be a great name for the paper, because the initials have come to be the rallying point for the movement—Fuck the Army. A friend of mine sent this."

Although Salt was speaking softly and they were separated from the remainder of the platoon in a bunker on the northwest quadrant of the hill, both for protection and effect, everyone looked around to make sure they had not drawn any unwanted attention.

"Well, I think you all know where my head's been on this from the beginning. I didn't want to come here, I don't want to be here, and I'd do anything short of getting blown up to get out of here," Hulk said—his normally engaging demeanor had vanished.

JR opened his mouth to speak, but closed it again and took some time deciding whether or not to expose his feelings. The others, anticipating him saying something, waited patiently.

It had been boiling up inside since the day Cricket had died— the same day JR had first killed another human being. Since then, the platoon had been in an increasing frequency of firefights—for what was becoming to JR increasingly uncertain objectives. They were losing comrades faster than they were being replaced. And most distressingly, he knew with certainty he had killed four other human beings and likely more. Unlike the blind shot into the Hill 254 thicket, each of these kills was fully visible, and he had looked into the blank stares of death for each of them during the body count.

Within this same timeframe, JR had been with others in the back of the lead troop transport truck in a convoy when he heard and felt a thump that brought the deuce-and-a-half to an abrupt stop. Train jumped out of the back of the truck hollering, "Secure the area!"

BODY NOT RECOVERED

The squad followed, taking positions and looking for Charlie. JR was located in the front of the truck and was the first, other than the driver and guy riding next to him, to see what had really happened. Laid out below the front of the transport was a Vietnamese civilian of indeterminate age, clearly dead with his hand still clutching the end of a rope that was tied to a water buffalo that was also on the ground; injured, but alive.

"Put the fucking animal out of its misery," the driver of the truck said, "I've already done the same for the gook."

JR couldn't believe what he heard, "You bastard, you killed an innocent civilian."

"No fucking way—he's clearly a VC sympathizer. I came around the bend, and there he was. He ran right into the front of the truck. Truck, one—gook and pet, zero," the driver said as he laughed.

"You probably want to add both him and his ox to the body count, you asshole." JR was fuming and realized his finger was adding pressure to the trigger.

He walked away to calm himself and heard the shot that killed the ox. "Pull them to the side of the road and get loaded up," Train shouted.

As the convoy started back up, JR tried to sort out his reactions. He came close to tears as he saw the man and his animal dead and alone on the side of the road and thought of the family that would be grieving. He could not believe that the driver, Train, and most of the others didn't seem to have a second thought about what just happened. And he knew from the look on Hulk's face that he was thinking the exact same things as was JR.

One week following the truck incident, JR was in a Huey on the way back to base camp from an operation, when the door gunner opened fire and was screaming, "Take that you Charlie gook bastards!"

JR strained to see out of the door opening over the gunner's shoulder. He expected to see enemy combatants with guns or rocket launchers firing at them. What he saw instead was a group of women who had obviously been working in a paddy field. Several lay lifeless in the wet field; the others were scattering.

JR pulled at the gunner's shoulder trying to get him to stop and yelled, "What the fuck are you doing?"

The gunner stopped firing, calmly turned toward JR, sneered, and over the noise of the chopper, hollered, "Target practice!"

Although he was tempted to throw the gunner out of the cabin door, JR could only settle into his seat with his head in his hands. He had never really thought about it before, but it was becoming apparent that his parents had instilled a set of values and that were being frequently violated. The hell that was Vietnam was becoming untenable.

The incident that served to solidify JR's thoughts was the most recent. Two weeks earlier, Bravo Company had been ordered to ferret out VC sympathizers who were suspected of harboring men and supplies in or near the village of Vung Dong. The plan for the mission was for Bravo One to investigate the village, while other platoons would surround it to ensure no Viet Cong could escape.

Bravo One's three squads approached the village from different directions with orders to interrogate residents and only return fire if fired upon. Two South Vietnamese interpreters accompanied them to manage the language difficulties, although some of the veterans of the war had picked up sufficient Vietnamese to believe they could get through the basics.

After deployment by helicopter and a three-klick trek, the company was in place. Train led his squad to the village, and they arrived just before the others, finding Vung Dong to be no different than other small rural villages. The thatched-roof, bamboo-wall huts were scattered in no apparent pattern. Poles supported each hut about three feet off the ground to protect it from monsoon season flooding. Shallow wells with buckets resting in them pock-marked the open area of the village. A rutted dirt road ran through and out of the village, likely used for carts to take goods to market. Dozens of dogs, a similar number of pigs, and a few water buffalo roamed freely.

When the villagers saw the soldiers, they ran to their homes, from which they were rousted and assembled in the central open area of the village, where it was quickly apparent that the several hundred crowded together were only women, children, and old men. The people of Vung Dong cowered in fear, and women hugged their children close.

"Ask them where their young men are," Lieutenant Grand said to one of the interpreters.

After a flurry of conversation with a number of the old men, one of the interpreters said, "They are working in the paddy fields."

"Don't fucking believe it, LT," Train interjected. "These gooks are VC for sure. Let's make an example of a few of them, and they'll tell us what we want to know."

He knocked a coulee hat off a young woman, grabbed her by the hair, and dragged her away from the other villagers.

The woman wailed and an old man rushed at Train to help the woman. Train hit the old man in the chest with his rifle butt, and the man went down in a heap. The staff sergeant then pointed the rifle at the temple of the young woman and shouted at her in broken Vietnamese, "Where the hell are they?"

The sound of screaming, crying, and wailing of the villagers increased, then came to an abrupt silence at the sound of the rifle shot. JR expected the woman to go down, but she was still standing. Train had purposely fired just above her head and shouted, "The next one is in your fucking ear. Where are they?"

The woman finally did go down when she fainted. Train grabbed her by the throat and pulled her up, stared into her expressionless face, then let her fall back to earth. "You know what, LT. Fuck the interrogation. Let's just burn this place down." His face was beet red, his eyes were maniacal, and his hands were shaking in anger.

Lieutenant Grand, seemingly frozen by the spectacle that was unfolding before him, hesitated just long enough for Trainer to turn to his squad and say, "Torch it."

JR was telling himself that there was no way he was going to obey that order. As it turned out, he did not need to. Train pulled a grenade from his belt and was about to throw it at a nearby hut, when Grand shouted, "No way, Sergeant! At ease!"

For the first time since JR had been in the platoon, he had witnessed Lieutenant Grand confront Trainer, "We're here to gather information, not to level a village! Stand down, Staff Sergeant!"

Trainer was taken aback, but relented and reluctantly deferred to his superior, "Yes sir."

It took some time for everything to calm down, and Grand began to work with the interpreters to approach the villagers again. Just as he did, someone in the platoon shouted, "Here they come!"

Down the dirt road came the young men of the village. Instinctively, Bravo One brought their rifles to the ready, but as the young men got closer, it was evident they did not have weapons in their hands, but had the tools they had been using in the paddy fields.

The platoon never learned for sure whether any of the villagers were Viet Cong or sympathizers. What most suspected was that the villagers were just plain folks trying to get by in an impossible situation. The platoon left behind an old man with a severe bruise on his chest, a young woman who had been close to death, and hundreds of people who had good reason to hate Americans. What they did not leave behind was a burned out village and piles of dead innocents.

CHAPTER 27

THAT GUY

September 3, 1966
Hill 356, Cam Ranh Bay Perimeter, Vietnam

JR had collected his thoughts and himself and was finally ready to share his feelings with his comrades. He raised his head, which was heavy with both weariness and despair, and spoke softly but resolutely, "It took me a long time to figure out what I wanted to do with my life, and I thought I made the right decision to enlist. For the first time in my life, I've felt I belonged somewhere, felt like my life had a purpose—no more blank pages or blank stares."

JR had relived that moment in the high school cafeteria over and over again; staring at his yearbook photo and space where his high school activities would have been listed, if he had any.

"But I'm not so sure anymore. Let me tell you a story."

Hulk, Peepers, Pucker, Salt, and Doc were riveted as JR told them of OD, Not So, and the Rawlings family, especially Walter. He told them of losing his parents and feeling as though he was part of a family again with the Rawlings. He told them about Karen as though she were his sister, although he mused to himself whether she was more than that. JR told them about Walter and him being beaten at work. And, with tears in his eyes, he told them about Walter's death and how it became clear in his last five minutes with Walter what was in his heart to do.

"So, I enlisted and here I am, right where I thought I would be and should be. I knew it wasn't going to be mom and apple pie. But, more and more, I think it was the wrong move. It's not about being in the army—that's been great for me. It's not about you guys— you've been great for me. It's about what we're being asked to do and who we're being asked to be.

"I've been trying to put how I've been feeling into words and think I finally figured it out. You know that asshole I told you about who beat us up and probably was the one who killed Walter? Well, somewhere in his background, somebody taught him to blindly hate.

"My folks loved the musical *South Pacific* and took me to see it when I was about ten. There's a song in there that they made me listen to over and over again after that; but I never really understood it at the time. The name of the song is 'You've Got to Be Carefully Taught.' It goes, 'You've got to be taught to hate and fear, you've got to be taught from year to year, to hate the people your relatives hate, you've got to be carefully taught.'

"That guy beat us up because someone taught him to hate blacks. He didn't know Walter; he didn't know me. He just saw the black skin and a white guy who was his friend. It set him off. I hate him for it, and I hate whoever made him that way.

"And guess what—I'm becoming that guy. I don't know who I'm shooting at. I just know that I've been taught to hate them. I don't know the people who live in the villages, but I'm being asked to burn their homes and shoot them. I'm hating myself for it, and I'm hating the people who are making me this way. I don't want to be that guy."

JR bowed his head and was silent. The only sounds were the breeze rustling the elephant grass, the mosquitoes in their ears, and the beating of their own hearts.

Hulk rose slowly, resettled next to JR, put his huge arm around his friend, and said slowly and emphatically, "You are not that guy, and you never will be if I have anything to say or do about it."

After another period of silence, Salt said, "We do need to do something about it."

"What the fuck can we do?"

Salt responded to Pucker, "We could disobey orders. We could try to convince others. We could start an antiwar newspaper. There's a lot we can do."

Pucker thought for a moment, "Well, a lot of fucking good all that'll do. We all end up in the stockade here and prison back home. And nothing changes."

Hulk, who was more concerned about JR than the discussion, finally joined in, "You guys know that I was drafted. Some of you know that I tried like the dickens not to be, but shit happens. I didn't like this war before I got my notification and don't like it now. I've been thinking about what to do about it—in fact, when I'm not being shot at, that's mostly what I think about.

"Salt, I agree with Pucker. There's a bunch we can do here, but none of it will make a difference. I think all of the real antiwar action is back home. Every new guy we get tells us about campus protests, marches on Washington, celebrities speaking out, and all of it showing up on TV. That's where I'd like to be—back in the states making a real difference."

"So, Hulk, why don't you just reserve a flight home and get to work? You can ask Train for a lifelong pass. Hell, he might even make the call to the airlines for you."

"Yeah, right, Doc, simple as that," Hulk laughed, but with no humor in it.

Then he got serious and continued, "But if there was a way to do it, I'd jump on it in a minute."

"Bullshit. You can fucking dream about that all you want, but we're stuck here for the duration."

"Pucker, I've actually been thinking about this, and there might just be a way."

Hulk looked around and met each guy eye to eye. "But I'm not having this conversation unless I'm dead-nuts sure that each of you would be willing to listen. Any one of you who would not be committed to taking a big fucking risk to get back home sooner rather than later, then I'm done talking."

He went around once more, but this time, he stopped on each face.

"Pucker?"

"I may not be thinking about this the same way as the rest of you. I know you guys say you want to do something to help stop the war. Well, I think that's a good idea, but it's an idea that's too big for me. I just want to get out of here because I'm scared shitless. The only reason I'm alive and Cricket and others aren't is pure dumbass luck. So, yes, count me in."

"Peepers?"

"Pucker, I hear you man. Scared? Yep. Ready to get out of here? Yep. Signed up for the antiwar thing too? Yep—I'm in."

"Salt?"

"You know how I feel."

"Yeah, but I need to hear it. And so does everyone else."

"Count me in."

"Doc?"

"Wow, this is moving faster than I'm ready for. I'm pretty close to rotating back anyway."

"Doc, no hard feelings. It's your call."

Doc stared at Hulk, waited a moment, then said, "I've seen too many guys die, too many blown to bits, too many lose a limb. This isn't really about me, is it? Hell, why not. I'm with you."

"JR?"

"Hulk, I need to get out of here, and I need to do something to stop this war. Apparently, those two things go together. So, yes. Tell us what you've got in mind."

CHAPTER 28

A DIFFICULT REQUEST

September 13, 1966
Bangkok, Thailand

The discussion on Hill 356 was interrupted before Hulk could begin to lay out his ideas about how to get them out of Vietnam and back to the states.

"OK, everybody listen up."

Train and the other squad leaders had rounded up everyone on the hill who was not on perimeter duty. Lieutenant Grand briefed them, "Tomorrow morning, we're heading south. We've got another concentration of sniper and mortar fire that we'll take care of before heading back to base."

JR and Hulk looked at each other and knew they were thinking about the same thing. Was this delay getting back to base camp going to screw up their R&R plans? Although they had been told the army was committed to pull them from the field almost regardless of what was going on, they were skeptical.

Hulk had convinced JR to put in a request for R&R in Bangkok; they had both been approved for the date they asked for; and they were scheduled to leave in a few days.

Thankfully, the remainder of the patrol was uneventful. Another platoon had already secured the area, and Bravo One was back at camp on Thursday. The following Sunday morning, the two friends were in a transport with a few others from Bravo Company on the way to Cam Ranh Bay to be flown to their R&R destinations.

Over the next 24 hours, they changed into civilian clothes, checked their jungle fatigues and other gear in a locker in one of those air conditioned Quonset huts, exchanged their military pay certificates and Vietnamese piasters for U. S. dollars, boarded a chartered commercial airline, and landed in Bangkok. Once they cleared customs in Bangkok and rented extra civilian clothes for the week, JR and Hulk tolerated a two-hour series of lectures about what was off limits and exchanged their dollars for Thai Baht.

JR and Hulk made their way toward their hotel and ducked into a nearby bar to escape the sensory overload that confronted them— the hordes of people, the growling noise of incessant car and motor scooter traffic, the mixture of odors from the outdoor cooking fires of street vendors and piles of uncollected garbage, and the vivid colors of the Bangkok streets.

The combination of beer and the local girls, who would have been glad to be their companions for the week, almost kept them at the bar all night. "Come on, Speargun. I know you're enjoying the wine, women, and song, but we have plans for the morning. Well, what I mean is for later this morning," Hulk said, checking his watch, and finding it to be 2:00am.

"Hey, I thought we were supposed to be getting an early start. I just woke up—it's almost noon," JR said as he shook Hulk to wake him up.

Hulk rolled over, flashed his signature grin, stretched his big body, and said, "It's remarkable what a real bed, no fear of being shot, and drinking a few too many can do for a good night's sleep. But right, we need to get started. I have a call to make."

An hour later, after cleaning up and getting a bite to eat, Hulk solicited the assistance of one of the hotel staff to help him phone the Jattawan family, hoping he could make arrangements to see Annan. But his serious business would be with Annan's father.

Hulk reached Khun Jattawan at his office, exchanged cordial greetings, and asked if JR and he could visit with the Jattawan family the next day. His father's friend offered to send a driver for Hulk and JR at the hotel the following morning. Having the rest of the day to themselves, they returned to the bar, hired two of the local girls and enjoyed a tour of the city and of their accommodating guides.

Despite another very late night, JR and Hulk were waiting for the Jattawan's driver just after breakfast, over which Hulk reviewed what he had in mind and the role he hoped the Jattawan family would play. JR was both excited and anxious about the possibilities, knowing all of their plans were contingent on whether Khun Jattawan was willing and able to help. The next few hours would be crucial. As they stood in front of the hotel, they were silent and somber.

The driver got out of the black sedan whose make and model neither American recognized, bowed slightly with his hands pressed together in front of his face as if in prayer, opened the back door for JR and Hulk, and said not a word as he navigated his way through narrow, bicycle-dense, and people-crowded streets. Thirty minutes of silence later, they stopped in front of the home that Hulk remembered so well. Annan was waiting on the terrace and rushed forward, yet stopped long enough to bring his hands together, bow slightly, smile, and say, "Sawatdee-khap."

Hulk and JR, as Hulk had taught him, returned the greeting.

Annan ushered them into the spacious, well-appointed, and dark teak-paneled drawing room, where they found his mother and father waiting. Greetings were repeated. After they lowered themselves into comfortable settees, which faced each other and were separated by an ornate teak coffee table, the talk was of Hulk's father, the business climate in Bangkok, reviews of the lives of other family members on both sides, and even a little about the war and the soldiers' role in it.

JR immediately knew why Hulk spoke so highly of this family. They were friendly and hospitable, making him feel at home these thousands of miles away from University City, Missouri, USA.

After tea and cakes were served and consumed, Hulk decided it was time to broach the subject, "Khun Jattawan, I have a difficult request to make of you, but I want to give you some background first."

"Before you continue, I will leave the business of the day to you men. It was wonderful to see you again, William. Please give my regards to your parents."

Hulk thanked Annan's mother for her hospitality and walked with her to the doorway as she gracefully left the room. When Hulk had returned to his seat, Khun Jattawan began.

"Mr. Carlson," he said in a formal manner to show respect for Hulk, for his family, and for the request Hulk was about to make, "I have been doing business with your father for many years and,

A DIFFICULT REQUEST

as you know, consider him a friend. When you visited our home, you also became my friend and the friend of my family. I am proud that Annan and you can come together as you did when you were younger. Before I hear what you have to say, allow me to tell you that I will do whatever I can to meet your request."

Four hours and a meal later, JR and Hulk left the Jattawan home and were driven back to the hotel. For the next two days, they enjoyed Bangkok; having made arrangements to tour with Annan, who made sure to take them to the places that could be most important to them in the near future.

Making sure no one else could hear them on the trip back to Vietnam, the two friends made sure they agreed on what they had arranged in Bangkok. They also talked about what they would have to do in Vietnam to make it all work. JR was surprised that while a lot of things still had to come together, he could actually begin to see his possible, albeit risky, future.

CHAPTER 29

LT'S BEEN HIT

September 24, 1966
Cam Ranh Bay Perimeter, Vietnam

It did not take long to transition from full nights of sleep, female companionship, cold beer, and the hospitality of the Jattawan family to the rigors, horrors, and fears of the war. Within days of returning from Bangkok, JR and Hulk joined Bravo One in the jungle. It had been quiet for the first two days of the operation when sniper fire rang out. Bravo One was along a tree line and able to easily find cover from the firing, which stopped as quickly as it had begun. Eyes and ears alert and weapons at the ready, the platoon awaited orders.

JR was crouched low near Staff Sergeant Trainer, and when he noticed the squad leader begin crawling up the tree line, JR followed; but stopped short of joining Train, Doc, and Grand's radio operator, who were huddled around and tending to the lieutenant.

Leadership assignments in Vietnam could be short-lived, because company, platoon, and squad leaders were prime targets. Snipers, intent on disrupting the chain of command, had little difficulty identifying a platoon leader from the single-bar insignia on his M-1 helmet and from the obvious actions that were different from those of other soldiers—frequently scanning maps, traveling close to their radio operators, and giving orders.

Lieutenant Grand was no exception. Jackson Grand was a Princeton graduate from the upper peninsula of Michigan whose family had a long tradition of serving in the armed services. Although he had plans for a future beyond the military, Grand made a personal commitment to join the army and graduated from 12 weeks of Officer Candidate School. Sharp, short, wiry, and bespeckled, Grand was respected by the men of Bravo One for his operations planning, but not necessarily for his strength of leadership.

Doc was focused on Grand's knee, which was bleeding and skewed at an angle JR did not know a knee could bend. LT was either unconscious, in shock, or had a miraculously high threshold of pain, because he was still and quiet.

JR could hear Train on the radio, but was not close enough to make out what was being was saying. That soon became clear. When the conversation was over, Train turned back toward the platoon, and made eye contact with JR.

"Spears, pass the word. LT's been hit. You just earned yourself a temporary field promotion. You're the new Bravo One Three squad leader. I'm commanding Bravo One for the time being. We've got two objectives. One—secure an LZ so we can evac LT. Two—find that sniper's nest and take it out."

Over the next eight hours, they met both objectives, but sustained two more casualties to be medevaced with the lieutenant.

CHAPTER 30

WE'RE THE OPPRESSORS

September 28, 1966
Cam Ranh Bay Perimeter Base Camp, Vietnam

Although he survived the sniper incident, Lieutenant Jackson Grand's shattered knee meant he was going home. A replacement platoon leader was expected, but the timeframe was uncertain. For now, Train would continue to lead Bravo One.

JR's squad leader days ended as soon they returned from the operation. Sergeant Wilson Parker, a nearly Hulk-sized black from Chicago, was assigned from Bravo Two to lead Bravo One Three, at least in the interim. Demanding but fair, Parker was quickly welcomed.

Time at base camp was brief. Parker informed his new squad that although they had been there less than two months earlier, they would be returning to Vung Dong. The brass still believed that the village was either a haven for Viet Cong or at least sympathetic to them.

"You know, if it wasn't for Grand, Vung Dong wouldn't even still exist. What do you figure will happen when there's nobody there to hold Train back? This can't end well," JR said, shaking his head and pursing his lips in despair.

"This might be the last straw," Hulk concurred. "We'll see."

"This Vung Dong thing means more to me than you know, Hulk," JR began, long past any concerns about sharing his deepest feelings with his friend. "One of the reasons I'm over here is something my friend Walter Rawlings said shortly after I met him. It was the first time that I had heard a rationale for the war that made sense to me, and in many ways, it was why I enlisted.

"Even though he and the other blacks in St. Louis were constantly being harassed, he said he believed that it was still right for us to be over here keeping the South Vietnamese from being oppressed. He related it to what would have happened if the world would have stepped up to prevent the holocaust. How many European Jews would have been saved? How much better off would mankind have been?

"Well, I really believed what he said, and I still believe it today. The problem is that if I put myself in the shoes of these villagers, it looks to me like we're the oppressors, not the saviors. I'm not sure what I'll do if we get into a bad situation in the village. There's no way those women and children and old men are the enemy."

Since returning from Bangkok, JR and Hulk had debriefed Doc, Peepers, Pucker, and Salt on what they had arranged through the Jattawan family. Their big problem now was finding a way to get to Bangkok. Although they could not have predicted it, the Vung Dong operation would serve both to further solidify the common purpose of the small but determined crew and to open up a possible yet daring solution to their problem.

CHAPTER 31

VUNG DONG REDUX

October 2, 1966
Vung Dong, Vietnam

The basic plan for Vung Dong was similar to the approach two months earlier—Bravo One's squads would enter the village from three directions. This time, however, the ground operation would be supported by one OH-23 Raven helicopter for reconnaissance and two Huey gunships to help make sure Charlie did not escape.

The objectives were to find and kill Viet Cong, uncover arms caches, collect intelligence about VC movements, and make sure the villagers were not supporting the enemy.

After deployment to the target area had occurred without incident, Train positioned himself with Bravo One One and was the first to have the village in sight. Parker ordered Bravo One Three to advance when he got the radio command, and the three squads converged on the center of the village.

At first glance, Vung Dong appeared to be the same—thatched-roof huts elevated on poles, shallow wells, the dirt road through and out of the village. But, JR observed, there were big differences as well. During their first visit, it had been mid-August, and the monsoon season had not begun. Now, although it was a rare day during monsoon season when it was not raining, the village was mired in mud from relentless seasonal rains.

Throughout and around the village, there were new huge craters, whose presence could have no other explanation than being the result of U.S. bombing runs. "What in the hell are we doing to these people?" JR thought to himself.

After JR and the others had milled around the central area of Vung Dong for awhile, the greatest difference became apparent.

The village seemed to be abandoned—no people, no dogs, no pigs, only a few water buffalo. Perhaps the bombing had frightened the residents sufficiently that they joined thousands of others in the refugee camps that had been established.

For that brief moment when it appeared there would be no confrontation with villagers, JR felt relief, thinking that at least on this day, he would not be faced with a menu of only bad options. That's when he and others heard a muffled sound of dogs barking and pigs squealing. Train raised his hand demanding silence and slowly walked toward the source of the noise.

He looked down into what seemed to be an innocuous hole in the ground, shot two rounds from his M-16 into the cavity, and hollered in poor Vietnamese, "Come out."

Three dogs and four pigs scurried out of the hole followed by four older women. Either the underground bunkers had been there a couple of months earlier and not used by the villagers or had been built since the earlier visit, perhaps in response to the bombings. Regardless, somehow the Vung Dong residents knew the soldiers were coming and had retreated underground. "Search for other bunkers," shouted Train.

Once they knew what they were looking for, the Americans found a number of bunkers in the central section of the village. Shouting and gunshots were used to coax the villagers into the open. Within a half-hour, the assemblage looked much the same as it did two months earlier—several hundred women, children, and old men crouched down and huddled together; this time in the mud. Not a young man was in sight.

Not waiting for help from the interpreter who was available, Train began shouting, mixing in a few phrases of Vietnamese, "Where are your young men? You're hiding weapons; where are they? Tell me or I'll burn this place down!"

It was apparent to JR that the villagers had no idea what they were being told or asked. Becoming more and more agitated, JR searched for, hoped for, but found no way to affect the situation.

Warrant Officer Pat Richardson had his OH-23 recon copter hovering over Vung Dong, having positioned it to be ready to help if needed. "Looks like it's under control, Three Spot," talking to his door gunner, Trey Paulson, over the comm system. "No resistance from the villagers, and we seem to have them all assembled."

"It's quiet enough, Balls. What say we go get some gas and then head back here?"

The crew and copter had been involved with another operation earlier in the day and had not had time to refuel. Although they probably would have had enough to complete the Vung Dung mission, Richardson wanted to be on the safe side and judged the ground situation to be low risk.

Tony Baltieri, Richardson's navigator in the three-seater, agreed. Richardson let the two Huey pilots know he would be back shortly and turned toward the fuel depot.

On the ground, women were wailing; children were crying. Train kept shouting. Soldiers were on edge, whether they were the ones primed to kill and burn or the ones who faced this day with foreboding and wanted no part of it. The noise was escalating, but abruptly stopped as if someone had flipped a switch.

The silence lingered—even the children seemed to know something was about to happen. Train had raised his weapon and was walking toward a woman on the edge of the amassed villagers—she was the only one who seemed to have remained calm to this point.

Train knocked off the woman's coolie hat, pulled her up by the hair, separated her from the others, and without hesitation, shot her in the head. Villagers and soldiers alike were stunned, and there was a moment of total silence, before the cacophony began again. The wailing was louder; the crying was more intense; and Staff Sergeant and Platoon Leader Elton Trainer hollered at the villagers again, "Where are your young men? Where are the weapons?"

He stopped, waited for a response, which for many reasons would not be forthcoming. Train then shouted the orders JR was dreading, "Kill anything that moves and torch the rest."

While many in the platoon were frozen in place by what they had seen and what they had been ordered to do, some immediately moved toward the villagers raising their weapons and toward the huts with Zippo lighters and grenades in hand. The man with the platoon's single flamethrower headed toward the densest concentration of huts.

"You can't do this! It's against international law! It's against human law! They're not resisting! They don't even have weapons!"

"Private Morton, one more word, and you're facing a court martial!" Train was red with anger.

"If that's what it takes, OK," Salt screamed. "Then everything that happens here today will be on the record! I'm reporting it one way or the other, and you can't stop me!"

"The hell I can't" Train bellowed back.

"You asshole, we can't just kill women and children!"

"They're VC or they're supporting Charlie!"

"How do you know?"

"Hell, even if we don't know, we'll kill them all and sort it out later!"

With just a flicker of change of facial expression, Train appeared to regret what he had just said, but he held his ground and his eye contact with Salt.

"Don't make us do something we'll regret the rest of our lives," Salt pleaded, this time more softly.

"Fuck you!"

The interchange had inadvertently served Salt's purpose. The killing and burning had been averted as the platoon stopped to watch Train and Salt toe-to-toe. But the reprieve was brief.

Train turned away from the confrontation and repeated the orders even louder than he had been screaming at Salt, "Kill them all and burn this fucking place to the ground!"

Then he added, "And if Morton gets in the way, shoot him too!"

M-16 and small arm fire broke out as villagers fell where they were squatting. Other Vietnamese and animals scattered in every direction, pursued by soldiers who had chosen to follow the orders.

There was a ditch along the road leading out of Vung Dong. Soldiers caught up with and forced about 30 women and children

BODY NOT RECOVERED

to line up between the road and the ditch—then they opened fire. Bloody and broken bodies fell into the ditch.

Every structure was ablaze and burned quickly, despite earlier rains and high humidity.

The sound of gunfire abated as the number of live targets diminished.

In 90 minutes, most of the village had been destroyed and most of its residents killed.

About half of Bravo One had participated in the killing. Some others chose to start fires to avoid being part of the human massacre. A few, JR among them, merely stood by, refusing to follow the orders. And one American soldier lay dead amid the bodies of Vung Dong. Jack "Salt" Morton had been shot in the back.

When Richardson and his crew returned from refueling, they could not believe what they saw. The huts of the village were smoldering. People and animals lay everywhere. "What the hell happened," Richardson asked one of the Huey pilots, who was also a close friend.

"Right after you left, all hell broke loose. I couldn't tell what prompted it. I didn't see any resistance or enemy fire. We've been asked to medevac one of ours—guy was shot; he's dead."

"We're going in for a closer look."

As the recon copter swooped down, the crew saw the end of the shooting of women and children along the ditch. It was clear that this was not a fight, but a massacre. Richardson was livid.

As he was trying to figure out what he could do about it, he noticed activity. Twelve people, mostly children, were leaving a bunker on the northern edge of the village. The villagers were running across a field toward the jungle. One mother was carrying a baby.

"There's more! They're coming out of that bunker! Bravo One Two, take care of them!"

Trainer was making sure they would complete his mission, "Find 'em, kill 'em, count 'em." He looked forward to reporting the several hundred enemy dead and would figure out later how to explain away the lack of weapons found.

Bravo One Two, several of the squad reluctantly so, headed toward the fleeing villagers. Now in open field, the shooting would be easy. That is until they saw the recon helicopter landing between them and their prey.

Richardson was out of the copter in a heartbeat, while Three-Spot, per his pilot's orders, aimed the door gun at the advancing squad. Richardson's sidearm was unholstered with the safety off when he confronted the squad leader, Sergeant Gerald Evans.

"Sergeant, stand down!"

"Get the hell out of our way, and get that bird out of here!"

"No way, Sarge. You've got no right to kill those folks, and you know it," Richardson tried to reason with the sergeant.

"I've got orders," Evans said with a tinge of regret in his voice. "Now move it!"

"Sarge, here's what we're going to do. I'm calling in our two Hueys to evac these villagers, because I can't fit them in the OH-23. You're going to get back to your platoon and get your casualty here in the next ten minutes. We'll evac him as well. You're going to tell your squad to stand down and let this all happen. You got it?"

Bravo One Two was motionless, waiting to see what Evans would do. The villagers had stopped running and were watching the scene unfold, apparently understanding what Richardson was doing.

"You got it," Richardson asked again, this time louder to make sure Evans and others could hear over the sound of the recon copter and the Hueys positioning themselves overhead.

"Yeah, I got it," Evans hollered without conviction.

He turned and gave an order, pointing at two of his men, "Go get Morton and bring him back here."

Before the confrontation between Richardson and Evans ended, the pilot further established his position. He turned to his crew and made sure Evans and the remainder of Bravo One Two understood him when he both hollered and pantomimed, "Paulson, Baltieri, if any of these guys makes a move toward those villagers, shoot them."

Richardson had one more thing to do. The bodies between the road and the ditch were about 50 meters away. He sprinted to the mangled frames, stopped, looked, and listened. What he had hoped for was true. The moaning he heard said that there was at least one survivor, maybe more. Richardson crawled through the bodies to kneel beside a young boy, apparently no more than four years old. The boy had wounds in his upper right arm and across both of his legs below the knees, and he had blood splattered on most of the rest of his body. It was unclear how much was his blood or that of others. The boy was the only sign of life.

Richardson cradled the boy in his arms, looked into his frightened eyes, and tried to give him as much of an expression of reassurance as he could muster. He carried the boy back to his chopper and nestled him in the small space that was available in the rear next to Three-Spot.

The Hueys were on the ground. Richardson gestured to the villagers to board the craft, which they did without hesitation, the few women shepherding the children. They instinctively knew Richardson was their savior. Moments later, the three choppers were in the air and heading to drop off their respective human cargo.

Richardson took the boy to an orphan hospital, explained the situation to a nun, and left. On the way, his two crewmen noticed Richardson was crying and remembered that he, at age 25, had a young son at home, about the same age as the boy in their chopper.

The Hueys flew to a nearby refugee camp and turned the surviving Vung Dong villagers over to a camp administrator. They continued on to deliver Salt to Cam Ranh Bay's morgue.

While this air mission of mercy was going on, Staff Sergeant Elton Trainer was wrapping up his operation. He assembled the platoon in the center of the village, "OK, note this—285 enemy killed. Lost one man to enemy fire. I'll be dealing with a number of you when we get back. Evans, you're the first on my list, and the rest of you know who you are. Let's do one more sweep of Charlie's nest, especially looking for weapons."

They found no weapons, never learned where the young men where, left the dead villagers and animals to rot, and moved out.

CHAPTER 32

WATCH YOUR ASS

October 8, 1966
Cam Ranh Bay Perimeter, Vietnam

JR was leaning against a support pole of the mess tent, unable to get himself to go in to eat. With his head hanging down, all he could see were Hulk's size 14 boots and the mud. In just above a whisper, he once again shared his innermost feelings with his friend, "The only other times in my life when I remember crying were when my folks were killed and when Walter Rawlings died. Since Vung Dong, I've either been in tears or close to it. We've got to do something."

Back from Vung Dong, the squads were told they would have some time at base camp to unwind. They were also told they would likely be questioned about the incident, but after a couple of days, not one soldier had been formally asked to describe what had happened.

The camp was eerily quiet and nerves were frayed, even more than usual. Hulk, knowing JR had more to get off his chest, guided him to a bunker just inside the camp perimeter where they could be alone.

JR continued, "We can blame Train for being an asshole. We can blame the fact that sometimes we can't tell enemy from friendlies. We can blame the heat and the rain and the jungle rot and the lack of sleep. We can blame seeing friends blown to bits and hoping we're not next. We can blame the fact that we're barely in our twenties, if that, and we've been trained to kill. We can blame anything and anyone we want. But, at the end of the day, there's really only two things to blame—this fucking war and the idiots who put us in this position.

"The war killed those poor people in Vung Dong and Cricket and Salt and all of the others. It's got us 9000 miles from home for reasons I can't understand any more. The war has us taking target practice at regular folks from copters and running over a guy and his buffalo and laughing about it. It has me killing a 14 year old boy with his family's photo in his pocket."

JR could not hold it back any longer. Through his tears, he told Hulk about the boy on Hill 254 and showed him the photo.

Hulk said nothing as he gave JR time to compose himself. When JR continued, he was less despondent, "Vung Dong confirmed for me that we're right—there's no way to change things while we're here. Look what happened to Salt when he tried to. Enemy fire, my ass. The Animals are right. 'We gotta get out of this place, if it's the last thing we ever do.'"

"Agree with all you've said, Speargun. Any ideas on how?"

"Actually, yes. Since Vung Dong, I've been thinking about a possibility. I have some checking to do, but I may have an idea. The next couple of days will be risky, but when I get back, we can hopefully get Doc, Peepers, and Pucker together and do the deed."

JR laid out how things came together for him after the incident in the village and what he planned to do.

"Do you want me to go with you?"

"No, it'll be hard enough to pull this off with just one of us."

"OK, man, go for it, but watch your ass," Hulk said, putting his arm around JR and maneuvering him back toward the mess tent. "Now can we get something to eat?"

Later that evening, JR stopped by the company quartermaster to talk to a guy that Hulk and he had shared a few beers with over the last couple of months. "Hey, Socks. I've got a favor to ask. Do you have one of your normal supply runs to the airfield in the morning? I'd like to tag along, if you'll be back by 1600."

"Yep—leaving at 0600. But we're staffed for the run."

"I just need to get out of here to break the monotony. We're not heading into the jungle for a few days."

"Have you cleared it with your brass?"

"Sure," JR lied, "and I'll be just one more weapon if you run into trouble."

"OK, we can squeeze you in. Be here at 0545, and you'll ride with me."

"Thanks, Socks, see ya in the morning."

JR jumped into the cab of the deuce and a half, one of three in the morning's convoy. The supply trucks were accompanied by three jeeps, two of them with M60 machine gun mounts. A Huey gunship provided air support. It was clear to JR that the supply run was no more safe than trekking through the jungle on patrol.

After tolerating a two-hour incident-free ride over rutted roads, JR asked if he could help load the trucks, but also said he had to take care of one thing. Socks gave him a pass on helping, but told his comrade to be back in no more than three hours.

JR headed straight for the officer's mess, hoping to find someone who knew where he could find Warrant Officer Pat Richardson. Immediately after the Vung Dong massacre, the story of Richardson's actions and his name spread like wildfire through the troop grapevine at Cam Ranh Bay and in the field.

"Haven't seen him today. He's been keeping to himself. You might check the horseshoe pits. That guy can pitch shoes all day long."

JR got directions to the pits, but already had a sense for where they were, remembering the first-day attack that injured Kit and the nearby horseshoe game that was interrupted. As he headed for the pits, he wondered whether Richardson was one of the players that day. Well before JR reached his destination, he could see a solitary figure.

As he got closer, JR noticed the man was a horseshoe-throwing machine and seemed to be in a trance. Throw four shoes in succession, listen to shoes two, three, and four clink on each other while not touching the peg, walk the 40 feet, pull the four ringers off the stake, and throw toward the other pit.

"Warrant Officer Richardson?"

No response.

"Sir?"

No response.

"I was on the ground in Vung Dong."

Richardson looked up, scanned JR slowly from head to toe, and, without a word, returned to his activity. Richardson was in a backswing when JR said quietly but resolutely, "We should have stopped it, but we didn't."

Richardson held the shoe. He stood a bit taller, looked JR in the eye, and finally spoke, "Why not?"

"There is really no excuse, and there are hundreds of them. It was chaos—guys shooting into the villagers, setting huts on fire, grenades going off, screaming, cursing. It spread so quickly—there was no place or way to intervene. When we saw your helicopter do just that, we had two thoughts. First, good for you. Second, why couldn't or didn't we find a way?"

"Whose 'we?'"

"That's why I came looking for you. That's what I want to talk to you about."

"I'm listening," Richardson said, still leery of JR and the conversation.

"I'm taking a risk here, sir. What I'm about to tell you would get us court marshaled if the wrong people found out. I'm guessing though, based on what you did in Vung Dong, that you may be thinking about things the same way we are, and if so, then you might be the final piece of a big puzzle. This is important enough for me and us that I'm ready to take the risk."

"Like I said, I'm listening."

JR stood face-to-face with Warrant Officer Pat Richardson for the next half hour and told him everything about what, who, why, and where. He also explained the how for those things he and the others had figured out. JR then proposed what Richardson could do to complete the plan.

When he was through, although he hoped for a positive response, JR was also prepared to hear something like, "Are you out of your fucking mind?"

Instead, what he heard was, "Spears, you're not going to believe it, but this is exactly the conversation Three-Spot, Balls, and I have been having since that day. We don't want any part of it any more. For us, what we did in Vung Dong was a small victory for decency in the midst of insanity, but we need a bigger victory, and the three of us have had no idea how to proceed.

"I've had death threats. Those who may agree with what we did don't want to be seen with me. I'd already heard what happened to your friend on the ground. There are guys who would kill Americans to make a point.

"OK, instead of rambling on about my problems, let me cut to the chase. What you're talking about is crazy and risky. It's a life-changer. But guess what, my life is already changed forever. Here's what I'm going to do. If you're OK with it, and I think you have to be, because we're not going to do anything without them—I'm going to talk to my crew. If they're in, I'm in.

"Assuming they're good to go, you and I are going to find a way to get back together to see if we can flesh this out a little more. And I have one thing to ask—no, call it a demand. It sounds like I'm the only one in your crew and mine that's married. I need to let my wife know that no matter what she hears in the next couple of months, I'm alive, I'm coming home, and I'll explain it to her when I get there.

"You know, Spears..."

"Call me Speargun," JR said and explained why.

"You know, Speargun, if I didn't sign on to your plan, I'd be in this hellhole another nine months. Until Vung Dong, despite seeing things no man should have to see in a lifetime, being on the verge of death several times, and missing my family, I thought I could do the time. But when I had to crawl through those broken bodies to get to that boy and when I thought of my own boy, I knew I couldn't stand it anymore. Thanks for showing up when you did."

Both men were fighting back tears, because the horrors of that day flashed back in their minds and because they realized they had made a personal connection that they each needed.

"Sir..."

"Call me Pat."

"OK, Pat. I'm not sure where this will all lead, but what I do know is that we have a core of guys who believe we have to do it. We

BODY NOT RECOVERED

need to find a way to get back in touch. I've got to get going or I'm going to miss my ride, and if that happens, all hell will break loose."

"You sure you can't stick around for a few minutes and throw some shoes?"

"No—like I said, I've got to catch my ride. Besides, the way you throw, I'd just be in your way. You know I started the day and will end it bouncing along in a truck with my friend, Socks. Now that I have a new friend who throws like you do, I'm sure you need a new name. So, I'm going to call you Shoes. Shoes and Socks—get it?"

"Yeah, I get it. OK, Shoes it is."

"See you as soon as I can, Shoes."

"Be safe, Speargun. Wow, what a day this turned out to be."

JR got back in time for his bumpy deuce and a half ride back to base, and found when he returned that he had not been missed, at least not by the brass. He found Hulk and filled him in, finishing with a grin, "Yeah, what a day this turned out to be. Shoes and Socks—get it?"

CHAPTER 33

I'M IN

October 9, 1966
Cam Ranh Bay Perimeter, Vietnam

"This is coming together, so I need to check with you one more time, are you in?"

JR had gathered Hulk, Peepers, Pucker, and Doc with the intent of bringing them up to speed, but he needed to know that they were still committed. The last time they had been through this drill, it was Hulk who went from man to man, but JR had now taken the leadership role.

"Hulk?"

"This war has got to stop, and I think there are only two ways to do that. One is to just stop fighting it, but I'm not naïve enough to believe that if we do, the whole war will shut down. The second is to protest and put political pressure on decision makers. And as we've talked, the only way for us to help with that is to get back to the world. So, yes, I'm still in."

"Peepers?"

"You know, when I got into the army, I had this vision...OK, no vision jokes...I had this vision of being able to say to people, 'Hey, I'm a veteran.' But what's the pride in saying you're a veteran, if you're a veteran of something wrong? I'm in, Speargun."

"Pucker?"

Pucker hesitated and the others held their collective breath.

He began, "I've got to tell you..." but another hesitation; this one longer.

"Remember, Pucker, we said that if anyone wants out, that's fine. We just need to know that you won't share what we've been talking about with anyone," JR said, hoping they would not need to confront that possibility.

"Look guys. I have to admit, I'm nervous about this whole thing. No, more than nervous—I'm scared."

"We all are," JR knew he was speaking for everyone.

"I just want you to know that I've been playing this all out in my head. I'll tell you my biggest problem. I'm having a tough time thinking about how my mom and dad will take it when they hear I'm missing in action. I wish there was a way I could fix that, but I can't figure out how. So, since we're all in this together, you need to know that I'm confused and scared. But, yes, I'm in."

"OK, Pucker, and like I said, I'm scared too," JR responded. "When we get back to the world, we'll all have to figure out how to deal with relatives and friends. To be honest, at least for awhile, I think we'll all be better off if we didn't make any connections until we figure out what our lives are going to be. That doesn't mean you can't get a message to your folks, but we'll all have to be really careful about it."

"OK, Doc. You still in?"

"I'm even more committed now. When I got to Salt and saw that he'd been shot in the back and at close range, there was no doubt in my mind that we need to help put a stop to this, and we're not going to be able to do that over here. I'm not sure who shot Salt, but I am pretty sure that if that guy knew what we were considering, we'd have to be watching each other's backs 24 by 7. It's hard enough fighting the enemy, but now we have to be concerned about guys on our side. This may look like a war to the higher-ups, but to me, it's just a free-for-all."

"Doc, I think we need to start watching each other's backs anyway. From here on out, it's going to get more and more risky, but no more risky than what we're already doing here. We're going to do what it takes to make this work. OK, let me fill you in on how I think this is going to play out."

JR and Hulk had already given the others a debriefing after they returned from Bangkok. Now, JR shared the conversation he had with Shoes, and laid out the whole plan in as much detail as he had. "It looks like the next big problem we've got to solve, assuming Shoes and his crew are in, is how to get the five of us alone with them in a chopper."

"I think I can help with that," Doc said.

CHAPTER 34

OFF THE RECORD

October 9, 1966
Cam Ranh Bay Airfield, Vietnam

"Richardson, I'm not exactly sure what we're going to do with you. Before your circle-jerk in that village, I was looking at you as a lifer who had all kinds of potential. But you really screwed the pooch."

Shoes had been summoned to meet with his Aviation Brigade Commander. Although Alvin Weiner's stature was far from impressive and his last name a constant target for attempted levity, his command bearing was irrefutable. Standing barely five-foot-seven, carrying some extra weight around his waist, having short, tightly curled, graying hair, and wearing wire-rim glasses made Weiner look more like an academic than a brigade commander. But the combination of his strategic intellect, steady bass voice, self-confident aura, and ability to be both demanding and compassionate earned the respect of those in his command and his superiors.

Standing just inside the door of the small, gray-drab, well-organized office, whose only wall hangings were marked-up maps, and feeling as though he had previously established both a professional and informal relationship, Shoes requested, "Permission to speak off the record, Sir."

"Did you ever need permission before," Weiner replied, causing them both to smile knowingly.

"Sir, it's been an honor to serve under you, and one of the reasons is that you do what's right. I have little doubt in my mind that if you were in my place over Vung Dong, you would've done the same thing and maybe even more."

"OK, Richardson, off the record. I don't disagree with what you did as a human being. I'm just trying to reconcile it with what you did as an army aviator in a war zone. You fucking pointed your weapons at our guys and acted the savior for a group of folks that the grunts identified as enemy. OK, I get it. They were a few women and a bunch of kids. Oh shit, what am I going to do with you?"

Immediately after JR had left him, Shoes sought out Three Spot and Balls. The first thing he told them was his new nickname—they bought it right away. Then he asked for their discretion and laid out the conversation he'd had with JR. Paulson's and Baltieri's feelings paralleled Richardson's—they thought as he did about what had happened in Vung Dong and how the war was warping their sense of values.

It took a couple of hours to talk through it, but in the end, the helicopter crew settled on what was an outline of a plan. When it seemed they had come to agreement, Three Spot declared, "All for one and one for all."

As they moaned at *The Three Musketeers* reference, the aviators raised their arms holding mock swords to salute their mutual commitment.

Shoes knew, therefore, Three Spot and Balls would be in agreement with what he was about to suggest to his commander.

"Sir, I've been piloting gunships, recon birds, and medevac missions since I've been here. I've got a great crew and we've been successful. If I might be so bold, we were even successful in Vung Dong, but let's call that off the record also.

"I would and have put my life in Paulson's and Baltieri's hands. They followed my orders in that madhouse, but I imagine you or someone else is going to have this same conversation with them. So, here's what I suggest, if I might."

"Proceed."

"At least for the time being, keep my crew together and order us to be limited to medevac missions. That way, we'll be in and out of landing zones only. If and when we're fired upon, it will be by real VC, so there'll be no reason to do anything like I did the other day. We'll know who the enemy is and we'll take the appropriate action.

"You can call it punishment, make the appropriate notes in my record, declare that it will limit our careers, and do whatever else you need to do. But I can still make a difference in your unit, sir, and I'd be proud to do so."

After a long pause, Weiner said, "Richardson, consider yourself limited to medevac flights only until further notice. Now, get the hell out of my office."

As Shoes turned to leave, he heard the commander say, "OK, once more off the record."

Richardson turned back to face his superior officer.

"I also have a young son, Pat. When I heard what you did, I couldn't help but hope that I would have had the balls to do the same thing. I did some checking. The boy from the village is going to be OK, at least physically. His wounds were not fatal, and the nuns had the wherewithal, with some help from a nearby army doc to sew him up."

Tears welled up in Richardson's eyes, "Thank you, Sir."

"I tried to find out more about your villagers at the refugee camp, but it's far from well-organized, and I couldn't find out anything definitive. But one thing for sure—they're alive because of you.

"So consider yourself duly punished on the record and thanked off the record."

Richardson left with tears in his eyes, but a smile on his face. The first step of his role in the plan had been taken. Little did he know that both he and a medic he had yet to meet were on the same wavelength.

CHAPTER 35

SHRAPNEL

October 23, 1966
Cam Ranh Bay Perimeter, Vietnam

"It's driving me crazy that we haven't found a way to reconnect with Shoes. All we do is talk about plans without actually making any progress," JR whispered his frustration to Hulk through the raindrops, when they found themselves away from others during a brief break in their jungle trek.

At the same time, on a bumpy medevac mission in the monsoon rain, Shoes was expressing similar frustration to Three Spot and Balls, "I've been keeping track of Speargun but haven't been able to make the connection happen."

When he was not on a mission, Shoes searched for ways to reconnect with JR, figuring the best way to increase the odds of doing so was to know where JR's unit was at all times. He struck up an ongoing conversation with a clerk who was new to his role in Vietnam—meaning he was one of the few who did not know who Richardson was and what he had done in Vung Dong, and he seemed unaware he was not supposed to share troop movement information.

For both the grunts and aviators, the momentum of the war and their role in it were relentless. Over the past couple of weeks, Bravo One had been on several missions, during which it had taken numerous casualties. Doc had his hands full keeping his boys alive and getting them to medevac landing zones. For the sake of self-preservation rather than for the greater overall strategy and tactics of the missions, JR, Hulk, Peepers, and Pucker fought the fight.

Shoes, Three Spot, and Balls flew their missions, frequently in monsoon rains and heavy fog; often finding themselves dodging enemy fire and doing their best just to stay alive.

After completing a medevac mission, Shoes was sitting alone with Three Spot and Balls in the mess tent—their isolation having become the norm. "We may have a break. JR's unit is heading out to put an end to some sniper and mortar fire on the airfield. And I know right where they'll be focused. Even though we just got back, I moved us up the duty roster, so stay ready."

JR, Hulk, and the rest of Bravo One Three were on the right flank in the direction of the suspected source of sniper and rocket fire. Pucker and Peepers in Bravo One Two were flanked left. Doc was positioned with Bravo One One nearby the new platoon leader, Lieutenant Sam Rogers, who had been in-country for only a few days. Staff Sergeant Elton Trainer had ceded his temporary platoon leader role to Rogers, and to everyone's surprise, he did not resume his assignment as squad leader.

The morning the operation began, Train was simply gone—no word on where he went or why. Train's departure could have been an opportunity for the platoon to put Vung Dong behind them, but each heart and mind knew the sights, sounds, and smells of that day would never leave them.

Although for now, it was beneath the surface, the tension between those who had fully participated in the massacre and those who held back continued to grow. Train had clearly been the instigator, but the platoon carried the collective guilt.

There was conjecture that an investigation of Vung Dong had been conducted, albeit quietly. The men speculated that if that were so and the brass wanted to defuse any possible fallout from the incident, perhaps it would help if they got Trainer out of the arena. Regardless of the reasons, he was gone, and no one seemed upset.

The platoon had been slogging through thick growth since early morning, which had begun with a dense low-lying fog. Having only stopped for a mid-day break, they were expecting to find a place to settle in for the night. It was about 1630 when they heard the firing. Ready to take cover, Lieutenant Rogers quickly realized his platoon was not the target. The barrage was aimed at the airfield.

Rogers ordered the platoon to double-time it toward the shooting. If he were right, the platoon would be approaching the enemy from behind and should be in prime position to disable the VC nests. When they were within a klick, Rogers slowed the pace and brought the flanks closer together to concentrate a ground assault if it were needed.

Once his men were positioned, Rogers was on the radio, calling in air support. The fog had cleared enough by noon for gunships to be effective. For several days, the VC had been firing briefly from one position and then quickly moving to a new location. Now that Bravo One was close enough to Charlie to focus an accurate air strike and in place to finish up the operation on the ground, the support had been called in.

As the platoon converged, the firing stopped. Rogers signaled to halt and await further orders and the air strike. That's when their position, which had seemed to be a tactical advantage, became anything but. The sniper and rocket fire began again, but this time had turned on them. The next two hours were chaotic and catastrophic.

Within seconds, Doc was challenged to respond to shouts of "Medic" from three directions. The first soldier he got to was Pucker, who had been close to a mortar strike. A piece of shrapnel had impaled his right thigh above the knee, fortunately missing the femoral artery. His bleeding had to be stopped, but it looked manageable, at least for now. Doc worked quickly to stabilize Pucker before moving on to the next casualty. Peepers pulled Pucker into a copse of trees to protect him, hoping that the air support would take out the gunner nests and that it would stay light long enough to bring in a medevac chopper for his friend.

Within moments, WHOP, WHOP, WHOP—three Huey gunships appeared and bore down on Charlie's gun emplacements. The pressure and the assault were off of Bravo One, at least long enough to give them some time to do a better job of digging in.

The hill from which the VC were firing was now ablaze from the side-mounted XM157 rocket launchers and M-60 machine guns on the attack copters. Just as it seemed there was no way for anyone to survive the air assault, a single mortar round rose from amidst the conflagration on the hill and hit the underbelly of one of the gunships.

The fuselage burst into flames and crashed into the hillside. Continuing to spin, the main rotor disengaged and hurtled toward Bravo One, imbedding itself less than 100 meters from their forward position. The tail boom and rotor separated from the fuselage and fell to the jungle floor.

The other two aircraft finished the attack, made sure there was no more enemy response, and tried to find a place to land to look after their fallen comrades, but there was no landing zone to be found. The pilots radioed Lieutenant Rogers, "LT, unless there's an LZ near you, we're heading back. Would you send a recon to the crash site? Likely no survivors, but we'd like our guys to be medevaced with yours."

"No LZ yet. We've got some work to do. Likely we'll be ready in the morning."

"Do you want us to call that in or do you?"

"We'll call in the medevac request. We're sorry about your guys. We'll get them out."

"Roger that." The Hueys were gone.

Rogers pulled his squad leaders and Doc together. "OK, what have we got?"

Not including the copter crew, they had two dead and Pucker needing evac.

"We'll send a squad to the copter site and get the bodies back here. It's not far, so we'll do that now, even though they'll be coming back in the dark. What's Planck's status, Doc?"

"Pucker, I mean Planck, is stabilized, and we have the gear to keep him that way tonight. But we really should get him out of here first thing in the morning. Much later than that, and I can't be sure."

"OK. I'll call in evac for the morning. Evans and Parker, we need an LZ by morning. Any ideas?"

"There was a clearing about half a klick back, LT. With some work, that should do it—just be harder at night."

"How about your squad handling that?" Rogers had addressed Sergeant Parker, who had been permanently assigned to lead Bravo One Three when Train moved on.

"Got it, LT. We'll set it up. When you call it in, tell them we'll have it lit—they'll need as much guidance as we can give them if it's as foggy tomorrow as it was this morning."

CHAPTER 36

ARE YOU SHOES?

October 24, 1966
Cam Ranh Bay Perimeter, Vietnam

Although they had slept little in the past 48 hours, the men of Bravo One worked through the night to recover the downed copter crew and clear an LZ for the morning's medevac. Those not on specific tasks provided security. As it turned out, none was needed. The VC on the hilltop had been wiped out by the air assault.

Doc had injected Pucker with one of the morphine syrettes he carried in his bag, and had given Peepers a supply for the night with instructions on how and how often to use the painkiller. Doc also set up a glucose drip in Pucker's arm and said he would be back in time to change the bag. Although he had stabilized his comrade, Doc knew that a morning evac would be important to saving Pucker's life.

The morphine would ensure Pucker would never remember the pain, but it did not stop his constant moaning. Peepers just had to tolerate that, but he had learned to tolerate a lot since being in-country. In the protection of the damp darkness and the copse of trees, he would hold his friend throughout the night for both Pucker's sake and his own mental well-being.

The crumpled fuselage was quickly located not far from Bravo One's position. The badly burned bodies of the four crewmen were extracted and respectfully carried on stretchers back to what had become Bravo One's base. It took two trips through the dense brush at night to get the job done.

Parker led his squad back to the small clearing. It looked large enough to handle one Huey at a time, but the squad spent hours hacking away at the perimeter to make it larger and less risky for the pilots, who would likely be landing in a fog. The squad positioned their unlit flares for the following morning and tried to get a couple of hours sleep.

At first light, Rogers reconfirmed the medevac need by radio and reported on-ground conditions, "Fog's not as thick as yesterday, but still soupy. We'll touch off flares and talk you in."

Turning from the radio to his squad leaders, Rogers said, "Bring the evacs to the LZ and let's do one final security sweep. One Three will handle the evac with the birds."

Rogers acted as though he had been in command for a long time instead of just days. The stress of the war brought out either the best or worst in a man quickly—for Rogers, it was the best. He personally led the two security squads into the brush and the foggy morning.

Sergeant Parker stayed close by his radioman anticipating contact from the choppers. "Bravo One, Mustang One over your position. Over."

"Mustang One, Bravo One. We're touching off flares and will talk you in. Fog is not as heavy as expected."

"Looks thick from up here, but we'll do this. You should be hearing us any minute."

"Roger that, we hear you now. Sounds like you're right overhead."

"We're dropping flares."

"We see them. We'll go silent unless needed."

The first of the medevac copters worked its way through the fog and with only a little guidance from the ground, landed dead center.

Doc ran to work with the pilot. "I'm the medic. We've got six dead and one seriously wounded."

"Let's get the wounded guy out of here first; then Richardson can bring Mustang Two down to pick up the dead after we leave."

"Pat Richardson?"

"Yeah."

"Hold on a minute; I'll be right back."

Doc ran to JR and found him with Hulk touching off more flares.

ARE YOU SHOES?

Barely able to speak through his excitement, Doc reported, "Speargun, you're not going to believe this, but your guy is flying the second copter. No time for planning; this may be our best shot."

"Are you shitting me, Doc?"

Doc took control, "Follow me—I know how we're going to make this work."

The three ran back to Mustang One, and Doc hollered to the pilot, "Let's get the dead on your bird. I've got to do one more thing down here to stabilize our wounded guy. Then I'll go with him on Mustang Two."

"You know the conditions better than I do," the pilot responded. "OK, get your guys to bring the dead on board."

Doc waved Rogers over and told him the plan. "Why not Pucker first?"

Doc, improvising as he went along, answered, "Need to hang another bag and give him another shot before we load him. Just enough time to get this first bird on its way and the second down here."

Trusting Doc's judgment, Rogers ordered the squad to move the fallen onto the helicopter. Mustang One's crew helped get the dead into body bags and position them in the available space. Within moments, Mustang One was cutting through the fog out of the landing zone and on its way to the field morgue.

"Mustang Two, Bravo One here. Mustang One is clear. We're ready for you."

"We're following Mustang One's coordinates and will be dropping flares in a minute or so."

"Roger that."

Mustang Two's landing was also successful. Doc ran to the chopper. He looked up into the cabin and saw the name Richardson over the pilot's right pocket. "Are you Shoes? I'm Doc. Speargun told me all about you."

"I've been hoping to run into you guys and finally got lucky. Good to meet you, Doc. Where's Speargun?"

"Sorry to be abrupt, Sir..."

"Call me Shoes."

"Shoes, this might be our last best chance to make this work. No time for planning. No disrespect, but is this your standard crew, and are they 'on board?'" Doc emphasized what he meant by gesturing quotation marks with his fingers.

"Yep, Doc. This is Three Spot and Balls. We're flying short a co-pilot today as we have been for awhile trying to find you guys without others getting involved. Hasn't been a problem—nobody wants to fly with us anyway and the brass don't seem to care. Besides, Three Spot has had enough training that he could fly this thing if need be."

"Then this is it, Shoes. If you're OK with it, follow my lead."

"You're in charge, Doc."

Doc's heart was racing, and he was sick to his stomach. After thinking and talking about this possible moment for so long, it was now about to happen. The series of events that would alter his life forever were about to begin. He took a couple of deep breaths while saluting Shoes, who returned the salute; both men being much more formal than the situation called for, but both knowing that it was time to get serious and that from here on out, their lives would be inextricably linked.

As Mustang Two had been landing, JR and Hulk guided Peepers, who was carrying Pucker, to the LZ. JR quickly let Peepers know who was flying and told him to just go with the flow.

Doc ran to Sergeant Evans, "Sarge, a request."

"What?"

"Since the platoon is trekking back to base camp right after we get the medevac done, I'd like to take Hulk, Speargun, and Peepers with me. All three were throwing up this morning and are dehydrated. I used most of my fluid for Pucker last night."

Evans hesitated, "I don't know. Let me check with the LT. He may know something else about our orders."

"Gotta be quick, Sarge. I'll position them all to go, and wait to hear from you," Doc said as he turned to head back to the copter, knowing full well that he was getting them all on board regardless. He just needed to plant the seed with Evans to make sure he had his ass covered if all of this went south.

When Doc returned to the helo, JR was shaking hands with Shoes and Hulk and Peepers were lifting Pucker through the door with help from Three Spot and Balls from inside.

Doc hollered to the few remaining Bravo One Three squad members, "Evans says he wants you with him. We can take it from here."

Doc then turned to JR, Hulk, and Peepers, "Get in; I'll explain later."

Within moments, the five grunts had joined the three aviators.

"Pleasantries later, gents, I've got to get this thing out of here," Shoes hollered to all on board.

As the helicopter took off, in the confusion of the moment, Doc had not checked on Pucker. Peepers reminded him when he said, "He's stopped moaning. Do you think he'll be OK?"

When Doc tended to Pucker, his heart and his shoulders sank. His body language had everyone on board except Shoes staring at him. Doc could only shake his head—Eddie "Pucker" Planck had died.

CHAPTER 37

COMMITTED TO THE ENDGAME

October 24, 1966
The Skies over Cam Ranh Bay Perimeter, Vietnam

"We have a decision to make, and we need to make it quickly," Shoes said over the comm system after everyone had donned a headset. "Three Spot, Balls, and I have been doing a lot of thinking about this. So, let me break it down for you."

"In about 20 minutes, I'm going to radio in that we're having trouble with our instruments and because of the fog, we can't get our bearings. Basically, we're not sure where we are. That won't surprise anybody—it's a frequent problem, especially when it's rainy or really humid, which by the way, is always. That will buy us time and give us a basis for disappearing. That's the easy part, and it will begin our separation from this place.

"The hard part is to figure out the best way to get to Bangkok. Two choices. The water option is to ditch the copter somewhere near the coast and commandeer a boat to make the trip along the Cambodian coast and to Bangkok through the Gulf of Siam. The other is to fly from here to Bangkok in several legs.

"In either case, we will need to find a way to ditch the copter after radioing in that we're in trouble and about to crash. We want them to come searching for us but not find our bodies. If we pull that off, then for all intents and purposes, we're believed to be dead and free to make the rest of the trip without being pursued."

JR's thoughts went immediately to M. J. Savoy—"Crash at sea; body not recovered." And he knew that Hulk was thinking about the incident as well. It was Mouse's letter about M. J.'s crash that became the foundation for JR's and Hulk's plan. And now that the plan was in action, JR could imagine the *St. Louis Post-Dispatch* article describing his own death.

Headline: *"Local Army Boy Killed—Lost at Sea"*

"University City High School graduate JR Spears was killed in Vietnam on October 24, when the Huey in which he was riding lost control and crashed into the South China Sea just off the southern coast. Similar to his classmate, M. J. Savoy, who died in a fixed-wing plane crash in the South China Sea off the coast of Vietnam on June 17, an extensive search for Spears' body was not successful. He is officially listed as 'killed in action—helicopter crash at sea—body not recovered.'"

Shoes had continued, "The water option has us interacting with fewer people, but we would need to find a boat, which I have no idea how to do. The biggest advantage of the water option is that it's the best way for us to ditch the copter and lose ourselves.

"The flying option avoids the need to find a boat, but the range on this thing means we'll have to stop to refuel a few times. At each stop, we'll need to talk someone into fueling us without raising suspicion. Then when we get to Bangkok or nearby, we'll still need to figure out what to do with the bird, and our story would be less credible that far from Vietnam.

"Since leaving the LZ, I've been flying toward Than Son Nhut airfield near Saigon. It's in the direction of our final destination. Once we get there, we can claim it was our best option when we got our instruments back and needed to refuel. We can say we found ourselves closer to them than trying to make it back to Cam Ranh Bay. But beyond Than Son Nhut, it would be more of a crapshoot. I have a buddy at the airfield in Saigon who would likely help us out without having to reveal too much. We're about 350 kilometers from there right now, and we've got enough fuel left for about 420.

"So, here's what I recommend—we continue to Than Son Nhut for refueling and use the two hours to talk about the rest of the plan. But we've got to decide now or we'll have a fuel problem."

Everyone looked at JR, who had been the one who had sought out Shoes and had pieced together the gist of the overall plan. JR was definitive, "Shoes, fly us to Saigon."

With his arm still wrapped around his friend, Peepers spoke almost too softly to be heard, "We need to do right by Pucker. We need to build that into whatever we do."

"Do you think your guy in Saigon can help with that," JR asked.

"Great idea. That would be best for us and best for your friend and his family. We'll try to make that happen. Or there may even be a better option."

In the tight confines of the cabin, Balls pulled out his navigation charts to show what it would take to make it to Thailand by air. Assuming they could get refueled when needed, the route would be first to Than Son Nhut and then to Binh Thuy airbase in the Mekong Delta. Binh Thuy would put them within less than 650 kilometers from a target airfield in Thailand, a stretch for the Huey's range, but their best shot.

They would need to do everything they could to extend the range—lighten the load, decide based on prevailing winds and topography what the optimum altitude would be, determine the best flying speed based on the altitude choice, keep the cabin doors closed to reduce wind resistance, and pray.

"There's two more issues," Shoes jumped in again. "Most of the trip at that point would be over Cambodia. That could get us shot down or cause a diplomatic incident—I care a whole lot more about the first than the second, but it's a risk.

"Then, even if all goes well, we'd be running on fumes when we land in Trat, which shows up on Balls' charts as a small civilian airport in the far southwest part of Thailand."

No one on board was greatly encouraged by either the water or air options, but they were committed to the endgame. They were on their way out of Vietnam and would reevaluate their choices depending on how things went at Than Son Nhut.

CHAPTER 38

VUNG TAU

October 24, 1966
The Skies over Southeastern Vietnam

"You know, Shoes, I hadn't put two and two together before, but there may be an easier way to do this."

Balls had been staring at the navigation charts for 15 minutes after using them to explain the air option to all on board. During that time, everyone was quiet, each alone with his own thoughts and fears, as the Huey droned relentlessly toward Than Son Nhut.

"Say more, Balls."

"OK, hear me out. About 130 kilometers southeast of Saigon is a resort town called Vung Tau," Balls said, as he pointed to it on the chart. Everyone strained to get a look.

"I've actually been there. It's a site for in-country R&R. There are two things there that we need. First, among other things, it's a fishing village. Fishing means boats, and we need a boat. More about that in a bit.

"Secondly, the Royal Australian Army has a logistics support group headquartered there. I did some drinking with some of their guys one night. That was a contest I was never going to win—they can sure put it away."

"Focus, Balls. Keep going," Shoes said impatiently.

"OK, OK. Well, they've got a full logistics operation. That means they've got aviation fuel. We could refuel there; telling our same story. And two added advantages. First, it's closer to where we are right now, so we won't be stretching our range to Than Son Nhut. But more importantly, I think, is that we won't be explaining ourselves to Americans. It should be easier to just get our fuel and go."

171

"Well, I'm not sure if that's true," Shoes said with more than a bit of skepticism in his voice.

"OK, maybe not. But, think about it all together—closer to our current position, fuel available, and close to boats. And speaking of boats, ready for this? Some of the fishing fleet makes money taking Americans and Aussies deep sea fishing when they're on R&R. I didn't go. I'd rather spend my hours in the local discos with the local women, but I was down on the dock with some guys who were negotiating for a trip. They were having boat captains bid to take them out. Guess what. Every one of those captains spoke passable English."

JR jumped into the conversation, "This sounds like a great option to me. We'd also be close enough to Than Son Nuit to be able to radio in our distress call. I say we head toward Vung...what's it called, Balls?"

"Vung Tau."

Peepers, who had continued to keep an arm around his dead comrade and who was almost too tired and emotionally drained to speak, squeaked out, "But what do we do about Pucker?"

"I've been thinking more about that," replied Shoes. "Try this out. When we're ready, we radio that we're in trouble and make it look like we crashed. We certainly don't want them to find our bodies—we want to be long gone by then. But what if they found Pucker's body on board? First, that'll make it for certain that his body gets home to his folks. Second, it will make the crash more realistic having one of us found with the bird."

Again, JR thought about M. J. Savoy. Only two of the 14 on M. J.'s plane had been found. The others were "lost at sea—body not recovered."

There was no direct response to Shoes's suggestion about Pucker. None was needed.

Shoes continued, "Nice job, Balls. You know, my dad always says, 'A plan is only something from which to deviate, but have a plan.' Let's change ours. Unless anyone disagrees, set us a course for Vung Tau. Let's go talk some Aussies out of some gas and a fisherman out of a boat."

CHAPTER 39

NO WORRIES, MATE

October 24, 1966
Vung Tau, Vietnam

"Balls, do we have a radio frequency for the Aussie logistics HQ?"

"Yeah, there's an approach plate in the Nav Bag. As long as the frequency update is accurate, we're good to go."

For the past hour in the cramped cabin, they had worked through the details of what they would be doing in Vung Tau and beyond. Although having a plan gave them a growing sense of confidence, they all knew that improvisation would likely be the order of the day.

During the flight, Pucker had been respectfully placed in a body bag that Mustang Two had brought on the medevac mission. It was all Peepers could do to let go of his buddy and help move him into the bag.

Although he was now part of a plot to desert, was likely breaking a bunch of federal laws, and was risking his life trying to get back to the world, all Peepers had on his mind was one question. Why did Eddie Planck have to travel 9000 miles to fight and die in a war that made no fucking sense instead of being back home in West Virginia getting on with the rest of his 19-year old life?

Shoes signaled for quiet to radio the Aussies. His passengers took a collective deep breath and instinctively leaned forward as if they needed to be closer to Shoes both to give him moral support and to listen.

Shoes dialed in the radio frequency Balls had provided, "Royal Australian Army Logistics HQ, this is Mustang Two, United States 1st Aviation Brigade out of Cam Ranh Bay. We have an emergency. Over."

Nothing.

Shoes repeated his call.

Nothing.

Twice more. "Balls, you sure we have this frequency right?"

"It's the one on the…"

Balls was interrupted and gladly so, "Mustang Two, this is Army Logistics. What's the emergency? Over."

Shoes loved the Aussie accent, but never more so. "We're about 50 kilometers east northeast of your position. We were on a medevac mission in the fog near Cam Ranh Bay and lost instruments. By the time we cleared the fog, regained instruments, and figured out where we were, we were closer to you than to our own field. Requesting permission to land and refuel."

Another collective deep breath in the cabin.

"No worries, mate. Are you fully functional now?"

"Thanks, mate. Roger that. Full power, full instrumentation. And we have charts to your location."

"Let's get you on the ground, and we'll sort things out from there. To confirm your charts, our helicopter landing area is at 270 from your position, on the beachside. Winds are calm."

Shoes stayed on with the controller for the next 15 minutes until he landed on the tarmac of the Royal Australian Army Logistics Supply HQ among several Aussie helicopters.

"Mustang Two, someone's coming out to work this out."

"Roger that, mate. Over and thank you."

As the staff sergeant walked toward them, Shoes turned to his passengers and reminded them what they were already thinking, "Let me do all the talking so we have the best chance to keep our story straight. One screwup and we're shit out of luck."

Not waiting for a response, Shoes exited to meet the Aussie. A formal salute and an informal handshake later, Shoes explained their situation, "Staff Sergeant, thank you for the hospitality. We were getting pretty short on fuel and weren't sure about making it to Than Son Nhut. It's been a long day, mostly for the grunts I have on board. We're a medevac unit carrying one dead and others who were dangerously dehydrated but better now."

"Sir, first of all, allow me to speak for our entire unit in expressing condolences for your lost comrade. Secondly, we are glad to help. We'll just need to slog through the paperwork. You know how that goes. But we're all in this together. Right?"

"Right you are, Staff Sergeant," Shoes replied, trying hard not to fall into the trap of emulating the Aussie's singsong accent. "If I might be so bold, here's what I'd like to see happen if it would not be too much to ask. First, I'd like to refuel the bird so we can get to Than Son Nhut to make arrangements for our fatality and then be able to head back to Cam Ranh Bay. Secondly, a good meal, a shower, and especially plenty of water would be great. And finally—you'll understand this is more a nice-to-do versus a need-to-do—I'll stay with the helo, but while we're in Vung Tau, I'd love for our guys to have just a few hours to relax. Do you have some civilian clothes they could use and get down to the water for a couple of beers and some fresh sea air? Maybe you could even take more time with that paperwork than usual."

Both men grinned. "Sir, give me a few minutes to make some arrangements, and I'd be honored to meet your requests, including what you call the 'nice-to-do.'"

"What everyone says about you Aussies is correct. Thank you."

"No worries."

This time there was no formal salute, just a sincere handshake. The Aussie returned to the building near the landing area.

"OK, so far, so good," Shoes reported when he returned to the helo. "Only thing to do now is wait for him to come back. Open the cabin doors, but let's stay on board to make sure we don't look too pushy. We won't know this is going to work out until it actually does."

CHAPTER 40

TAKE US TO THAILAND

October 24, 1966
Vung Tau, Vietnam

A half hour later, Shoes was alone in his helicopter with Pucker, and the others were inside the building. Having showered and changed into civilian clothes, they were lunching with members of the Aussie logistics staff eating sausage sizzlers, a barbecue of sausages and onions on bread with a tomato sauce. The entrée, piles of fresh vegetables, plentiful water, the hospitable company, and actually eating on tablecloths in air conditioning made it a very special meal. The only difficulty was trying to minimize any talk of the war and their part in it, not wanting to get into any discussion that would jeopardize their plans.

The staff sergeant had delivered a meal and water to Shoes and asked if he would also like to shower and change to head down to the waterfront. Shoes declined, not wanting to leave the bird or Pucker. He did, thinking ahead, ask that he have civilian clothes brought out just in case he changed his mind.

"Do you think you can take those few hours to get the paperwork done?"

"Can't imagine doing it any faster than that," a broad grin creasing the staff sergeant's ruddy face.

"The name's Pat Richardson, but folks call me Shoes," he said as he reached out his hand.

The staff sergeant completed the handshake, "Aaron Taylor; they call me Wino."

"OK, I'll bite. Wino?"

"Family owns a vineyard. Oh, and I do appreciate a glass or two. Shoes?"

"Ever play horseshoes? It helps me relax in the midst of the horror of this war."

"Played back home all the time. We've got pits around the back of the building if you'd like to throw now."

"No," said Shoes, glancing at Pucker, "Need to stay with my bird."

"Understood. Again, we're sorry about your loss. I'll get those civilian clothes out to you anyway, just in case. Enjoy the meal, and let me know if you want anything else while your guys are away. By the way, we'll bring a fuel truck out to you."

"Thank you, Wino. For everything. We'll want to be taking off by 1600 to make sure we're at Than Son Nhut in plenty of time"

Warrant Officer Pat Richardson sat quietly in the open cabin door of his Huey, feet hanging over the edge. For the first time since taking off this morning, he had a quiet moment to reflect on what had happened in his life and what was about to happen. He knew what he had chosen to do would have a profound effect on his wife and son. He knew that there were both physical and emotional risks ahead. He knew that regardless how all of this turned out, his life would be on a new and unpredictable course.

Was he still ready to make the leap? He had one more chance to change his mind. All he would need to do, he thought, was get to Than Son Nhut, refuel and head back to Cam Ranh Bay. The others would try to talk him out of it, but at the end of the day, they had no choice. He had the helo.

He went through his decision-making process for what he told himself would be the last time. Vung Dong had happened, and as best he could tell from what he was hearing, although perhaps not to the same extent, similar incidents were occurring. He had seen more death and destruction than any one human being should ever see. If he stayed in Vietnam, all of that would only continue—then what effect would that have on him, his wife, and his son?

He was being ostracized and had even received less-than-veiled death threats. He had heard about what happened to Salt on the ground in Vung Dong. What would happen to his wife and son if he were killed either by the enemy or friendly fire?

He hated what the war was doing to him and others. He saw that if he stayed, the effect on his wife and son would likely be worse when he got home than if he went through with the plan.

And his final reason for staying the course was a new thought. He was now part of a group of guys with a common objective derived from a mutual philosophy and shared experiences. And these guys now relied on him.

"OK," Shoes said out loud, with no one but Pucker in earshot, "I'm in. I'm committed to this thing, and I'll work everything else out if and when I get home."

Feet still dangling outside, comfortable with his decision, Shoes laid back into the cabin, nestled Ball's navigation bag under his head, and fell asleep in the sea breeze that wafted through the open doors.

Despite the comfort of the company and the food, the Americans had more pressing matters to attend to. They thanked their hosts, excused themselves, and asked for directions to the waterfront. The Aussie's Logistics HQ compound was about three kilometers across the peninsula to the waterfront entertainment area and to where the fishing boats were docked. The next thing they knew, their hosts had piled them into two jeeps and driven them to the area that Balls had accurately described as the center of R&R activity.

One of the Aussie drivers asked, "Do you need a ride back?"

"No, you've done too much for us already. We'll find our way back in a few hours," Doc replied, wanting them to be able to maintain full flexibility depending on how it went with hiring a boat. "Thanks for everything."

Once the jeeps had departed, JR said, "First order of business is the boat. Balls, since you've been here before, why don't you take the lead, and let's see what we can make happen."

It did not take much leading. The tops of the fishing boats were visible from where the Americans had been dropped off. A short walk later and with just enough discipline to make it past the bars, girls, discos, and street entertainers, they were huddled together staring at a ramshackle collection of fishing boats that looked like they could barely make it out to sea, let alone all the way to Thailand. And each one was resting atilt on the dry beach being barely tickled by incoming waves.

"OK, now what?" Each face was filled with disappointment, with one exception.

"As our new Aussie friends would say, 'No worries, mates,'" Balls said as he began walking toward the closest boat.

The wooden hull was in dire need of paint. Every metal piece carried years of rust, especially the two 55-gallon drums that served as gas tanks and were exposed to the elements in the aft portion of the deck. Unruly piles of netting filled the front half of the deck, some spilling over the sides. The cabin, if it could be called that, was little sturdier than the huts in the Vietnamese villages and filled the remainder of the deck space. It was pieced together with scrap clapboard, and its roof served as a storage space for burlap bags of unknown contents. On one outside wall was painted "VT1466," indicating some semblance of a boat registration system. It was unclear whether there was anything or anyone below deck, but a best guess based on the odor would have been an open hold for fish.

"What the hell do you mean, 'No worries,'" Three Spot prodded his fellow crewman.

"First of all, my friend, these things aren't beached here permanently, it's low tide. See the water line on this boat. In a few hours, the boats will be floating. That's why they're tied off. It's a damn good thing you guys aren't in the navy. Secondly, they may not look like it, but the fishermen who own these boats earn their living sailing into and back from deep water every day. When I talked to guys who spent a couple of hours out at sea, they had a blast."

"I hope you're right, Balls. I don't know what I was expecting, but this wasn't it."

"You want go fishing?" The voice came from behind them as they were approaching the boat.

"Yes, something like that. Is this your boat," JR asked.

JR had to smile, as the person closest to the Vietnamese was Hulk, who seemed huge among any group of people. Standing next to the fisherman, who was no more than five feet tall and could not have weighed more than 110 pounds, he looked like a fairytale giant.

"My boat. Can take you fishing. Americans? Five American dollars to fish for two hours. OK?"

During the flight to Vung Tau, they had pulled their money into a single pot and put it in JR's keeping. It would have to get them to Bangkok with some reserve for emergencies. They figured they had enough to do so, and were about to test that proposition.

JR sustained the conversation with the fisherman, "We were thinking a much longer time."

"OK. Four hours. Eight dollars."

"What would you charge if we rented your boat for ten days?"

Taken aback, the fisherman needed some time to think. His boat was his livelihood, and the combination of selling his unpredictable and often scanty daily catch and offering short excursions to soldiers on R&R allowed him to eke out a living, but every day was a struggle. Although he did not understand why the Americans wanted his boat for ten days, he was not sure he really cared. At least for awhile, this would help him and his family. But maybe he did care. What could they possibly want? Would it be dangerous? He decided there was only one way to find out. He would ask why they wanted it before deciding whether to do it and what to charge.

"Where you go for ten days?"

"We want you to take us to Thailand."

The fisherman did not seem fazed, and for the next hour they worked out a plan. Between the fisherman's knowledge and Ball's studying of the charts, they agreed that Pham Cong Ha would take them all the way to Bangkok. The 1000 kilometer route would go around the peninsula at the far southwest extension of Vietnam, northwest through the Gulf of Siam, into the Bay of Bangkok, and finally up the winding Chao Phraya River to the city.

The Americans would pay half up front and the other half when safely in Bangkok. They would also pay for two extra 55-gallon drums of fuel and other provisions to be brought on board. The price worked for the Americans, and Pham Ha was very happy with the arrangements.

That is until they said they'd like to leave in about three hours. When they told him that the only way they could do the trip is to leave on that short notice and that they would be glad to see if another fisherman would do it instead, Pham Ha gladly agreed to the schedule.

After arrangements were made and the relationship among the Americans and Vietnamese fisherman seemed to be on good footing, JR felt he was ready to enlist him to help with the details of the copter crash—for an additional and attractive fee, of course.

Pham Ha listened to the plan with no expression on his face, thought about his family and how they would benefit from the extra money he would be making, and only asked one question, "Bring son to help? OK? Long trip. Go night and day. Son can help."

The Americans looked at each other, could think of no reason for his son not to join them, and agreed. Their new Vietnamese friend smiled, made a gesture with his arm, and a young man was by his side. The two spoke in Vietnamese for a couple of minutes. The young man looked directly at JR, who, because he was leading the negotiations, was standing in the front of the group, and said in perfect English, "I will make arrangements for fuel, food, and water. The tide will be up in three hours and we can leave."

JR returned the gaze and asked, "Do you have a radio on board?"

"No, but I can get one."

Fifteen minutes later, JR had added the extra fee for the radio to the payment and worked out the details of communications with the son. The father and son indicated they were about to head off to see to the fuel, food, water, and radio, but JR signaled them to wait a moment.

He gathered the Americans together, "I'm going to stay here with the boat. You get back to Shoes and let him know what's up. On the way back, figure out what to tell the Aussies if they notice we're a man short. It's hard to know whether we can really trust our new fisherman friends, and without them, this doesn't work. So, someone needs to stay with them, and that's me."

"OK, we'll figure something out," Doc said.

Balls wrote down a frequency that JR could use to contact the helo, and the group started their three-kilometer walk back. They had plenty of time, but decided to stay focused enough to make it past the bars, girls, discos, and street entertainers.

CHAPTER 41

IT'S SHOW TIME

October 24, 1966
Vung Tau, Vietnam

Shoes was startled awake by the sound of the fuel truck's arrival and instinctively reached for his sidearm. Realizing where he was, he relaxed, assisted in the refueling process, and thanked the truck driver. A few minutes later, Wino returned to ask Shoes to sign the paperwork that verified he had, in fact, landed and refueled.

"I'm about to end my shift. Too bad we don't have time to have a glass or two, but I suspect you'll need to be going as soon as your mates return. If you need anything, Staff Sergeant King will be available. I've briefed him. Since all of the paperwork is complete, your departure timing is your call. I wish you Godspeed."

"Wino, I feel badly that we didn't get a chance to throw some shoes and drink some wine. I would've liked that. I hope you understand that we've got other priorities right now. Thank you again, and please pass along our thanks to your entire staff."

Following a strong, long, and final handshake, Staff Sergeant Aaron Taylor was gone.

After their casual walk back across the peninsula, the Americans, minus JR, returned to the Aussie compound. Taylor had briefed the incoming Logistics HQ staff, and they were eager to let the Americans into the building and out to the tarmac.

Because of the shift change, no one noticed that JR was missing. This oversight was fortunate for the returning crew, because the excuse they had devised for why one of them was missing had been weak at best.

They picked up their military clothing, including JR's, and walked out to the helo, saying nothing about keeping the civilian clothes—and no one asked. Hulk gave Shoes a quick update, and they piled onto the craft.

"It's show time," said Shoes, assuming the pose of a circus ring master for effect before getting in his seat. He worked fluidly with Balls and Three Spot to go through the checklist to power up the Huey.

When the helicopter was sufficiently warmed up, Shoes got on the radio, "Army logistics, this is Mustang Two. Over."

"Go ahead, Mustang Two. Over."

"Thanks again for your hospitality. We're going to hover over the water to make sure we have full instrumentation."

"You're clear, Mustang Two. And no worries, mate."

As the copter lifted off, Shoes turned it toward the South China Sea. When he had gained sufficient altitude and was well off shore, he said, "OK, back into uniform and start sorting out what you'll need to take with you and what you'll leave behind."

Shoes double checked the radio frequency for Than Son Nhut and said to his crew, "We need to get to 5000 feet or more to make sure we have the radio range for Saigon, so we're about five minutes from our first call to the airbase. But let's see if we can raise Speargun first. Balls, what was the frequency you gave him?

"Speargun, this is Mustang Two. Speargun, this is Mustang Two."

On shore, JR had attached himself to the fisherman and his son as they scurried around the commercial section of the dock area procuring extra gas, food, and water. That was the easy part. The radio would turn out to be much more difficult. The fisherman's son knew a guy who knew a guy who might have what they needed.

JR and the two Vietnamese wandered well away from the boat and were wending their way through narrow bustling alleyways lined with dilapidated shanties, open-air food markets, and shops of all sorts. JR was getting more uncomfortable as they got deeper into the maze and was now questioning whether he could really trust his new partners. His muscles and mind were tensed, ready to spring to action, but his fears were allayed when they came upon a shop that had electronic devices of all types piled indiscriminately on wooden planks supported by saw horses.

The fisherman's son and the shop owner spoke for some time before JR was let in on the discussion, "He has a radio, and if we pay him enough, he will even come to the boat to set it up. He has batteries also."

"How will we know it'll work?"

"When your friends call."

"Not good enough. How can we test it?"

Ten minutes later, after harried discussions and some jerry-rigging, the radio was set up and the power was on, but there was only static.

"Now what?" JR's concern and sense of urgency increasing.

The shop owner slowly turned the frequency dial, but the sound of the static was constant. JR was about to ask if there were another shop they could try, when the static lessened. JR's first thought was that the battery had already begun to fail, but he was pleasantly surprised when he heard in English, "Nothing showing on our screen. Over."

"Roger that."

After eavesdropping for about five minutes, JR happily concluded that they had happened on the frequency of a nearby U.S. radar installation. He did not care how far away it was, because they would not need much range. The radio worked.

JR was perfectly fine with the price after he reconfirmed that the shop owner would get the radio set up on the boat. JR added two things to the arrangement. He asked for and paid for extra batteries, and he told the fisherman that when the trip was over, he could keep the radio. Everyone involved in the deal was happy, and they walked together to the boat.

"Mustang Two, this is Speargun."

"Holy shit, we got you. Nice work. Are you still in dry dock or afloat?"

"We're working our way out of the harbor now. What's your status?"

"Just lifted off and are heading out to sea."

JR controlled his excitement and got down to the business at hand, "Let's get eyes on each other. Can you swing by the harbor? Once we see you, we can head your way. We have this radio, but all of the navigation on board is done in the heads of our two hosts. They have a few raggedy nautical charts on board, but I don't know if they'll be helpful."

"Roger that, Speargun, we're on our way. When you see us, get out on deck to let us know we've found each other."

"OK, Shoes. It's about to get hairy. Let's do this."

"Hairy is right. We'll find you and then contact Than Son Nhut. Fingers crossed. Out."

CHAPTER 42

THE CRASH

October 24, 1966
South China Sea, Vung Tau, Vietnam

Shoes took the Huey over the harbor and hovered at 1000 feet.

"I've got eyes on him," Three Spot hollered, keeping his binoculars trained on the boat.

"Are you sure it's the right boat?"

"Well it's got VT1466 on the cabin and there's a guy that looks just like Speargun jumping up and down waving his arms. So, yeah, I'm sure."

Ignoring Three Spot's sarcasm, Shoes circled the fishing boat several times at lower altitude to make sure JR could see the number 38566 on the tail boom and Doc and Hulk hanging out of opposite cabin doors waving back.

Shoes reset the radio frequency, calmed himself, pulled back on the stick, rose to 5000 feet guessing that would give him the radio range he would need, and made his first try.

"Than Son Nhut tower, this is Mustang Two, 1st Aviation Brigade out of Cam Ranh Bay. We have an emergency. Over."

Shoes was ready to gain altitude to increase his radio range but did not need to.

"Mustang Two, Than Son Nhut tower. Did I hear you right? Cam Ranh Bay? Over."

"Roger tower. Long story. Short version. Huey on Medevac mission. Heavy fog. Lost instruments. Ended up closer to Vung Tau than home field. Just refueled with the Aussies. One dead on board and seeking clearance to your position."

THE CRASH

"What's your current status, Mustang Two?"

"Hovering over South China Sea off of Vung Tau to make sure we have instruments before we head your way. OK for now. Want to confirm for ten minutes or so."

"Roger, Mustang Two. Stay on this frequency and let me know when to expect you. I'll be on station through your flight."

"Affirmative, tower. Appreciate the help. Will keep you posted."

Shoes thought of something he had not considered before and asked, "One favor, tower?"

"Go ahead."

"I'll give you the names of those on board. Would you contact the 1st Aviation Brigade at Cam Ranh Bay to let them know our status and our plan to get back tomorrow? Ask them to let the grunts' brass know also."

"Roger, Mustang Two, will do. Do you want us to arrange to process your casualty?"

"Affirmative, tower. Thank you."

Shoes gave the tower the name, rank, and serial number of JR and each of those on board, starting with Eddie Planck. He hoped that when a search was started, the rescue teams would know who they were looking for and, more importantly to those on board, who to report missing in action when the bodies were not recovered. The plan was taking shape.

Shoes kept the helo at 5000 feet and contacted JR.

"Speargun, we're all set. It'll be dark soon, so I want to time this to allow you to get us out of the water while there's still light but make it likely any search will be ineffective until morning. So here's what we're going to do. I'll make my next couple of calls to Than Son Nhut as planned. When you see me descend, let's get as close as we can so we can minimize time in the water."

"Got it Shoes. We're ready."

"Than Son Nhut tower, this is Mustang Two."

"Go ahead Mustang Two."

BODY NOT RECOVERED

"The instruments are not holding up. So far intermittent. Can't resolve. Will likely head back to Aussie logistics and figure it out from there."

"Roger that, Mustang Two."

"Tower, we're going to stick with this a little longer to see if we can resolve the instruments. We'll keep you posted. Over."

"Roger, Mustang Two. Do you want us to send out another chopper to help out if needed? Over."

"Not necessary. We have Aussie HQ in sight and can make it back there if need be. Over."

"Roger and out."

Five minutes later, "Than Son Nhut tower, Mustang Two. Got a problem, tower. Instruments still out, and the helo just threw itself into a big-assed right bank."

Shoes assumed a voice that would be expected if the problem were real, urgent, but professional and short of panicked.

"We've got a vibration that's getting worse. If we don't ditch now, we might just shake ourselves to pieces. Can't be precise about coordinates, but we're about five klicks southeast of the Aussie logistics compound."

"Mustang Two, stay on the radio. Do the best you can to keep us posted on your position. We'll get support heading your way immediately. Getting dark, but we'll have folks in the water as soon as we can."

"Roger that, tower. We're going to fight this thing. See if we can stabilize."

Because the timing of the staged crash and the setting of the sun could not be perfectly coordinated, Shoes had purposely given the tower the wrong location—close enough to ensure the crash site would eventually be found, but far enough so that the search would need to be continued in earnest in the morning.

"OK, guys," Shoes turned his attention to his passengers. "We need to do this and do it fast. Three Spot, do you still have eyes on the boat?"

THE CRASH

Shoes had already begun a rapid descent. Just before he did, he heard, "Mustang Two, Than Son Nhut tower. Over. Mustang Two, tower. Over."

Shoes did not answer. Game on.

Three Spot responded, "Yep, I've still got eyes on 'em. They're at our five o'clock position."

Shoes eased the helo down to 100 feet within a half kilometer of the fishing boat.

"OK, I'm going to get us just above the waves," Shoes instructed his passengers. "Get out on the landing skids and hit the water. Speargun has the boat coming this way."

For the grunts, this maneuver was similar to how they exited a chopper when being deployed in a hot fire zone. The craft would get just short of touching down, and the troops would jump out, hitting the ground running. The chopper would then ascend without ever landing.

Shoes had the copter positioned, "OK, everybody out!"

"I'm staying with you, Shoes!"

"No fucking way, Balls! Get out of here! I'll ditch it and get to the boat!"

"Shoes, no arguments! You have no idea how the bird will react when it hits the water. You may need help getting out. So, I'm staying!"

"Balls…"

"Shoes, that's final, unless you want to come back here to throw me out, and you have more important things to be thinking about! Let's do this, get out, and get to the boat!"

"Roger that."

Hulk, Doc, Peepers, and Three Spot were in the water, swimming to the boat. JR and the fisherman's son were on deck while Pham Ha was delicately guiding the boat toward the swimmers. JR was astonished at how precisely this little man handled the rusty tub.

Shoes guided the helo farther away from the boat to make sure it did not injure the swimmers or damage the boat when he hit the water.

"Balls, buckle up! We're going in! As soon as it settles, we're out of here!"

Shoes brought the Huey down gently, but as he approached the water, the rotor caused a constant and heavy spray to envelop the craft. Unable to see where he was relative to the water, Shoes pulled back on the stick to slow down and get the nose up, trying desperately to regain visibility.

He began to see through the spray, when he felt the helicopter jerk. Shoes immediately realized that the nose-up position put the tail down enough to impact the water. The tail rotor instantaneously went from 3000 rpm to zero.

Without the anti-torque control provided by the tail rotor, the main rotor drove the fuselage into an uncontrolled counterclockwise spin.

Recognizing that the main rotor was going to hit the water, Shoes shut down the power. It was too late—the blades hit a wave, stopped abruptly, and fragmented. Pieces flew in all directions.

The force of the rotor hitting the water put the craft on its side. Shoes knew he had little time before his copter sank, taking Balls and him with it.

The sound of the blades shattering combined with the screeching of metal made it difficult for Shoes to hear what sounded like Balls screaming something to him. Then there was silence. As Shoes ripped off his headset, he could only hear the sea lapping against the side of the helicopter.

Lying sideways in his pilot's seat of the capsized cabin, Shoes struggled to get out of his harness. He grabbed the top of the control panel with his left hand and pulled to relieve the pressure on the belt and unclipped his restraint with his right hand. Finally freed, Shoes half-crawled half-fell out of his seat and looked back to find a way out—he threw up.

The tail boom had dislodged and broken through the back of the cabin. A jagged metal extension had penetrated Tony Baltieri's back and was protruding through his chest cavity. His friend was dead.

Shoes knew that he had no time to waste grieving. He crawled past Balls to the cabin's left door, which was out of the water and facing skyward, pulled himself up, climbed out of his Huey,

THE CRASH

and jumped into the water. Shoes frantically swam to distance himself from the crash site, the danger of the helo sinking rapidly and sucking him down with it, and the scattered debris from the broken craft and everything the crew left behind, including Pucker and Balls.

When Shoes sensed he was out of immediate danger, he turned to look at the Huey. What he had envisioned would be a gentle water landing had turned out to be a real crash. Shoes turned his pained face away from his helicopter and his friend, both which had dropped below the surface of the water, to continue toward the fishing boat.

Having watched the crash, JR and the fisherman's son focused their attention on the first four swimmers. They had rigged the fishing nets to create a functional ladder to help everyone into the boat. Americans and Vietnamese then had a moment on deck to look at the Huey in the water and notice only one man was swimming their way.

When Shoes had made his way to the boat and on board, he did not need to nor was he able to say a word. Everyone could tell from the look on his face that Balls had joined Pucker as the copter went down.

It was near dark as they solemnly headed southwest toward the tip of Vietnam as fast as the vessel would go, wanting to be nowhere near the crash site when a search began.

When they had planned for this day over the past couple of months, there had been nine who had committed themselves to the course of action. They were down to six, having lost Pucker to combat, Salt to what they knew was an assassination, and now Balls to their plan.

CHAPTER 43

I'M JR

October 25, 1966
South China Sea off Southern Vietnam

Monday, October 24, 1966 had been the longest of days. Already exhausted, they had started in the jungle in the middle of the night—clearing the dense thicket for a landing zone, tending to a wounded friend, and guiding a helicopter down through the morning fog. Through the course of the day, they had made quick and life-changing decisions, united with new comrades in common purpose, improvised and executed a risky plan, and watched two friends die. Now in darkness, interrupted only by the three-quarter moon, the six remaining warriors were gathered on the deck of a small fishing boat passing the Mekong River Delta and heading southwest toward the Gulf of Siam along the Vietnamese coast, which was illuminated only by an occasional light from a village cooking fire.

Sleep deprived and emotionally spent, they lay on piles of netting, each lost in his own thoughts. The demons of the day and of the previous months prevented sleep from coming despite the dire need. Eventually each of the Americans on their floating island in the South China Sea succumbed to exhaustion.

One by one, they awoke the next day in full sunlight and open sea with the Vietnamese coast still in sight to starboard. The boy was at the helm, and Ha had prepared something for them to eat. They were at the beginning of a journey to Bangkok, Thailand and toward the rest of their lives.

"Where are we, or do we know?"

"We lost Balls's charts in the crash."

"No worry, sirs. We have charts, and my father is very good with the stars and the sun," the boy said, staring down at them from inside the open wooden cabin.

"Until now, you only know me as Pham Cong Ha's son, the fisherman's son. My name is Pham Huu Hieu. Our family name is Pham. My given name is Hieu. It means 'dutiful to parents.' My middle name, Huu, means 'very much.' My father's middle name, Cong, means 'skillful.' His given name is Ha; it means 'ocean.' So," he said smiling, "my father is skillful with his boat on the water and I am very much dutiful to him. As I have heard other Americans say, 'You are in good hands.'"

Every man on board found himself smiling with the young man and enjoying seeing the smiles on each other's faces. A long sleep, the breakfast, plentiful fresh water, and the sea breeze invigorated them. Regular and restful sleep, meals, hydration, and the seemingly therapeutic nature of the salt air would be the norm on their voyage—the healing being both physical and emotional.

Doc broke out his medical kit. A priority for JR, Peepers, Hulk, and himself was to soothe the jungle rot that they had become accustomed to. The salve from his kit, the air, and the fact that they were not slogging around in the damp jungle promoted rapid recovery.

Following the advice of their captain and first mate, they spent some time getting all of their supplies either tied to the top of the cabin roof or down in the hold, where it was hard to spend too much time. The overwhelming smell of fish permeated the space, and the advantage of the breeze was lost. Although the deck was crowded, almost all of their time was spent outside.

While little training was necessary, the father and son taught each of the Americans to pilot the boat. Shoes had done some sailing when he was growing up, and his flight experience made him comfortable with the charts that were available. When he noticed there were no tide charts, Shoes asked how they were going to manage. Pham Ha smiled and said, "Open water, deep water, no problem."

Not fully satisfied with the answer, Shoes pushed back, "What about near Bangkok? Have you ever been to Bangkok?"

"We have never been that far. But we have heard about the harbor and river. When we get close, we will follow the big ships," Huu Hieu answered matter-of-factly.

With growing confidence in the fisherman, his son, and the boat itself, there was little more to do than lie back and enjoy the voyage. The Americans had plenty of time to share details of their pasts, express hope for their futures, enjoy indeterminate spans of silence, and attempt to put their individual and collective feelings into words.

The rolling of the boat was mesmerizing. The drone of the boat's engine was soothing. The warmth of the sun and cooling of the sea breeze were comforting. The darkness of night and light from the moon were spiritual. The war in their past and the promise of their future were transformational. The memory of Salt, Pucker, and Balls was sobering. The length and quality of their sleep were therapeutic. The good humor of the fisherman and his son was joyful. The recalled reasons they were on this new life course were encouraging. The conversation and camaraderie were uplifting. The laughter was healing.

But the voyage was not without incident, as they tolerated storms and high seas, deciding to stay on deck and holding fast to the secured netting to allow the breeze to help fend off seasickness. Having become resourceful in the rainy jungles, the grunts taught the others to use ponchos to keep reasonably dry and to jerry-rig a collection system to turn rain into a resupply of drinking water.

One morning JR awoke to a strange silence—the engine had stopped and neither the fisherman nor his son were in sight. "Hey, get up! We have a problem!"

Their combat experience kicked in, and they were on full alert with weapons in hand in a moment. Before they could decide what to do, the two Vietnamese emerged from the hold, with grease on their hands. They were smiling, until they saw the guns.

"At ease, troops," JR said with mocking authority.

All of the Americans stowed their weapons, except Peepers, who instead raised his sidearm and pointed it directly at the fisherman. Peepers' face was contorted in anger; his breath was labored; his trigger finger was tensed.

Doc stood to Peepers' right and was the first to realize that Peepers was not yet ready to separate his jungle instincts from his new life. As he was about to grab his comrade, Doc thought better of it. Instead, he took three careful steps to stand between Peepers and the fisherman.

With both hands raised in front of him as if to signal Peepers to stop, Doc spoke calmly to his comrade, "It's OK, Peepers. It's OK. At ease. We're safe. You're safe."

Confusion mixed with the anger in Peepers' expression, but he neither lowered his weapon nor released the tension on the trigger.

Doc stayed as calm as he could, "I know you're angry at losing Pucker. But these men had nothing to do with that. They're our friends."

With Peepers' attention on Doc and the fisherman, Hulk moved slowly behind to physically control Peepers if needed.

Doc continued quietly, "At ease. You're OK. Everything's going to be OK. They're not the enemy."

About to bear hug Peepers from behind, Hulk noticed a slight change—Peepers' body had relaxed a bit and he had perceptibly lowered his sidearm. Hulk stayed in position. Doc kept his hands raised.

Peepers then dropped his weapon into the netting at his feet, slumped his shoulders, lowered his eyes, and whimpered, "I'm sorry. I'm sorry."

And he wept.

Doc put his arms around Peepers to comfort him until he had composed himself. Then Peepers stood straight and began walking toward the Vietnamese. Hulk stayed right behind him, but Peepers turned around, put his hand gently on Hulk's chest to signal that it was not necessary, and said, "I'm OK, big guy. Just give me a minute."

Hulk stopped, but he and the others stayed alert and ready to step in as Peepers entered the cabin where the Vietnamese had been frozen in place since the incident began.

"I'm sorry," Peepers said softly to the man and boy.

He held out his hand and each of the Vietnamese hesitantly shook the hand that had moments before was ready to shoot them. Peepers turned around and held up his hand to show his comrades, and his smile grew into a full-blown laugh. The hand was full of grease. Still wary, the father and son nodded as if to recognize the joke, but they were not yet ready to join the laughter.

For now, everything seemed resolved, but the Americans knew it would take Peepers some time to really be back to normal. And each of them also wondered if that would be true for them as well.

Still shaken from the incident, the son spoke as he climbed to the top of the cabin and refilled and tied down bags of tools, cans of oil, and spare parts, "We fixed the engine. No problem."

Ha restarted the engine, looked guardedly down at his passengers, and they were on their way.

After breakfast that same day, JR opened a conversation with his comrades, "Since we're going to be together for awhile, hopefully all the way to South Dakota and maybe beyond, I think we should decide whether our nicknames are still what we want to be known by. For one, I want to leave Speargun behind me. I don't want to be known for something that has to do with a weapon. So, I'm JR."

"What does JR stand for?" Three Spot asked.

JR was reminded of the friendly harassment he used to get from Mouse and Swish about his name. "Nope, doesn't stand for anything. JR is what's on my birth certificate."

"I was Hulk back in school—I brought it with me and plan to take it back."

"Don't think I ever told you this, Shoes, because I didn't want to hurt your feelings. When you gave me the name Three Spot, I got it. Trey—three in a deck of cards—three spot—I got it. But I really don't care for it. So, while we're at it, Trey will do for me."

"Shit, man. I didn't know. You got it, Trey."

"Well, speaking of names we don't like..."

"OK, Peepers, I get it. Sorry," Hulk said.

"No big deal, but either Dan or Prince works for me."

"Prince...I like that. Should have used it from the beginning. Again, Peepers...er, uh, Prince, I'm sorry."

"Doc, what do you think?" JR asked.

"Well, to be honest, I never really liked the name my folks gave me anyway. I was happy when my friends back home called me Arnie instead of Arnold. But it's deeper than that. Every medic seems to get the nickname Doc. And, in fact, I've been proud of it, because I've been able to help a lot of guys over the months.

"But on balance, I'm not sure where I come out. Doc carries with it not only all the guys I helped, but all of the horror I've seen and the guys I couldn't help."

Doc's body shook and months of bottled-up emotion came pouring out in tears. Every man understood that this was exactly what Doc needed. After giving him some time to just let it out, JR rose, sat down next to Doc, and put his arm around him. No words were necessary.

Doc, tears still running down his cheeks, slowly looked from man to man, wordlessly telling each one with his expression that he was thankful for their compassion. He needed their friendship as much as he had needed to cry. The last face he made contact with was JR's, only inches away. Then he nestled his head against JR's shoulder and slowly stopped crying.

"So, as I said, on balance, I'm really not sure."

"Welcome aboard, Arnie," JR tightened his hold on his friend.

Arnie raised his head, nodded a thank you to JR, and was able to muster a smile.

"Well, I guess that leaves me. For me, it's pretty simple. I'll be Pat when I get home to my family, but until then and for you guys, if you don't mind, I like Shoes. Although I didn't have the nickname until I met JR, I feel it's my bond to Balls."

Shoes stared into the horizon and continued, "He and I would throw for hours at a time; sometimes gabbing away, sometimes not saying a word."

JR was even more convinced that it was Shoes and Balls throwing horseshoes that first day in Vietnam when Kit had been injured. Things had come full circle.

CHAPTER 44

CONFIDENCE AND MATURITY

October 29, 1966
Gulf of Siam

After Pham Ha's fishing boat cleared the southern tip of Vietnam, he set a course directly for Bangkok through the Gulf of Siam. To help ensure that winds and tides would not take them too far off course and lengthen the trip, Ha kept them within sight of the Cambodian and then Thai coasts while also keeping a safe distance so as not to draw attention.

As they would approach the Bay of Bangkok at the northern end of the gulf, it would be especially important to steer clear of Sattahip, Thailand, which jutted out of the southeastern section of the mouth of the bay. Sattahip was a deep-water port and site of a large Royal Thai Navy base, and its local airport was used extensively by the U.S. Air Force—Balls had pointed out the two military installations when he was describing the option to fly to Bangkok.

They wanted nothing to do with either the Thai Navy or the U.S. Air Force. The plan was to travel westerly across the Gulf of Siam before reaching Sattahip and enter the bay along its western edge before entering the Chao Phraya River.

On the morning of the fifth day of the voyage, Sattahip could be seen through binoculars, as could Thai Navy patrol boats. It was time to make the course correction. The Americans spent the morning in the hold and were glad to come back on deck once the boat was well clear of any risk of discovery.

Ha turned the helm over to his son and joined his passengers on deck, where JR rose to make room for the Vietnamese fisherman, whom everyone had come to appreciate for his skill and good humor. JR joined Huie in the shade of the cabin.

"Where did you learn to speak English so well?"

"I went to a school where the nuns teach English, and for many years, I help my father take Americans and Australians on our boat. I wanted to visit America and go to school there."

"What do you mean wanted? Don't you still want to go to the United States?"

"No," Huie said and then hesitated. Not wanting to offend his passenger, he continued, "I like you and the others, but I do not like what you are doing to my people."

JR was glad that he was having this conversation well after the incident when one his fellow Americans had been close to shooting this boy and his father. In fact, Prince had gone out of his way since then to be nice and helpful to the Vietnamese.

Huie concluded, "It makes me not want to go to America."

"You may not understand this," JR began, as he spoke to the short, thin boy whose age was difficult to guess. "We are going to Bangkok, because we also do not like what we are doing to your people."

JR was about to continue when Huie said, "My father has a sister, and she has a family. They are farmers. The American planes bombed their village. My father's sister and her family were not hurt, but they cannot live there. And they cannot farm. They are in a camp that is very bad. My father wants to help them, but we cannot. If Americans do this, I do not want to go to America."

JR was conflicted. His reflex was to defend his country and argue that before American troops arrived, North and South Vietnamese were already killing each other, and there were already many village incidents. He wanted to say that many South Vietnamese villagers are communist sympathizers and are helping the Viet Cong. He wanted to say that with the support of some villagers, North Vietnamese had killed friends of his.

But he said none of this, because he knew that even if most of it were true, he fully agreed with Huie. He had made a risky decision that would affect the rest of his life, because he too profoundly believed that what the boy was saying was right.

"Let me tell you more about Americans, Huie. Back in the United States, many Americans agree with you and are protesting against the government to stop the war. Do you know what protest means?"

Huie nodded that he did.

"My friends and I are going back to the United States, because we want to help stop the war. That is part of what is great about America. We keep trying to get things right when they're wrong. I hope someday you can visit America and learn more about us than what we are doing in your country."

JR was not only speaking but was also listening to himself. Just a couple of short years ago, he was a lost young man about to graduate high school with no idea of a future in mind. He recognized that he was now speaking to Huie with confidence and a maturity he had developed and grown into.

Huie tilted his head and stared as if to see within the mind and soul of the man standing across from him. After a moment's thought, the young Vietnamese smiled and said, "Maybe someday I will go to America."

JR spent the next couple of hours trying to describe America to a boy whose life had been limited to a small corner of a small country thousands of miles and a culture away. What made the conversation even more interesting was that JR had experienced little of the United States himself.

CHAPTER 45

SINGHA

October 30, 1966
Chao Phraya River, Bangkok, Thailand

"You said this would work," Shoes nodded and smiled at Huie after spotting and pointing out the large ship on the horizon, the first of many they would encounter as they made their way across the Gulf of Siam.

Ha positioned the small fishing boat among the cargo vessels, making sure to be neither too close nor caught in the wakes, and followed them through the Bay of Bangkok toward the Chao Phraya, their route to the heart of Bangkok.

As Hulk finished going through the Bangkok plans once again, Arnie pointed over the bow at the mouth of the Chao Phraya. Shoes stood as if to indicate that what he was about to say was of utmost importance. When he began, he was choked up, "I know we all had a piece of getting us this far. But, Hulk and JR, with your Bangkok connections, your idea to stage the crash, and your guts to put this together, I want to especially thank you. I know we have a long way to go, but we've also come a long way. I can actually envision being with my wife and son."

While nodding appreciation of Shoes' comments, Hulk cautioned, "Still a lot that can go wrong, so let's stay on our toes. The Jattawans expect us at some point, but there was no way to let them know it would be today. Let's get upriver and find a reasonable place to dock, so we can contact the family."

As they entered the Chao Phraya, the feeling of the open sea dissipated. There were places along the river that were less than the width of a football field and others as wide as a mile. The new surroundings and the sights in and along the winding river served to distract the Americans from their thoughts about coming up on yet another major and uncertain milestone in their journey.

The river was busy with traffic of all sorts. Pilot boats were guiding the large cargo ships to and from their berths in the ports along the river. Brightly painted and decorated motorized long-tail boats, some as long as 30 meters, crisscrossed the waterway ferrying passengers.

Floating markets overflowed from opposing banks and into the channel on both sides of the river. Bamboo-hatted vendors paddled small boats laden with fruits, vegetables, and flowers to sell to customers both on land and on water. The brightly-colored boats, produce, and vendor's garb overloaded the senses of the Americans who had become accustomed to the constant grey of fog and monsoon, brown of mud, and green of jungle. Even JR and Hulk, who had recently been to Bangkok, were unprepared for the display.

The river was also dense with fishing boats not unlike their own, giving the Americans a feeling of comfort as their craft blended in.

"Pham Ha," Hulk took the lead, "we need to find a place to dock near a hotel or someplace else where I can find a telephone. Do you understand?"

Ha nodded as did Huie, both of whom had stationed themselves in the cabin before the boat approached the mouth of the river. Fifteen minutes later, Vietnamese fishing boat VT1466 worked its way slowly through a dense floating market to find its way to a dock. Prince and Arnie tied up and they all looked to Hulk for instructions.

Hulk got them started, "I'm going to find a phone to call the Jattawans. Someone should come with me in case I need some help."

"Shoes, do you want to go with Hulk," JR asked, resuming his leadership role. "Pham Ha, I know you need to resupply for your trip back. Do you want help with that? Huie should stay with the boat."

"I'll go with Pham Ha," Arnie offered. "JR, do you have the rest of the money we owe them? This would be a good time to settle up."

"Sounds right," JR said as he reached into his pack to make the final payment.

"Prince and Trey, how about joining me in the hold to empty all of the packs? Later, we'll sort through what we want to take and what we'll leave with Ha and Huie. I'm thinking everything having to do with war stays with them, including uniforms and weapons. They can decide if they want to dump things at sea or figure out what to do with them when they get back to Vung Tau."

"I'm OK with M-16's staying with the boat, but I think we should hold on to sidearms until we really know that everything's working out," Shoes said, his brow wrinkled with concern.

"Damn right," Prince declared as his expression morphed into one similar to the one when he had drawn a bead on the fishermen earlier in the trip. "I'm not giving up my weapon."

"Makes sense to me," JR agreed calmly to defuse Prince and the situation. "Let's see what it all looks like when we spread it out."

Doc sidled next to Prince, put his hand firmly on his friend's shoulder, "Everything's OK. No one is taking our weapons."

Prince's face relaxed and reddened, "I keep having to say I'm sorry. I just can't help it. I'm cool."

With Prince calmed down and a plan in place, Hulk, Shoes, Arnie, and Ha left the boat. Huie stayed on deck, and the others went below.

When JR, Trey, and Prince had finished below, they came back on deck to wait. Huie pulled JR aside, "Our boat trip together is the first time I really know Americans. I want you to know I have been thinking about what you said. And I have been thinking about you and your friends. I want to visit the United States and even go to school there if I can. I am going to talk to the nuns at my school."

"That's great. I'm glad, and I hope you do come to the United States."

"Where will you be? If I come, I want to visit you."

"Huie, I wish I knew. I won't know about what my life will be until I get back. It is likely we'll never see each other again, but I want you to know that I'll never forget you and your father."

"And I will never forget you and your friends."

"Hey, how about a Singha," Shoes announced as he and Hulk came on board, both holding their already-open beers.

"You look like everything worked out," JR said.

Hulk took a swig of beer and said, "I spoke to Annan. His father was in the room. They gave us instructions about where to be tomorrow, and they'll pick us up. And there's more. They're contacting my father to get the wheels turning. So for tonight, let's celebrate our arrival in Bangkok. We've got the beer and we're surrounded by a floating market. It's banquet time."

When Ha and Arnie returned with the boat's provisions for the journey back to Vung Tau, JR confirmed with Ha that he agreed with staying docked overnight and parting ways in the morning.

"I will miss you," Ha said as he looked at his son. "We," he emphasized the word, "will miss you."

With everyone back on board, they had a couple of things to do before morning; sort out the belongings that were spread throughout the hold and celebrate being in Bangkok.

Organizing the contents of their packs would be more than a matter-of-fact exercise. Their gear had helped sustain them through basic training and AIT, through the jungles and in the muddy bunkers of Vietnam, and even on the boat ride during which they had finished their remaining C-rations. They had carried the packs and weapons on their backs, just as they had carried the burden of war in their hearts. Parting with their gear was a symbolic step on their journey to separate themselves from what had become abhorrent— relieving themselves of both physical and emotional weight.

Although they had been living in them for a week, the Americans remained in their civilian clothes to avoid undue attention. Arnie kept what was left of his medical kit. Everyone held on to their sidearms, the complementary ammo, and a few odds and ends. Prince reluctantly relinquished his M-16, which along with everything else went to the father and son—uniforms, helmets, ponchos, rifles, bayonets, bandoliers of ammo, grenades, field shovels, an extra pair of binoculars, and some girlie magazines.

Having attended to those details, they purchased their banquet from floating market vendors and settled in for a meal and a couple of Singha beers.

JR held up his beer, "Here's to Balls, Pucker, and Salt...and to M. J. Savoy."

CHAPTER 46

THE ENEMY IS THE WAR

October 31, 1966
Bangkok, Thailand

It had begun as a financial arrangement—payment for the long boat ride, during which six Americans and two Vietnamese learned a lot about each other. They spoke openly about their lives, their plans, their hopes, and their fears.

During their celebration the evening before, Pham Ha, with help from his son, shared the story of his family. He spoke of his sister and her family and of the American bombing of her village. He shared that his first instinct was to hate all Americans, but then he realized that many of his fellow countrymen were acting no more honorably.

Pham Ha, despite language limitations, eloquently expressed what they had all been thinking. The enemy is not the North Vietnamese. The enemy is not the Viet Cong sympathizer in the South Vietnamese village. The enemy is not the American pilot who is dropping bombs. The enemy is the war itself.

When he had learned early in the voyage that the Americans had chosen to no longer fight and wanted most of all to stop the war, he knew that his job was to make sure they got to Bangkok safely. He, Pham Ha, a humble Vietnamese fisherman, was proud to play a role in this plan. He knew that this was something he could do for his sister and her family—to play a part in stopping the war.

In the morning, they ate breakfast in silence. The Americans were on edge, as they tried to envision what would happen next with the Jattawan family. And both the Americans and the Vietnamese knew they would soon say good-bye.

Before breakfast, the Americans had gathered what they planned to take with them and secured what was to stay on board in the hold. When the meal was finished, JR was the first to speak, bowing modestly from the waist, "Tam biet; Cam on."

Huie returned the greeting in English, extending his hand, "Good bye; thank you."

After they shook hands, Huie leaned toward JR, whispering in his ear, "Thank you for helping me think about America. And thank you for helping my father learn how to help his sister."

The next five minutes were filled with bowing and hand-shaking and hugging and English and Vietnamese. Perhaps the most heartfelt good-bye was when Prince approached Ha. "Again, I'm sorry for what I did," Prince said as he extended his hand.

The small Vietnamese fisherman took Prince's hand in his and covered it with his left hand. Ha then began speaking in Vietnamese.

When he finished, he looked at his son, who translated to Prince, "My father says he could not express himself in English and to please pardon him. He says you do not need to be sorry. It is not your fault. He wishes that the demons the war brought to you will soon go away. He also wishes your journey to be swift and safe."

Prince said nothing but covered Ha's hand with his and gently nodded.

It was time to part ways.

"Safe travels," JR called when they were off the boat.

"Safe travels," the fisherman and his son waved from the boat.

The Americans turned and were quickly out of sight in the narrow alleys across from the dock.

Hulk took the lead to return to the hotel from which he had made the phone call the day before. They had about an hour to wait for the two cars that were to pick them up and take them to the Jattawan home.

CHAPTER 47

FOREVER GRATEFUL

October 31, 1966
Bangkok, Thailand

Although JR and Hulk were comfortable as the cars approached the Jattawan home, the others' senses were on full alert. While they trusted JR and Hulk, the Thai family was an unknown to them personally. Shoes, Trey, Prince, and Arnie were excited to be at what promised to be their jumping-off point for home, but they had been conditioned over the previous months to assess the threats of any new place they approached. What and where were the risks?

The two cars had entered the gated private drive, which had a canal running parallel to the road on one side. On the other side of the road were huge houses, barely visible through the dense foliage made up mostly of diverse species of palm trees.

As they pulled into the Jattawan's driveway, the large dark-red oiled teakwood house remained barely visible. Only the three peaked roofs, one for each section of the structure, could be clearly seen over the palms that hid the house from view in an oasis-like setting.

As they approached the house, the Americans saw small ponds surrounded by lush vegetation in the courtyards on either side of the terrace entrance, which was guarded by large Chinese lion sculptures.

Shoes whispered to Trey, "This place has the feeling of a compound. We should be able to go unnoticed here. So far so good. Let's meet the family and hope they're OK too."

JR ushered Hulk through the door first in deference to his relationship with the family, and then stepped forward toward Khun Jattawan and his son, Annan, both who were waiting for their guests on the terrace. "Sawatdee-khap," Hulk said, placing his hands together and bowing slightly, as the young man from Mitchell, South Dakota entered the Jattawan home in Bangkok, Thailand for the third visit of his life.

JR repeated Hulk's greeting and introduced the remaining Americans. The Jattawans formally returned each man's respectful greeting.

"Welcome to our home. We were uncertain whether this day would come, but it is here and we are prepared. Mr. Carlson, thank you for sharing your friends with us. Let us have some coffee and talk," Khun Jattawan said as he added a sweeping arm gesture to welcome his visitors into the same drawing room in which Hulk had made his initial request for help.

As they made their way, Annan sidled next to Hulk, put his arm around the big man, and whispered, "It is good to see you, my friend. It is my wish that all of this works out well for you and your friends."

"Me too, Annan. Me too."

"My mother will not be joining us, as she is not feeling well. She wants you to know that our home is your home."

Hulk could tell by the look on his friend's face that there was something more to what he was saying, but he chose not to press for an explanation, at least not yet.

It did not take long for Shoes, Trey, and the others to feel comfortable with the Jattawans. Once they were seated with coffee and cakes served, Khun Jattawan skipped pleasantries and got down to the business at hand, "Since Mr. Carlson and Mr. Spears visited us, we have been working with Mr. Carlson's father. Here is what we have planned."

He scanned each of the eager young faces and continued, "As soon as we heard from you yesterday, we contacted Mr. Carlson. He is leaving on a plane in the next hour and will be here tomorrow. He and I have many friends in our business, and we are going to take full advantage of that to get all of you home to the Carlson ranch."

For the next fifteen minutes without interruption, Khun Jattawan methodically shared the outline and some of the details of the plan. When he finished speaking, he paused and asked, "Are there any questions?"

Before anyone could ask a question, JR stood, faced Khun Jattawan, and said, "I know that I am speaking for all of us. Thank you for your help. We know that you could have chosen not to do this, and we know that you are taking a risk. We will be forever grateful."

Each of the Americans was nodding. After a few minor questions, Khun Jattawan, said, "We will cover all the details tomorrow when Mr. Carlson arrives. For now, I am sure you are tired from your journey. Annan will show you to our guest rooms. He will also inform you of all of the other house arrangements."

On their voyage from Vietnam to Bangkok, they had only begun to shed the physical and emotional weariness of their months in Vietnam. In the comfort of the Jattawan home, the comrades had no difficulty sleeping that night. It was as though they had reached the peak of a mountain. They had experienced the challenge and uncertainty of the climb and were joyful at having reached the summit. But they each knew that the downhill portion of the adventure carried its own risks, and the adrenaline would return soon.

CHAPTER 48

AN ORDER

November 20, 1966
Mitchell, South Dakota

"Well, if I ever wanted to hide out in the U. S., which I guess is actually what I'm doing, this would be the place," Shoes said as he sipped his cold Budweiser. "Mr. Carlson, would you mind if I used your phone to make a long distance telephone call? I won't be long."

"Take as much time as you need, son. I understand. And to remind you, it's John, not Mr. Carlson."

Everyone in the expansive, high-ceilinged, rough-hewn living room of the Carlson ranch house knew that Shoes would be making this call. He had reminded them a number of times of the agreement he had struck with JR—his wife already knew not to believe what she heard had happened to him. He now needed to hear her voice, explain the situation, and begin to work out plans. Out of respect for his comrades, Shoes once more scanned the room to get the go-ahead nods, which he received.

The deserters, for that is what they were, had easily settled into their newest home when they arrived the day before. And they knew they were there because of both their own ingenuity and John Carlson.

Carlson had taken charge as soon as he arrived at the Jattawan home. Since having heard of his son's request from Khun Jattawan, John Carlson had been doing everything he could to arrange for Hulk and his buddies to get home safely without being discovered. From the moment he was introduced to Hulk's friends until they were sitting comfortably in the remote Mitchell, South Dakota ranch house, John Carlson had it all mapped out.

AN ORDER

"OK, here's what we're going to do," he had declared in the Jattawan sitting room.

Although they were a bit overwhelmed by the scope of the plans he was laying out for them, each of the young men relying on him to get them back to the world hung on Carlson's every word. Their months in Vietnam as well as the week of the crash and voyage to Bangkok had been filled with uncertainty. Yet sitting before them was a man who was powerfully bringing certainty to their lives. All they would need to do was follow his instructions.

"It's Tuesday. On Thursday morning, we'll be driven to the airport," Carlson paused and looked at his Thai friend, who nodded confirmation. "I've arranged for a private plane to fly us to Nagoya, Japan with a stop in Taipei. The plane belongs to a company that Khun Jattawan and I do business with. They can and will manage to get us from country to country without papers or questions.

"Once in Nagoya, we'll be driven to the docks. I'll fly back to the states after making sure you're situated on board the Seacrest. She's a Panamanian-flagged cargo ship we frequently use, and she'll deliver you to Seattle after stopping in Hawaii."

"Wow, Hawaii! I wanted to go there for R&R, but never made it," Trey said.

"Whoa boy. The ship will be in Hawaiian waters, but you won't get off. It's too dangerous, and there's really no way to manage papers if you try to go ashore."

"Oh, yeah, sorry," Trey said sheepishly as he slouched in his seat.

"I've brought you some reading material for your time on the ship. You already know of the growing antiwar movement. You'll see that the press has picked it up big time. In the last few months, *TIME* and *LIFE* magazines and all of the major newspapers have been covering the horrors of the war you guys had been asked to fight and the protests that are cropping up everywhere. Well, not quite everywhere—most of it is centered in the Bay Area and on a number of college campuses. But it's starting to spread.

"Anyway, the Seacrest gets you to the Port of Seattle, and I will have made arrangements for a private boat to come out and pick you up to avoid any official entry. From there, it's one more private plane and you're home. Questions?"

"Mr. Carlson..."

"It's John, Arnie. It's John."

"John, I don't have a question, but I do want to let you know how much I appreciate all that you're doing. I've only known your son for a pretty short time, but have come to respect him. Now I know where he gets it. You're a standup guy. How can we ever repay you?"

"Just make sure you follow the itinerary carefully and don't take any chances."

Two days later, the morning was filled with words and gestures of appreciation and parting. Hulk wrapped his huge arms around Annan and said with confidence, "I don't know when, but I know I'll see you again."

"I am hoping that is true, my friend. May your travels be safe and your return to your home comforting."

The others had assembled at the cars that would take them to the airport and waited patiently for Hulk and Annan to separate. As Hulk walked toward his comrades, he turned once more to wave to Annan and his father before folding himself into the car.

"Dad," Hulk said to his father on the ride to the airport, "I was surprised that we didn't see Mrs. Jattawan at the house. I heard she wasn't feeling well. Is she OK?"

"She's fine son. She just didn't agree that her husband and son should be taking the risk they did to help us out. It caused quite a rift in the family. She was staying with her sister until we left. I'm not sure what the penalty would have been if they were discovered, but they definitely stuck their necks out."

"How's mom taking all of this?"

"She's fine. Scared, but fine."

"Dad...," Hulk halted to get his composure, "Thank you."

As Carlson had promised, the company plane was waiting for them. The flights on the small but well-appointed corporate jet to Taipei and Nagoya were uneventful. Parking the plane on the far end of the apron across from the private terminals in each location minimized the risk of time on the ground. Limos seemed to magically appear at planeside in Nagoya and drove the men to the docks.

Carlson confirmed the arrangements with the Seacrest's captain, got everyone on board and settled, then left for his flight home. The young men began a 14-day journey of additional sleep recovery, healing, and boredom. Their cabin had three bunk beds with a small head and minimal standing space. Although it was cramped, they agreed it was much more comfortable, dryer, and safer than a rainy jungle base camp, a hillside bunker, or a helicopter cabin in a hot zone.

"Pucker! Pucker!"

On the third morning of the voyage, JR, Hulk, Arnie, Trey, and Shoes were awakened to Prince's screams. Arnie, who had assumed an informal responsibility for Prince since the incident on the fishing boat, was out of his top bunk and approaching his comrade, when he noticed the gun.

While still at the Jattawan home, the young Americans had assembled in the walled-in back terrace. Shoes had asked them to get together and opened the conversation, "Hulk, no disrespect to your father, but we have a long way to go until we're sitting in your ranch. I suggest we keep our sidearms until we're there. Even though we have a plan, there's still a lot we don't know.

"In fact, let me put it another way. I'm going to keep my weapon and just bury it in my duffle. I think you should all do the same. We're not out of the woods yet."

"No offence taken, Shoes," Hulk began. "I've been thinking about this too, and I'm with you. Let's keep the weapons and not even bring the point up. This is just among us. OK?"

Everyone had agreed, and now they were facing Prince with gun in hand. It was unclear whether he was asleep or awake, but his eyes were open.

"Prince, this is Arnie. Give me the gun."

"Doc, you've got to do something for Pucker. He's moaning. He just keeps moaning. Can't you do anything to help?"

"OK, Peepers," Arnie reverted to the jungle nickname, recognizing that was where Prince was in his mind. "Give me your gun, and I'll see what I can do."

"I've got to protect him. You fix him, Doc. I'll keep him safe."

Just as he had done on the fishing boat, Hulk began moving in behind Prince to be in a position to physically control him if needed. But Prince, who they now knew was awake but in another world, saw Hulk and trained the gun on him, "You take one more step toward Pucker and you're dead."

"Peepers, it's Hulk, not the enemy," Arnie said, straining to keep his voice as calm as possible. "He's going to help protect Pucker. You can put down your gun."

As an expression of recognition crept onto Prince's face, he began to lower his weapon and relax, which caused the others to calm down as well. Then, without warning, the expression was gone. Prince raised his gun and aimed it point-blank at Hulk's chest. His finger tensed on the trigger.

JR, who was on the closest lower bunk and on full alert, leaped toward Prince to grab him and the gun at the same time. He hit Prince's arm just as he fired.

The explosion inside the small cabin was deafening, as the bullet missed Hulk by inches and went through the closed compartment door. Before he could fire again, JR and Hulk were on top of Prince and disarmed him. Arnie grabbed the gun from the deck and was holding it when the ship's captain rushed into the cabin followed by an armed sailor.

"What the hell is going on?"

Thirty minutes later, the Americans had a tenuous agreement with the captain. Prince, who was still in JR's and Hulk's grasp, was no longer resisting. He was shaking and whimpering. After Arnie had explained what had happened and why, the captain agreed to allow the Americans to control their friend instead of restraining him in another part of the ship. But the captain demanded that they surrender all of their weapons, which they agreed to do without argument.

When everything had calmed down, Arnie took Prince topside and in the cold ocean breeze, explained what had happened and why he thought Prince was acting out. They agreed to spend time alone each day talking about it.

Prince found himself on edge several times, but there were no further serious incidents. More than once, he apologized to everyone, but especially to Hulk, "Can you forgive me?"

"I know you weren't thinking straight," Hulk said, reflecting on the explanation of battle fatigue that Arnie had given to everyone. "But man, if there was anyone you could pick to look like a North Vietnamese, the last person you'd pick would be me."

When Prince had a hearty laugh at that, they knew that although it might take awhile for him to recover, he would probably be OK.

As the Seacrest approached the Strait of San Juan de Fuca, the captain told the Americans of a slight change in plans. Instead of entering the channel and going all the way to Seattle through the Puget Sound, they would drop anchor just south of the far western point of the strait on the American side. Mr. Carlson would come to them from Port Angeles, which he had decided would be a lesser risk.

As he promised, John Carlson was on the deck of the yacht that picked the men up from the Seacrest and took them to a secluded dock area at the far western end of Port Angeles where they could disembark without issue. As they thanked the captain for the voyage and for his understanding, JR spoke for the group, "You can keep the weapons."

"I was planning to," the captain said, sporting an expression that made it clear he was glad to be having this set of passengers off his ship.

When the young men disembarked and stepped onto the dock, Shoes said what they were all thinking, "We're back in the world."

Over the next five hours, they were driven to a small airport, boarded another private jet, and flown 1400 miles to land on an air strip on the Carlson ranch. They were home—or what would serve as home for at least awhile.

Just before Shoes could depart for the phone call to his wife, Vivian Carlson walked into the room and said, "I know each of you is anxious to get on with the rest of your lives, but I have one request."

"Yes ma'am," JR answered for the group.

"Thursday is Thanksgiving, and we have a lot to be thankful for. You all are staying until then."

"Mom, that sounds more like an order than a request."

"Son, I learned that approach from your father."

Shoes, who had stopped at the doorway on his way to the phone, stood at attention, saluted, and said, "Ma'am, that's an order we'd be glad to follow."

CHAPTER 49

WE'RE GOING TO BERKELEY

November 24, 1966
Mitchell, South Dakota

The large table in the spacious dining room could have easily accommodated two of the squads of Bravo One. The six young men joined John and Vivian Carlson at one end for all of the Thanksgiving fixings.

Hulk's brother, James, who knew Hulk was coming home and how and why but had been sworn to secrecy by his father, was spending Thanksgiving week with his fiancé's family and planned to return home late Sunday to see Hulk.

Each person at the Carlson's Thanksgiving table had both shared and personal reasons to be thankful. JR summed it up for his friends, "Mr. and Mrs. Carlson, thank you for having faith in us, for supporting us, and for your hospitality. I mean, you made all of the arrangements to get us home; when we got here, each of us had a full duffle of clothes waiting for us; and you've made us feel like part of the family. Mostly, thank you for your son. He has been and I hope will always be a big part of my new life—because that's what I have—a new life.

"Shoes, Trey, Arnie, Prince—thank you for your friendship and for your guts to risk everything to get us to this point. We lost Pucker, Salt, and Balls along the way. They should be here with us, but they're not. We'll always remember them."

After Shoes proposed a toast to what JR had said, Hulk stood, looked JR directly in the eye, and said, "JR, I'm thankful for you. When we first met, you were quiet and disconnected. I had to drag you places. Now you're a leader in every sense of the word. You're the primary reason we're here today. You're a good friend—

BODY NOT RECOVERED

the best, and I'm going to miss you. I know you are committed to figure out how to make a difference in the antiwar movement, and I know you will. I want to also, but I'm going to stick around here for awhile, spend some time with James, and see if I can get my head together first."

"Son, we're glad you'll be here for awhile, but we also understand how strongly you feel about the war and stopping it. If and when you're ready to do something about that, you know you have our full support," Vivian Carlson said, fighting back tears. "Boys," she looked around the table, "what are your plans?"

Shoes spoke first, "I'm leaving tomorrow to see my wife and son. It's taken her these few days to work out the details. We live near Minneapolis, but we didn't want to deal with the chance of me running into anyone we know after being declared a war casualty. We're going to meet in Fargo day after tomorrow and begin figuring out the rest of our lives. It would be helpful to get a ride to Sioux Falls, and I'll get a bus from there."

"We can do that," John Carlson said.

JR was next. "Everything I've heard and read says that the center of the antiwar activity is in the Bay Area, so that's where I'm heading. I'm not exactly sure what I'll do when I get there, but I'll figure it out. Hell, we made it from the jungle to Vung Tau to Bangkok to here. I'm sure figuring out the Bay Area is doable. Arnie, Prince, and Trey are going to join me—we'll still have each other's backs."

"Actually," Prince said, shrugging his shoulders, "I've been doing some more thinking about all of this. You're right, JR, I was planning to join you, but I've decided I've got a couple of things to do first. I feel like I need to go see Pucker's parents in Beckley, West Virginia. Guess I'll hitch my way across the country. Then I may get in touch with my older sister. Our folks are gone and she lives away from where we grew up, so the risk of going to see her is low. From there, I'll figure it out. You may see me in San Fran at some point."

As Prince was talking, Arnie's expression of concern grew more intense, "Are you sure you'll be OK hitchhiking cross-county on your own?"

Prince smiled knowingly and said to Arnie, "Yeah, I do, unless you want to join me as my traveling shrink. Seriously, I hope I've got all of that out of my system—thanks to you."

WE'RE GOING TO BERKELEY

"OK, but at least stay away from weapons for awhile," Arnie said, his look of concern having only somewhat dissipated

"Boys...I keep calling you boys. You're not. You're men. You've been through hell and if you're not men by now, you never will be. So, men, Vivian and I want to do one more thing. Right now, all you have are the clothes in your duffle and your plans. Although you've proven to be about as resourceful as any group of people on the planet, you're going to need some seed money to get you started. So, we're going to take care of that."

"Mr. and Mrs. Carlson, thank you," JR spoke for the group.

"You brought our son back to us in one piece—it's the least we can do," Vivian said, having lost the battle with her tears.

"Well, with all you've done, I hesitate to make one more request," JR said.

"Fire away," Mr. Carlson responded.

"Since Shoes won't know where he's going to settle until he and his wife figure that out and since Prince is heading east and doesn't know where he'll end up, it would be helpful to be able to keep track of each other. Would you mind if each of us keeps you informed about our whereabouts? That way, if we want to get in touch, we can start with you."

"Great idea, we'd be glad to do that. Just keep us posted."

They decided they would all depart when Shoes was ready to leave to meet his wife and son. Plans were made to get him along with JR, Arnie, and Trey to the bus station in Sioux Falls, where the three would also take a bus to the Bay Area. Prince reconsidered, but decided he would rather hitchhike than take the bus, but that the Sioux Falls bus station was as good a place as any to get started.

Saturday morning was emotional as everyone parted ways in phases. Hulk would have taken up too much room in his father's Ford pickup truck, so he and his mother said their goodbyes, shared hugs in the two-story foyer, and extended them to the front porch. Hulk could not help but walk his comrades to the truck. On the way, he pulled JR aside, put his huge arm around his shoulder and whispered, "I love you like a brother. If you ever need anything, you find me. If I ever need anything, I'll find you."

Reluctantly leaving the bear-like arms of his friend, JR forced himself to turn and walk to the truck. While the others were loading, JR reflected that every time he felt part of a family, it was taken from him in one way or another. This parting with Hulk and the Carlsons, while certainly less severe than losing his parents and losing Walter, was still painful. Hulk and he had been joined at the hip through the hell that was Vietnam and would be forever bonded by the risks they had taken together. Although he hoped it would not be the last time he saw his friend, JR was already feeling the depth of his loss.

Having packed the cab and the back of the pickup with bodies and duffle bags, Mr. Carlson and the five travelers made the 75-mile drive to the bus station in Sioux Falls. Everyone thanked Mr. Carlson, who returned to the truck for his drive home.

All but Prince bought their bus tickets; Shoes having to move fast to make it on board in time. He quickly said goodbye, then added, "You guys are saying goodbye to Shoes, but I'm getting off the bus and greeting my wife and son as Pat Richardson."

He turned and ran to his bus.

Prince was the next to depart, wanting to get as far down the road as possible during daylight. In a moment, he too was gone.

JR looked down at his bus ticket then up at his two traveling companions, "Arnie, Trey, we're going to Berkeley."

CHAPTER 50

I'M JR

December 8, 1966
Berkeley, California

Both before and after the draft card burning rally at Stanford and the bombing of the VDC office in Berkeley, Maggie and Bernie collaborated with others to look for more opportunities to get their message out. They helped organize and joined a march of several hundred to the Berkeley Draft Board, where the staff was presented with a black coffin as a mock gift and a number of students burned their draft cards. They joined a women-only march from the steps of Sproul Hall on the Berkeley campus to the Oakland Armed Services Induction Center, and they joined a sit-down protest around a Navy recruiter table in the Berkeley Student Union. When they resisted police action to break up the demonstration, Maggie and Bernie were taken into custody, but later released without being charged.

Although Bay Area protests, as well as those on campuses around the country, were primarily focused on disrupting the military recruiting and induction machinery, activists were also targeting the Dow Chemical Company. Dow had developed and was manufacturing napalm, a petroleum jelly that burned at over 2200 degrees and stuck to whatever or whoever it splashed on. Being used prolifically in Vietnam, napalm was killing both enemy combatants and innocent women and children in a horrific way, as well as, mistakenly, the occasional American soldier.

An interview with a local Vietnam veteran by a San Francisco news outlet served to further inflame those who had already detested Dow Chemical. The veteran described napalm and lauded its continued development by the company, "We sure were pleased with those backroom boys at Dow. The original product wasn't so hot - if the gooks were quick, they could scrape it off. So the boys started adding polystyrene - now it sticks like shit to a blanket. But then if the gooks jumped under water, it stopped burning, so they started adding Willie Peter, that's what we called white phosphorus, so's to make it burn better. It'll burn under water now. And just one drop is enough; it'll keep on burning right down to the bone so they die anyway from phosphorus poisoning."

Maggie and Bernie involved themselves with the Stanford Coalition for Peace in Vietnam, which led a protest at the Dow Plant in Torrance, 400 miles south. They supported the Women Strike for Peace, housewives who were arrested when trying to block napalm shipments out of San Jose. And as activists aimed frequent campus protests against Dow's on-campus recruiting, research, speaking, and investment practices, Maggie and Bernie were there.

It was a time of high energy and growing tension, both between antiwar and pro-war advocates and among the antiwar protestors themselves. The conversation about the extent to which they should resort to more aggressive and violent tactics continued unresolved. Was it ethical to fight violence with violence? Would doing so help or hurt the cause? How far should they go?

Hoping to ensure unity among all of the antiwar organizations and the broader support network, key leaders organized a meeting in Pauley Ballroom in the Berkeley Student Union to discuss plans for 1967, including the possibility of an all-out student strike. The flyer announcing the meeting stated, "Just as in 1964, the Free Speech Movement was incited by the power structure's attempt to crack down on the Civil Rights Movement, the present conflict stems from the continuing attempt to crush the antiwar movement in this country. The right of dissent is imperative to the continuance of opposition to American suppression of self-determination in Vietnam, and it is a fundamental right upon which any democratic enterprise must be based."

Expecting the issue to be on the table alongside that of the student strike, many feared the disagreement about violence would both disrupt the meeting and cause a rift in the fabric of the movement. The ballroom, which had been arranged with tightly-packed rows of folding chairs, was crammed, and it did not take long for the room to get hot and stuffy. The meeting was also heated, but orderly. Each speaker was given the reasonably respectful attention of those assembled.

Vietnam Day Committee leaders started the meeting by highlighting the continued refusal of the university administration to negotiate with the student groups and introduced the idea of organizing a student and faculty strike. SDS leaders followed, emphasizing the need for action and offering options about how the strike might work. Several professors added their perspective and support. Although there was no formal agenda, each speaker seemed to know when it was his or her turn.

Maggie and Bernie were sitting in the first row to the right the podium. When there was a brief gap during which no one was sure who was going to speak next, Bernie surprised Maggie by heading up the stairs to the stage and toward the microphone.

"My name is Bernie. I'm a former Berkeley student and have been working against the war across the country for several years. All we've done this evening is bemoan the current situation and suggest a tactic that is little different from what has been tried before with only minimal and local success. It's time to do something more dramatic to bring the war home. It's time to get more aggressive. It's time to show people here what it's like to live in fear in a village in Vietnam and what it's like to live in fear as a soldier trekking through the jungle.

"I know that you won't all agree that we need to be more violent—there, I said the word—so I'm not going to suggest we agree this evening. But if you want to talk more about it, I'll be in Sproul Plaza after the meeting."

There was a brief hush throughout the room, and then the meeting erupted into a spontaneous roar as everyone shouted out agreement or disagreement with Bernie, who had waited a moment for effect before making her way from the podium back to her seat.

As she was descending the stairs amidst the turmoil she had instigated, she was passed by a young man who had risen from mid-room during the outburst. He made his way to the front, climbed the stairs to the podium, politely nodding to Bernie on her way down, quietly faced the crowd, and stared. His demeanor calmed the room. Without saying a word, he had restored order. Everyone settled down and was leaning forward to hear from this person none of them knew.

"I didn't plan to speak this evening. I'm brand new to the antiwar movement, but my friends and I want to help. I decided to speak because of what Bernie just said. I'm JR, and my friends and I are Vietnam veterans."

Arnie and Trey sat agape when JR unexpectedly left them and headed for the front of the room. Although they were proud of him as he spoke both quietly and confidently, they were on high alert, eyes darting around the room hoping not to see authorities that could bring their short-lived Bay Area experience to an abrupt end.

JR continued, "We're here because of what we saw in Vietnam. Violence is a word that doesn't come close to describing seeing a friend bleeding to death from a neck wound. It doesn't come close to the feeling of shooting and killing another human being, even if they are called Viet Cong or Charlie or gook or enemy. It doesn't describe the fear on the faces of women and children and old men huddled in the center of their village, knowing that they may soon be killed and their homes set on fire. Violence doesn't describe our planes and helicopters dropping napalm and Agent Orange and bombs on villages and countryside. And it doesn't describe how one American can shoot another in the back simply for arguing with an order to kill innocent people."

JR stopped for a moment. The ballroom was dead silent, waiting for him to continue. Nobody else in that room other than JR, Arnie, and Trey had experienced the war firsthand.

"I don't know all of the reasons that Bernie argues for becoming more violent. I'm sure some of them are good reasons. But after experiencing violence or whatever word better describes what we saw in Vietnam, I know one thing. I can't support trying to stop violence with more violence.

"I've heard and read that the police have used force to break up peaceful protests. I've heard that protestors have been beaten with clubs, dragged down steps by their feet so their heads bang along the concrete, and assaulted with tear gas, fire hoses, and rubber bullets. Is that a justification for us being violent?

"There has to be a better way. We can't become violent to stop the violence in Vietnam and the violence of our police. Violence is the enemy. War is the enemy."

JR was done. He simply left the podium. When he was nearly back to his seat, the first clapping broke the silence and grew into a thunder of applause. Not everyone participated, as there were those who disagreed, but even they found themselves respecting the young man and what he stood for.

Two people in the crowd who were not applauding, but for different reasons, were Arnie Timlin and Maggie Blessings. When JR got back to his seat, Arnie yanked JR close to him, and in a loud whisper said, "JR, that was great, but are you out of your mind? Here we are at our first rally. We have no idea how this works. We have no idea if we're at risk of being recognized. And the first thing you do is get up in front of all these people and basically say, 'Here I am. Come get me.'"

"Oh shit, Arnie, you're right," JR whispered back. "I didn't really think. One minute, I'm in my chair, the next thing I know, I'm speaking. But, I gotta tell you. It felt pretty damn good up there."

"Well, let's hope for the best this time, my friend, but a little more thinking before acting would help," Arnie responded as he smiled and slapped JR on the back.

Maggie simply sat stunned. JR had evoked memories of Matt's letters. There was no doubt in her mind that JR had made the speech that her brother Matt would have made had he been able. Her eyes followed JR back to his seat. She knew that she needed to meet this young man and vowed to do it.

CHAPTER 51

ANY SUGGESTIONS?

December 8, 1966
Berkeley, California

The campus was dimly lit, but Bernie was easy to find on the steps of Sproul Hall. A small band had responded to her plea and gathered in the chilly evening to discuss whether and how to proceed with more aggressive antiwar tactics.

Maggie was also there, but she had no interest in anything violent, or for that matter and that moment, anything antiwar. She was there to meet JR. As the session in Pauley Ballroom was winding down, she had found her way to where JR was sitting, leaned across Trey, who was on the aisle, and said, "Excuse me. I'd like to talk to you. When this is over, could you meet me in Sproul Plaza?"

"Sure, be glad to. But, where is it and who are you?"

"Oh, sorry. I'm Maggie. I liked what you said tonight."

"Thanks. I'm JR."

"So you said."

"OK, so where are we meeting?"

By now, Trey had stood up to get out of the way, and Maggie was sitting next to JR.

"Exit out the back door," Maggie pointed, "look for the building with the columns and the steps. We'll be somewhere near the steps."

"Who's we?"

"Well, you met Bernie on the way up to the podium. I'm with her."

Hearing that, Trey, who was standing nearby, craned his neck to get another look at Bernie.

JR caught Trey's maneuver, smiled, and said to Maggie, "OK, but as you could tell, I wasn't really in favor of her violence speech."

"Actually, I'm not either. That's part of what I want to talk to you about."

"OK, see you there. By the way, this is Arnie and the guy who's trying to get a better view of your friend is Trey. We'll see you later."

Bernie was in heated conversation with the small group that surrounded her, when Maggie saw the trio coming toward her with their duffels in tow. JR and Arnie stopped in front of Maggie, but Trey made a beeline for Bernie.

"Now that it's a little quieter, let me reintroduce myself. I'm Maggie Blessings."

"JR."

"Do you have a last name?"

"No, just JR."

JR, Arnie, and Trey had decided to use only first names to minimize the risk of being identified. They had also thought through whether to assume new first names, but concluded it was complicated enough to remember not to use their nicknames.

"Well, just JR, good to meet you. And I think you said your name is Arnie."

"That's it," Arnie bowed at the waist with a gallant flourish of his arm.

Maggie appeared not to notice Arnie's gesture and returned her attention to JR, "For someone who just made a very moving speech, you don't say much."

"Well, to be quite honest, I'm really not sure who that guy was up there speaking. I had no intention of saying anything, but it just seemed like the right thing to do. Are you a student here?"

"No, Bernie and I came out here to be part of the protest movement. Things are happening all over the country, but this area is the center of the action. We've been out here about a year."

"Well, we think alike. Arnie, Trey, and I came here because we didn't really know how to get started and how we could help. We also chose Berkeley because of all the activity. When we got in the area, we kept our ears open. That's how we found out about the meeting."

"Where are you guys crashing?"

JR instinctively recoiled at the use of the word 'crash' and backed away. His confused expression prompted Maggie to rephrase, "Where are you staying?"

"Oh. Uh. We haven't really figured that out yet. We were hoping to find a cheap place until we knew what to do next. Any suggestions?"

CHAPTER 52

INSPIRATION

December 9, 1966
Berkeley, California

Maggie, JR, Arnie, and Jill were walking to get some breakfast near Jill's apartment, where the four had crashed the night before.

"Thanks for making room for us," Arnie said as he walked next to Jill on the sidewalk making small talk. "Have you been in this neighborhood long?"

"I found it when I was a student and fell in love with it. It's filled with active, caring folks, and there's always something going on. I work part time at a local bakery—in fact that's where we're heading. So, tell me more about your Vietnam experience."

Arnie was not quite ready for that and certainly did not want to get into details, so he kept it simple, "I was a medic."

"Really, that's great. You know, there's a drop-in clinic right around the corner that a friend of mine organized. It's staffed with doctors and nurses who volunteer their time when they can, but they're always short of help. I'll bet they could really use someone who has your training and experience."

For Arnie, the discussion had just turned from small talk to inspiration. "Great idea! Where's the clinic?"

"We're going to pass it on the next block. We could stop in on the way back from breakfast," Jill said, as the aroma of the bakery reached them before it was in sight.

"I'm in."

The previous evening, Maggie, JR, and Arnie had walked over to the periphery of Bernie's conclave. What they heard disturbed them.

BODY NOT RECOVERED

"So, what you're saying is that the best way to get people's attention is to take credit for a couple of bombings and use the platform to voice our demands."

"That's it," Bernie said to the tall bearded man standing across from her. "But let's be clear about this—we already know that we need to be careful about protecting our identity. A commitment to this path is a commitment to going fully underground. It won't just be local police on our asses but the FBI as well. Now, for me, I say fuck 'em. But if you're in, make sure you're all in."

"Do we need to decide now," asked a black woman who had progressively stepped closer to Bernie and was now face-to-face.

"No," Bernie said. "We still have a lot of planning to do—figuring out how to make and detonate bombs, finding the materials, and picking the best targets. And, I'm not looking to kill or hurt anyone. So, we need to figure out how and when to do the bombings so only buildings suffer.

"If you're interested in even considering this, let me know now, but until we make a move, you can always back out—assuming you're willing to keep your fucking mouths shut."

Five of those assembled drew closer to Bernie as the black women relinquished her space. Trey had worked his way to be closest to Bernie, who had vetted him earlier when he stepped into the group and she asked, "Who the fuck are you?"

"I'm a Vietnam vet, and I came here with them," Trey had responded while pointing to JR and Arnie.

Bernie thanked everyone, "I'll be in touch."

The group disbanded leaving Maggie, JR, Arnie, Bernie, and Trey alone on the steps of Sproul Hall. Maggie introduced JR and Arnie to Bernie, "You already know Trey apparently."

"Yeah, he appears to be my new best friend," Bernie said as she sidled up more closely to Trey and put her arm around his waist.

Trey smiled and returned the gesture.

"We were just talking about finding a place for these guys to crash," Maggie said.

"Mags, I think I know where Trey and I are going to be tonight. You can take JR and Arnie back to Jill's place. I'm sure she won't mind."

Before anyone had a chance to confirm arrangements or bring up the bombing discussion, Bernie and Trey, still joined at the hip, were walking across the plaza inadvertently doing their Jimmy Durante impersonation, being visible from lamppost to lamppost.

"Well," Maggie said as she smiled sheepishly, "I guess you guys are with me."

Bernie was right—Jill did not mind. Separate corners of the small apartment were divvied up and bedding was improvised, and the four spent a little time getting to know each other before deciding to get some sleep and talk more in the morning.

After coffee and a muffin at the bakery, Arnie announced, "Well, I'd love to stay here surrounded by these smells and have another one of those melt-in-your-mouth muffins, but I'd really like to see that clinic. Is this a good time?"

"Sure, let's go now. I volunteer as a receptionist a couple of days a week for a few hours. Today's one of my days, but I'm not scheduled until noon. We can go early, and I'll show you around and introduce you to the director. She can help you figure out if you want to get involved."

"While you two are at the clinic, JR and I are going to the park to talk," Maggie said without consulting him.

CHAPTER 53

BROTHER AND SISTER

December 9, 1966
Berkeley, California

Maggie grabbed JR's hand to get him started on the two-block walk, then released it as he got in step with her. A few minutes later, they entered the small urban park nestled among three-story apartment buildings, found a bench in the warming late morning sun, and settled in.

"I thought what you said last night was courageous. It must have been awful in Vietnam. Do you mind talking about it," Maggie asked meekly, not knowing JR well enough to anticipate his willingness.

"You probably don't want to hear all of the details, but I don't mind talking about it. Telling the truth about the war seems like one way to get people to oppose it. You know, when I decided that I wanted to help protest the war, I had no idea what that meant or how to proceed, but getting up last night just felt like the natural thing to do."

"Well, I love Bernie, but she can certainly be overwhelming. You just followed her up there and said what you thought. That was great."

"Thanks. So, you said you and Bernie came out here to get involved. From where?"

"Took us awhile, but we came from Washington, DC."

"Is that where you're from?"

"JR, that question is why I came back to talk to you last night. Since meeting you, I've been struggling with how much to tell you. And I've decided that I want to tell you everything. For some reason I can't understand yet, I trust you and want you to know."

BROTHER AND SISTER

JR did not respond but merely waited for Maggie to go on.

Before she had fallen asleep the previous night, Maggie had decided to tell him about her family, about Matt, about the letters, about everything. But even having made the decision, it was difficult to get started. Taking a deep breath and following her instincts, Maggie looked into JR's eyes, felt a calm come over her, and told him the whole story up to when he had stepped up to the podium the night before; only leaving out her more intimate relationship with Bernie.

Then she said, "I found you last night after you spoke, because for the first time in over a year, I felt like there was someone I could talk to like I was talking to Matt. And someone I could talk to who would know what Matt went through to help me understand. I think that someone is you."

JR reached out and took Maggie's hand in his. "Mags...I hope you don't mind if I call you that...I do know what Matt was trying to tell you when he wrote that he was scared and that he hated what he was being asked to do. That's exactly why I'm here; trying to help make sure others don't have to deal with all of that and other families don't have to lose someone."

Maggie pulled her hand out of JR's and then scooted forward to put her arms around him. It was clear to each of them that this was not a romantic hug, but one of a brother and sister reuniting after being apart much too long. Maggie had lost a brother; JR had never had a sibling. As only a long-lost brother and sister could, they had immediately bonded.

"JR," Maggie said hesitantly after a few moments, "tell me about Vietnam."

"Are you sure?"

"Yes, I need to hear it for two reasons. One reason is Matt, and the other reason is you. I want to know what you've been through."

"OK, Mags, I'll tell you, but I'd prefer that my story, like yours, is just between the two of us."

She nodded and waited.

JR had thought about this moment—what would he say to people who asked him about his past? He knew he would tell Karen and Mary Rawlings the whole story if and when he saw them again,

233

but they were a special case. He knew instinctively that Maggie was different than most people, but should he tell her everything? He decided to start and see where his gut took him.

JR then told her his story from enlisting to leaving Vietnam. Although he did mention losing his folks, that was the only pre-enlistment part of his life he revealed. And he made no mention of how he left Vietnam, leaving it to Maggie to assume that it was a normal military discharge. "Would he ever tell her more," he wondered to himself. Time would tell.

After JR had shared his experiences with Maggie, they hugged again, and he asked her for more details about the antiwar movement and how he might help. They were just getting into it when they saw Arnie walking their way, his face in full grin.

"What are you so happy about, Doc?"

The grin disappeared as Arnie glared at JR, who had immediately caught his error.

"Sorry, Arnie."

But the grin returned, "OK, JR, let's put it this way—either Arnie or Doc works for me."

"Why the change?"

"I just spent the last hour at Jill's clinic. They do great work. Lots of locals either can't afford medical care or they're too far from a hospital. The clinic fills both needs. Jill introduced me to the director. Believe it or not, she's been looking for a part time employee with my skills. So, I told her, 'Yes.'

"Jill's really excited and says I can stay at her place as long as I like. But she's not as excited as I am. I can really make a difference here.

"Oh, I'm not backing off of the antiwar work. I'm sure Jill and you will make sure that doesn't happen. But this is something I really want to do. Who knows, maybe it will become full time work."

"Arnie, how did you handle the paperwork," JR asked, referring to the fact that officially, Arnie was dead and any documentation he completed would put him and the others in jeopardy.

"That's another good part. I'm not sure why, but there wasn't any. If there was, I would have probably just volunteered."

JR realized they were having this conversation in front of Maggie, who definitely looked perplexed.

"Mags, nothing to worry about. There was a mix-up in Arnie's discharge paperwork, so it's a little confusing."

He did not feel good about lying to Maggie, but upon reflection, maybe he was not really lying. Arnie's discharge paperwork was mixed up, because he was not discharged—and to say the least, in that regard, things were confusing.

"So anyway, JR, I'm back in the medic business. You can call me Doc."

CHAPTER 54

DEAR KAREN

December 11, 1966
Berkeley, California

Dear Karen,

First of all, I am so sorry that I couldn't contact you before to let you know that I'm alive and OK. I know that you heard that I had died in Vietnam, but as you can see, I didn't. I wish you didn't have to go through that, but I had no choice. I ask that you please only tell your mom, OD, and Not So. I ask you to not even tell Walter, Jr. I hope you can understand.

I'm safe. I'm in the United States, and I'm getting involved in the antiwar movement. As you can probably figure out, if the government finds out I'm alive and where I am, I'd be in big trouble. I need to be very careful. I don't know how all of this will play out, but I had to do it. Hopefully, someday soon, I can explain to you in person.

I think about you and your mom all the time. Although we haven't been in touch much and although I've put you through another round of grief, I want you to know that I still think of you both as family. As soon as I can be more certain about things, I will call and try to make plans to come to St. Louis to see you.

I wish I could let you know how to get in touch with me, but I just can't. Please trust me. Please believe in me. I will get in touch as soon as I can.

With Much Love,

JR

CHAPTER 55

I REALLY MISS HIM

December 15, 1966
St. Louis, Missouri

Mary and Karen sat at the dining room table side-by-side and hand-in-hand. They read JR's letter out loud for the fourth time and continued to sob, which started when Karen opened the envelope and came running to her mom. Mary released Karen's hand, rose slowly, walked to the bureau drawer in her bedroom, and retrieved the newspaper article, which she brought back to Karen.

The *St. Louis Post-Dispatch* report of JR's death had been devastating. They had grieved privately, consoled only by their friends, OD and Not So. And they had been grieving for nearly two months, carrying the additional burden of knowing how Walter would have felt had he been alive to hear the news.

Mary handed the newspaper clipping to Karen, who ceremoniously balled it up and threw it in the trash.

"Mom, I want to be mad at him for what he put us through, but I just can't. I really miss him."

"I know you do. I do too."

"Mom, we both miss him like that," Karen said, allowing a small smile and a twinkle in her eye to shine through the tears, "but I miss him in a special way."

"I know that too. Hopefully, someday you'll be able to tell him."

"Mom, I also wish I could tell him that Walter Jr. would understand."

"At some point, I hope we can get both of our boys together."

CHAPTER 56

BIG PROBLEM

February 3, 1967
Mitchell, South Dakota

"Dad, I think I have a big problem. In fact, I think we have a big problem," Hulk said with emphasis on the word "we."

Hulk and his father were sitting together, warmed by their morning coffee, by the heat emanating from the fireplace, and by the comfort of looking at the rolling hills of South Dakota out of the ceiling-high windows that filled the south side of the ranch's great room.

"What's wrong, son?"

"Well, I was going to tell you last night, but needed to think about it some. You know I've been trying to figure out what I'm going to do. I can't just sit around here anymore. There's a lot of open space, but I'm getting cabin fever and I need to set a direction for my life.

"So, yesterday afternoon, I took the truck to get some air and think about things. After driving around for awhile, I got antsy and...I know it was wrong...but I headed for town. I just needed a change of scenery, but it turned out to be a mistake."

"You're right—bad idea. What happened?"

"I was driving down Main Street, coming up on the Corn Palace, and feeling pretty good about being in town. I knew enough to have my hat and sunglasses on and to keep my head down, but then I had to stop at a red light. Of all the people to be walking by—it was Mr. Jennings."

"You've got to be shitting me!"

Charlie Jennings owned the land adjacent to the Carlson ranch and was one of the members of the local draft board who made certain that John Carlson's boy received no special treatment. In fact, he helped make sure that the big kid was at the top of the draft list. There was no love lost between Charlie Jennings and John Carlson.

"Did he see you or didn't he?"

"I think he did, but as soon as I saw him, I tilted my face away and couldn't see if he recognized me. But based on where he was, it would have been hard for him not to. I'm pretty recognizable, and he likely knows our truck."

"Since you thought about it last night, what do you suggest?"

"Dad, there's two problems here. One is that if I'm recognized and caught, I'm heading for prison. And if I do, problem two is that Mom and you are also in trouble for...what do they call it...harboring a fugitive. So, I think the only answer is that I have to get out of here. And, to be quite honest, I was about ready to do that anyway."

"We knew you were getting close. Your mother and I have been talking about it."

Resisting his natural tendency to take charge and solve his son's problem, Carlson simply stopped talking and waited for Hulk to continue.

"Well, as I see it, I have a few options. One is to stay here and help around the ranch—that used to seem a real choice, but not anymore—and maybe never was. Another is to head for the Bay Area and join up with JR and the others doing the antiwar thing. I could head for Canada and just start all over until this dies down. Maybe I could settle someplace near James, but I don't want to put him at risk. Or I could throw a dart at the map and start over wherever in the country it hits. You probably know that my preference would be to head for Berkeley."

"We haven't been in touch with those guys since they left except for the letter we got from JR letting us know they were OK and how to contact them if need be. What do you think, Dad? Any ideas on how I should decide?"

"First of all, you know we'll certainly miss you, but you're right, it seems like it's time. Jennings is only part of the problem. We all know you can't spend the rest of your life cooped up here. But there's one option you haven't mentioned that I think should be on the table. And to be honest, I'm surprised you haven't considered it."

"What's that?"

"Bangkok."

Hulk was stunned, not because of his father's suggestion, but because he had not thought of it himself. After a bit of recovery time, Hulk said, "You're absolutely right. I have no idea why I didn't think of Bangkok. I'm comfortable there; I have the Jattawans to help me get started; and I really think of Annan as a friend.

"Every one of my options has big issues attached, but the one that comes to mind about Bangkok is how to get my passport and other paperwork managed given that I'm supposed to be dead."

John Carlson smiled and said, "William Carlson, what do you think fathers are for?"

"Thanks, Dad. Let me think about this through the day, and I'll let you know by dinnertime. I think we'll need to act fast. Can we?"

"I'll make some calls today assuming you decide that's what you want to do."

"One more question. You think Mom would be OK with me going that far?"

"As she and I have talked about it, she knows you'd be happy there, and your happiness is foremost on her list of priorities."

"I love you both."

That evening at dinner, Hulk jumped right to the point, "Mom, Dad, I'm going to Bangkok."

"I've almost got all of the arrangements made. And I think you should be ready to leave first thing in the morning. I got a call from Charlie Jennings this afternoon. He wants to talk to me. The last time he called, it was to let me know that there was no way I would be influencing the draft board. So, I can't imagine this one is just a courtesy call."

John Carlson's face transitioned from anger and concern to glee, "It'll be a pleasure when I talk to him tomorrow and tell him how offensive it is for him to be inquiring about our dead son."

BIG PROBLEM

Over the next several hours, Hulk's father made a few more calls. Hulk packed and got a full set of instructions, said his goodbyes to his mother, and prepared to begin his journey back to Southeast Asia.

Before he went to sleep, he asked for one more favor, "Dad, would you please get in touch with JR and let him know?"

"Sure son, good night."

CHAPTER 57

WE'LL SEE

February 6, 1967
St. Louis, Missouri

JR sat with Mary and Karen Rawlings, huddled together on the sofa, reliving the pain of two deaths and celebrating one resurrection.

Immediately after writing Karen in December, JR had begun to plan his trip to St. Louis, dealing with two major concerns. First and foremost, would the Rawlings ever forgive him for putting them through another period of grief? Secondly, how could he ensure that he would not be recognized in his home town?

There was nothing he could do about the first concern but confront it. And if he could get Not So to pick him up at the downtown bus station and go straight to the Rawlings's home, there should not be a problem being recognized by anyone he did not want to see.

It had been relatively easy to write the letter to Karen. It was much more difficult for JR to pick up the phone and call her to make plans to visit. He knew he had put her and her mother through so much pain. There was no way to get around that, and he needed to see them. With the clicking of each number dialed, he almost set the phone back in its cradle, but JR stayed the course.

"Hello."

"Karen?"

"Oh my god. JR. Are you OK? I can't believe it. When I got your letter..."

Karen broke down and could not continue.

JR immediately picked up the conversation to give her a moment, "Karen, I'm so sorry, but it was the only way I could think of to get out of Vietnam and get back to the states to see what I could

242

do to help end this terrible war. My only regret is not having been able to contact you beforehand."

"JR," Karen had calmed somewhat, "I understand. When are you coming home?"

"That's what I'm calling about. I'll only be coming for a visit, but we can figure everything else out from there. I'm coming to celebrate your birthday."

JR laid out his plans. Karen said she would make sure that Mitch was at the bus station.

"Mitch?"

Karen understood the question, "Ever since Dad died, they decided that Not So and OD were no longer appropriate. So, it's Mitch and Oliver."

"Tell them I can't wait to see them. And especially tell your mom."

"She's not going to be happy that she missed your call. She's at church. She spends a lot of time there."

With his head down to reduce the risk of being recognized, JR's transition from the bus through the St. Louis station and to Mitch's car went well. Twenty minutes and a non-stop discussion later, Mitch had dropped JR off at the Rawlings house. It was a bitterly cold and windy day, so none of the neighbors were out to see the arrival. Knowing JR, Mary, and Karen needed time alone, Mitch said he would get Oliver and be back for dinner. A hug later, Mitch was gone and JR was at the front door.

Hugs, kisses, and tears moved Mary, Karen, and him en masse from the door to the sofa. When they were able to talk, JR pointed at Karen, and said, "You first."

She explained about her passionate commitment to become a nurse, "Even though they couldn't save Dad, I was moved by the care and caring he got. That's what I want to do for others."

She told him of trying unsuccessfully to get into the Barnes Hospital School of Nursing, but was admitted to the school at Homer G. Phillips Hospital, which had always admitted blacks. Karen was also working part time as a receptionist in a doctor's office. "I'm definitely committed to the medical profession," she said proudly.

BODY NOT RECOVERED

JR, sitting between Mary and Karen on the couch, found himself unable to take his eyes off of Karen as she spoke and sensed his hand had melted into hers. He felt both the warmth of her skin and the warmth of her being. It was becoming clearer to him that she was more than just Walter's daughter and a friend.

"Karen's so busy with work and school that she's had no time for dating."

"Mom," Karen whined the word and winced at the implication of Mary's comment. "Well, I am actually pretty busy, but I get out with friends every once in awhile."

Mary put her hand on JR's shoulder. "What do you want to tell us?"

He had anticipated this moment and had thought about it on the long bus ride from California, during which he convinced himself that he could and would trust the Rawlings—he needed to tell them the whole story. They deserved to know, and he yearned to get it all out to someone he cared about—yes, someone he loved.

"This is going to take awhile," JR began.

When JR had brought them right up to the moment, Mary said, "Thank you, JR, for two reasons. One, I know that was difficult to live through and to tell, but we needed to know. And two, when Walter Jr. got home, he wouldn't tell us one thing about Vietnam. He just didn't want to talk about it.

"We certainly didn't push him either. He just moped around the house and then tried to find a job, but really didn't have his heart in it. And he had a hard time sleeping. I think it was a combination of the war and missing his dad.

"He was here for a couple of months and announced one day that he was going to visit a cousin in Chicago, where he decided to stay. We hear from him, and he says he's working and doing OK, but I'm not so sure."

"I wish he'd come home," Karen added. "He said he'd be here for my birthday, but then said he couldn't make it. I might just head to Chicago soon and really see how he's doing for myself."

They sat silently for a few moments before Mary said, "Well, I better start dinner."

"We'll help, mom."

"No, you two visit, I'll be fine."

When Mary had hugged each of them and gone to the kitchen, JR and Karen were left in an awkward silence, until Karen placed her free hand on JR's cheek, "I've really missed you, and when I heard you were..."

JR stopped her by placing his index finger on her lips and even surprised himself when he blurted out, "Come back to California with me."

For the first time in a couple of hours, Karen's hand released JR's and she pulled her other hand from his cheek. She needed both of her arms to wrap around JR; her face snuggled into the side of his neck, which she then gently kissed. Karen then pulled her head up to face him, and moved the kiss to his lips. With his arms tightly wrapped around her as well, they held the kiss.

"I hope you know that I'd love to go with you, but I don't think I should. I've worked hard on my nursing degree, and I'm so close to finishing. Let's make the most of your visit and phone as much as we can. I could come visit; you could come back. Once I have my degree, we'll see. What do you think?"

"I didn't plan to ask you to come with me. It just came out, but I really mean it. I want you to be happy. So, OK, we'll see."

"I'm so glad you're here."

"So am I."

CHAPTER 58

AURA

February 9, 1967
St. Louis, Missouri

Mary had planned a small celebration for Karen's birthday with JR, Mitch, and Oliver. There would be a larger party for her at church for neighbors, family, and friends, but Mary was helping JR minimize the risk of being recognized.

"It's hard to believe our little girl is 20 today. Before Mitch and Oliver get here, I just want to say," Mary hesitated briefly and looked at her daughter, "your father is here today celebrating with us. He loved you so much."

"And I loved him, Mom. I still do."

JR's visit had passed quickly but had been eventful and was about to become even more so. At dinner on the evening he had arrived, JR warmed in the glow of those he now considered family. They rejoiced in being together, and they remembered the loss of their friend, husband, and father.

About an hour into a wonderful dinner, Oliver said to JR, "You know a commitment made should be a commitment kept."

Although Oliver had not heard JR's whole story, he had gotten the gist of it, or at least figured he had. Since no one responded to what he said, he continued, "I can only imagine how difficult it was over there, and I've talked to others who came back. But it's tough for everyone who enters any struggle. Tough doesn't mean quit.

"Others stuck it out. Walter Jr. stuck it out. You didn't. But I think you should have. For your own good. If you make a commitment and don't keep it, it's easier not to keep the next one."

"Oliver, this isn't the time or place..." Mary began with a chiding tone, but JR interrupted her.

"Pardon me, Mary, but it is the time and place. When Walter used to tell me things about myself, they weren't always easy to hear, but I needed to hear them."

JR turned his attention back to Oliver and continued, "OD...uh... Oliver, I understand what you're saying, and thank you for saying it. It sounds exactly like something Walter would've said. I can't tell you how difficult the decision was for me to do what I did. I could hear Walter in my head the whole time. When I finally decided, one of the things I considered was whether I could've explained to him what I was going to do. When I convinced myself that I could have—when I knew what was in my heart to do, I knew it was right.

"But I can tell you, Oliver, I'll take to heart what you said. Thank you. I'll make sure that a commitment made is a commitment kept."

Oliver stared at JR for a moment, contemplating what JR had said, "I gotta tell you, that first day Walter asked you to join us for lunch, I thought he was nuts. Young, puny white boy. What was he thinking? But like most things, he knew exactly what he was doing. You've grown up a lot since then, JR. Oh, and you weren't bad to start with. Walter could sure judge people."

"Then why the hell did he have you as a friend," Mitch asked while laughing and slapping Oliver on the back.

"Good question," Oliver laughed and slapped back.

JR would see Oliver and Mitch off and on over the next couple of days, but he spent most of his time with Mary and Karen, who had asked for some time off from work and minimized studying to be with JR. Mary went to church each day and on the day before Karen's birthday, left early, "I'll be back after lunch—I'm helping at the food pantry all morning."

When she was gone, Karen, still in her pajamas, walked up to JR, put her arms around his neck, and kissed him deeply. Then without saying anything, she took his hand and guided him to her bedroom. In the Bay Area, JR had been living in an environment of free love and had plenty of opportunities, but he had chosen to abstain. He found himself sufficiently satisfied living with Maggie's deep friendship, his dedication to the movement, and his thoughts of Karen.

The next two hours with Karen felt so natural, and JR found himself bonded to her both physically and emotionally. Although she may not be coming back to California with him for now, he knew that somehow, somewhere, sometime, they would be together.

The big problem was hiding the aura that now engulfed them both from Mary and the others.

When Mary came home, she came into the kitchen where JR and Karen were eating lunch. "Did you have a good morning?"

"Yes, mom," Karen said rather stiffly, "did you?"

Mary simply said, "Yes," and began working on the arrangements for Karen's birthday dinner for the following evening. While JR was relieved, Karen suspected her mother knew, but neither would speak of it.

Karen's birthday had arrived, and Mitch and Oliver were expected soon to help celebrate. Mary was scurrying around making last-minute preparations. JR and Karen were helping as best they could; mostly by staying out of the way.

Exactly on time, there was a knock on the door. Mary, closest to the door, went to greet Mitch and Oliver.

"Hi, Mom."

Mary's knees buckled at the sight of her son, and Karen screamed from across the room and flew into Walter Jr.'s arms.

"Happy birthday, sis."

In an instant, Walter Jr.'s expression turned from glee to hatred and he was across the room in JR's face, "What the hell are you doing here?"

CHAPTER 50

NEXT TIME

February 9, 1967
Palo Alto, California

Despite his growing leadership role in the Bay Area antiwar movement, JR's absence did not dissuade Maggie and others from acting on their own. They had learned from Berkeley SDS leadership that Vice-President Hubert Humphrey would be speaking at Stanford University later in the month and joined a meeting in Palo Alto to plan a demonstration. Bernie and Trey chose not to go, having little interest in anything that would be no more than a peaceful rally. Joining others, Maggie, Doc, and Jill made the one-hour trip from Berkeley.

When the meeting at Stanford had finished and plans made, the Berkeley contingent took advantage of the sunny day to walk around campus. Jill saw a sign that read "Campus Police" and headed that way. "Let's go check out the local rent-a-cops."

As they approached the police building, the group heard Maggie say out loud but mostly to herself, "Beautiful campus—when the war is over, I'm going to be looking for a school. Wouldn't be bad going here."

Just as Maggie had finished her musing, a tall clean-cut young man exited the police offices not more than 20 feet from her, stopped, and stared—a look of recognition on his face.

Mooch knew he had seen the redhead before, but could not place her. Still staring and feeling the urge to approach the girl, her group moved on. As he was about to turn away to head to class, he noticed the girl look back at him, seemingly recognizing him as well, but she broke eye contact and kept walking.

"I've seen that guy somewhere before, Doc," Maggie said as they walked shoulder to shoulder. "I just can't place him."

Doc grinned, gave Maggie a playful elbow in the side, and said, "Good looking guy—maybe next time you see him, you'll say something."

CHAPTER 60

YOU DESERVE IT

February 9, 1967
St. Louis, Missouri

"You deserted, you bastard, you deserted!"

"Walter, leave him alone," Karen was pleading with her brother as she tried pulling him away from JR.

Mitch and Oliver, who had been excited about being part of the birthday surprise and had stood back while Walter Jr. greeted his family, raced into the room to help Karen separate the two young men.

"You left them there to die! You left your buddies there to die! You're a deserter, and now you're going to die for this, you white bastard," Walter Jr. screamed.

"Walter, what are you talking about," Karen pleaded, searching for both answers and peace and being both angry and perplexed.

"Karen, didn't you know," Walter Jr. had a sneer on his face and a know-it-all tone in his voice, "the penalty for desertion is death. You don't think I considered deserting? You don't think most guys do? There's two things that kept us from doing it. You can be sure it wasn't some noble belief in the war—we didn't give a shit about that. It was the threat of the death penalty, and it was the disgrace of leaving your buddies behind. Neither of them seemed to matter to your friend here."

"They mattered—both of them did," JR finally spoke.

His calmness brought the tension in the room down a couple of notches, but not enough to keep Walter Jr. from firing back, "If they mattered, what the hell are you doing here?"

BODY NOT RECOVERED

"You think I didn't think about both of those? I did, but the horror of what I was being ordered to do and who I was being told to become was worse. We could have gone to Sweden—did you know they take in military deserters? We could have gone to Canada. But no; we decided to come back here to fight the war in another way. I decided to take the risk."

JR then took two steps toward Walter, who was still being held by Mitch and Oliver, stood erect as if at attention, and said, "So Walter, what are you doing about the war? You said you thought about deserting, that everybody does. Well, if you thought about it, then there was something about Vietnam that made you want to get out. If it was that bad, what are you doing to stop it? Don't take your frustration out on me. Live with it or do something about it."

Walter Jr. wriggled his right arm free enough to take a swing at JR, but he missed and Mitch and Oliver regained control.

JR went on as though the swing never happened, "And one more thing. Your father used to tell me about the holocaust, when Hitler killed all the Jews in Europe. He also told me about Nuremberg. Do you know what that is? Well, it's where the Nazis were on trial for all they did. The Nazis claimed they were just following orders, but they were found guilty anyway. Do you know why?

"It was decided that even if ordered to do something, we each have a responsibility to make moral choices. Was killing innocent women and children in a village moral? Was killing a 14 year old in the bush moral, even if he was shooting at you? Was losing friends taking a hill and then giving the hill up the next day moral? Was dropping napalm on anyone, enemy or innocent, moral?

"I went to Vietnam because I thought we were fighting to keep people from being oppressed. Your father taught me to do what was in my heart to do. When I got there, I realized that in many ways, we were the oppressors, and dammit, that's not what I signed up for. Was that what you signed up for?"

Since first being controlled by Mitch and Oliver, Walter Jr. had furiously resisted their grasp. Now, after listening to JR instead of holding Walter Jr. back, Mitch and Oliver were holding him up. His body had gone slack. He shuddered and for the first time since coming home from Vietnam, Walther Jr. broke down and sobbed, realizing that JR had said what he had been feeling, but could not put into words.

When Walter Jr. had regained some composure, he nodded to Mitch and Oliver, who instinctively knew it was safe to release him, and walked slowly to JR. The two young men were different in so many ways, but they had also shared the same profound experiences and realized they were much more alike than different. Walter Jr. reached out a hand, but JR did not take it. Instead, he took one more step and put his arms around Walter Jr., who returned the hug.

Walter Jr. stepped away, nodded knowingly to JR and walked over to his sister. "I'm sorry Karen. I ruined your birthday."

"Welcome home, big brother," Karen said, gently wiping the remnants of tears from Walter Jr.'s cheeks. "I love you."

He hugged and kissed his sister and went to his mother. "Mom, I'd like to stay for awhile, if you don't mind."

Mary could not speak, but her embrace gave Walter Jr. the answer he was hoping for.

"So, I thought this was supposed to be a birthday party, and I'm starving."

"Thanks, Oliver," Mary said, smiling. "You always seem to know how to get a party started. Dinner is served."

Karen took JR by one hand and Walter Jr. by the other and walked them to the dinner table. When they were out of hearing range of the others, Walter Jr. leaned over between JR and Karen and whispered, "Well, now that that's all resolved, I guess I'll be sleeping downstairs in the basement where you've probably been staying, JR. And based on the look in my sister's eyes, maybe you could move into Karen's room with her."

Karen gasped and gave her brother a knowing, yet both solid and playful jab to the upper arm. The three shared a laugh and refused to tell the others what the joke was.

After Mitch led grace and before the birthday meal began, JR, still holding Karen's hand, said, "Now that I know this family is in good hands," nodding at Walter, Jr., "I think it's time for me to get back to California. But, you've not seen the last of me. We'll keep in touch and I'll try to visit soon. But for now, happiest of birthdays, Karen, you deserve it."

CHAPTER 61

COLUMBIA

August 17, 1967
New York City, New York

During his first week at Columbia Law School, Mooch walked into his faculty advisor's office, introduced himself, and said, "What do I need to do to get my degree in two years?"

Just a few weeks earlier, he was at the end of his third summer session at Stanford, finishing the course requirements that would complete his three-year Bachelor's in Political Science. He would have just enough time to say his few good-byes, pack, drive cross-country to New York in the 1957 Chevy his father had given him as a Christmas gift the previous year, find a place to live, and begin the fall semester at Columbia.

Despite his personal commitment to steer clear of the increasingly frequent student demonstrations at Stanford, Mooch had remained curious and continued to seek out campus activists. He would leave Stanford with a degree and a growing sensitivity to the antiwar and civil rights movements.

Mooch had been especially influenced by several long conversations with Stanford student body president, David Harris, who had been elected on a platform that included demands for the university to end its cooperation with the war effort. During one meeting, Harris gave Mooch a copy of the text of Martin Luther King's "Beyond Vietnam" speech that King had delivered in April at the Riverside Church in New York City.

In part it read, "Perhaps a more tragic recognition of reality took place when it became clear to me that the war was doing far more than devastating the hopes of the poor at home. It was sending their sons and their brothers and their husbands to fight

254

and to die in extraordinarily high proportions relative to the rest of the population. We were taking the black young men who had been crippled by our society and sending them eight thousand miles away to guarantee liberties in Southeast Asia which they had not found in Southwest Georgia and East Harlem. So we have been repeatedly faced with the cruel irony of watching Negro and white boys on TV screens as they kill and die together for a nation that has been unable to seat them together in the same schools. So we watch them in brutal solidarity burning the huts of a poor village, but we realize that they would hardly live on the same block in Chicago. I could not be silent in the face of such cruel manipulation of the poor."

Mooch reread the entire speech from time to time and was moved by its passion and logic as well as its continued commitment to non-violence. Upon reflection, Mooch realized there had been something bothering him about what he was hearing from some activists—a growing belief that violence would be necessary to make their point. Mooch's deep-seated respect for the law disallowed his support of protests, regardless of the justice of the cause, if they were destined and, perhaps, even designed for violence.

Mooch's attention to antiwar and civil rights matters waned somewhat later in his Stanford tenure, as he dedicated every bit of extra energy and time he had to studying for his Law School Admission Test. His efforts paid off. Mooch scored 173 of a possible 180, which along with his 3.975 GPA and strong references from Political Science Department Chairman Almond, Special Agent Marcus, and Chief Davis, locked him into acceptance to Columbia University School of Law, his first choice.

His application to Columbia had also required an essay, a personal statement of how attending the university fit into his life plans. Writing the essay flowed easily, as Mooch detailed how Columbia suited his long-sought path to the FBI and explained why he wanted to be an agent. Since his first meeting with Paul Marcus, Mooch had been refining his answer to that question.

Included in his essay was, "A career in the FBI would fulfill my desire to make a positive difference in the lives of victims, perpetrators, and society in general. I am convinced that this is my motivation—what is in my heart to do."

After hearing Mooch's question about finishing his law degree in two years, the faculty advisor maintained his stoic expression and replied, "Mr. Muccelli, you can't complete a law degree in two years. It's a three-year curriculum."

"How about two and a half years?"

"You can't. It's a three-year curriculum."

Throughout his first months at Columbia, he searched for a way to get around the system, but to no avail. Frustrated but undeterred, Mooch decided to spend the energy he would have spent on another accelerated degree on getting a head start toward getting a job with the FBI.

CHAPTER 62

FETAL POSITION

October 16, 1967
Oakland, California

The long-planned Stop-the-Draft-Week demonstration was underway. Organizers, JR and Maggie among them, were in front of the protestors, who were poised to march on the Oakland Armed Services Induction Center. JR's command of the Pauley Ballroom had drawn attention, and shortly thereafter, he and Maggie, who were now inseparable, found themselves not only active, but accepted into the elite circle of protest organizers.

"Maggie, before this gets started, look around at who's here," JR said as he scanned the gathering of nearly 3000 demonstrators amassed at one end of Clay Street in downtown Oakland.

"What am I looking for?"

"Just months ago, this demonstration would've been mostly students and mostly white. But now we've got businessmen, gray-hairs, black men and women. We're making progress."

JR was speaking from growing experience in the movement. Since meeting, he and Maggie had been deeply involved in Bay Area activities. They had joined 30,000 others at the "human be-in" in Golden Gate Park.

They had played a minor role in organizing a march in San Francisco from Second and Market Streets to Kezar Stadium. An estimated 100,000 marched, filled the venue, and roared in response to Vietnam veteran, decorated Green Beret, antiwar activist, and keynote speaker Donald Duncan, who said, among other things, "Protestors are the best friends the soldiers in Vietnam have."

Later in the year, the antiwar movement was bolstered when 600 faculty members at California colleges and universities signed a "declaration of conscience," pledging "full and active support" to "all who determined that they will not participate in this war."

On this day in Oakland, JR and Maggie were without their close friends. Doc and Jill were working at the clinic and Bernie and Trey had chosen not to participate, becoming increasingly frustrated with demonstrations and marches in lieu of what they believed should be more aggressive action.

The plan for the Stop-the-Draft-Week protest was to have a contingent large enough to bring the work of the induction center to a halt. The size of the rally grew after people learned they would be joined by human rights and peace activist Joan Baez.

The marchers reached the induction center, sat down in the doorway, overflowed into the street, and forced inductees to climb over them to enter the building. As the inductees were doing so, protestors handed them antiwar leaflets and chided them to refuse induction and join the protest. To further their point, some protestors burned their draft cards and held them in the faces of the inductees.

Clay Street looked like a parade route, as the police followed the protestors. Fully aware of and prepared for the demonstration, police with nightsticks, white helmets, and face shields marched five abreast and ten deep toward the protest. Other officers lined the street to keep pro-war demonstrators from entering the fray and bystanders safely separated from the anticipated melee. Motorcycle police followed to help control what they believed would likely become a major confrontation. Two buses brought up the rear of the police echelon, each filled with reinforcements and rigged to help collect those arrested. Behind those were six more buses filled with inductees. Paddy wagons had been prepositioned near the induction center.

The noise from the antiwar and pro-war demonstrators and marching police and the din and odor from the exhausts of the motorcycles and buses accumulated and magnified through the canyon of downtown buildings. People, vehicles, and signs were everywhere. Although JR and Maggie were focused on their role in the demonstrations, each had a sense that the event was already out of control. Then perception turned to reality.

The police advanced to clear a path for the inductees to enter the building; the protestors passively resisted; and the police attacked with clubs. Protestors closest to the center doors were soon bloody, and many were arrested. Among those arrested was diminutive Joan Baez, who, surrounded by officers seemingly twice her size, walked calmly to the police paddy wagon.

When an older woman saw Baez being led away, she rose and began singing "We Shall Overcome," a song Baez had sung in demonstrations across the country. For a few moments, the scene turned from violence to reverence. En masse, the thousands of protestors rose and joined the woman.

"We shall overcome, we shall overcome, we shall overcome, some day. Oh deep in my heart, I do believe, we shall overcome, some day."

The police seemed to be mesmerized by the chorus and reverberations of the song echoing off of brick walls and windows. But the respite was short-lived. With shouted commands from ranking officers, the police resumed their mission of clearing the demonstration from the induction center, bringing the chanting to an abrupt halt.

Nearby, three cops had a young man on the ground—his arms over his head to protect himself. The police dragged him by his feet facedown to the police van. Two other officers held a gray-haired balding man against the wall of the center. Protestors surged forward to help, but the elderly man calmly held up his hand as if to say, "I'm fine—let it be," and he was escorted to the van without further incident.

The police were indiscriminant about whether they swung at heads or legs. Maggie found herself in the midst of the melee, curled herself into a fetal position, and put her arms over her head for protection. Her position and the fact that her eyes were shut tight in fear kept her from seeing whether the swing was meant for her. She felt the blow on the upper right thigh and screamed in pain.

JR, who was not far away helping an older protestor get to his feet, heard the scream above the general din, turned to see it was Maggie, and moved quickly in her direction. He pushed the

BODY NOT RECOVERED

cop away and was about to be clubbed himself, when his combat training kicked in. He disarmed the policemen, pushed him well back, and was about to strike the cop with the man's own club—but JR caught himself, realized what he was about to do, dropped the nightstick, and returned to Maggie.

He carried her to safety through the mass of demonstrators and away from the induction center doorway. He was sure the officer would follow, but the cop, who had needed some time to regain his footing and his club, had lost his two tormentors in the confusion.

CHAPTER 63

IN THE SAME BOAT

October 20, 1967
Berkeley, California

Maggie's leg, which Doc tended to, was painful but not enough to keep her from participating during the remainder of Stop-the-Draft-Week. On Tuesday, the number of arrests more than doubled to nearly 100. By Wednesday, the demonstration had grown from 3000 to 10,000. Everything was escalating, and on Friday, the confrontations with police would grow to a new level.

The dark red of the blood stains on streets and sidewalks and the trash from each day were only superficially cleaned up before the next day's protest began. Owners had shuttered the doors and windows of nearby buildings. News organizations had established permanent reporting posts.

Each evening, JR, Maggie, and other leaders got together to plan the following day's tactics. Bernie, who had begun coming to the meetings after Maggie had been clubbed, spoke up on Thursday night, "So what have we really accomplished? I agree that we've gotten media attention and have made our point. But the fucking induction center is still in business and not one inductee has changed his mind.

"I'm thinking there's only one way to shut it down. It's time to use the same tactics on them that they're using in Vietnam. Bomb it!"

"No way," JR was adamant while standing and looming over Bernie to emphasize his point. "That's not the answer. Besides, there are thousands of people there every day. I'm not going to be part of killing anyone—I had enough of that in Nam!"

Bernie, not one to be intimidated, stood to meet him face-to-face, "I'm not talking about doing this when everyone's there. I don't want to kill anyone either. But Stop-the-Draft-Week hasn't stopped the fucking draft! I say we extend the week until Saturday and sometime early in the morning, when nobody's around, do the deed.

"If no one else is with me, I'll do it on my own," Bernie challenged as she looked around the room, face by face, asking for support.

She started with Trey, "I'm with you, Bern."

JR leaned over and whispered to Doc, "Trey's with Bernie's tits—wherever they go, he'll follow."

JR and Maggie as well as Doc and Jill, in whose cramped apartment the planning meetings were being held, declined as did the others in the room, some of whom had sympathy for Bernie's position but were not yet ready to sign up for that level of violence.

"Bernie and Trey, to be clear, you're on your own."

"No regrets," she responded. "It's the right thing to do."

"That being said," JR, shifting focus from Bernie back to the meeting, continued, "I think we need a different tactic in front of the center tomorrow. We've been passively resisting all week, and the result is that some get arrested, some get beaten, and we all get cleared out of the way so that the inductees can get through. Our strength is in our numbers—let's take advantage of that.

"Every time a group of police head toward the doorway to clear us out, instead of just sitting there, let's calmly stand and walk toward the police van. They'll need to deal with that group of us, and then another group will come in behind to sit in the doorway. It's like a war of attrition."

Doc stood up, put his hand on JR's shoulder, and said, "Why don't we take a break so everyone can think about that for awhile. JR, can I talk to you?"

JR and Doc made their way into the hallway outside Jill's apartment. "Hey," Doc began, "you know what I think? I think you're not thinking?"

"Doc, if you don't agree with what I'm suggesting, just say so in the meeting."

"It's not that. You almost got arrested on Monday, or so I hear. And you've been on the front line of this thing since then. I applaud you for that, but what if you do get arrested? What are you going to tell them about who you are? 'Hi, Mr. Officer, I'm JR Spears, and I'm a deserter from the United States Army. You might have heard of me. I'm the dead guy who's leading these protests. Can I go free now?'

"JR, you can't afford to get arrested. Since you've become a leader, the movement can't afford for you to get arrested. If you do, we lose you forever—you'll be chanting antiwar slogans from a federal prison somewhere. And by the way, I can't afford to lose you either, my friend."

"I can't..." JR began to argue, but then stopped.

"Doc, you're right," he conceded. "Of course, you're right. So what am I supposed to do? Quit?"

"No, not quit. Just find a way to continue to energize these people while getting off the front lines when we're on the streets. You may have noticed that I've not been sitting in the doorway with you, because I'm in the same boat as you—and this one's not a Vietnamese fishing boat."

"OK, OK, I get it. Thanks, Doc."

"One more thing, how are we going to get Trey's mind out of Bernie's crotch before he gets himself in big trouble or blown up somewhere?"

"I don't know how to solve that one. He's got to make his own decisions. Have you talked to him?"

"Tried once—no dice. He's been mesmerized by Bernie since he saw her for the first time. I believe that he wouldn't rat us out if he got arrested, but I'm still worried about him."

CHAPTER 64

LET'S GET OUT OF HERE

October 21, 1967
Oakland, California

At 3:00 AM, Bernie called the telephone number of the Oakland Armed Services Induction Center. "No one's there. Let's go."

"What about people in the buildings on either side, Bern?"

"Office buildings. Who the fuck is going to be there at this time on a Saturday morning? And besides, all those buildings have been boarded up."

Bernie, stark naked, was standing next to the sleeping bag she and Trey had been sharing in a small bedroom at a friend's apartment. Trey, still lying on the bag, grabbed her legs playfully. She pulled away, "You'd rather fuck than anything, but not this time. You can stay there and play with yourself or you can get dressed and come with me."

Within five minutes, they were out of the apartment, duffle bag in hand. Thirty minutes later, they had rested the bag against the glass double doors of the induction center, inserted a long fuse into the dynamite bundle, and extended it well outside the bag. Bernie lit the fuse, and she and Trey ran up Clay Street.

As they did, they heard sirens that were getting louder. Not imagining the sirens had anything to do with them, they stopped about five blocks away to wait for the explosion.

Over the last few months, Bernie and Trey had been learning how to make and detonate bombs and had been collecting materials. Finding out about bomb making was easy—a visit to the UC-Berkeley campus library provided a multitude of resources. The raw materials were not as readily available, but Bernie located a nearby construction site where an older apartment building was going to be imploded to make room for a new one. Trey climbed the fence surrounding the site, located and broke into the explosives cabinet, and filled his duffle bag with dynamite sticks and fuses.

Now, tucked into a dark doorway to make it difficult to see them from the street, they waited for what seemed like an eternity. No explosion. Louder sirens. "Fuck! Let's get out of here."

Out of breath, they were back at their apartment 20 minutes later. Worked up over the failed bomb attempt, Bernie was both livid and passionate, neither of which bothered Trey, who wrestled her down onto the sleeping bag and helped Bernie work off her tension.

A few blocks away and that afternoon, Maggie was reading the *Oakland Tribune,* looking for coverage of the week's protests. Yesterday's final day of the Stop-the-War-Week protests had drawn 10,000 demonstrators who tried JR's surge-and-fill strategy. Although the approach delayed the eventual clearing of the induction center doorway by police, it also increased the numbers of protestors being injured and arrested.

JR and Maggie had worked their way through the demonstrators giving instructions, but JR made sure that when the physical confrontation began, he was far enough away to reduce the risk of being arrested. He felt badly about not being right up front, but knew that if he were arrested, it would put an end to any involvement.

"Oh, my God! JR, you've got to see this," Maggie screamed as she handed him the newspaper.

"Bomb Plot Discovered"

"A bomb was discovered overnight at the Oakland Armed Services Induction Center. The bomb, which failed to detonate, was disassembled to make sure it remained harmless. Because of the recent demonstrations at the induction center, the police had the building under surveillance.

"An officer who was patrolling the area saw two figures running from the scene. He found the bomb, pulled the fuse, and called in the incident. Bomb specialists arrived within minutes as did other officers who scoured the area looking for the perpetrators but without success."

The article went on to describe the previous week's protests and provided details documenting how the antiwar movement had clearly chosen to turn violent.

"This is going to make the police even more aggressive," JR said when he finished the article. "And we're going to be under much more scrutiny. Not a reason to stop what we're doing, but it could get much uglier."

Later in the day, Bernie heard a report on the local news. "Fuck!"

CHAPTER 65

YOU BETCHA

October 26, 1967
New York City, New York

"Agent Paul Marcus, please. John Muccelli calling." Mooch needed to wait only a few seconds.

"Hey, Mooch. Great to talk to you. How's Columbia treating you?"

"Hi Paul, we haven't talked in awhile, so I thought I'd give you a call. Columbia's great," Mooch said while thinking it would be better if I could get done in less time. "Is this a good time for you to talk?"

"Well," Paul hesitated. "Sure, I'm really up to my neck in work, but what the hell. Last week, I learned that I was being transferred. I'm heading for the mother ship—going to headquarters in D. C. So, I've got to wrap up here, start learning about my new job, and make all of the personal arrangements for the move, but other than that, not much going on."

Mooch chuckled, then stammered, "Er...Uh...I was hoping to get some advice."

"Sure, what's up?"

"Well, as you know, I was able to cut a year off my Stanford degree, but as best I can tell, there's nothing I can do about accelerating my law degree. Actually, based on the intensity of my first-semester classes, I'm not sure I could pull it off anyway."

"Problems with classes, Mooch?"

"No, it's not that—I'm doing just fine. They're just taking more study time than I was expecting. Anyway, I was hoping to be applying to the FBI in a couple of years, but now it looks like it'll be three. I talked to Dad about it, and he advised me to just dig in and make the best of it. Good advice, but I thought I'd bounce it off of you also."

"Well, as usual, your father is spot on. Law school is not just a check box that you have to get through—it's an opportunity to build your skills for the future. Making the best of it sounds like a pretty good plan. That being said, I have a couple of ideas."

"I'm all ears."

"One of them I mentioned to you before, and the other is a new thought. For both of them, you'll need to nail your first-year classes."

"I can make that happen, Paul. What are your ideas?"

"Well, the one I told you about is that the FBI has been thinking about beginning volunteer summer internships for prospective agent candidates who are in their graduate programs. If you're interested and can handle the volunteer part, which, by the way, translates to unpaid, I'd be glad to see what I can do to help. It's likely that your internship after year one would be in an office-support kind of role; then after year two, you might be able to expect more agent-like activities. Interested?"

"Holy cow!" Mooch responded, borrowing the expression of St. Louis Cardinals baseball play-by-play announcer Harry Caray.

"I'll take that as a 'yes,'" Paul snickered. "Tell you what—let's talk about this more in a few months once you've got your grades well established, and I'm settled in to my new job."

"What will you be doing, Paul?"

"I can't talk about it yet—in fact, I'm not sure if I can ever talk about it. But if I can, I'll let you know."

"I don't mean to be pushy, but you mentioned a second idea."

"Oh yeah, right. The FBI is interested in getting the best candidates committed to the bureau as soon as possible. So, we actually interview candidates for the job after their first year of graduate school. That is assuming they've earned the interview. You should have no trouble getting on that list."

"Will 'Holy cow' work again? I'd love to take a shot at it, Paul. I didn't think to check out the campus placement center this early, but I will, and I'll find out how to proceed. If I run into questions, I'll get back to you if that's OK."

"You betcha."

Mooch and Paul spent a few more minutes catching up on personal items, then Paul said, "Mooch, it's been great talking with you, but I really have to dig into the pile here."

"Paul, once again, thank you for everything you've done for me. I just hope I can pay you back some day."

"I'm sure you will, Mooch. Now, go hit the books. There's law to be learned. And remember, as I've told you before—no promises."

CHAPTER 66

OCCUPATION

April 23, 1968
New York City, New York

Mooch had done exactly what Paul Marcus and he had talked about in the fall. He focused on his studies, even more so than usual, to ensure he would be poised to compete for a prized summer internship with the FBI and that he would be sought after by FBI recruiters for a full-time post-law-degree job. His dedication had paid off—he was scheduled for early May interviews for both intern and permanent positions.

As the year proceeded, despite his best efforts, Mooch recognized that his interviews and even his first law school year were in jeopardy for circumstances beyond his control. Columbia, campuses across the nation, and the nation itself were becoming increasingly restless.

The war was escalating, casualties on both sides were mounting, and reports of atrocities by U. S. troops were becoming commonplace. Less than three weeks earlier, Martin Luther King had been assassinated, and American cities were burning. There was growing racial tension on the Columbia campus and in nearby black communities.

On this Tuesday, tensions boiled over on campus when a jointly planned protest by the Students for a Democratic Society and the Student Afro Society targeted a new gymnasium being built near the university in Morningside Park, a green space that buffered the campus from the predominately black Harlem neighborhood. Students were outraged, because the justification to allow Columbia to lease public land was predicated on ensuring the facility would be available to the nearby neighborhood residents. But the plans for the building showed the multistory complex having only limited

270

facilities in the basement for the black residents, and their only access would be through a back door.

The protest, which assembled at the sundial, a traditional campus meeting place, moved toward the site of the gym. Although it was unplanned, over the course of the day, SDS and other white organizations split off from the SAS. Instead of following their initial intent to highlight the Morningstar Park issues, the white contingent entered and occupied five university buildings, including the president's office. Over the next days, the occupiers attempted to negotiate with the administration, pro-war demonstrators held counter-protests outside the buildings, and the police tried to maintain order and decide what to do.

One night during the occupation, Mooch was studying when he heard police sirens nearby. The previous week, he had walked by the mobs assembled outside the occupied buildings on his way to what he hoped would be his classes. Only self-discipline and his fear of having to explain himself to Paul kept him from getting closer to see what was happening at the core of the protests. But on this night, his curiosity overwhelmed his hesitation.

Mooch took a deep breath and headed for the center of campus. The sirens wailed for a few more moments, then were ominously quiet. By the time he reached the periphery of the mob, he could hear the police captain announce himself through the bullhorn and read the orders to clear the occupied buildings. The city had deployed the New York City Tactical Police Force.

Students within the buildings were given a chance to leave on their own, but few did. Mooch worked his way through the rings of those assembled around the buildings. The outer ring was made up mostly of press reporters, TV cameramen, and interested bystanders. The next ring was made up of students and some faculty who supported the occupation. Signs were prevalent. "STRIKE" "A Free University in a Free Society" "Columbia Supports Murder of Women and Children" "REVOLUTION" "COLUMBIA-ENEMY OF ALL BLACK PEOPLE"

Mooch continued to push his way forward, drawn by the sound of the captain's voice blasting from the bullhorn. He reached the inner ring, comprised of what the protestors called "jocks," a group that had been positioned there all week. This pro-war group included many of Columbia's athletes but also members of conservative campus organizations. Throughout the occupation, they disrupted the supply of food and other provisions intended for the students who had taken over the buildings.

Intermingled among each of the circles were New York City Police officers. As Mooch approached the jocks, he was also able to see a concentration of what seemed to be hundreds of TPF officers, donned in full gear. The captain had finished reciting his prepared statement to the protestors. Without hesitation, he ordered the TPF into the buildings.

For the next two hours, the buildings were cleared of students, who exited holding their hands aloft with fingers making a "V" to indicate peace and chanting "no violence, no violence." Their chant was not a plea to police but rather a reminder to themselves.

Despite their peace signs and chanting, the police immediately and continually brandished batons and beat the protestors inside the buildings and as they left. Blood and fallen bodies were everywhere. Mooch was horrified. Is this the role of the police? Is this the best tactic? What would I do if I were in their place?

A group of students that had been in a building rushed out trying to avoid the cadre of TPF officers and ran directly toward Mooch. The three outside rings of people had morphed into a single solid mass, making any escape difficult if not impossible.

The police followed closely behind the group of students, indiscriminately wielding clubs. When the group ran into the mass outside, there was no place to go. Mooch was close enough to hear the crack of clubs hitting skulls and more muted sound of blows to backs and legs. He was close enough to get splattered with blood. He was close enough to be at risk of being clubbed himself.

His first instinct was to run. His second stopped him from trying to escape, as he turned toward the police to demand that they stop even though he knew he wielded no influence. He then heard Paul Marcus's voice in his head, "Mooch, what are you doing here? Is this the way you stay out of trouble? Don't you have an interview coming up? What are you going to tell them if you're beaten or arrested?"

Mooch's adrenaline rush enabled him to force his way through the mob pushing aside anyone who was in the way. When he reached the periphery, he was barely able to catch his breath from both the

OCCUPATION

physical and mental exertion. Only then did he risk taking the time to look back. What he could make out were the flashing lights of ambulances and police vans, into which arrested protestors were being packed.

Back in his room, still gasping for breath, he ripped off his bloody clothes and took a long, hot shower. He could still not process what he had witnessed, and he would find out later that about 700 were arrested. Many who were badly injured were not afforded medical care until after they were processed through the justice system.

For weeks, although the school was not formally shut down, it was unclear whether his classes and his interviews were on or off. Students, even more determined after the police actions, were calling for another strike. Ad hoc antiwar rallies were being held on lawns, and students were being asked by activist leaders not to attend regular classes. The students' demands were stated and restated—shutting down of the Morningside Park gymnasium project, amnesty for those who protested, and disassociation of the university from the Institute of Defense Analysis, an organization that funded weapons research for the Department of Defense. The activists claimed that the university's support of the IDA made the school complicit in the use of these weapons to kill and overkill innocent Vietnamese.

Mooch had not heard whether his FBI interviews would still take place and could not find anyone who could tell him with certainty if he would be allowed to complete his first year of law school. He anxiously awaited news of his future.

CHAPTER 67

RIGHT NOW

May 7, 1968
New York City, New York

Dressed in coat and tie, Mooch headed toward West 81st Street. A week earlier, he had received a telephone call from the FBI recruiter, who explained that the bureau would not be intimidated into cancelling these important interviews because of the campus unrest but at the same time, had chosen not to conduct them in university facilities.

Mooch enjoyed the two-mile walk to the Excelsior Hotel on the clear Manhattan day. The sights, sounds, and smells of the city acted as a buffer to allow him to be alone with his thoughts. His single-minded focus on the interviews grew with each step.

Although Mooch understood both sides of the on-campus confrontation, on a personal level, the preceding two weeks had been filled with uncertainty and frustration. The successful completion of his first year of law school was a prerequisite for both the summer internship and a career job offer. Yet, because some faculty supported the antiwar and civil rights agenda, they would occasionally express that support by cancelling classes. And even when classes were held, students needed to show two ID's to gain access to the buildings.

More than once on his way to class or the library, Mooch passed groups who were burning University President Grayson Kirk in effigy, blaming him for turning the police on students. There was a constant threat of such incidents escalating into another round of violence among students or with police, risking a total shutdown of the campus and Mooch's loss of access to FBI opportunities.

Perhaps most difficult was passing groups of students and faculty that he knew were discussing the pros and cons of the war, the civil rights movement, and campus activism. His curiosity continued to pique his interest in those discussions, but he successfully struggled to remain uninvolved. His close call and his recollection of the blood on his clothes, as well as the constant voice of Paul Marcus in his head, had moved Mooch resolutely from room to library to class.

By the time he finished his walk to the hotel, the uncertainty of previous weeks had faded. He located the room that the FBI recruiters were using to conduct their interviews, awaited his appointed time, took a deep breath, and strode confidently into the room and his future.

Mooch knew the interviews, throughout which he had sensed the presence and support of Paul Marcus, Chief Davis, and his father, had gone well. At the end of the process, the interviewer who seemed to be in charge said, "Mr. Muccelli, based on your record, your references, and what we've learned about you today, I'm authorized to offer you a summer internship with the FBI at bureau headquarters in Washington, D. C. During that internship, we plan to have others in the bureau interview you, and should you continue to perform at a high level in law school, we would look forward to further discussing a career in the FBI with you.

"We laid out the details of the internship for you during our discussions today. So, unless you have any further questions, we would like an answer on your commitment to this summer's internship within the next week."

"I have one question, sir. What will happen if Columbia shuts down and instead of getting my grades, the semester is marked incomplete?"

"We'll just need to deal with that if and when it happens. Will you be getting back to us by the end of next week?"

"I have no reason to wait to commit to the internship. I can give you my answer right now."

CHAPTER 68

THEY'LL GET THE POINT

November 6, 1968
San Francisco, California

Their failed bombing attempt more than a year earlier had not dissuaded Bernie and Trey from continuing to look for ways to amplify antiwar violence. But their friends' intransigence did not dissuade JR, Maggie, Doc, and Jill from staying the course on more traditional demonstrations.

They had been among 500 demonstrators protesting the draft at the San Francisco Federal Building and had joined hundreds who picketed the San Francisco Fairmont Hotel, where Secretary of State Dean Rusk, a strong pro-war voice, was speaking. Police in full riot gear aggressively broke up that demonstration, but JR and Doc were careful to be on the periphery when the police began to deploy.

Later in the year, nearly 900 Berkeley seniors and graduate students assembled on Sproul Plaza for what they called a "Vietnam Commencement" and signed an oath that stated, "Our war in Vietnam is unjust and immoral. As long as the United States is involved in this war, I will not serve in the armed forces." JR had worked closely with student activists to organize the event.

The tension between the two factions with differing points of view about how violent the movement should become was growing, putting a continual strain on JR's, Maggie's, and Bernie's friendship.

"Bernie, we're making progress without resorting to bombing," Maggie implored.

Bernie was predictably unyielding. "Not enough and not fast enough."

Although he knew he was not going to change Bernie's mind, JR felt compelled to try once more to make the case for moderation, "Bernie, public opinion is more antiwar than ever and half of Americans think Vietnam has been a mistake. That photograph that showed the street execution—you know, the one where the South Vietnamese National Police Chief shot the guy in the head—that had more impact than a bombing ever will.

"And remember when Cronkite got back from Vietnam where he saw the results of the Tet Offensive? He reported that he thought that the best we could expect from the bloody experience of Vietnam was that it would end in a stalemate. Johnson's exact words when he heard what Cronkite had said were, 'If I've lost Cronkite, I've lost middle America.'

"You don't think that had something to do with Johnson deciding not to run for reelection?

"People are pressing for an end to the war. After Bobby's and King's assassinations and after the police riots at the Democratic National Convention, folks are more scared about what's happening here at home than they are about winning a war 10,000 miles away.

"The last thing we need is for the antiwar movement to look like part of the problem instead of the solution. Bernie, please think again about what you're planning to do."

Bernie was as inflexible as ever, "I've thought about it and am convinced Bob Dylan is right, 'You don't need to be a weather man to know which way the wind blows.'"

Bernie turned and stomped away, leaving JR and Maggie to look at each other and simultaneously shrug their shoulders and hang their heads.

Although JR and Maggie were disappointed they were not in Chicago for the convention demonstrations, they remained active in the Bay Area throughout the remainder of the year. In what would be one of the most significant and highly publicized antiwar demonstrations, students at San Francisco State University went on strike and shut down the campus for five months. Throughout that period, University president S. I. Hayakawa called in police, resulting in countless injuries and scores of arrests.

On the first evening of the strike, JR joined student marchers who had assembled at the Speaker's Platform on campus and were intent on confronting Hayakawa at the Administration Building. A tall blonde coed walking next to JR along Holloway Avenue held a sign that read, "On Strike! Shut it Down!"

"Would you hold this for a sec," she asked JR, as she pulled a pack of Kool cigarettes from her purse.

"Sure," replied JR as he took the sign and kept it raised above their heads.

When the girl finished lighting her cigarette, JR reached out to return her sign when the police arrived in force. Most of the marchers maintained order, but a number, including the coed, panicked and fled.

JR, still holding the sign, found himself closer to the action than he would have liked as the police contingent deployed. Recalling Doc's caution about the risks of being arrested, JR looked for a way to get out of the middle of the crowd. The first thing he did was to hand his sign to one of the students.

Unlike other protests JR had attended, the police did nothing to approach the demonstrators. Instead, in an orderly fashion, they positioned themselves shoulder-to-shoulder between the marchers and the administration building. As he moved to the furthest periphery of the marchers, JR allowed himself to relax and judged that the march would continue peacefully.

"This is the San Francisco police. Please disperse. Return to your dorms and your classes."

The bullhorn announcement put JR back on full alert. His combat training and his experience at previous demonstrations kicked in when he saw the line of police take two steps forward. Then two more.

The students, sensing they were going to be pushed across Holloway Avenue, determined en masse to hold their ground. As the police line advanced a step or two at a time, they were soon within arm's length of the marchers. Each officer then raised his baton to chest height and extended in front of him, a hand at each end of the weapon.

THEY'LL GET THE POINT

For several minutes, the marchers succumbed to the physical pressure and allowed themselves to be pushed across the street.

"Please disperse. This is your last warning."

The word "warning" seemed to change the mood of the marchers.

JR heard a young man's voice above the general din, "Warning my ass. We're here to shut it down."

JR was close enough to notice it was the student to whom he had handed the sign. He was also close enough to see the young man swing the sign at the closest policeman and hit him in the neck just below the officer's helmet. The officer instinctively put his hand where he had been struck. He looked at his hand, saw the blood, and furiously swung back, striking the student just below the ear. The boy went down.

What had been a tense but peaceful confrontation changed in an instant. The flash point incident was as if a stone had been dropped into a still pond. The ripples spread, as nearby policemen anticipated further attacks and took the offensive. The wave moved down the police line in both directions. Clubs that had only been used to push the marchers backwards were now being swung.

JR had become all too accustomed to the scene of injuries and arrests. Although not proud of it, he remained on the periphery while others threw themselves into the fray.

That evening, after JR described the incident, Bernie was quick to jump at the opportunity and defiantly said, "JR, you just don't get it. We can't wait. We need to bomb the closest police station while the cops are busting heads. It's the only way they'll get the point."

CHAPTER 69

EXPLOSION

July 20, 1969
San Francisco, California

The crowds were amassing, and it appeared that this would be a meaningful event after all. At one point, there was a possibility that Joan Baez would join the protest and would be singing. Largely because of her arrest in 1967 for being among those who blocked the entrance to the Oakland Armed Forces Induction Center, the Bay Area antiwar community adored Baez.

After the Oakland incident, Baez had met David Harris, founder of The Resistance, an organization that urged young men to refuse to cooperate with the Selective Service System, and they had married. Not only was Baez pregnant and not likely to be singing, but just days before, Harris had been arrested for refusing to be inducted.

Even though they knew she would not be there, the crowd seemed to be assembling out of love for Baez, to express outrage about Harris, and to take advantage of a beautiful Sunday afternoon in Buena Vista Park.

Although most entering the park were headed for the lush grassy hill where the demonstration would be held, the green-space was also populated by families whose children romped around the playground, people sitting alone on benches reading, and vagrants rummaging through trash cans. Despite being in the middle of Haight-Ashbury, a densely-populated area of the city, the park created a refuge amongst its mature trees.

JR and Maggie sat quietly by themselves, awaiting the action to begin. The moment allowed JR to reflect on the contrast of these bucolic surroundings to the hell that was Vietnam. For now, his consciousness was only filled with grass, trees, the breeze, and his friend Maggie.

The two had played a part in organizing the day's event but were content to sit in the grass away from the demonstration's center to just let it happen. They had walked across the street from the Victorian rooming house on Haight Avenue, where they had been living for the past week. Saying she needed a place of her own and inviting Trey, Maggie, and JR to stay there, Bernie had rented an apartment for $25.00 per month

Although reluctant because Bernie had been growing increasingly distant and agitated, JR and Maggie had decided to move in. Since her failed bomb attempt at the Oakland Induction Center, she had been searching for another opportunity and for compatriots to share her philosophy and tactics. Trey had stayed by her side, but she was also growing distant from him.

One night, with a joint in hand, she declared, "God dammit. This country is blowing up villages and people in Vietnam while people here are fat, dumb, and happy. I've been working on a new bomb. This one's gonna fucking work!"

"You've got to quit this, Bernie. It's making you crazy," Maggie pled, caring deeply even though the friendship waned as Bernie became more radical and spent most of her time with Trey or by herself.

"Dammit, Mags, we need to blow something up! It's the only real way to bring the war home."

"No way," JR jumped in. "We've been through this over and over. How can you justify stopping killing by killing?"

"That's the fucking justification the US government is using. You're right, it's a shitty rationale, but if we do the same, it will help everyone see how stupid it is."

"Whoa, Bernie, I've told you before that I'm not going to be a part of hurting someone. I just can't," Maggie said, clearly expressing the frustration she felt.

Bernie softened for a moment. "And, Mags, I've told you before that I don't want to hurt anyone either. Just like the induction center, I think we should pick a target and learn enough about it to make sure we plant the bomb when no one is going to be around."

"To be clear, Bernie, I'm not going to be part of blowing anything up." JR had enough of blowing up things and people.

He looked at Bernie, trying to see into her mind, and asked, "Where's the bomb?"

"If you don't want any part of it, then stay out of it," Bernie said and abruptly turned and walked toward the stairs, which led to the small loft where she had been spending much of her time.

For now, Bernie and bombs were the farthest things from JR's mind as he sat with Maggie in the brilliant sunshine. Their reverie was broken when a hefty, curly red-haired guy about their age sat down a couple of yards from them, laid back, stared at the cloudless sky and said, as if speaking only to himself, "Fucking war!"

Seemingly surprised by his own outburst, he looked around, noticing JR and Maggie for the first time. "Oh, hi, sorry—I just hate what's going on."

"We do too," JR mused, "that's why we're here."

"Bill Ritter," he said, holding out his hand.

"I'm JR. This is Maggie."

"Well, Maggie, looks like you and I have started the redheaded section."

"Guess so," said Maggie smiling back at the likeable guy.

"Are you very active in the movement? I am."

JR and Maggie looked at each other with knowing smiles.

Ritter continued, "I've been trying to do everything I can to stop this thing. I hated the war even before I was drafted. Then since I dodged the draft, I've been protesting, trying to get my parents and their friends involved, writing everyone I know."

"Wait, Bill," JR interrupted, "if you dodged the draft, why are you here and not in Canada or hiding or whatever?"

"Oh, I dodged it legally. I'm 4-F, unfit for service." Ritter's grin broadened across his freckled face, shot up, did 10 jumping jacks, and then sat down again.

JR and Maggie studied their new acquaintance. He looked fine and fit. "OK, Bill, I'll bite. How did you manage the 4-F?"

"Well, I was out of college, having ridden that deferment as long as I could. I went to work, but was not in a critical industry, so no deferment there. I began looking into my options. I considered everything—Canada like you said, the Reserves, refusing induction, faking illnesses—anything I could think of.

"The Selective Service forced the issue when I got my draft notice and was ordered to report for my induction in six weeks.

"I was trying to figure out what to do, so I began reading the draft regulations to find something that would work. Came across the Army's height and weight chart. For each height, there are limits to how light or heavy you can be. I'm five-ten. At the time I found this, I weighed 210 pounds, the same weight I was when I played high school and college baseball. I had continued playing in softball leagues and pickup basketball games almost every day after college. So, I was in reasonable shape.

"Well, I check out the chart and it says for five-ten, the upper weight limit to pass your draft physical is 219 pounds. That was it! My ticket out!

"I began eating anything that wasn't nailed down, including a quart of ice cream and half a cake every night. I didn't trust the Army, so I sailed past 219 pounds. I went from a 36-inch waist to a 42.

"My mom lined up a draft attorney for me. He helped me understand what I needed to do at the induction physical to make sure that the Army followed their own regulations. Well, I show up at the physical and start going through the procedure. I get to the part where I get weighed, and the guy looks at the reading and at me and says, 'Get off and try again.'

"He looks at me and the scale reading again. 'OK, I guess it's right,' he says and writes down the number. I ask him what I weighed. 'Well, you're a big guy, but this doesn't seem right. You weigh 262 pounds.'

"I did my best to look concerned, but I'm celebrating on the inside. Now it's crunch time. Will they try to ignore the number or follow the regs? I'm ushered into a small room with classroom-like desks and told to wait with a few others. The room is filling, and I find out that these guys had failed their physical or psyche exams.

"I'm in there about an hour when a sergeant comes in, looks around the room, opens one of the files, and starts with me. 'Well, Ritter, you're a little overweight, but we can fix that. If you sign this waiver, we can put you in the fat boys' platoon and get you in shape in no time.'

"He shoves the waiver at me and holds out a pen. 'No sir, I'll pass on the waiver. What should I do next?'

"He looks at me like what self-respecting fat guy wouldn't want the Army to help him fix that problem? I look back at him like I'm done here, when can I leave?

"He shakes his head, points me toward the door, hands me my file, and tells me to give it to the clerk on the way out. I'm checked out of there in no time and on my way. A couple of weeks later, I get a 1-Y classification card from the Selective Service. Every six months, they called me in and checked to make sure I had not miraculously taken off the weight. Each time I weigh in at 236. Then it comes—my new Selective Service card. I'm 4-F, physically unfit for the service. Wanna see my card?"

"OK, what do you weigh now?"

"I'm at about 215, back to playing softball and pickup basketball, as well as being in a flag football league. But, I'm physically unfit for the Army. Fat boy's platoon, my ass!"

JR, Maggie, and Bill are all grinning at Bill's elation, and Maggie is reaching to see Bill's 4-F when they see Trey walking toward them across the park. As he gets within earshot, he says, "Too nice a day to be holed up inside, so here I am."

As he extended his hand to introduce himself to Bill Ritter, they heard and felt the explosion.

CHAPTER 70

HELLO, MRS. WILLIAMS

August 25, 1969
San Francisco, California

"JR, I have to go," Maggie said with conviction. "It's the only way I can keep it together. I have to see Bernie's parents, and the more I think about it, I may see mine as well. I don't know if I have the guts, but it's been so long, maybe things have changed."

"Do you want me to come with you," JR took Maggie's hand.

"No, I have to do this on my own. But thank you. You're the best. Maybe this would be a good time for you to visit St. Louis, and I could just meet you back here at some point."

"I've already been thinking about a St. Louis trip. But I'm concerned about Trey. He's threatening to pick up where Bernie left off and is talking about bombing everything in sight. He's out of control, and that's not good for him or us."

JR and Maggie were sitting on the same grassy knoll as they had on the day of the explosion only five weeks before. The chaos of that tragic day and the days that followed had subsided, but the sense of the loss of Bernie Williams ran deep.

JR waited for Maggie to respond, but she only released his hand and slowly pulled her knees toward her chest and held them there with clasped hands.

Maggie was silently reliving her time with Bernie, from first seeing her in the D. C. bus station through their growing and then intimate relationship and her concerns with Bernie's increasingly erratic behavior. Maggie stared at the site that was once Bernie's rooming house, which had been cleared as if it had never existed.

The rooming house explosion had ignited a fire that consumed the remnants of the structure and caused secondary gas line explosions. Windows were shattered throughout the neighborhood and nearby buildings were damaged.

The protestors assembling in Buena Vista Park had quickly joined neighbors as bystanders, as JR, Maggie, and Trey tried unsuccessfully to break through the perimeter that had been set up by police, who were already on hand to help monitor the demonstration. Even though the three friends knew immediately what had happened and that Bernie was gone, their instincts were to try to save her.

Only after the fire had been controlled did firefighters find Bernie's remains. No one else was in the building at the time nor injured nearby. If the explosion had occurred just an hour earlier, the loss of life would have been much higher and would have included the three of them.

After the police also found unexploded sticks of dynamite, a live military antitank shell, blasting caps, and several large metal pipes packed solid with explosives, they announced that it was miraculous the explosion was not even more intense.

Not even Trey had any idea of the arsenal that Bernie had amassed or how extensive her plans apparently were. They now better understood why Bernie had insisted on renting her own place where she could store her wares and work on her plans more discreetly.

Not only had they lost their friend, but they had also lost their possessions. With one exception, those losses were of little concern, because their lifestyle was such that they lived light and had little to lose.

The one exception—Matt's letters were irreplaceable.

One day after the explosion, Maggie had picked up and replaced the phone several times before mustering the wherewithal to dial. She had been about to hang up as the phone was ringing.

"Hello."

Maggie froze.

"Hello, is anyone there?"

Finally with her voice cracking, Maggie responded, "Hello, Mrs. Williams. You don't know me, but my name is Margaret Blessings, and I'm a close friend of your daughter. I have some terrible news for you, but I felt that I needed to be the one to tell you. Bernie would have wanted me to."

Through the difficult conversation, Maggie felt herself bonding with Bernie's mother and knowing that she needed to visit. Despite JR's concerns about Trey, there was little she could do to help, and she began planning her trip. She replaced her clothes at a thrift shop and bought her bus ticket.

CHAPTER 71

TORE OUR FAMILY APART

September 5, 1969
Brick, New Jersey

The Brick, New Jersey bus station was a counter at a Shell gas station, but it served the purpose. Maggie asked the attendant how she could get a cab and 20 minutes later was knocking on the door of the Williams' house. Though fully confident she was doing the right thing, Maggie's chest was tight. Bernie and she had grown distant, but that did not lessen the pain. For her own benefit and hopefully for that of Bernie's parents, she needed to be here.

On her cross-county bus ride, Maggie had the time to reflect on her past, present, and future. She concluded that she was well settled into and comfortable with her new life, initially because of Bernie and now primarily because of JR. She felt she had made a difference in the antiwar movement that was growing in the Bay Area and across the country.

Events in which she had taken part had fueled the fires of the movement, which had begun with students and young activists, but was now penetrating the mainstream. Older individuals, prominent organizations, politicians, and celebrities were joining the cause.

Maggie saw progress everywhere. Peace talks had begun in Paris, although they were proving frustrating, because there were more arguments about the shape of the negotiating table than legitimate discussion about ending the war.

Despite the progress, she knew there was a lot of work to be done as the war wore on relentlessly. U. S. troop levels in Vietnam had grown to nearly 550,000 and fatalities to nearly 35,000, and the *New York Times* had reported on the previously secret bombing of Cambodia.

On her trip, Maggie read *LIFE* magazine, which had printed photos of 242 Americans who had been killed the previous week in Vietnam, including many who had died in the battle for what became known as "Hamburger Hill." More than 70 American servicemen died and over 370 were wounded during the frontal attack to take the hill, which was of little strategic value. Once the hill was secured, the troops were ordered to abandon it. Maggie thought of Matt as she cried at the useless loss of life, but she knew that events like these and the ensuing media attention were serving to infuriate the public.

And when Maggie picked up a newspaper at the Philadelphia bus station, one stop before Brick, she knew that another event would soon move public opinion. Lieutenant William Calley had been charged with murder for his role in the massacre of unarmed South Vietnamese civilians in the village of My Lai. As she read the article, she thought of Matt and his letters and of JR and his stories of Vung Dong.

Despite the progress and her recognition that there was still much to do, a nagging question accompanied her all the way to New Jersey. Had she done enough to meet her commitment to Matt and to herself?

A striking woman answered the door, and Maggie was struck by how much she resembled Bernie. "Hi Maggie. Thank you for coming. Please come in."

"Thank you, Mrs. Williams. I'm sorry to be here for this reason, but I'm glad to meet you."

"Please call me Doris, dear. Marvin will be home shortly."

Bernie had been away from home for many years, but her presence permeated the spacious and well-kept home. Photos of her were everywhere. A scrapbook on the coffee table in the formal living room was labeled, "Bernice: The California Years." It was clear that Doris and Marvin Williams had been keeping track of their daughter as best they could. Although curious, Maggie was determined not to peek in the scrapbook, and it was not offered.

"Did you know that I talked to Bernice pretty often?"

"No, I didn't. She kept that to herself."

"She told me about you, always referring to you as 'my new best friend,' even after she knew you for quite awhile."

Close to tears already, Maggie lost it. Doris followed suit as they embraced to comfort each other.

As the two women were releasing each other, Marvin came through the door. The tall distinguished man with an athletic build was less animated than his wife, yet the moistening of his eyes made it clear that he continued to love his daughter and was stricken by her loss.

Doris and Marvin said they had wanted to believe that their Bernice would come home one day and return the family to an earlier and happier time, but were accepting the fact that it would never happen.

Doris Williams summed up their anguish, "This war tore our family apart just as if we had a son who fought and died in Vietnam."

At their request, Maggie stayed with the Williams family for several days. At dinner one evening, Doris asked, "What are your plans, Maggie?"

"Well, as I told you, I haven't seen my family for a long a time. I regretted leaving, even though I knew I needed to. And from time to time, I've tried to figure out how to fix everything. I have no idea what I'll say when I get there, but my visit here has taught me that it's time. As soon as I figure out how to get there, I'm going home— at least for a visit. After that, I'm really not sure."

Since leaving home, Maggie thought about her parents often, but if she were honest with herself, the frequency had become less so as time passed. She had written the letter prior to leaving for the Bay Area. She had picked up a phone so many times, but could never envision what she might say or how it would affect her parents—so each time, with one exception, she replaced the phone in the cradle before her finger touched the dial.

Her heart told her to get in touch, and she deeply regretted not having done so. But she could not get those final months at home out of her mind. She had convinced herself that before she left home, her parents had literally abandoned her.

Yet, just after she was struck on the leg during the Stop-the-Draft-Week demonstrations almost two years earlier, Maggie's physical and emotional state overcame her apprehension. She needed to talk to her mother, and although she still had no idea what she would say, she dialed the number. No one answered. Maggie never called again.

Seeing how losing Bernie had affected Doris and Marvin caused her to reconsider everything. Was it time to go home and live with the consequences of both leaving and returning?

"We have two cars," Marvin said. "If you plan on coming back through here after your visit, you can borrow one."

Doris looked at her husband and smiled for the first time since learning of Bernie's death. She knew that he had warmed up to Maggie and had begun to treat her like his own.

"Marvin, I can't tell you how much I appreciate that. Thank you. I'll take good care of it," Maggie said, not mentioning that she no longer had a valid license or that the last time she drove was when she left her parents' car at the bus station nearly four years earlier.

CHAPTER 72

ABJECT SADNESS

September 10, 1969
Tunkhannock, Pennsylvania

With Marvin's car, a set of maps he gave her, and a generous gift of more-than-ample funds to make the trip, Maggie found her way. Just as she had stopped by Matt's grave after leaving home, she was compelled to do so again before returning.

She parked in the cemetery lot and made her way to the gravesite, slowly at first but with more pace as her confidence grew. She planned on telling Matt all about Bernie and JR and what she had been doing to fulfill her promise to him to do everything she could to stop the war. As she turned onto the walkway to his site and lifted her head to find Matt's stone, she barely kept her balance as her knees weakened.

Almost touching Matt's gravestone was another one, too close to be for anyone other than a family member. Maggie slowed her pace, feeling the urge to turn and run. But she kept her bearings and reached the site. Her wobbly legs could no longer hold her. Falling to her knees and through tear-filled eyes, she read the engraving on the newer stone, "Jennifer Louise Simpson Blessings; 1921-1967; Beloved Wife and Mother."

"Oh my God, Mom, what happened? Why didn't Dad let me know?"

"Because he couldn't. He didn't know where I was."

"This is all my fault. I was selfish. I need to find Dad."

"But I can't face him now."

"Matt, what would you do?"

"Yep, face it head on. You're right. Thanks."

"I'll go find Dad. He needs me, and I need him."

"I love you both."

Maggie finished her conversation with her mother and brother and with herself and having no sense of time, caressed the gravestones and wept.

Finally forcing herself to her feet, Maggie took the long walk to the car and crying all the way, made the drive to what once was her home. Her tears were of both sadness and guilt. All the way, she tried to think of what to say to her father, but nothing seemed to sound anywhere near right. During all of her preparation for this moment, she had assumed her reconnection with her family would be through her mother. Finally, with no other option than turn around, she decided to just play it by ear and live with the consequences. She owed him that.

But when the house came into view, she had the same sinking feeling as when she saw her mother's gravestone. The house was in obvious disrepair and there was a tilted "For Sale" sign barely visible through the overgrown front lawn.

Once again, Maggie fought to remain standing as she exited the car. On shaky legs, she walked along the path to the front door, sidestepping huge weeds that had worked their way through the cracks between the pavers. Her father had prided himself in the appearance of his home and its environs. Everything was just wrong.

She knocked on the door. No answer. She kept knocking until her knuckles were sore. Still no answer. After walking around the house to look in windows and try other doors, Maggie concluded no one was home, got back in the car, and sat there, making no effort to stop crying while trying to figure out what to do next. Only one possibility came to her, and she headed down the road to the Swansons, the couple to whom she had misaddressed the postcard she sent to her parents the day she left.

After a less-than-cordial greeting, they did not invite her in, but stood shoulder-to-shoulder in the doorway and explained what had happened after Maggie had left home. The burden of Matt's death had been magnified by her leaving. Despite having no identifiable illness, her mother's health deteriorated rapidly, and she finally succumbed to what the Swansons called "abject sadness."

Still mourning the loss of his son, Maggie's father did little to help. It was hard to tell what effect Maggie leaving had on him—he was already non-communicative. Soon after her mother died, Maggie's father put the house up for sale and literally disappeared.

Local and state police tried to track him down, but to no avail. His former friends, coworkers, and even the real estate agent who worked with him to put the house on the market had no idea where he had gone. Harold Blessings had vanished.

Maggie had no doubt that the Swansons blamed her for what had happened, and she could not disagree. There was nothing left for her to do but say a superficial "Thank you" and leave, hearing the front door slam after she had turned away.

Too overwhelmed to either cry or drive, Maggie sat in the car staring out the front window. Eventually gathering herself enough to decide to begin her drive back to the Williams house, she pulled away and caught a glimpse of the home that was once happy and hers in the rearview mirror.

All she could think and feel was how truly alone she was. Even though she had been gone and not talked to her parents in four years, somewhere in the back of her mind she assumed they would always be there for her if she ever decided to return. That was no longer an option.

She forced herself to think of her friends, especially JR, and her antiwar cause in California. But that did not make her feel any better.

Would her own feeling of abject sadness pass? What should she do? Did it really matter?

She found herself pulling up to the Williams' home after the long drive, much of which she literally could not remember.

"Hi Maggie. Come on in. You look as white as a ghost. Are you OK?"

"Doris, can I stay here a little while?"

"Stay as long as you like, dear. What can I do to help?"

Maggie had just enough energy to tell Doris Williams what happened in Tunkhannock.

"Oh Maggie. I'm so sorry. Please, as long as you'd like, consider this your home. When you're ready to figure out what to do next, we'll be glad to help."

Maggie, who had her head down through the whole conversation, looked up at Doris and realized that the woman was still grieving the loss of her daughter and yet reaching out to her.

"Thank you," Maggie said as she embraced Doris as she would have her mother. "I'd like to stay awhile. Are you sure Marvin wouldn't mind."

"He'd only mind if I didn't ask you or if you said 'no.'"

CHAPTER 73

I LOVE YOU TOO

September 13, 1969
Brick, New Jersey

"Hello."

"JR, is that you?"

"Mags, how are you?"

"It would take a long time to answer that question, but I'll give you the short version."

Five minutes later, Maggie concluded with, "So, JR, I'm going to stay here awhile—maybe a long while."

"Mags, do you want me to come to you?"

"No, JR, I'd love to see you, but I have to spend some time sorting things out on my own."

"Well, OK, but I'll miss you. And you know, if there's anything I can do, and I mean anything, you let me know. Promise?"

"Yes, I promise. Thank you. JR, how are you?"

"I'm doing fine. Trey is acting crazy, and I can't get through to him. Bernie's death has really twisted him. Doc tried to talk to him the other day, and he actually shoved Doc away. We've lost track of where he is and what he's doing. It can't end well."

"I know you'll do what's right for him and for you. JR, I'm going to say something I've never said before, and I want you to understand it the way I mean it. You're like a brother to me, and for that I love you."

"I understand, Mags, and I love you too."

CHAPTER 74

SPECIAL REPORT

May 6, 1970
St. Louis, Missouri

JR and Karen were entwined on Karen's living room sofa. Although the television was on, they were paying little attention.

Karen had finished nursing school a year earlier, was working as a floor nurse at Jewish Hospital, and had moved into her own apartment in early January.

JR had been back in town for three days, and except for dinner with Mary, Walter Jr., Mitch, and Oliver each night, he and Karen had spent most of their time wrapped around each other. Mary had no apparent qualms about the sleeping arrangements, and Walter Jr. gave JR a playful elbow and a knowing look every time he saw him.

Walter Jr., who had found a job at a small manufacturing firm that produced ceiling speakers for public buildings, was attending evening classes at the new St. Louis Community College—Forest Park Campus, and had begun to meet with a group that was creating a chapter of the Vietnam Veterans Against the War. And Walter Jr. continued to be grateful to JR for helping him get his head screwed on straight.

Although JR would have liked to be involved at Berkeley and other Bay Area campuses following the killing of four students by National Guardsmen on the Kent State campus in Ohio just two days before, antiwar activities were the farthest thing from his mind. His full attention was on Karen, but a familiar voice on the television caught his ear, "We are interrupting this program to bring you a special report."

JR diverted his attention for a moment to watch local news anchor Max Roby, "The Air Force ROTC building on the Washington University campus is burning and surrounded by about 2500 people, predominately students. The incident should not be a total surprise to university officials. In late February, arson leveled the Army ROTC. Since then, there have been specific threats to the Air Force building.

"In March, 700 students marched from a meeting at Holmes Hall and nailed signs reading "Condemned" over the windows and doors of the remaining ROTC building.

"Washington University has apparently joined campuses all over the country that have been in turmoil, especially since the incident on the Kent State campus. We will bring you more about the ROTC building fire.

"We will return you to your regularly scheduled program shortly, but we just received a report that is eerily similar to a story from last year, when Lieutenant William Calley was charged for his role in the massacre of the unarmed civilian villagers in My Lai, Vietnam.

"Similar charges were filed today against Staff Sergeant Elton Trainer for his role in the killing of civilians in the village of Vung Dong. But unlike Calley, Trainer is also faced with an additional charge.

"During the incident, Trainer is alleged to have also shot and killed Private Jack Morton, a member of the platoon Trainer was leading, who apparently tried to stop the killing of the villagers."

JR gasped and stood up when photos of Train and Salt in uniform were displayed side-by-side on the screen. Sensing JR's need for support, Karen hugged him as his knees buckled.

"Are you OK," Karen asked softly.

"It took awhile, but it looks like in this case, justice will be done," JR responded, as he stood erect, the strength having returned to his legs.

"If you're happy about what's happening to this guy, why the long face?"

"There's no justice for your father," JR pursed his lips in anger. "I don't know what I can do, but someday I'll find a way. That guy is

SPECIAL REPORT

not going to get away with what he did! But that's for another time. For now, we need to get over to Washington U."

As JR began dressing, Karen tried to push him back onto the couch, "You can't be anywhere near there. What if you're recognized?"

"It's dark and everyone will be focused on the fire."

"Not everyone. The police will be trying to figure out who did this, and they'll be watching the crowd."

"If I promise to be careful, will you drive me to campus?"

"OK, but when we get there, I'm in charge of where we stand and whether we stay or leave."

"Yes, ma'am," JR said and saluted, then hugged Karen, who was still naked.

They were out of the apartment in five minutes and to the Washington University campus ten minutes later. They parked on the street in the well-to-do neighborhood across Wydown Boulevard, which bordered the university dorm area, and trotted across campus to join hordes of students who were curious about the fire that was lighting up the nighttime sky. JR and Maggie could feel and smell the smoke well before they got close.

Because Washington University is on the border of the communities of Clayton and University City, police and firefighters from each of those communities as well as from the campus were on hand. Also on hand were student demonstrators chanting, "Kent State, Kent State."

By the time JR and Karen got close enough to see what was going on, the building was gutted. JR's attention was drawn to a melee to his right where a student was attempting to raise a Vietcong flag up the ROTC flagpole. Police moved in both to keep that from happening and to break up the mob before it got out of hand.

Karen was applying constant pressure as she held JR's right arm above the elbow while guiding him away from the center of the activity. He looked at her, smiled, stopped resisting, and turned to walk away from the activity toward where they had parked the car.

"I've seen all I need to, Karen. Thank you for indulging me. This Kent State thing is going to be a rallying cry for the movement for a long time. Let's get out of here."

BODY NOT RECOVERED

Karen moved her hand from the tight grip it had on his upper arm to a loving grip of his hand. They each put the fire behind them and began a leisurely walk across campus.

Although neither of them would ever know it, JR Spears walked within five feet of University City Police Chief Mike Muccelli.

CHAPTER 75

WELCOME TO SQUAD 47

May 7, 1970
New York City, New York

Mooch was preparing to leave for class, when his apartment phone rang. "Mr. Muccelli, this is Special Agent Paul Marcus. Do you have a moment to speak?"

Responding to Paul's formality, Mooch said, "Yes sir."

Paul got right to the point, "Mr. Muccelli, I am authorized to formally offer you a full-time job with the Federal Bureau of Investigation. Your assignment will be the one we have talked about previously. Do you continue to be interested in employment with the FBI?"

Two years earlier, Mooch had taken an important step when he accepted his first summer internship with the FBI, but at the time, his future remained uncertain, because Columbia University was on the brink of closing the campus.

Although the confrontation between campus activists and the administration had continued and student and faculty actions had disrupted class schedules, the university officially remained open. Graduation was held, but that had given many of those graduating the opportunity to make one final point to university administrators by walking out in the middle of the ceremony en masse.

But because the university had remained open, John "Mooch" Muccelli would earn the grades necessary to lock in his volunteer summer internship with the FBI.

Mooch spent the next two summers at bureau headquarters in Washington, D. C. The first summer, as Paul had predicted, was mostly office support, helping agents manage their paperwork.

301

Although he would have preferred to be doing something more actively associated with law enforcement, Mooch knew he was learning a lot about how the bureau worked as a whole and how agents as individuals thought and acted.

His second summer was spent with an FBI section that received and analyzed information regarding the Top Ten Most Wanted fugitives. Although he was not allowed to do any field work, this assignment drew him one step closer to the action.

Both summer experiences were complemented by his keeping in frequent contact with Paul Marcus, who had transferred to headquarters and worked several floors above Mooch. It was not until well into Mooch's second summer that Paul opened up, albeit just a bit, about his work. And he only did so because he wanted to get a feel for whether Mooch would be interested in getting involved when he completed his law degree.

Because of his excellent grades and the high ratings he received from the FBI personnel he worked with, Mooch had been offered full-time employment at the bureau. His dream was coming true, and it was shaping up to be even better, because it looked like he was going to work with Paul, and although it was unusual, he was going to be in the field seeing action almost immediately.

Hoping that he would be offered an FBI job and that his first assignment would be the one Paul and he had talked about, Mooch had done something exactly the opposite of what would normally have been expected of him. He spent the second semester of his third year at law school growing a scruffy beard and letting his hair get long.

"Yes sir, I am definitely interested. I have already considered all that I have learned about the bureau and its employment policies during my internships. If I might, I would like to formally accept your offer immediately."

"Mr. Muccelli, welcome to the Federal Bureau of Investigation. I will followup this phone call by sending you all of the paperwork you need to complete. We will expect you in Washington as soon as you can arrange it after you successfully complete your degree."

"Thank you, sir."

"Mr. Muccelli, welcome to Squad 47."

CHAPTER 76

IT'S A PLAN

May 7, 1970
St. Louis, Missouri

"Karen," JR began after they had returned to her apartment from the ROTC fire on the Washington University campus, "come back to California with me."

She stared into his eyes.

JR continued, "There are so many reasons. The most important is that I want to be with you. I love you."

Her stare deepened.

Not knowing exactly what to do next as Karen remained silent, he went on, "We'll be much more accepted in California. You could easily find a nursing job there. If I continue to come visit here, you're right, there's a greater chance that I'll be recognized, and I, in fact we, can't afford that. And let me go back to the first reason. I love you."

Still no response. JR's expression turned quizzical. As he was about to speak, Karen preempted him, "I love you too."

"Wow, OK, so you'll come back with me?"

"I don't know," Karen replied, clearly torn. "My gut tells me to do it. But Mom's here; Walter Jr. is here; my job's here; I have friends here; and Dad's grave is here. St. Louis is my home. I'm afraid that if I go, I'll never be back. That doesn't feel right."

He held eye contact but was concerned about what she would say next.

"So, can I think about it? And I need to talk to Mom."

BODY NOT RECOVERED

"I wouldn't want you to be in California and be unhappy. You should only come if you really think it's right for you, that it's in your heart to do."

They both smiled as they thought about Walter.

"JR, I'm going to think about it and probably little else. When I'm ready, I'll know it. Can we leave it at that for now?"

"Well, given that you said 'when' and not 'if,' I can live with that. I'm going to head back as planned in a couple of days. If you know by then, we'll make arrangements. If not, I'm a phone call away, and we can arrange it at the right time."

"There are two things I do know now. I love you and I'll miss you. Just give me some time."

"It's a plan."

CHAPTER 77

I NEED SOME ADVICE

October 8, 1970
San Francisco, California

With law degree in hand, Mooch reversed his cross-country trek of three years earlier and was ready for work by July 1. Sporting scraggly long hair and a beard to match, Mooch settled into his new life, his third-floor walkup apartment near Union Square, and his Squad 47 assignment in San Francisco.

Although he would report through Squad 47 hierarchy to Paul Marcus, Mooch would be working out of the San Francisco office. When Mooch had entered the bureau offices for the first time dressed in sandals, worn blue jeans, a blue bandana around his neck, and a "Peace Now" tee shirt revealed by an unbuttoned, wrinkled, threadbare, denim, long-sleeved shirt, he was met with suspicious stares from nearby agents and staff as he walked up to the reception desk .

"Miss Morgan, my name is John Muccelli. I was told to report to the Squad 47 offices," Mooch said to the matronly receptionist after reading her name plate.

Morgan's apprehensive air transformed to a welcoming smile when she found his name on the papers in front of her. "Please follow me, Agent Muccelli."

"Thank you, ma'am, and call me Mooch."

"I'm Emily, but I think I'll stick with Agent Muccelli."

When Emily stopped at an office door, Mooch, seeing no signage to indicate they were at the right door, asked, "Is this Squad 47?"

With a knowing smile and before she pirouetted to return to her desk, Emily said, "Yes, sir. You're in the right place. And again, welcome."

Although Paul had told Mooch enough about Squad 47 to get him interested, his orientation, albeit brief, gave him a more detailed understanding. Squad 47 agents, who were assigned to operations across the country, were part of a larger covert activity within the FBI. COINTELPRO, the Counter Intelligence Program, had been created to infiltrate, discredit, and disrupt domestic political organizations that the FBI, primarily Director Hoover, deemed subversive.

Because Hoover had become increasingly frustrated by and insistent about the growing antiwar movement, a segment of which had become more violent, Squad 47 targeted individual antiwar activists and organizations.

Among these targets were the members of The Weathermen, a radical breakaway faction of the SDS, that had organized violent antiwar demonstrations, lost three members in a Greenwich Village townhouse when a bomb they were assembling prematurely detonated, claimed responsibility for the bombing of the New York City Police Headquarters, and issued a "Declaration of a State of War" against the United States government. Their stated objective was to "bring the war home" by showing the public and the government what it was like for there to be the constant threat of bombings, similar to what was occurring in Vietnam.

Because of Director Hoover's sense of urgency to dismember these radical left organizations and bring individual antiwar fugitives to justice, new agents like Mooch were given accelerated training and rapidly deployed to their field work. Paul chose the Bay Area for Mooch because of his familiarity with the area from his Stanford days, and because he believed there would be little risk that Mooch would be recognized, having been away from the area for several years, but more so, having drastically altered his appearance.

The San Francisco Squad 47 unit was the largest in the country behind New York and Chicago. The unit was also among the busiest because of the high degree of protest activity in the Bay Area.

Mooch learned that he would join other Squad 47 agents to investigate bombing incidents when they occurred, but most of the time, they would conduct surveillance anywhere they were hopeful of identifying protest instigators and to capture those who were already fugitives from previously issued arrest warrants. Agents attended protests large and small.

When intelligence uncovered where friends and family of likely suspects lived, Squad 47 agents would visit those homes on special occasions, hoping a fugitive would come home for a birthday, holiday, or some other event. Agents also identified and investigated individuals, who, while they might not be directly involved on the streets, supported the antiwar movement financially.

Because the activists had developed a very disciplined approach, Mooch found the work to be rigorous and dangerous. Activists only used pay phones, moved frequently and thoroughly cleaned each house and car with rubbing alcohol to erase fingerprints, spoke and wrote in code, assumed many different names, used full and fake identification packages, and, perhaps most importantly, those who had gone underground had totally cut themselves off from their families. To add to the painstaking attention required to make progress, even when agents had a strong reason to believe that a targeted activist was going to be at a protest, the sheer size of the demonstrations, which could include thousands of people, made it hard to find the individual in the crowd.

The danger derived from the agents' appearance and dress. When on surveillance at a rally, the Squad 47 agents, by design, could not be distinguished from the protestors. When the police would fire tear gas canisters into a crowd or wield nightsticks to break up a demonstration, it was not uncommon for agents to feel the full physical brunt of the onslaught. In just a short time, Mooch was subjected to tear gas several times, and his occasional proximity to aggressive police tactics brought back memories of the New York City Tactical Police Force on the Columbia campus in 1968.

Despite the difficulty and occasional danger, Mooch was excited to be in the FBI and in Squad 47. But there was one concern that was brewing for him and perhaps other Squad 47 agents, although he did not discuss it with them. When an agent had a strong suspicion that a targeted individual or possible associate was living or meeting in a building, there was a procedure to follow to get approval from FBI hierarchy to enter and search the building without a court-authorized warrant.

Based on everything he had learned in law school and from his father about suspects having rights secured by the constitution, Mooch did not feel right about the procedure, and when he felt comfortable to do so, mentioned his concern to his supervisor.

"Agent Muccelli, we distinguish between gathering intelligence and gathering evidence. As long as we're not intending to introduce what we find in court, we don't consider our actions to be limited by constitutional prohibition against unreasonable search and seizure."

"Sir, we're not only entering the homes and bugging suspects but also their relatives and acquaintances. Is that OK also?"

"The Director has interpreted the laws to allow us to enter homes without warrant and to bug those homes in the pursuit of the FBI mission to bring espionage agents, possible saboteurs, and subversive persons to justice."

Mooch was not mollified but felt that pursuing it would not be helpful. He was getting the bureau's policy position without regard for what he felt were legitimate concerns. "Thank you, sir."

Being so new to the bureau and the lack of satisfaction he got from his supervisor, Mooch was concerned about bringing the issue up again in his San Francisco office, but it continued to gnaw at him.

"Dad, I need some advice."

CHAPTER 78

COMING TO CALIFORNIA

October 8, 1970
San Francisco, California

Mooch's call home for advice was not the only San Francisco to St. Louis call that day made by a member of the University City High School Class of 1964, "Karen, how are you?"

"Hey, JR. Am I ever glad you called! I've been thinking about you and was about to try to get in touch."

"Must be those West Coast to Midwest vibes I've been sending," JR said and laughed.

"Well, you won't have to be sending them for long. I'm coming to California."

JR was speechless.

"I've talked a lot to Mom and even asked for Walter Jr.'s opinion. I'm sure you'll guess what advice they've each been giving me."

"Do what's in your heart to do?"

"Yep. And there is no doubt in my mind and in my heart that I want to be with you. I have to tell you though that I'm really nervous about this. I've never been away from home for long before. I've certainly never lived with anyone other than my family before. And although you've explained it to me, I'm really not sure what risk I'm taking with your antiwar work and your relationship with the army. But I've thought through all of that, and I'm ready to take the leap."

"I can't wait for you to get here. I love you."

They spent another ten minutes making plans and decided to call each other nightly, if only briefly, until Karen left for San Francisco.

"JR, I have one last request. I need you to promise me that we'll find some way to get back to St. Louis."

"I can't promise that we can get back permanently or when, but I'll do everything I can to make sure you see your family and friends. Good enough?"

"Good enough."

CHAPTER 79

JUST FOLLOWING ORDERS

October 8, 1970
San Francisco, California

"Sure, son, what's up," responded Mike Muccelli when Mooch said he needed some advice.

"Just today, the Weather Underground claimed responsibility for three bombings; one at the University of Washington, one nearby here at the Marin County Courthouse, and one in Santa Barbara. These folks clearly need to be found and stopped."

"That seems pretty obvious to me. So what's the issue?"

"Dad, this really needs to be between you and me. I know when I tell you, you'll want to do something about it, but for now, I just need you to help me figure out what to do."

"OK, Mooch, between you and me."

"One of the things we're doing to identify and catch up with these the Weather Underground and others is to break into suspicious homes and install wiretaps and bugs. When we do, it's been approved by higher ups in the FBI, but there is no court-approved warrant. Just the other day, I was involved in listening to a conversation in an apartment that we bugged. I didn't actually do the break in, but I was involved. It doesn't seem right."

Mike Muccelli sensed the tension and concern in his son's voice, but Mooch's feelings were not Mike's only consideration, "Son, I have to agree with you and for two reasons. First, I'm not sure why or how the FBI can or should get away with violating constitutional rights. Second, for me there's a bigger personal issue. There are felony wiretap laws that would probably put you at risk."

"Ooh, I'm not sure why, but I didn't even think about the felony issue. There's a whole lot of this going on, and I've heard no concerns about that from any of the agents. Guys are just following orders."

"Mooch, what are you thinking about doing?"

"Dad, I was concerned when I called you for advice; now I'm scared based on the felony thing. I'm not really sure what to do. So, advise away."

"I think you have three options. Ask a superior about the felony issue and how you're protected. Just refuse to do any of this. Or keep doing what you're told. My guess is that you're not OK with number three, or you wouldn't have called me. Number two will get you disciplined at the least. So, what do you think about option one?"

Mooch was able to relax a bit as his dad's advise was helping solidify his thoughts. He tested an idea with his father, "I wonder if I can go straight to Paul Marcus on this one. Now that I'm in the bureau, it seems like I can't or shouldn't count on the same relationship. I'll be going over people's heads to talk to him."

"This whole thing sounds like something that Paul wouldn't condone anyway. If you could talk to him off the record, that might be the best option. It seems like the risk of doing that is lower than the risk of continuing to do what you've been doing. Doable?"

"I'm willing to take that chance to get this sorted out. Let me think about how to pull it off. Thanks, Dad."

"Anytime, son. Your mother's waving from across the room. Want to say 'hi?'"

"You bet, and thanks again, Dad. I'll keep you posted."

CHAPTER 80

ARRESTED

February 10, 1971
San Francisco, California

"Read this."

Doc handed JR the previous day's *San Francisco Chronicle* and pointed to the page-two headline.

"War Deserter Arrested"

"Trey Paulson was arrested last evening before he could detonate a bomb he had planted at the Oakland Army Induction Center. The induction center has been under close surveillance because of frequent antiwar demonstrations and previous bombing attempts. A police officer observed Paulson leaving a package in the doorway and confronted him before he left the area. Experts diffused the bomb, which they say would likely not have exploded, because it was so poorly constructed.

"When interrogated, Paulson, an African-American, claimed to be a Vietnam veteran but was later found through Army records to have been listed as killed in a helicopter crash off the Vietnam coast.

"Paulson maintains he was supposed to be on the helicopter after it refueled at an Australian base in Vung Tau, Vietnam. He further claimed that during the refueling, he went to a local bar having told the pilot to leave without him. When he heard the helicopter had crashed and all on board were killed, he decided not to find another way back to his unit. Instead, he deserted and found his way back to the United States.

"Paulson also admitted that he had made a previous attempt to bomb the induction center with the late Bernice Williams. Williams

was killed in the rooming house explosion in the Haight-Ashbury neighborhood on July 20 last year. It was suspected that she had been building a bomb that detonated prematurely. Paulson, who was across the street at an antiwar demonstration in Buena Vista Park when the explosion occurred, confirmed that suspicion.

"Although the frequency of bombings associated with radical antiwar groups has increased since late 1969, police and FBI spokesmen indicate that Paulson seemed to be acting alone and was not associated with the Weather Underground or any other group."

"Prosecutors say Paulson will be charged with desertion as well as the attempted bombing of a federal building. He faces the possibility of spending the remainder of his life in a federal prison."

Shaking his head in sorrow and being thankful for Doc's advice to stay off the front lines of demonstrations, JR said, "I feel sorry for him. The feds don't fool around. You know, even though he had been obsessed with Bernie and bombing, we have to be thankful he had the wherewithal to protect us. At least for now."

CHAPTER 81

CAN WE ALTER A PHOTO?

March 3, 1971
San Francisco, California

"I want to come with you," Karen cooed as she wrapped her arms around JR's neck.

His arms around her waist, JR said, "You just got here. Why don't you focus on finding the nursing job you want and getting settled in? Then, when you're ready and if you still want to, you can get as deeply involved in the movement as you'd like."

Although they had planned for Karen to be in California shortly after the call during which she told JR she was coming, the trip was delayed when Walter Jr. had an accident at work. While installing a speaker in a high ceiling, he lost his balance and fell. Karen was not willing to leave town until Walter Jr.'s compound leg fracture was sufficiently healed.

In the meantime, JR had rented a one-bedroom furnished apartment not far from the rooming house on Haight Avenue in which Bernie was killed. It was the first time since being in the Bay Area that JR would have a place of his own, and he was thrilled about sharing it with Karen. Although JR's jobs as a waiter in various restaurants had easily paid for his simple living expenses, the apartment would stretch his finances. He knew that Karen was bent on finding a nursing job, and she had agreed to the cost of the apartment.

He was also able to add work hours, because while waiting for Karen to arrive, JR found that he had quite a bit of time on his hands. The protest movement had seemed to take on a life of its own. Activism was less likely to spring from the college campuses or the streets of the Bay Area. Celebrities, politicians, the Vietnam Veterans Against the War, and others were staging events throughout the country. And the Weather Underground was drawing significant attention, having claimed responsibility for bombings in multiple cities. Public opinion continued to become more antiwar, only 34% approving of the Vietnam strategy and half of all Americans believing that the war was morally wrong.

Karen's job in St. Louis had enabled her to afford a flight to San Francisco, and JR met her and her four overstuffed suitcases at the airport. From the moment they embraced at her arrival gate, they were inseparable for a week, focusing on each other and getting acclimated to their new life together. But it was time to also pursue their individual interests.

"OK, JR, maybe you're right. You go today, and I'll join you another time. I'm going to head over to the hospital to apply for that nursing job Doc told me about. And I'm glad you took me by the clinic. In fact, I'm thinking about volunteering there even when I get a nursing job."

"They'll really appreciate your help. Good luck with the job application. I can't wait to hear how it went. I'm going to head out. There's a group planning to demonstrate across the bay at the Oakland Induction Center this afternoon. I'm going to be there for just a few hours, and I'll be back."

At the same time JR and Karen stood in the doorway of their apartment, reluctant to release their hug, Mooch was in a meeting of the San Francisco Squad 47 agents at the bureau office. Although Mooch preferred street work to meetings, he was glad to attend this gathering, because Special Agent Paul Marcus would be there. Marcus had been on a cross-country tour, visiting each of his Squad 47 offices to review progress and plans.

The local Squad 47 lead agent conducted the meeting, "Special Agent Marcus, we're glad you're here. A group has been analyzing surveillance photos from the past six months and categorizing them in an attempt to help identify key activist leaders. We've combined this work with intelligence from our agents to select targets, and we'd like to share our approach and findings with you."

"It's an honor to be here, and I'm looking forward to hearing what you've found. If this approach works, we'll reapply it in other cities."

CAN WE ALTER A PHOTO?

Paul responded as he looked from face to face, stopping just a split second longer on Mooch, who caught the gesture and smiled.

"OK, what do we have," the lead agent asked, prompting the discussion.

For the next 45 minutes, the analysis group shared their findings, which focused on 11 people they believed to be key leaders. Some of the targets were known by name, and the bureau had some information in their files other than just photos. But there were others for whom the photos were the only lead.

The clearest photo of each potential target was circulated to those in the room to see if anyone else had any information that had yet to be shared. Mooch looked at each photo and commented on a couple based on his experience. When one particular photo was in front of him, he stared at it longer than he had at the others. The face looked familiar, but he could not put a finger on why.

When there was a break in the conversation, Mooch asked the squad's imaging expert, "Can we alter a photo to see what a person would look like with shorter hair and no beard?"

"Sure can, but it'll take awhile," the expert replied, beaming at the attention.

"See what you can do with this guy and let me know when you have something I can look at. He really looks familiar," Mooch said, continuing to stare at the photo.

Paul Marcus was thanked again for coming, assignments were given, and the meeting was adjourned, giving Paul a chance to corral Mooch in the hallway for a moment.

"How are things going, Mooch?"

"In general, pretty well. But there is one thing I'd like to talk to you about off the record if we get a chance."

"I'm staying in town tonight. I have a dinner with some of the local brass, but I could get together after that."

They exchanged phone numbers and agreed on a plan to get together later, then shook hands. Mooch headed for the Oakland Induction Center to check on a demonstration that they had heard would be held that afternoon.

CHAPTER 82

WHO IS THAT GUY?

March 3, 1971
Oakland, California

JR took a bus across the Oakland Bay Bridge, never tiring of the view of San Francisco and the bay, and made his way to the induction center. He had not been a part of organizing the protest, which was expected to be small, but he wanted to show his support. When he got there, he found only a couple of hundred relatively lackluster demonstrators, who appeared to be outnumbered by local police, who were always in full force whenever the induction center was involved.

JR spent some time talking to the organizers and some others that he knew, realized that this demonstration, compared to so many others, would not make a meaningful difference, and decided to leave to get back to Karen.

As he turned from a conversation he was having, he was face-to-face and about 20 yards from a guy who was staring at him. JR, who was sensitized to the risk of being recognized, would have normally averted his eyes and walked the other way as calmly as possible. In this case, for some reason he could not explain, his gaze remained riveted. Despite being surrounded by several hundred demonstrators and police, JR felt as if he were alone with the man standing in front of him.

There was the look of recognition on the face of this tall long-haired, bearded man who faced him. And, JR realized, the guy looked familiar to him.

Mooch's first thought was, "This is the guy in the photo at the meeting today."

His next thought was, "But I also know him from somewhere else."

JR, despite the risk of being recognized, actually found himself taking a step toward this man. And he noted that the man had already taken two steps toward him. That realization shocked JR into his normal reality. He was about to turn and leave when he heard, "Bomb!"

The demonstrators, police, and bystanders scattered. JR would find out later that one of the demonstrators had brought a fake bomb to the protest just to make a point. The frenzy had separated him from the induction center, the scurrying mob, and the man.

"Who was that guy?"

Both men had the same lingering thought.

CHAPTER 83

THIS STINKS

March 3, 1971
San Francisco, California

Mooch went back to the office with the intent of finding out more about why the guy at the protest looked so familiar. He looked for the imaging expert to see if he had altered the photo but could not find him. After checking through some files and finding nothing, Mooch shifted his focus to his meeting with Paul.

Marcus got in touch with Mooch at his apartment at 9:30 and 20 minutes later they were face-to-face in a booth at a soda shop near Paul's hotel.

"You sure look scraggly, Mooch. It's really good to see you."

"Likewise, Paul, only not the scraggly part. When I heard you were coming out, I hoped we could find some time."

"How are your mom and dad?"

"Talked to them just the other day, and they're doing well. Sounds like Dad's dealing with a downsized version of what we're doing out here. I'm sure you heard about Washington U's ROTC building. Dad was there."

"It's spreading nationwide and quickly. The bureau brass are frantic. That's why our work is so important."

"It's our work that I was hoping to talk to you about, Paul, if you don't mind me going off the record for a bit."

"Let's start that way," Paul said warily, "but if I feel you're getting too far off, I'll call a halt. Fair enough?"

"Works for me."

"OK, what's up?"

"You know how much the bureau means to me and how much I care about the rule of law."

Mooch had spent a lot of time thinking about what to say to Paul and how.

"Well, I have personal concerns with some things that we're doing, and I need some guidance on how to think about it. I can't think of anyone better than you to provide that guidance."

Paul looked concerned, but Mooch could not tell if it was concern about the issues he was about to hear or about having this conversation at all.

Mooch decided he needed to lay out the issues regardless of how Paul reacted—he forged on, "Let me see if I can do this in a concise way. I firmly believe in people's right to demonstrate, but I also know that many of the activists are breaking laws. I'm certainly against the rising violence and bombing being advocated and executed by the Weather Underground and others. And I know that the FBI and Squad 47 are tasked with bringing perpetrators to justice.

"What bothers me is that we're conducting searches and wiretaps without court warrants. This puts the rights of individuals at risk and perhaps, puts me at risk as well. So that leads me to two questions. Why is it right for us to be conducting warrantless searches and buggings and am I at risk of committing a felony myself?"

Paul listened patiently, but Mooch could tell he had opened a difficult subject.

Mooch finished with, "I hope that I'm not imposing on our friendship by sharing these concerns with you. If you don't want to or can't talk about it, I'd understand."

Paul was silent for several moments, all the time maintaining eye contact with Mooch while slowly stirring his Coca-Cola with his straw.

"I want to talk about this with you, but I'm not sure I can. Would it satisfy you if I were to say that I have similar concerns and am working on them without telling you more than that?"

"So, I don't want this to sound like it's all about me, but am I at risk legally?"

"I can't talk about that."

Paul had gotten very serious. In the absence of any specifics, Mooch studied Paul's facial expressions and body language. He came to the conclusion that Paul was also seriously conflicted, and that raised a big red flag for Mooch.

"Paul, I don't want to cause any problems—at least, I don't think I do. What would happen if I refused to continue to participate?"

"If you're asking me as your boss, I would say that the bureau would have to treat that as insubordination, which it would not take kindly."

"What if I'm asking you as a friend?"

"Without being more specific, I would tell you to take good care."

Mooch was becoming more agitated, "I've wanted to be an FBI agent my whole life, and I'm blessed that my dream has come true. But now I'm in a position to have to make a choice whether to continue to pursue my dream by looking the other way about what I feel is wrong.

"And to top it off, I may be breaking the law myself. I'm beginning to think that this stinks."

"Mooch, you know how much I want to make this right for you, but I'm in a position where I need to do it behind the scenes and not share with you what that means. What are you going to do?"

"First of all, Paul, I understand the position you're in, and you know I trust you to do everything you can to make it right. But as I see it, I have several choices. Just continue on as though nothing has changed. Decide not to follow orders that I think are illegal and take the consequences. Blow the whistle on this whole thing. Or just leave the bureau and keep my mouth shut."

Mooch's shoulders were slumped and his head was down looking at the floor in front of him. Then he raised his head, looked Paul in the eyes, and said, "I just don't know."

"At this point, I can't help. I wish I could. But if I get to the point that I can, I'll definitely let you know."

For the first time since the incident at the Berkeley draft card burning, Mooch and Paul parted ways on a down note.

CHAPTER 84

EFFECTIVE IMMEDIATELY

April 2, 1971
San Francisco, California

Mooch stopped by the office before heading out on the streets to followup on a lead he had received about one of his target suspects. When he checked his mail box, he found one sheet of paper, an organization announcement. Although the text was very brief, it would have huge implications for the struggle Mooch was having to reconcile his values with what the bureau had been doing and asking him to do.

Since meeting with Paul a month earlier, Mooch had continued to do his job but was able to work with his Squad 47 counterparts to manipulate assignments and keep from actually being a part of warrantless searches and wiretaps. He had also had several phone calls with his father trying to sort out a course of action.

He was still uncertain about what he would do but feeling increasingly anxious about needing to do something and to do it soon. When he read the organization announcement, he found it initially added only more confusion, but as he reflected on it, he sensed the beginnings of clarity.

"Special Agent Paul Marcus has resigned from the Federal Bureau of Investigation effective immediately. Leadership of Squad 47 will be assumed by Special Agent James Lansing effective immediately."

Mooch tried to reconstruct the conversation he had with Paul. What had Paul meant by, "Would it satisfy you if I were to say that I have similar concerns and am working on them without telling you more than that?"

Mooch had many more questions than answers. Had Paul confronted FBI leadership? Even Director Hoover? Did he really resign or was he asked to leave? How does all of this affect what I'm trying to decide?

"May I speak to Special Agent Marcus please?"

"Mr. Marcus is no longer with the FBI and cannot be reached at this number."

Mooch tried Paul's home number. No answer. He continued to try throughout the day. No answer.

Another question without an answer—would he ever see or talk to Paul again?

As Mooch continued to struggle with the possibilities, a new thought emerged, "Paul knew I was concerned about what the FBI was doing. Paul cares about me as both a mentor and a friend. Paul would not have left in this way without getting a message to me. He knew I would get the organization announcement. That is his message. Paul knew I would assume that he left because he could not affect what was going on and he, like me, could not reconcile it with his values. Paul left for his own reasons, but his leaving was also a signal to me."

Mooch sensed a course of action becoming more clear. It was time to talk to his father again.

CHAPTER 85

HAPPIEST OF MY LIFE

April 1, 1973
San Francisco, California

JR and Karen had settled into a loving and comfortable relationship. She was working as a floor nurse at San Francisco General Hospital, and JR continued to earn tip money as a waiter at a nearby bistro. They had been back to St. Louis several times, and Mary had visited them in San Francisco.

"I wish I could find the words to tell you how much I love you and how thankful I am that you came out here to be with me. These past two years have been the happiest of my life. And this is not an April Fool's joke."

JR had come to Berkeley to surprise Karen and meet her after her shift at the clinic. They had walked to the park and the bench where JR and Maggie had first shared their pasts and connected as surrogate brother and sister.

JR and Karen held hands and twisted on the bench to face each other. JR continued, "As much as I love you and our life, I need to tell you that I'm feeling a bit useless these days. It's good news—the movement has taken on a life of its own, and the pressure on Washington is finally paying off."

JR and Karen religiously watched and read the news about the war. Walter Cronkite showed them Vietnam veteran John Kerry calling for an immediate withdrawal of troops when he testified before a Senate committee. During his testimony, Kerry asked, "How do you ask a man to be the last man to die in Vietnam? How do you ask a man to be the last man to die for a mistake?"

They saw TV news footage of 200,000 protestors demonstrating on the Mall in Washington, and they participated with over 150,000 who demonstrated in San Francisco, the largest antiwar rally ever on the West Coast.

They read *The New York Times* and *The Washington Post* reporting of leaked secret government documents, later known as the "Pentagon Papers," which indicated that the Johnson administration had fabricated information to convince the public and congress to continue to escalate the war effort.

They watched coverage of three paraplegic veterans, including Ron Kovic, interrupt Richard Nixon's acceptance speech at the Miami Republican National Convention, shouting, "Stop the bombing! Stop the killing!" and then be roughly ejected from the convention.

And they were watching on January 23, 1973, when President Nixon announced a peace agreement had been reached in the Paris talks. Four days later, an agreement was signed ending American involvement in the Vietnam War. By March 29, the last U.S. troops left Vietnam.

JR went on, "I've taken huge risks and have dedicated myself to the movement. What's my purpose now?"

"How about me being your purpose," Karen asked, squeezing his hand.

"That's why I started this conversation by telling you how much I love you. I can't imagine what I'd do if I didn't have you."

"I know how much it means to you that the war is over," Karen said. "And I know that even though our lives will never be normal, we can start settling into what should at least be a quieter time. You'll find another cause. You care too much about things not to."

"I hope you're right, but that's the other thing I'm worried about. I have no regrets about the decisions I made, but I do wish there was a way that we'd not have to live with the constant threat that I'd be recognized and arrested."

CHAPTER 86

AMNESTY

September 17, 1974
San Francisco, California

"You're not going to believe this," JR said after Doc had answered the phone.

As Karen was getting ready to go to work, she and JR had been watching the local morning news, and JR ran down to the corner to get a newspaper to confirm what they had heard. The *San Francisco Chronicle* article aligned with the TV news report.

"Believe what?"

"Let me read this to you. It's from this morning's *Chronicle*.

"*President Gerald Ford has signed a proclamation that...*

"Oh hell, Doc, let me just tell you. There's an amnesty for deserters. We have until January 31 to report to Camp Atterbury, Indiana and do two things, sign a declaration of our loyalty to the United States and commit to two years of public service. If we do that, we're free to move on with the rest of our lives."

Silence.

"Doc, are you still there?"

"Yes," Doc could barely talk. "Are you sure?"

"We need to get the details, but it looks and sounds real. They played a tape of Ford's speech this morning, and he said two things that are quoted in the paper. I'll read to you what he said.

"*I did this for the simple reason that for American fighting men, the long and divisive war in Vietnam has been over for more than a year, and I was determined then, as now, to do everything in my power to bind up the Nation's wounds.*

"The primary purpose of this program is the reconciliation of all our people and the restoration of the essential unity of Americans within which honest differences of opinion do not descend to angry discord and mutual problems are not polarized by excessive passion."

"It also says here that Ford had announced plans for this program back in August, but I sure didn't hear anything about it. I'm going to call Mr. Carlson and have him get in touch with Hulk, Pat, and Prince, although last time I talked to him, he still hadn't heard anything from Prince. Then Karen and I are coming over to take Jill and you out for dinner to celebrate. Then we're going to make plans to get to Camp Atterbury. Sound right?"

Doc, still finding it hard to speak, forced out, "I just can't believe this. Sure, let's get together and figure this out. We have to be sure it fits our special circumstances."

CHAPTER 87

HELLO MOUSE

September 20, 1974
San Francisco, California

As they learned more about the details, their excitement about the pending amnesty increased. When they met for dinner, JR, Karen, Doc, and Jill began to make more specific plans.

JR took the responsibility to confirm the amnesty proclamation and process. Over the past couple of days, he had anonymously contacted local military offices and got the number of the right office in Washington. He made the call and got all of the information he needed, all of it verifying the understanding they had derived from the news reports.

With confirmation in place, JR made three phone calls. The first was to the Carlsons. After he had told him why he was calling, John Carlson confirmed that he too had heard of the amnesty, looked into it, had already informed his son, and was about to contact JR, but JR had beat him to it. Carlson then agreed with JR's suggestion, "I would be honored to coordinate the reunion at Camp Atterbury, but no, I've never heard from Prince and have no idea how to contact him."

The second call was to Maggie. Although they had not seen each other for five years, JR and she had stayed in touch, albeit infrequently. Over that time, Maggie had settled into a family-like relationship with Doris and Marvin Williams, attended the newly-opened Ocean County College in nearby Toms River, worked part time mucking stalls at Tricorn Farm in Colts Neck, and was contemplating going on to earn her degree at a four-year university.

"Maggie, you're not going to believe it."

JR went on to tell her about the amnesty and Karen's and his plans. Maggie, who had regained much of her zest for life over the years of stability at the Williams, was excited about the news. "You know, JR, I've been thinking about where I'd like to go to college. Since visiting the campus when I was out there, I've had my heart set on Stanford. But another I've been considering is Washington University in St. Louis—it's a great school and not as far from home. If you're going to be in St. Louis, that may be my reason to choose Washington U."

The third call was the most difficult. "Hello Mouse."

CHAPTER 88

DON'T LEAVE THE BASE

October 23, 1974
Camp Atterbury, Indiana

Pat Richardson drove the Hertz rent-a-car from the Howard Johnson's on the south side of Indianapolis. The last time he had been at the controls with this crew, there were eight of them—now there were four. Pucker had died in the jungle; Balls had died in the crash. Three-Spot was in federal prison, and Peepers had disappeared.

The white 1974 Ford LTD four-door sedan, which Pat's wife, Lucy, had rented for them, because she was the only one of the entire group with a driver's license, approached the gates of Camp Atterbury. "It's show time," Pat said, bringing knowing grins to each of their faces.

"Can I help you, sir," asked a guard at the gate.

"Yes, you can. The four of us are here to surrender as deserters."

"Had you previously surrendered elsewhere?"

"No, we haven't."

Deserters around the country were being urged to surrender at a local military facility and were then being assembled for charter flights to Camp Atterbury. JR had suggested to Mr. Carlson, through whom all of the plans were coordinated, that the four comrades reunite near Indianapolis and then surrender at the camp together.

Two days earlier, JR, Doc, Hulk, and Pat converged on the motel, and Karen, Jill, Lucy and Pat's son, Brent, accompanied their men. Although in general the mood was one of excitement and relief because of the opportunity that the amnesty presented, the reunion was bittersweet. They had a lot to celebrate and catch up on, but they also continued to carry the burden of their experiences in Vietnam, the loss of their friends, and the stress of living underground.

Although the motel pool was covered for the winter, the group commandeered a corner of the deck, bundled up against the October Indiana breeze, and reveled in their reconnection.

The women bonded quickly. Although their individual stories were very different, each had signed on to the conspiracy on a deep personal level. Pat had told Lucy the whole story as soon as he reached her from the Carlson ranch. JR had told Karen and Mary Rawlings everything that happened when he first visited in St. Louis. And when Doc and Jill realized they had a relationship far beyond just a common place to live, he trusted her with his history.

Hulk told stories of Bangkok and updated everyone on the Jattawan family, including Annan's marriage. The Jattawans, even Annan's mother, had sent their regards. Pat told of his family's unsuccessful effort to find a place to call home. JR and Doc talked about the antiwar movement, trying hard not to offend Hulk and Pat for not having joined the cause.

The most energetic conversation, however, was about their future plans—now that they envisioned having a future.

Hulk jumped in first, "After my two years of public service, I'm going to live part time in the States and part in Bangkok. I'm slowly taking over dad's business and am working with the Jattawan family on some new ideas. And the best news is that Annan is also getting more involved in the business."

With Brent at his side and an arm around Lucy, Pat said, "As soon as I heard about the amnesty, I contacted a Vietnam flying buddy. Do you guys remember the guy who was flying the Huey over Vung Dong and transported the surviving villagers to the refugee camp? He has a helicopter touring business at the Grand Canyon and offered me a job.

"I found out that I can get the amnesty without having to do the two years of public service. When you guys do your two years, you'll get what's called a clemency discharge. Mine will be called an undesirable discharge. As best I can tell, the difference is that you'll have an easier time finding a job.

"Anyway, we've been bouncing around way too long. We're just going to head straight for the Grand Canyon and try to put down some roots."

Pat tightened his arm around Lucy and drew Brent to him with the other. Pat's wife and son hugged him back—they were united and happy about their plan.

"I'm hoping to convince the administrators at Camp Atterbury that I could offer a lot if I got a medically-related public service assignment. Once we know where we'll be, Jill and I are planning to get married."

When the whoops and hollers died down, Doc continued, "Then we're planning on me going to medical school and getting back to the Bay Area as soon as possible. I know I'm getting a late start on schooling and my profession, but I can't imagine doing anything else.

"And," he happily reminded them, "I'm already Doc."

JR and Karen had squeezed themselves into one of the pool's lounge chairs and somehow made it look comfortable, "We're going to start by heading home to St. Louis. My ten-year high school reunion is coming up, and I feel like I need to reconnect with my class, even though I wasn't really close to them in the first place. Karen's going to return to her nursing career there. Then I'll do my two-year stint, wherever it is, but hopefully nearby.

"St. Louis is still not ready for a mixed-race couple, but we are. And we think it's time to let the cat out of the bag. We got married a year ago when Karen's mom was visiting."

More whoops and hollers.

JR continued, "We've learned a lot about organizing and think we can make a difference in race relations and civil rights. Don't know for sure, but maybe we'll join the Congress of Racial Equality.

"I'm not sure what I'll do for work, but I've learned a lot about playing it by ear. So, I'm not worried about it."

Not knowing how long the processing would be, the women and Brent stayed at the Howard Johnson when the men went to Camp Atterbury.

"Sir, if you drive to the end of this road and report to the last building on the right, they can help you out."

Camp Atterbury, a one-time basic training camp, was now a ramshackle facility that had clearly been neglected for some time. The military had chosen it because of its central location in the country and because it was no longer an active military compound; eliminating the risk of tension between the surrendering deserters and active forces.

When the four signed in, they were ushered to a room and given a full briefing about how the processing would take place and what their legal responsibilities and rights were. On day two of what was expected to be a four-day process, an officer ushered the four into a barracks area.

"Gentlemen, we've investigated each of you and determined that your case is very different. You're the only ones listed as missing in action, presumed dead.

"And we know, or at least suspect, that you crashed an army helicopter into the sea as part of your desertion plans. That creates a much different scenario. Will you confirm that we understand your situation correctly?"

The four comrades looked at each other, but could not read each others' thoughts enough to gain consensus on what to say. After several more moments of silence, the officer began, "Gentlemen, I'm asking you again..."

"Yes sir," JR took the lead, "we staged the crash of a helicopter for the purpose of deserting. The plan was my idea."

"There were others in the helicopter with you. Where are they?"

JR stepped up again, "Pucker...er...Eddie Planck and Tony Baltieri had died earlier that day, and before we decided to ditch the copter, we were trying to get them to a field morgue. We lost track of Dan Prince when we got back to the States, and Trey Paulson is in federal prison on a bombing charge."

In the brief moment he had to figure out what to say, JR realized that because Balls died in the crash, they could have been charged with his death. He decided to lie and hoped the others would not challenge what he said. They did not.

"OK, for now, we'll continue with your processing, but I need to investigate this further to make sure you're still eligible. Don't leave the base."

He walked out leaving four stunned, speechless, and dejected men behind.

CHAPTER 89

INDEPENDENCE DAY

October 24, 1974
Camp Atterbury, Indiana

"Gentlemen," the officer began as he entered their barracks the following morning.

In the 20 hours since learning they might not be granted amnesty, JR, Hulk, Doc, and Pat had talked about nothing but options and implications. They were not only at risk of losing the amnesty, but of being arrested and imprisoned.

Being isolated in the barracks building gave them the opportunity to speak in confidence. Sitting on their cots and leaning into each other, the conversation was intense but controlled. These comrades had trekked through the jungle together, planned and executed a staged helicopter crash, made their way to Bangkok on a rickety fishing boat, and had lived underground since then. They were used to adversity, trusted each other implicitly, and were adept at improvisation. Now they had another problem to solve.

Pat summed up their conversation, "As I see it, it comes down to this—wait to hear what the army decides and live with the consequences or find a way off the base, back to Indianapolis, and back to our former lives."

"I'll do some recon to figure out how we can get to our car and get out of here," JR volunteered. "In the meantime, we also need a plan B. What happens if we can't get to the car?"

As it grew dark, JR drew a mental map of the camp as he prepared to check out an escape plan. Although not in the jungles of Vietnam, he recognized the feeling of fear and adrenaline coursing through his body. Once again, his future was at stake.

INDEPENDENCE DAY

When he judged it was dark enough, JR stepped out of the barracks door, ready to head for the visitor's parking lot. It only took him two steps to realize there was a part of their recon plan they had not anticipated. Not only had the officer told them to stay on base, but he had also placed armed guards to make sure that happened.

JR nodded to the guards, who had brought their weapons to the ready, as though he had just stepped out to get some air. He had no choice but to turn around and walk back through the door to the shocked look on his friend's faces, "We're out of options."

"We're never out of options," Hulk stood and responded.

JR was disconsolate, "There are two guards, both armed, and that's the only door. Although we could probably surprise and overpower them, we risk them or us getting hurt or killed. And even if we handle the guards, we'd likely still have to fight our way off the base. It doesn't look good."

"So what do we do, leave it up to the army's good graces," Hulk challenged. "Doc, Pat, what do you think?"

Pat responded quickly, "For the last eight years, I've been haunted by the reality that I killed Balls. Let's not argue about that. He was alive until I crashed the copter. I'll have to live with that the rest of my life. So, I can't and won't be part of being responsible for another death, either a guard or one of us."

Hulk sat down and did not respond. Nor did the others.

The four sank despondently into their cots, each alone with his thoughts for the night.

In the morning, the officer continued, "We've looked into your situation in more detail. As best as we can determine, it seems that everything you told us is true. Thank you for your honesty. The remaining issue is that you purposefully destroyed an army helicopter. We needed to look into the implications of that.

"We've concluded that holding you accountable for that aircraft at this point would not meet the intent of President Ford's proclamation of amnesty. You are free to continue through processing."

The officer was patient and, in fact, smiling, as the four men leaped into each other's arms, whooping with delight. He allowed the tumult to wind down and even for the men to wipe away their tears of relief.

"Sorry, sir," Doc said.

"No problem," the officer responded as he regained a professional bearing, "I also have news about Prince and Paulson. Paulson's attempted bombing conviction will preclude him from pursuing amnesty. He'll be locked up for a long time.

"A Dan Prince has surrendered himself in West Virginia, and we expect him here for processing in several days. I'll make sure he doesn't get caught up in the helicopter issue."

JR spoke up, "Thank you, sir, and can I ask a favor?"

"Go ahead."

JR scribbled something on a piece of scrap paper on the table in front of him. "Would you please give Dan Prince this telephone number?"

Within 24 hours, each of them received their appropriate discharge and except for Pat, they had their public service appointments. Although these were being assigned, they had been asked for a preference. Doc ended up helping in a Public Health Service clinic that served Indian tribes around Taos, New Mexico.

Although he was disappointed not to be assigned to Thailand because the volunteer quota was full, Hulk would be joining the Peace Corps and would be stationed in the nearby Philippines.

And JR could not wait to let Karen know that they would be located in St. Louis, where he would be working with a federal child literacy program.

During the drive back to Indianapolis, the mood was generally light and lively. But just under the surface was the realization that without extra effort, they might not see each other again.

JR decided to deal with that head on, "OK, today is October 24, 1974. It's our Independence Day. I propose that we come together every year on this date to celebrate our holiday. Hulk, do you think your parents would mind hosting our annual celebration at the ranch?"

"They'd love it."

"All in favor."

Not surprisingly, the vote was unanimous.

CHAPTER 90

ARRANGEMENTS FOR TWO

November 29, 1974
St. Louis, Missouri

JR stared into the mirror. Although he had entered the bathroom ten minutes earlier with the express intent of shaving the beard that he had grown shortly after arriving in the Bay Area eight years earlier, he had yet to pick up the razor.

JR recalled the day in the high school cafeteria when he had stared at his yearbook photo—a blank reflection. What he saw now was strength, contentment, and self-confidence.

He recalled the blank space in the yearbook where his high school activities would have been listed had he had any. What he recognized now was that he had a list of experiences that would fill a book.

Ten years earlier, he had no idea what the future held. That was still true. But now, he knew his future would be built on a foundation of experience, solid relationships, demonstrated leadership, and both physical and mental toughness.

Ten years ago, he could not have envisioned attending his high school reunion. Yet, later this evening, that was exactly what he would do.

Although the call he had made to Mouse after learning of the amnesty proclamation had begun as an awkward apology, the two friends quickly warmed up and promised to get together in St. Louis. Mouse then told JR about the upcoming reunion and convinced him that his classmates would love to see him. Although JR was not quite sure of that, he told Mouse that he would make every effort to attend.

Mouse offered to take care of all of the arrangements with the reunion committee, to which JR said, "Thank you, and make that arrangements for two. Let me tell you about Karen."

When JR finally got around to shaving his beard, he checked with Karen to see how she was doing.

"What's wrong," Karen asked, sensing JR's tension.

"It's hard to explain. I've been through a lot over ten years. Although there were plenty of times I was scared, I found a way to get through them all, and I feel really good about my life and where we're headed. But I don't think I've ever felt nervous like I do about tonight."

"Oh, do you mean just because you were dead and now you're not. Or is it because you're walking into an all-white party with a black woman? Why should either of those bother you," Karen asked sarcastically, trying to lighten his mood.

JR snickered, hugged Karen, and said, "OK, maybe a little of each. Maybe also because I was never really part of my high school class, and now I'm going to an event that's celebrating it. It just feels strange."

"Do you think that anyone in high school feels totally connected? They should call it insecurity school. Even the folks who appear to be involved and popular have their issues. Besides, what's the worst thing that can happen? If it doesn't work out, we can always leave."

JR just stared silently and smiled.

"What are you grinning about," Karen prodded.

Maintaining his smile, JR said, "You have your father's wisdom. I love you."

"So I've heard," Karen said, as she pushed him away, turned him toward the closet, and patted his behind. "Get dressed, and let's go to a party."

Dressed and ready to go, they held hands as they left their new St. Louis apartment, got in their new car, and drove to University City High School, where the Friday night reunion event would be taking place.

ARRANGEMENTS FOR TWO

JR and Karen walked hand-in-hand through the cold evening across the dimly-lit street from the parking lot, entered the warmth of the school, and followed the signage to the gymnasium.

CHAPTER 91

WE NEED TO TALK

November 29, 1974
St. Louis, Missouri

When JR saw him, John Muccelli was talking with Swish—the two former basketball teammates standing 15 feet from and to the right of one of the baskets on the hardwood floor in the bandbox of a gymnasium, where ten years earlier, they were running Coach Greenblatt's offense. Swish took a mock jump shot, and it looked as sweet as ever.

JR had connected with Swish earlier, and as he approached, he saw Swish shake Mooch's hand and walk away, leaving JR and Mooch to be alone. And that is how JR felt—despite being amidst the noise of several hundred classmates, their spouses, and a DJ playing "Wake Up Little Susie" by the Everly Brothers, JR felt as if he and his hopefully former adversary were by themselves in the gym.

"Hi Mooch, I'm JR Spears. We need to talk."

"Was that you in Oakland?"

"Yes. Small world."

Earlier in the evening, JR was pleased with the generally sincere and warm reception he and Karen received from classmates. People he knew in high school, but mostly those he did not, came up to tell him how devastated they had been to hear he had been killed and how glad they were to see him. And, with but few exceptions, classmates treated Karen as if she were one of theirs.

JR thoroughly enjoyed Mouse, who had recently ended marriage number two, acting as their personal escort and as though he had single-handedly brought JR back to life. Not only

342

WE NEED TO TALK

had JR reestablished his relationship with Mouse, but he had also connected with a class that he had not felt a part of ten years earlier.

During a recent phone call with Mouse, JR had asked him if Mooch would be at the reunion and prepared himself for the conversation. When JR and Mouse simultaneously saw John Muccelli across the gym, Mouse offered Karen his arm and whisked her away to meet more classmates.

"It occurred to me that it might be you, but I discounted that possibility, because I had heard about you dying in the copter crash."

"And I thought it was you, but decided it couldn't have been, because of how clean cut you always were. How could it be you behind the beard and long hair?"

"JR, you need to know that I left the FBI, in part because I didn't agree with many things we were doing. But you also need to know that I could never condone what you were doing—destroying property, putting lives at risk, breaking the law—all not OK in my book."

"Whoa, Mooch. In that regard, we were on the same side. There were plenty of folks in the movement who were very much opposed to violence. We did everything we could to try to talk down the bombing advocates from what they were wanting to do, but just couldn't get through to some.

"In fact, I lost a close friend when a bomb she was making exploded prematurely. Do you recall the Haight-Ashbury rooming house explosion?"

"That was about a year before I got into the FBI, but I heard all about it during my orientation. Perhaps she had it coming to her."

"No one deserves that. And I gotta tell you, although she was obsessed with and advocating for bombing, she was also dedicated to making sure she didn't hurt anyone."

"OK, I'll take your word for that. I have a lot of questions, but there's one at the top of my list. Why did you do it? Why did you take the risk of the crash, being caught, and prosecuted as a deserter?"

JR said nothing as he reached into his pocket to get his wallet. He opened it and extracted a tattered, faded photo of a smiling Vietnamese family. Before handing the photo to Mooch, JR looked at it one more time, focusing as he normally did on the young boy.

He extended the photo toward Mooch and simply said, "This is why."

Although Mooch certainly did not know the whole story, he could tell from the photo and the expression on JR's face that the reasons ran deep.

"Maybe someday, you can fill in the details," Mooch said as he respectfully returned the photo. "This is neither the time nor place. What are your plans?"

"Well, as you might imagine, I've gotten pretty good at organizing for a cause. I have a two-year public service commitment to complete, and I'm going to see if I can make a difference for racial equality. Not really sure what that means, but for now, it's a direction."

JR hesitated, but it was clear to Mooch to give him a moment. "Oh, and there's this guy in town here that I need to track down. Might take some time, but I'll find him. It's a long story, but shortly after we graduated, he killed a friend of mine and got away without being arrested. I have no idea how to proceed, but he needs to pay for what he did."

"Another story I'd like to hear about. Maybe I can help."

JR cocked his head as he mused how that might play out. "How about you? What are your plans?"

"Even though I left the FBI..."

"Sorry for interrupting, but why did you leave?"

"Well, in the same way you were opposed to what some antiwar folks were doing, I didn't like some of the things we were doing. I thought they were illegal.

"In fact, not long after I resigned, a lot of agents, including me, were called before a Federal Grand Jury. Thankfully, we were granted immunity in exchange for our testimony.

"One of my bosses was convicted," Mooch stopped for a moment as he thought of Paul Marcus, who was not implicated in the federal investigation. Mooch also thought with deep regret that he had never heard from Paul again.

"Well, that's probably enough," Mooch suggested. "This is neither the time nor the place, but I'd be glad to fill you in at some point.

"Anyway, even though I left the FBI, I still believe in the law. I have my law degree from Columbia. I've passed the Missouri bar and have joined a law practice. But that's only temporary. I'm trying to get into a prosecutor's office."

"High ambitions. I wish you luck."

"Well, we'll see how it works out. You know, I like what you said about making a difference for racial equality. When you get around to tackling that one, get in touch, will you?"

"Works for me," JR said, finding himself liking Mooch.

"Oh, and I'm thinking about one more thing," Mooch added. "I think I'm going to write a book about the FBI—about what it could and should be and about what it definitely should not be."

"You know, Mooch, maybe we should write a book together about our experiences. We saw the same thing from two very different angles."

"Well, that just might be a possibility. What would you call it?"

"*Body Not Recovered,* and I'd dedicate it to M. J. Savoy."